THE HARVARD CLASSICS
SHELF OF FICTION

HOUSE WHERE VANITY FAIR WAS WRITTEN

HOUSE WHERE VANITY FAIR
WAS WRITTEN

THE HARVARD CLASSICS
SHELF OF FICTION
SELECTED BY CHARLES W ELIOT LL D

VANITY FAIR

VOLUME I

BY

WILLIAM MAKEPEACE
THACKERAY

EDITED WITH NOTES AND INTRODUCTIONS
BY WILLIAM ALLAN NEILSON PH D

P F COLLIER & SON COMPANY
NEW YORK

CONTENTS

VANITY FAIR, A NOVEL WITHOUT A HERO

i

CONTENTS

BIOGRAPHICAL NOTE

WILLIAM MAKEPEACE THACKERAY was born at Calcutta, India, on July 18, 1811, the son and grandson of officers of the East India Company. His father died when William was six, and the following year the future novelist was sent to England to be educated. After some years at private schools, he entered the Charterhouse in 1822, and remained till 1828. Neither there nor at Cambridge, where he was a member of Trinity College for a year and a half, did he distinguish himself as a scholar; and he finally left the university because he felt he was wasting his time, and determined to finish his education by travel. During a stay of several months at Weimar he met Goethe, and years afterwards used his reminiscences of the Grand Ducal Court there in his description of Pumpernickel in "Vanity Fair." On his return to England he took up the study of law, and though he was later called to the bar he never practised.

Thackeray's father had left him a considerable fortune, most of which had disappeared by the time he was twenty-three, part lost in an unsuccessful newspaper, part in unfortunate investments, and part through gambling. Finding that he had to earn his bread, he resolved to study art, and in 1834 went to Paris for this purpose. Two years later he was appointed Paris correspondent of a short-lived paper, "The Constitutionalist," and on the strength of this he married Isabella Shawe, the daughter of an Irish officer. After four years of happy married life, Mrs. Thackeray's mind gave way, and though she lived till 1894 she never recovered. For a number of years he had to struggle to keep his head above water, writing for newspapers and periodicals and doing a good deal of illustrating. Though he never acquired great technical skill as a draughtsman, he had a gift of turning out amusing sketches, and for ten

iii

years he was on the staff of "Punch" as both artist and author. It was in that publication, with "The Snobs of England," that he first achieved popularity, his earlier novels, "Catherine" and "Barry Lyndon," having failed to hit the popular taste. In January, 1847, "Vanity Fair" began to appear in monthly numbers, and by the time it was concluded in the July of the following year he was generally awarded a place in the first rank of English novelists. Dickens was then at the height of his fame, and, though the two men appreciated each other's work, their admirers were fond of debating their comparative merits—a form of criticism which, though futile enough in the case of talents so dissimilar, has not yet entirely gone out of fashion.

"Pendennis," the most autobiographical of Thackeray's novels, came out in 1848-50, and still farther strengthened his reputation. In 1851 he took up lecturing, beginning with the series on the English Humorists of the Eighteenth Century, which he delivered first in London. These were in a sense a by-product of "Esmond," published in 1852, in the autumn of which year he carried them across the Atlantic. He lectured at Boston, New York, Philadelphia, Baltimore, Richmond, Charleston, and Savannah, was received with great hospitality, made many friends, and went home the next spring the richer by some $10,000. A second tour in America, with "The Four Georges," followed in 1855, and was also successful. Meantime he had completed "The Newcomes," and while in Rome with his daughters for the Christmas season of 1853, he wrote and illustrated for some children the amusing burlesque of "The Rose and the Ring."

Thackeray was now one of the notable figures of English society and was financially at ease. In 1857 he stood for Parliament for the city of Oxford, but missed election by a narrow margin. Apparently little downcast, he returned to his literary work and issued "The Virginians," 1857-59. It is commonly felt that with this book the quality of his work begins to fall off, and none of his subsequent novels achieved great success. In 1860 he undertook the editorship of the newly founded "Cornhill Magazine," and to it he contributed his delightful essays, "The Roundabout Papers."

But his health, which for years had been far from good, unfitted him for the labor of editorship, and he resigned in 1862. On the morning of December 24, 1863, he was found dead.

The death of Thackeray was keenly felt through a wide circle both in England and abroad. His striking figure—he was six feet, three inches in height, with a massive head—had become familiar not only through his appearances on the platform but through the caricatures of himself that he had whimsically introduced into many of his drawings in "Punch" and elsewhere; and he was held in affectionate reverence by thousands who had never seen him. Though he first made his reputation as a satirist, he was a man without malice and of extraordinarily tender sensibilities. He had had to struggle hard to gain a footing in letters, and suffered more than his share of domestic sorrow; but he was generously helpful to others, even when he could little afford it, and found his greatest delight in brightening the lives of children. He used to be blamed for cynicism, but it has long been clear that it was the keenness of his appreciation of the loftier possibilities of human nature that lay at the root of his sadness that these possibilities are so seldom realized.

Though he achieved brilliant success in the fields of the burlesque and the essay, it is, of course, on his work as a novelist that his great reputation is chiefly based. But when the attempt is made to rank his novels among themselves, great diversity of opinion appears. Some specialists would give first place to the comparatively little read "Barry Lyndon"; more favor "The Newcomes." His style nowhere reaches greater perfection than in the astonishing reproduction of the diction of Queen Anne's reign in "Esmond." Yet, all in all, it is safe to say that he never surpassed his first great success, "Vanity Fair." Here we find at their height his distinguishing qualities: his power of conveying the spirit and atmosphere of an epoch, of delineating a throng of people and making them all living men and women, of conceiving great dramatic situations and presenting these so as to display character with the utmost vividness, of stripping away the veils that hide our motives not only from others but from ourselves. It is doubtful if any English novel possesses a heroine more completely vitalized than Becky Sharp, a creature so amazingly real that critics are occasionally to be found taking sides with her against her creator. And in his description of such figures, in his painting of their backgrounds, and in his characteristically intimate discussion with his readers of their faults and follies, he wields an English style unsurpassed for clarity, ease, and grace, capable of lofty eloquence, extreme tenderness, and fiery scorn, but always appropriate and always sincere.

W. A. N.

CRITICISMS AND INTERPRETATIONS

I

By James Hannay

WHEN Thackeray wrote "Vanity Fair," in 1846-7-8, he was living in Young Street, Kensington, a street on your left hand before you come to the church; and here, in 1848, the author of this sketch had first the pleasure of seeing him, of being received at his table, and of knowing how essentially a kind, humane, and perfectly honest man he was. "Vanity Fair" was then unfinished, but its success was made and he spoke frankly and generally of his work and his career. "Vanity Fair," always, we think, ranked in his own mind as best in *story* of his greater books; and he once pointed out to us the very house in Russell Square where his imaginary Sedleys lived—a curious proof of the reality his creations had for his mind. The man and the books were equally real and true; and it was natural that he should speak without hesitation of his books, if you wished it; though as a man of the world and a polished gentleman who knew the world thoroughly, literature to him only took its turn among other topics. From this point of view, his relation to it was a good deal like that of Scott. According to Lockhart, people were wrong in saying that Sir Walter declined at all markedly to talk about literature, and yet his main interest was in active life. Just so, Thackeray was not bookish, and yet turned readily to the subject of books if invited. His reading was undoubtedly large in memoirs, modern history, biography, poetry, essays, and fiction—and, taken in conjunction with his scholarship, probably placed him, as a man of letters, above any other novelist except Sir Bulwer Lytton. Here is a characteristic fragment from one of his letters, written in August, 1854, and now before us: "I hate Juvenal," he says; "I mean I think him a truculent brute, and I love Horace better than you do, and rate Churchill much lower; and as for Swift, you haven't made me alter my opinion. I admire, or rather admit, his power as much as you do; but I don't admire that kind of power so much as I did fifteen years ago, or twenty shall we say. Love is a higher intellectual exercise than Hatred: and when you get one or two more of those young ones you write so pleasantly about, you'll come over to the side of the kind wags, I think, rather than the cruel ones." Passages like this, which men who knew him will not need to have quoted to them, have a double value for the world at large. They not only show a familiar command of writers whom it is by no means easy to know well, but they show what the real philosophy was of a man whom the envious represented to the ignorant as a cynic and a scoffer. Why, his favorite authors were just those whose influence he thought had been beneficial to the cause of virtue and charity. "I take off my hat to Joseph Addison," he would say, after an energetic testimony to his good effect on English life. He was, in fact, even greater as a moralist than as a mere *describer* of manners; and his very hatred of quackery and meanness was proved to be real by his simplicity, humanity, and kindliness of character. In private, this great satirist, whose aspect in a crowd was often one of austere politeness and reserve, unbent into a familiar *naïveté* which somehow one seldom finds in the demonstratively genial. And this was the more charming and precious that it rested on a basis of severe and profound reflection, before the glance of which all that was dark and serious in man's life and prospects lay open. The gravity of that white head, with its noble brow, and thoughtful face full of feeling and meaning, enhanced the piquancy of his playfulness, and of the little personal revelations which came with such a grace from the depths of his kindly nature. When we congratulated him, many years ago, on the touch in "Vanity Fair" in which Becky "admires" her husband when he is giving Lord Steyne the chastisement which ruins *her* for life, "Well," he said, "when I wrote the sentence I slapped my fist on the table, and said '*that* is a touch of genius!'" The incident is a trifle, but it will reveal, we suspect, an element of fervor, as well as a heartiness of frankness in recording the fervor, both equally at variance with the vulgar conception of him.—From "A Brief Memoir of the late Mr. Thackeray" (1864).

II

By Doctor John Brown

LOOKING at Mr. Thackeray's writings as a whole, he would be more truthfully described as a sentimentalist than as a cynic. Even when the necessities of his story compel him to draw bad characters, he gives them as much good as he can. We don't remember in his novels any utterly unredeemed scoundrel except Sir Francis Clavering. Even Lord Steyne has something like genuine sympathy with Major Pendennis's grief at the illness of his nephew. And if reproof is the main burden of his discourse, we must remember that to reprove, not to praise, is the business of the preacher. Still further, if his reproof appears sometimes unduly severe, we must remember that such severity may spring from a belief that better things are possible. Here lies the secret of Thackeray's seeming bitterness. His nature was, in the words of the critic in "Le Temps," *"furieuse d'avoir été désappointé."* He condemns sternly men as they often are, because he had a high ideal of what they might be. The feeling of this contrast runs through all his writings. "He could not have painted 'Vanity Fair' as he has, unless Eden had been shining brightly before his eyes."[1] And this contrast could never have been felt, the glories of Eden could never have been seen, by the mere satirist or by the misanthrope. It has often been urged against him that he does not make us think better of our fellow men. No, truly. But he does what is far greater than this—he makes us think worse of ourselves. There is no great necessity that we should think well of other people; there

[1] Essays by George Brimley. Second Edition. Cambridge, 1860. A collection of singularly good critical papers.

is the utmost necessity that we should know ourselves in our every fault and weakness; and such knowledge his writings will supply.—From "Thackeray's Literary Career," in "Spare Hours" (1866).

III

By Hippolyte Adolphe Taine

NO writer was better gifted than Thackeray for this kind of satire because no faculty is more proper to satire than reflection. Reflection is concentrated attention, and concentrated attention increases a hundred-fold the force and duration of emotions. He who is immersed in the contemplation of a vice, feels a hatred of vice, and the intensity of his hatred is measured by the intensity of his contemplation. At first anger is a generous wine, which intoxicates and excites; when preserved and shut up, it becomes a liquor burning all that it touches, and corroding even the vessel which contains it. Of all satirists, Thackeray, after Swift, is the most gloomy. Even his countrymen have reproached him with depicting the world uglier than it is. Indignation, grief, scorn, disgust, are his ordinary sentiments. When he digresses, and imagines tender souls, he exaggerates their sensibility, in order to render their oppression more odious. The selfishness which wounds them appears horrible, and their resigned sweetness is a mortal insult to their tyrants: it is the same hatred which has calculated the kindliness of the victims and the harshness of the persecutors.[1]

This anger, exasperated by reflection, is also armed by reflection. It is clear that the author is not carried away by passing indignation or pity. He has mastered himself before speaking. He has often weighed the rascality which he is about to describe. He is in possession of the motives, species, results, as a naturalist is of his classifications. He is sure of his judgment, and has matured it. He punishes like a man convinced, who has before him a heap of proofs,

[1] See the character of Amelia in "Vanity Fair," and of Colonel Newcome in "The Newcomes."

who advances nothing without a document or an argument, who has foreseen all objections and refuted all excuses, who will never pardon, who is right in being inflexible, who is conscious of his justice, and who rests his sentence and his vengeance on all the powers of mediation and equity. The effect of this justified and contained hatred is overwhelming. When we have read to the end of Balzac's novels, we feel the pleasure of a naturalist walking through a museum, past a fine collection of specimens and monstrosities. When we have read to the end of Thackeray, we feel the shudder of a stranger brought before a mattress in the operating-room of an hospital, on the day when cautery is applied or a limb is taken off.

In such a case the most natural weapon is serious irony, because it bears witness to concentrated hatred: he who employs it suppresses his first feeling; he feigns to be speaking against himself, and constrains himself to take the part of his adversary. On the other hand, this painful and voluntary attitude is the sign of excessive scorn; the protection which apparently is afforded to an enemy is the worst of insults. The author seems to say: "I am ashamed to attack you; you are so weak that, even supported, you must fall; your reasonings are your shame, and your excuses are your condemnation." Thus the more serious the irony, the stronger it is; the more you take care to defend your adversary, the more you degrade him; the more you seem to aid him, the more you crush him. This is why Swift's grave sarcasm is so terrible; we think he is showing respect, and he slays; his approbation is a flagellation. Amongst Swift's pupils, Thackeray is the first. . . .

One step added to serious irony leads us to serious caricature. Here, as before, the author pleads the rights of his neighbor; the only difference is, that he pleads them with too much warmth; it is insult upon insult. Under this head it abounds in Thackeray. Some of his grotesques are outrageous: for instance, M. Alcide de Mirobolant, a French cook, an artist in sauces, who declares his passion to Miss Blanche through the medium of symbolic dishes, and thinks himself a gentleman; Mrs. Major O'Dowd, a sort of female grenadier, the most pompous and talkative of Irishwomen, bent on ruling the regiment, and marrying the bachelors will they nill they; Miss Briggs, an old companion born to receive insults, to make phrases and to shed tears; the Doctor, who proves to his scholars who write bad Greek, that habitual idleness and bad construing lead to the gallows. These calculated deformities only excite a sad smile. We always perceive behind the oddity of the character the sardonic air of the painter, and we conclude that the human race is base and stupid. Other figures less exaggerated, are not more natural. We see that the author throws them expressly into palpable follies and marked contradictions. Such is Miss Crawley, an old maid, without any morals, and a free-thinker, who praises unequal marriages, and falls into a fit when on the next page her nephew makes one; who calls Rebecca Sharp her equal, and at the same time bids her "put some coals on the fire;" who, on learning the departure of her favorite, cries with despair, "Gracious goodness, and who's to make my chocolate?" These are comedy scenes, and not pictures of manners.—From "History of English Literature," translated by H. Van Laun (1864-65).

IV

By William Samuel Lilly

I SHALL inquire, presently, of what kind Thackeray's philosophy of life was. First let me say what it was not. There are those—Taine is among them—who find him a misanthrope; a charge which, by the way, was brought against Balzac. The accusation seems to me wholly unjust in both cases. To speak of Thackeray merely, he drew the world around him, as he saw it, extenuating nothing, but, assuredly, setting down nothing in malice. He saw clearly enough—as who that has eyes must not see?—the seamy side of society: its littleness, its meanness, its selfishness, its baseness, its false religionism, its secret impurities—in a word which sums all up, its worldliness. I remember hearing a very learned and pious divine, the late Father Dalgairns, once tell a particularly smart congregation, "society is the devil's church." I do not know whether Thackeray would have gone as far as that. Certainly, however, "Vanity Fair" might stand as the title of every one of his books. But clearly as he saw, and vividly as he painted, the scamy side of society, he was no misanthrope, as Taine fancies. He saw with equal clearness, and painted with equal vividness, the truth and incorruptness, the purity and goodness, the love and pity which exist side by side with the abounding evil. He discerned in these things the real goods of human existence, and felt for them that reverence which Ruskin has happily called "the chief joy and power of life." Taine seems to me particularly unhappy in calling him a disciple of Swift. In my judgment there is hardly anything in common between his genial humor and the *saeva indignatio,* the savage wrath, of that arch-inquisitor of human nature. Pungent as his satire often was, the man was overflowing with the milk of human kindness. "If Fun is good, Truth is still better, and Love is the best of all," are the words with which he concludes his "Book of Snobs." They seem to me an accurate expression of his mind.

Again, I cannot agree with Taine in his complaint—which has been made by hundreds of others—that the good people in Thackeray, if I may so call them, are contemptible and uninteresting. Colonel Newcome, George Warrington, nay, even Arthur Pendennis, particularly interest me as admirable specimens of what I take to be the best kind of man now extant on this planet, the English gentleman. And then his women, his good women. Surely Amelia Sedley is the very type of all that is "pure womanly": Laura, in her "finished chasten'd purity," "the queen of marriage;" while in Ethel Newcome we have "a perfect woman, nobly planned, to guide, to counsel, and command." Thackeray, happily, lived at a time before the strong-minded woman had come into fashion—at a time when it was generally received and believed that "woman is not undeveloped man, but diverse."

But I am treading on dangerous ground. Let me go on to notice another of Taine's complaints of Thackeray, whom he finds a cynic. The complaint is echoed by thousands, by hundreds of thousands. I confess it seems to me that those who make it, speak unadvisedly with their lips; that they have not realized what a cynic is. I find no cynicism in

Thackeray's pages. If you want to see what real cynicism is take up "Candide." In that incomparably witty book you have a perfect specimen of it. There Voltaire, under pretense of stripping off our illusions, strips us of our primary moral sympathies, of our fundamental ethical beliefs. But it is precisely to those sympathies and beliefs that Thackeray appeals, "those high instincts," as Wordsworth calls them in magnificent verse familiar, doubtless, to all here—

> "High instincts, before which our mortal Nature
> Did tremble, like a guilty Thing surprised,"

and which are the most certain of all our certainties. To those sympathies, beliefs, instincts, I say, Thackeray ever appealed, to recall us from the worship of Mammon, the worship of rank, the worship of notoriety, to the worship of goodness, and truth, and love. Nor is it true, as Taine complains, that he has turned the novel into mere satire. True it is that in him we have a satirist who, to quote Pope's description of Horace, "without method talks us into sense." But true it is also that beneath his satire, there are springs of tenderness and pathos which are ever welling up. He is full of those "thoughts that do often lie too deep for tears." He knew well that we apprehend moral verities not only with the intellect, but also with the heart; σὺν ὅλῃ τῇ ψυχῇ as the Greeks said; with the whole of our spiritual being. Nor let it be objected that he presents us with nothing better than trite moralities, "copy-book maxims." Sidney Smith, in whom the very voice of common sense seems often to speak, has happily said, "It is the calling of great men not so much to preach new truths, as to rescue from oblivion those old truths which it is our wisdom to remember and our weakness to forget." —From "Four English Humorists" (1895).

V

By William Shepard Walsh

THE reason that Thackeray's real nature was so generally misunderstood by his contemporaries is not so far to seek. He was a reaction against the spirit of his age. He came upon the world at the time when the grotesque sham into which Byronism had degenerated at the hands of Byron's admirers was emasculating literature; when the Great Soul was the popular ideal,—the gifted, gloomy, mysterious being who did not love the world nor the world him, but who usually had an amiable weakness for the world's wife. He was a protest against all this. He was a protest, too, against the rampant egotism that found its fullest expression in the fiction of that period, in the earlier novels, for instance, of Bulwer and Disraeli, mere clever poseurs without any earnestness or sincerity, who were continually proclaiming their own merits from the house-tops, and inviting public attention to the beauty of their own emotions. In the vigor of his protest against all this brag and bluster, Thackeray may have gone to the opposite extreme. A man who is anxious to keep straight is liable to bend over on the opposite side. So, in the reaction against unreal enthusiasm Thackeray habitually talked under what he felt. He veiled his deeper feelings beneath a self-respecting reticence; he would have shrunk from making a public exhibition of the pulsations of a troubled heart. A friend who knew him and valued him, and who tells us that in the discussion of serious subjects he was apt, when pressed, to have recourse to banter, acknowledges that much of his light talk was intended not so much to conceal as to keep down a sensibility amounting almost to womanliness which belonged to his nature, and which contrasted, one might almost say struggled, with the manliness which was equally its characteristic. "He could not read any thing pathetic without actual discomfort, and was unable, for example, to go through with the 'Bride of Lammermoor.' I have heard him allude to some early sorrows, especially the loss of a child, in a way which showed how sharp and painful was the recollection after the lapse of many years. That he could sympathize warmly with others I infer from much that I have heard. His well-known sensitiveness sprung perhaps from the same root as his sensibility. 'I like Thackeray,' an English critic once said in my hearing, 'but I cannot respect him—he is so sensitive.' But his sensitiveness made harsh things distasteful to him even when ne was not himself the object of them. 'You fiend!' he said to a friend who was laughing over a sharp attack on an acquaintance of both, and refused to hear or read a word of it."—From "William Makepeace Thackeray," in "Pen Pictures of Modern Authors" (1882).

VI

By James Oliphant

TO sum up on this point, it must be granted that while Thackeray was unrivalled in his power of representing all types of character on which it was possible for him to direct his satire, we must place against this great merit three serious considerations:—his satirical habit often led him into caricature; he failed entirely in creating types of ideal beauty, lapsing always into vagueness or inconsistency; and finally in number and importance, as well as in truth to nature, the contemptible figures in his portrait gallery are so preponderant that the whole effect is an utter travesty of human life. In a novelist this is an unpardonable sin. The avowed satirist purposely limits his vision, and we accept his pictures with the knowledge that they do not represent the whole truth. But the artist in fiction stands in a different position. He professes to tell us what life is. If it is not necessary that every novel should be a synthesis, the sum of the writer's work must at least give us a reflection of reality that is faithful up to the measure of his capacity. Thackeray was either insincere, or he was blind to the greater part of those elements in life which all of us hold most dear. There is no writer whom it is more delightful to dip into in certain moods; he ministers so admirably to the innate malice of human nature. His books have indeed a more justifiable value than this; as a corrective to conceit, to self-deception, to excess of enthusiasm, his barbed words may often yield a wholesome moral tonic. But as a whole his novels do their readers the greatest disservice that lies within the possibility of any one man's influence upon others. They strike at the root of the noblest sentiment that can animate the human spirit; they would destroy man's faith in man. We never rise from his books with brighter hopes or quickened energies.

One respect in which Thackeray stands supreme among novelists is the perfect naturalness of his conversations. It was perhaps easier for him to attain this, owing to his dealing mainly with the superficial aspects of life, but it is a gift of the highest order, and one which few of the great novelists have possessed even in a moderate degree. In the mouths of his characters as well as in his own person, his style has many of the qualities of his very best prose. It does not rise to the passion and melody of the finest imaginative writers, but it is a model of ease, and purity and grace. Having such a command of expressive language, and so keen a power of minute observation, it is somewhat strange that he should have attempted so little in the way of description. Very seldom in his novels have we any graphic picture of the outward surroundings of his scenes. The beauties of nature do not seem to have appealed to him strongly. He was a denizen of cities himself; London and Paris formed by far the greater part of his world, and the country was little more than an indefinite background, suggestive rather of dulness than pleasure.

That Thackeray was one of the chief literary figures of our century, and that his individuality has had a marked influence on the work of his successors there can be no manner of doubt. As a painter of manners, as a satirist, a critic, a stylist, he takes a very high rank, but the qualities which enabled him to excel in these various capacities do not of themselves constitute a great writer of fiction. If he must also be called a great novelist, it is not because he possessed in an eminent degree the special gifts which form the chief glory of the artist, but that his genius in certain faculties which should be subsidiary to the main purposes of creative art, was so forcible as to make him largely independent of the forms of expression he adopted, and to cover his many and serious deficiencies. His influence on the development of the novel has been almost entirely indirect. Following Miss Austen and Dickens in drawing his material from contemporary life, he helped to widen the range by dealing with new phases of society. Following the same writers, but reaching a higher success, he touched the limits of realism in dialogue. But he did little to help in guiding the art of fiction into its true channels. In his general methods he has fortunately had no imitators. He sought to turn his novels into vehicles of instruction, and the art he thus treated with indignity has revenged itself on him. With all his wonderful and manifold gifts he stands now in the history of fiction rather as a warning than as a model.— From "Victorian Novelists" (1899).

VII

By Gilbert K. Chesterton

THE mere title of "Vanity Fair" was certainly an inspiration; for it is both the strength and weakness of the book that it produces on the mind (I might say, even on the *nerves*) the same impression of mixed voices and almost maddening competition as a crowded square on market day. The force and fault of Thackeray was always to be irrelevant; but here irrelevancy rises till it reaches to a sort of deafening distraction. Elsewhere in Thackeray digression was destined to be slow; but here even digression is swift, swift as the dance of death at the balls of Lord Steyne or the swoop of all the vultures to the sick bed of Miss Crawley. Everyone in this tale is filled with a futile energy. The reader is purposely left wondering at so much courage in that craven battle, so much endurance in that strange and selfish martyrdom. Newman said once, I believe, "Evil always fails by over-leaping its aim and good by falling short of it." Whether true or not this might almost be a motto for "Vanity Fair." Here Thackeray is right in calling himself so constantly a moralist. He is genuinely a moralist in this essential sense that he insists that actions shall be judged not by their energy, but by their aim.

Many strenuous critics have sneered at the softness of Amelia Sedley and openly exalted Rebecca along lines of the will to live. It would be hard to persuade modern critics that Thackeray may be deeper or even more daring than they are. But I hardly think that they see Thackeray's point. His point surely is that Amelia was a fool; but that there is a certain sanative and antiseptic element in virtue, by which even a fool manages to live longer than a knave. For after all when Amelia and Becky meet at the end, Amelia has much less energy, but she has much more life. She is *younger;* she has not lost her power of happiness; her stalk is not broken. She could really, to use Thackeray's own metaphor, grow green again. But the energy of Becky is the energy of a dead woman; it is like the rhythmic kicking of some bisected insect. The life of the wicked works outwards and goes to waste. The life of the innocent, even the stupidly innocent, is within; if anyone dislikes the battered sentiment of the word "love," I will say that innocence has more *zest,* more power of tasting things. Hence Thackeray's thought is really suggestive; that perhaps even softness is a sort of superiority; it is better to be open to all emotions as they come than to reach the hell of Rebecca; the hell of having all outward forces open, but all receptive organs closed. For the very definition of hell must be energy without joy.

It was very specially in connection with "Vanity Fair" that the great accusation of "cynicism" broke about Thackeray's ears. The argument is a mere logomachy, the trick of taking a vague word and then asking if it applies precisely. If cynicism means a war on comfort, then Thackeray, to his eternal honour, was the reverse of a cynic. It is absurd, in this sense, to call a man cynical whose whole object it is to show that goodness, even when it is silly, is a healthier thing than wickedness when it is sensible. The truth in the accusation is probably this; that his vile characters are drawn a little more vididly than his virtuous characters. So, in the small artistic sense, Dante is more successful with hell than with the beatific vision. Virtuous characters are always drawn less vividly than other characters; because they are so much more worth drawing.—From the Introduction to "Thackeray" in "Masters of Literature" (1909).

VIII

By HAROLD WILLIAMS

"A BEAUTIFUL vein of genius lay struggling about in him," said Carlyle of Thackeray, with an aptness which does not always belong to his comments upon his contemporaries. Thackeray was a shy and diffident man, reserved and very sensitive, and we feel that never, either on paper or to his friends, did he wholly reveal himself; he was garrulous and wrote diffusively, he constantly made personal intrusions into his books, he is the most charming of friends and guides through the narrative, but something is kept back from us, and to the last page there is still an unknown element in the personality of the man who has talked so much about himself and of his books. Dickens showed what he was, and the least percipient could divine what his opinion would be on any given subject, what his mental attitude was to life in general. But Thackeray was a riddle; he was alternately accused of cynicism and sentimentalism: at one time he was unfeeling and represented life as worse than it was: at another he was inclined to hope too much in human nature. And why not? Every man who both thinks and feels will have his alternations of hope and depression, tender-heartedness and stoical contempt. And, though Thackeray mixed with his fellows in crowded places all his life, though he was a man of cities and a frequenter of clubs, an indolent Epicurean who loved to talk and lounge through

life, he kept a chamber of his soul closed to the world; he
was never completely off his guard, he never set the whole
of his genius free. It was always, as Carlyle said, struggling
about in him. For, though everyday philosophy was one of
his weaknesses, he never conceived a whole and clear view
of what life meant for him; and he appears, according to the
mood of the moment, as the censor of morals, the indifferent
cynic, the sentimentalist, the large-hearted man sensitive to
the pain rather than the joy of life, and the Epicurean dil-
ettante. . . .

Thackeray described himself as carried away by his characters till he lost control over their movements. The statement may be accepted and the inconsequent movement of
the narrative goes to prove it; but it may be doubted whether
he ever lost himself so completely as Dickens, who wept and
laughed with the characters he created. There is always a
degree of aloofness in Thackeray's attitude; even Arthur
Pendennis is not so much to him, not so dear to his heart
and his memories of youth, as David Copperfield was to
Dickens. Thackeray's interest in his characters is the interest of the student, the analyst, and the theorist: he did
not possess the faculty of absorption and identification. He
consistently acts the part of censor and showman. He is
always at our elbow, nudging and jogging us, pointing out
and supplying, sometimes, it must be confessed, rather com-
monplace reflections we are to draw from the narrative.
His pages are liberally provided with rubrics, stage-direc-
tions, marginal annotations, and textual commentary. We
are, for instance, told that "the present chapter is very
mild." Well and good, but the discovery might have been
left to the perspicuity of the reader. The part of showman
is deliberately and unashamedly adopted.

"And as we bring our characters forward, I will ask
leave, as a man and a brother, not only to introduce them,
but occasionally to step down from the platform, and talk
about them: if they are good and kindly to love them and
shake them by the hand; if they are silly, to laugh at them
confidentially in the reader's sleeve; if they are wicked and
heartless, to abuse them in the strongest terms which politeness admits of."

It is the mere pedantry of criticism to insist upon the artistic impertinence of this lecturer-with-pointer attitude of Thackeray's. We have learned to prefer the absence of the author; and in the majority of cases he is well-advised not to appear; but few would wish to see Thackeray out of his books. There may be books we can read without any desire for personal acquaintanceship with the author. If Thackeray were not in the habit of breaking off into commentary and personal intrusion, we should begin to wish for it; it is impossible to read his novels without a sense of personal interest in the figure of the author standing behind the narrative. But, as it is, he is always at hand as a delightful guide and instructor and friend.—From "Two Centuries of the English Novel" (1911).

LIST OF CHARACTERS

Miss Barbara Pinkerton, presiding over an Academy for Young Ladies.

Jemima Pinkerton, her sister.

Amelia Sedley, afterwards Mrs. George Osborne, an accomplished young lady, yet with more heart than brains.

John Sedley, Esq., of the Stock Exchange, father of Amelia.

Mrs. Sedley, his wife.

Joseph Sedley, older brother of Amelia, in the East India Company's Civil Service.

Mrs. Blenkinsop, housekeeper of the Sedleys.

Sambo, coloured servant of the Sedleys.

Rebecca Sharp, afterwards Mrs. Rawdon Crawley, daughter of a poor English artist and a French dancer. A fascinating, clever and unscrupulous adventuress.

Miss Swartz, a mulatto heiress from St. Kitt's, a school friend of Amelia's.

Sir Pitt Crawley, a miserly, hard-drinking, disreputable old baronet.

Rosa Grafton, second wife of Sir Pitt—a colourless and neglected invalid.

Rose,
Violet, } daughters of Sir Pitt by his second wife.

Pitt Crawley, a conventional prig—elder son of Sir Pitt by his first wife.

Rawdon Crawley, younger son of Sir Pitt Crawley by his first wife —a heavy young rake in the Dragoons.

Horrocks, Sir Pitt Crawley's butler.

Miss Horrocks, his daughter.

Rev. Bute Crawley, younger brother of Sir Pitt Crawley—a worldly minded country parson.

Mrs. Bute Crawley, his wife, a managing, scheming little woman.

James,
Frank, } children of Bute Crawley.
Four girls,

Mr. Osborne, a prosperous merchant in the city, who owes his start in life to Mr. Sedley.

Jane, spinster daughter and slave of Mr. Osborne.

Maria, afterwards Mrs. Frederick Bullock, younger daughter of Mr. Osborne.

George Osborne, son of Mr. Osborne, and godson of Mr. Sedley, a conceited young officer.

Miss Wirt, a "raw-boned vestal," governess to the Misses Osborne.

Miss Crawley, half-sister to Sir Pitt Crawley, a shrewd rich old spinster.

MISS BRIGGS, Miss Crawley's companion.

MRS. FIRKIN, servant of Miss Crawley.

BOWLS, butler at Miss Crawley's.

MR. RAGGLES, former butler at Miss Crawley's, and owner of the house on Curzon St. rented by the Rawdon Crawleys.

CAPT. WILLIAM DOBBIN, afterwards Major and Lieutenant Colonel, good angel of George Osborne and Amelia Sedley.

The MISSES DOBBIN, his sisters.

COUNTESS SOUTHDOWN, a strong-minded woman favourably known to the serious world.

LADY EMILY HORNBLOWER, her daughter, "author of several delightful tracts."

LADY JANE SHEEPSHANKS, afterwards Mrs. Pitt Crawley, younger daughter of Countess Southdown.

MR. CLAPP, Mr. Sedley's clerk with whom he takes refuge after his failure.

MRS. CLAPP, his wife.

MISS MARY CLAPP, their daughter.

FREDERICK BULLOCK, of the house of Bullock, Hulker & Bullock, who marries Maria Osborne.

ENSIGN STUBBLE, } subalterns in George Osborne's regiment.
ENSIGN SIMPLE, }

MAJOR O'DOWD, commander of Osborne's regiment at Waterloo.

PEGGY O'DOWD, his wife, commander of the Major.

GLORVINA O'DOWD, a good-natured Irish girl who fails to ensnare Major Dobbin.

GEORGE OSBORNE, JR., son of Amelia and George Osborne.

RAWDON CRAWLEY, JR., son of Rawdon Crawley and Becky Sharp.

GEORGE GUSTAVUS, Marquess of Steyne, Earl of Gaunt, Viscount, Hellborough, Baron Pitchley and Grillsby, Knight of the Most Noble Order of the Garter, etc., etc., etc., an elderly roué

LADY STEYNE, his wife.

LADY GAUNT, his daughter.

MR. MOSS, the bailiff.

FIFINE, Becky Sharp's maid.

CAPT. MACMURDO, Rawdon Crawley's friend in his affairs of honour.

MR. WENHAM, Lord Steyne's confidential friend.

REV. MR. VEAL, little George Osborne's tutor.

REV. BEILBY BINNY, curate of the District Chapel, an admirer of Mrs. Osborne.

ISIDOR, Belgian servant of Joseph Sedley.

KIRSCH, Joseph Sedley's courier.

FICHE, servant of Lord Steyne.

Doctors, apothecaries, solicitors, clerks, officers, servants, gate keepers, German students, noblemen, auctioneers, school boys, etc.

VANITY FAIR
A NOVEL WITHOUT A HERO

CHAPTER I

CHISWICK MALL

WHILE the present century was in its teens, and on one sunshiny morning in June, there drove up to the great iron gate of Miss Pinkerton's academy for young ladies, on Chiswick Mall, a large family coach, with two fat horses in blazing harness, driven by a fat coachman in a three-cornered hat and wig, at the rate of four miles an hour. A black servant, who reposed on the box beside the fat coachman, uncurled his bandy legs as soon as the equipage drew up opposite Miss Pinkerton's shining brass plate, and as he pulled the bell, at least a score of young heads were seen peering out of the narrow windows of the stately old brick house. Nay, the acute observer might have recognized the little red nose of good-natured Miss Jemima Pinkerton herself, rising over some geranium-pots in the window of that lady's own drawing-room.

"It is Mrs. Sedley's coach, sister," said Miss Jemima. "Sambo, the black servant, has just rung the bell; and the coachman has a new red waistcoat."

"Have you completed all the necessary preparations incident to Miss Sedley's departure, Miss Jemima?" asked Miss Pinkerton herself, that majestic lady; the Semiramis of Hammersmith, the friend of Doctor Johnson, the correspondent of Mrs. Chapone herself.

"The girls were up at four this morning, packing her trunks, sister," replied Miss Jemima; "we have made her a bow-pot."

1

"Say a bouquet, sister Jemima, 'tis more genteel."

"Well, a booky as big almost as a hay-stack; I have put up two bottles of the gillyflower-water for Mrs. Sedley, and the receipt for making it, in Amelia's box."

"And I trust, Miss Jemima, you have made a copy of Miss Sedley's account. This is it, is it? Very good—ninety-three pounds, four shillings. Be kind enough to address it to John Sedley, Esquire, and to seal this billet which I have written to his lady."

In Miss Jemima's eyes an autograph letter of her sister, Miss Pinkerton, was an object of as deep veneration as would have been a letter from a sovereign. Only when her pupils quitted the establishment, or when they were about to be married, and once, when poor Miss Birch died of the scarlet fever, was Miss Pinkerton known to write personally to the parents of her pupils; and it was Jemima's opinion that if anything *could* console Mrs. Birch for her daughter's loss, it would be that pious and eloquent composition in which Miss Pinkerton announced the event.

In the present instance Miss Pinkerton's "billet" was to the following effect:—

"The Mall, Chiswick, June 15, 18—.

"MADAM,—After her six years' residence at the Mall, I have the honour and happiness of presenting Miss Amelia Sedley to her parents, as a young lady not unworthy to occupy a fitting position in their polished and refined circle. Those virtues which characterise the young English gentlewoman, those accomplishments which become her birth and station, will not be found wanting in the amiable Miss Sedley, whose *industry* and *obedience* have endeared her to her instructors, and whose delightful sweetness of temper has charmed her *aged* and her *youthful* companions.

"In music, in dancing, in orthography, in every variety of embroidery and needle-work, she will be found to have realised her friends' *fondest wishes.* In geography there is still much to be desired; and a careful and undeviating use of the backboard, for four hours daily during the next three years, is recommended as necessary to the acquirement of that dignified *deportment and carriage,* so requisite for every young lady of *fashion.*

"In the principles of religion and morality, Miss Sedley will be found worthy of an establishment which has been honoured by the presence of *The Great Lexicographer,* and the patronage of the admirable Mrs. Chapone. In leaving the Mall, Miss Amelia carries with her the hearts of her companions, and the affectionate regards of her mistress, who has the honour to subscribe herself,

"Madam,

"Your most obliged humble servant,

"BARBARA PINKERTON.

"P.S.—Miss Sharp accompanies Miss Sedley. It is particularly requested that Miss Sharp's stay in Russell Square may not exceed ten days. The family of distinction with whom she is engaged, desire to avail themselves of her services as soon as possible."

This letter completed, Miss Pinkerton proceeded to write her own name, and Miss Sedley's, in the fly-leaf of a Johnson's Dictionary—the interesting work which she invariably presented to her scholars, on their departure from the Mall. On the cover was inserted a copy of "Lines addressed to a young lady on quitting Miss Pinkerton's school, at the Mall; by the late revered Doctor Samuel Johnson." In fact, the Lexicographer's name was always on the lips of this majestic woman, and a visit he had paid to her was the cause of her reputation and her fortune.

Being commanded by her elder sister to get "the Dictionary" from the cupboard, Miss Jemima had extracted two copies of the book from the receptacle in question. When Miss Pinkerton had finished the inscription in the first, Jemima, with rather a dubious and timid air, handed her the second.

"For whom is this, Miss Jemima?" said Miss Pinkerton, with awful coldness.

"For Becky Sharp," answered Jemima, trembling very much, and blushing over her withered face and neck, as she turned her back on her sister. "For Becky Sharp: she's going too."

"MISS JEMIMA!" exclaimed Miss Pinkerton, in the largest capitals. "Are you in your senses? Replace the Dixonary in the closet, and never venture to take such a liberty in future."

"Well, sister, it's only two-and-ninepence, and poor Becky will be miserable if she don't get one."

"Send Miss Sedley instantly to me," said Miss Pinkerton. And so venturing not to say another word, poor Jemima trotted off, exceedingly flurried and nervous.

Miss Sedley's papa was a merchant in London, and a man of some wealth; whereas Miss Sharp was an articled pupil, for whom Miss Pinkerton had done, as she thought, quite enough, without conferring upon her at parting the high honour of the Dixonary.

Although schoolmistresses' letters are to be trusted no more nor less than churchyard epitaphs; yet, as it sometimes happens that a person departs this life, who is really deserving of all the praises the stone-cutter carves over his bones; who *is* a good Christian, a good parent, child, wife, or husband; who actually *does* leave a disconsolate family to mourn his loss; so in academies of the male and female sex it occurs every now and then, that the pupil is fully worthy of the praises bestowed by the disinterested instructor. Now, Miss Amelia Sedley was a young lady of this singular species; and deserved not only all that Miss Pinkerton said in her praise, but had many charming qualities which that pompous old Minerva of a woman could not see, from the differences of rank and age between her pupil and herself.

For she could not only sing like a lark, or a Mrs. Billington, and dance like Hillisberg or Parisot; and embroider beautifully; and spell as well as a Dixonary itself; but she had such a kindly, smiling, tender, gentle, generous heart of her own, as won the love of everybody who came near her, from Minerva herself down to the poor girl in the scullery, and the one-eyed tart-woman's daughter, who was permitted to vend her wares once a week to the young ladies in the Mall. She had twelve intimate and bosom friends out of the twenty-four young ladies. Even envious Miss Briggs never spoke ill of her, high and mighty Miss Saltire (Lord Dexter's granddaughter) allowed that her figure was genteel; and as for Miss Swartz, the rich woolly-haired mulatto from St. Kitt's, on the day Amelia went away, she was in such a passion of tears, that they were obliged to send for Dr. Floss, and half tipsify her with sal-volatile. Miss Pinkerton's attachment was, as may be supposed, from the high position and eminent virtues of that lady, calm and dignified; but Miss Jemima had already whimpered several times at the idea of Amelia's departure;

and, but for fear of her sister, would have gone off in downright hysterics, like the heiress (who paid double) of St. Kitt's. Such luxury of grief, however, is only allowed to parlour-boarders. Honest Jemima had all the bills, and the washing, and the mending, and the puddings, and the plate and crockery, and the servants to superintend. But why speak about her? It is probable that we shall not hear of her again from this moment to the end of time, and that when the great filigree iron gates are once closed on her, she and her awful sister will never issue therefrom into this little world of history.

But as we are to see a great deal of Amelia there is no harm in saying, at the outset of our acquaintance, that she was a dear little creature; and a great mercy it is, both in life and in novels, which (and the latter especially) abound in villains of the most sombre sort, that we are to have for a constant companion, so guileless and good-natured a person. As she is not a heroine, there is no need to describe her person; indeed I am afraid that her nose was rather short than otherwise, and her cheeks a great deal too round and red for a heroine; but her face blushed with rosy health, and her lips with the freshest of smiles, and she had a pair of eyes which sparkled with the brightest and honestest good-humour, except indeed when they filled with tears, and that was a great deal too often; for the silly thing would cry over a dead canary-bird; or over a mouse, that the cat haply had seized upon; or over the end of a novel, were it ever so stupid; and as for saying an unkind word to her, were any persons hard-hearted enough to do so—why, so much the worse for them. Even Miss Pinkerton, that austere and god-like woman, ceased scolding her after the first time, and though she no more comprehended sensibility than she did Algebra, gave all masters and teachers particular orders to treat Miss Sedley with the utmost gentleness, as harsh treatment was injurious to her.

So that when the day of departure came, between her two customs of laughing and crying, Miss Sedley was greatly puzzled how to act. She was glad to go home, and yet most wofully sad at leaving school. For three days before, little Laura Martin, the orphan, followed her about, like a little dog. She had to make and receive at least fourteen presents,—to make fourteen solemn promises of writing every week: "Send my letters under cover to my grandpapa, the Earl of Dexter," said Miss Saltire (who, by the way, was rather shabby): "Never mind the postage, but write every day, you dear darling," said the impetuous and woolly-headed, but generous and affectionate Miss Swartz; and the orphan little Laura Martin (who was just in round-hand), took her friend's hand and said, looking up in her face wistfully, "Amelia, when I write to you I shall call you Mamma." All which details, I have no doubt, JONES, who reads this book at his Club, will pronounce to be excessively foolish, trivial, twaddling, and ultra-sentimental. Yes; I can see Jones at this minute (rather flushed with his joint of mutton and half pint of wine), taking out his pencil and scoring under the words "foolish, twaddling," &c., and adding to them his own remark of *"quite true."* Well, he is a lofty man of genius, and admires the great and heroic in life and novels; and so had better take warning and go elsewhere.

Well, then. The flowers, and the presents, and the trunks, and bonnet-boxes of Miss Sedley having been arranged by Mr. Sambo in the carriage, together with a very small and weather-beaten old cow's-skin trunk with Miss Sharp's card neatly nailed upon it, which was delivered by Sambo with a grin, and packed by the coachman with a corresponding sneer—the hour for parting came; and the grief of that moment was considerably lessened by the admirable discourse which Miss Pinkerton addressed to her pupil. Not that the parting speech caused Amelia to philosophise, or that it armed her in any way with a calmness, the result of argument; but it was intolerably dull, pompous and tedious; and having the fear of her schoolmistress greatly before her eyes, Miss Sedley did not venture, in her presence, to give way to any ebullitions of private grief. A seed-cake and a bottle of wine were produced in the drawing-room, as on the solemn occasions of the visits of parents, and these refreshments being partaken of, Miss Sedley was at liberty to depart.

"You'll go in and say good-by to Miss Pinkerton, Becky!" said Miss Jemima to a young lady of whom nobody took any notice and who was coming down stairs with her own bandbox.

"I suppose I must," said Miss Sharp calmly, and much to the wonder of Miss Jemima; and the latter having knocked at the door, and receiving permission to come in, Miss Sharp advanced in a very unconcerned manner, and said in French, and with a perfect accent, "Mademoiselle, je viens vous faire mes adieux."

Miss Pinkerton did not understand French; she only directed those who did: but biting her lips and throwing up her venerable and Roman-nosed head, (on the top of which figured a large and solemn turban,) she said, "Miss Sharp, I wish you a good morning." As the Hammersmith Semiramis spoke, she waved one hand, both by the way of adieu, and to give Miss Sharp an opportunity of shaking one of the fingers of the hand which was left out for that purpose.

Miss Sharp only folded her own hands with a very frigid smile and bow, and quite declined to accept the proffered honour; on which Semiramis tossed up her turban more indignantly than ever. In fact, it was a little battle between the young lady and the old one, and the latter was worsted. "Heaven bless you, my child," said she, embracing Amelia, and scowling the while over the girl's shoulder at Miss Sharp. "Come away, Becky," said Miss Jemima, pulling the young woman away in great alarm, and the drawing-room door closed upon them for ever.

Then came the struggle and parting below. Words refuse to tell it. All the servants were there in the hall—all the dear friends—all the young ladies—the dancing-master who had just arrived; and there was such a scuffling, and hugging, and kissing, and crying, with the hysterical *yoops* of Miss Swartz, the parlour-boarder, from her room, as no pen can depict, and as the tender heart would fain pass over. The embracing was over; they parted—that is, Miss Sedley parted from her friends. Miss Sharp had demurely entered the carriage some minutes before. Nobody cried for leaving *her*.

Sambo of the bandy legs slammed the carriage door on his young weeping mistress. He sprang up behind the carriage. "Stop!" cried Miss Jemima, rushing to the gate with a parcel.

"It's some sandwiches, my dear," said she to Amelia. "You may be hungry, you know; and Becky, Becky Sharp, here's a book for you that my sister—that is, I—Johnson's Dixonary, you know; you mustn't leave us without that. Good-by. Drive on, coachman. God bless you!"

And the kind creature retreated into the garden, overcome with emotion.

But, lo! and just as the coach drove off, Miss Sharp put her pale face out of the window and actually flung the book back into the garden.

This almost caused Jemima to faint with terror. "Well, I never,"—said she—"what an audacious"—Emotion prevented her from completing either sentence. The carriage rolled away; the great gates were closed; the bell rang for the dancing lesson. The world is before the two young ladies; and so, farewell to Chiswick Mall.

CHAPTER II

In Which Miss Sharp and Miss Sedley Prepare to Open the Campaign

WHEN Miss Sharp had performed the heroical act mentioned in the last chapter, and had seen the Dixonary, flying over the pavement of the little garden, fall at length at the feet of the astonished Miss Jemima, the young lady's countenance, which had before worn an almost livid look of hatred, assumed a smile that perhaps was scarcely more agreeable, and she sank back in the carriage in an easy frame of mind, saying—"So much for the Dixonary; and, thank God, I'm out of Chiswick."

Miss Sedley was almost as flurried at the act of defiance as Miss Jemima had been; for, consider, it was but one minute that she had left school, and the impressions of six years are not got over in that space of time. Nay, with some persons those awes and terrors of youth last for ever and over. I know, for instance, an old gentleman of sixty-eight, who said to me one morning at breakfast, with a very agitated countenance, "I dreamed last night that I was flogged by Dr. Raine." Fancy had carried him back five-and-fifty years in the course of that evening. Dr. Raine and his rod were just as awful to him in his heart, then, at sixty-eight, as they had been at thirteen. If the Doctor, with a large birch, had appeared bodily to him, even at the age of threescore and eight, and had said in awful voice, "boy, take down your pant . . .?" Well, well, Miss Sedley was exceedingly alarmed at this act of insubordination.

"How could you do so, Rebecca?" at last she said, after a pause.

"Why, do you think Miss Pinkerton will come out and order me back to the black-hole?" said Rebecca, laughing.

"No: but——"

"I hate the whole house," continued Miss Sharp in a fury. "I hope I may never set eyes on it again. I wish it were in the bottom of the Thames, I do; and if Miss Pinkerton were there, I wouldn't pick her out, that I wouldn't. O how I should like to see her floating in the water yonder, turban and all, with her train streaming after her, and her nose like the beak of a wherry."

"Hush!" cried Miss Sedley.

"Why, will the black footman tell tales?" cried Miss Rebecca, laughing. "He may go back and tell Miss Pinkerton that I hate her with all my soul; and I wish he would; and I wish I had a means of proving it, too. For two years I have only had insults and outrage from her. I have been treated worse than any servant in the kitchen. I have never had a friend or a kind word, except from you. I have been made to tend the little girls in the lower schoolroom, and to talk French to the Misses, until I grew sick of my mother-tongue. But that talking French to Miss Pinkerton was capital fun, wasn't it? She doesn't know a word of French, and was too proud to confess it. I believe it was that which made her part with me; and so thank Heaven for French. *Vive la France! Vive l'Empereur! Vive Bonaparte!*"

"O Rebecca, Rebecca, for shame!" cried Miss Sedley; for this was the greatest blasphemy Rebecca had as yet uttered; and in those days, in England, to say, "Long live Bonaparte!" was as much as to say, "Long live Lucifer!" "How can you—how dare you have such wicked, revengeful thoughts?"

"Revenge may be wicked, but it's natural," answered Miss Rebecca. "I'm no angel." And, to say the truth, she certainly was not.

For it may be remarked in the course of this little conversation (which took place as the coach rolled along lazily by the river side) that though Miss Rebecca Sharp has twice had occasion to thank Heaven, it has been, in the first place, for ridding her of some person whom she hated, and secondly, for enabling her to bring her enemies to some sort of perplexity or confusion; neither of which are very amiable motives for religious gratitude, or such as would be put forward by persons of kind and placable disposition. Miss Rebecca was not, then, in the least kind or placable. All the world used her ill, said this young misanthropist, and we may be pretty certain that persons whom all the world treats ill deserve entirely the treatment they get. The world is a looking-glass, and gives back to every man the reflection of his own face. Frown at it, and it will in turn look sourly upon you; laugh at it and with it, and it is a jolly kind companion; and so let all young persons take their choice. This is certain, that if the world neglected Miss Sharp, she never was known to have done a good action in behalf of anybody; nor can it be expected that twenty-four young ladies should all be as amiable as the heroine of this work, Miss Sedley (whom we have selected for the very reason that she was the best-natured of all, otherwise what on earth was to have prevented us from putting up Miss Swartz, or Miss Crump, or Miss Hopkins, as heroine in her place?)—it could not be expected that every one should be of the humble and gentle temper of Miss Amelia Sedley; should take every opportunity to vanquish Rebecca's hard-heartedness and ill-humor; and, by a thousand kind words and offices, overcome, for once at least, her hostility to her kind.

Miss Sharp's father was an artist, and in that quality had given lessons of drawing at Miss Pinkerton's school. He was a clever man; a pleasant companion; a careless student; with a great propensity for running into debt, and a partiality for the tavern. When he was drunk, he used to beat his wife and daughter; and the next morning, with a headache, he would rail at the world for its neglect of his genius, and abuse, with a good deal of cleverness, and sometimes with perfect reason, the fools, his brother painters. As it was with the utmost difficulty that he could keep himself, and as he owed money for a mile round Soho, where he lived, he thought to better his circumstances by marrying a young woman of the French nation, who was by profession an opera-girl. The humble calling of her female parent, Miss Sharp never alluded to, but used to state subsequently that the Entrechats were a noble

family of Gascony, and took great pride in her descent
from them. And curious it is, that as she advanced in
life this young lady's ancestors increased in rank and
splendour.

Rebecca's mother had had some education somewhere,
and the daughter spoke French with purity and a Parisian
accent. It was in those days rather a rare accomplishment, and led to her engagement with the orthodox Miss
Pinkerton. For her mother being dead, her father, finding
himself not likely to recover, after his third attack of
delirium tremens, wrote a manly and pathetic letter to Miss
Pinkerton, recommending the orphan child to her protection, and so descended to the grave, after two bailiffs
had quarrelled over his corpse. Rebecca was seventeen
when she came to Chiswick, and was bound over as an
articled pupil; her duties being to talk French, as we have
seen; and her privileges to live cost free, and, with a few
guineas a year, to gather scraps of knowledge from the professors who attended the school.

She was small and slight in person; pale, sandy-haired,
and with eyes habitually cast down: when they looked
up they were very large, odd, and attractive; so attractive,
that the Reverend Mr. Crisp, fresh from Oxford, and curate
to the Vicar of Chiswick, the Reverend Mr. Flowerdew, fell
in love with Miss Sharp; being shot dead by a glance of
her eyes which was fired all the way across Chiswick Church
from the school-pew to the reading-desk. This infatuated
young man used sometimes to take tea with Miss Pinkerton, to whom he had been presented by his mamma, and
actually proposed something like marriage in an intercepted
note, which the one-eyed apple-woman was charged to deliver. Mrs. Crisp was summoned from Buxton, and abruptly
carried off her darling boy; but the idea, even, of such an
eagle in the Chiswick dovecot caused a great flutter in the
breast of Miss Pinkerton, who would have sent away Miss
Sharp, but that she was bound to her under a forfeit, and
who never could thoroughly believe the young lady's protestations that she had never exchanged a single word with
Mr. Crisp, except under her own eyes on the two occasions
when she had met him at tea.

By the side of many tall and bouncing young ladies in
the establishment, Rebecca Sharp looked like a child. But
she had the dismal precocity of poverty. Many a dun had
she talked to, and turned away from her father's door;
many a tradesman had she coaxed and wheedled into good-
humour, and into the granting of one meal more. She sate
commonly with her father, who was very proud of her wit,
and heard the talk of many of his wild companions—often
but ill-suited for a girl to hear. But she never had been a
girl, she said; she had been a woman since she was eight
years old. O why did Miss Pinkerton let such a dangerous
bird into her cage?

The fact is, the old lady believed Rebecca to be the
meekest creature in the world, so admirably, on the occasions when her father brought her to Chiswick, used Rebecca to perform the part of the *ingenue;* and only a year
before the arrangement by which Rebecca had been admitted into her house, and when Rebecca was sixteen years
old, Miss Pinkerton majestically, and with a little speech,
made her a present of a doll—which was, by the way, the
confiscated property of Miss Swindle, discovered surrepti-
tiously nursing it in school-hours. How the father and
daughter laughed as they trudged home together after the
evening party, (it was on the occasion of the speeches,
when all the professors were invited,) and how Miss Pinkerton would have raged had she seen the caricature of herself which the little mimic, Rebecca, managed to make out
of her doll. Becky used to go through dialogues with it;
it formed the delight of Newman Street, Gerrard Street,
and the Artists' quarter: and the young painters, when
they came to take their gin-and-water with their lazy, dissolute, clever, jovial senior, used regularly to ask Rebecca
if Miss Pinkerton was at home: she was as well known to
them, poor soul! as Mr. Lawrence or President West.
Once Rebecca had the honour to pass a few days at Chiswick; after which she brought back Jemima, and erected
another doll as Miss Jemmy: for though that honest creature had made and given her jelly and cake enough for three
children, and a seven-shilling piece at parting, the girl's
sense of ridicule was far stronger than her gratitude,

and she sacrificed Miss Jemmy quite as pitilessly as her sister.

The catastrophe came, and she was brought to the Mall as to her home. The rigid formality of the place suffocated her: the prayers and the meals, the lessons and the walks, which were arranged with a conventual regularity, oppressed her almost beyond endurance; and she looked back to the freedom and the beggary of the old studio in Soho with so much regret, that everybody, herself included, fancied she was consumed with grief for her father. She had a little room in the garret, where the maids heard her walking and sobbing at night; but it was with rage, and not with grief. She had not been much of a dissembler, until now her loneliness taught her to feign. She had never mingled in the society of women: her father, reprobate as he was, was a man of talent; his conversation was a thousand times more agreeable to her than the talk of such of her own sex as she now encountered. The pompous vanity of the old schoolmistress, the foolish good-humour of her sister, the silly chat and scandal of the elder girls, and the frigid correctness of the governesses equally annoyed her; and she had no soft maternal heart, this unlucky girl, otherwise the prattle and talk of the younger children, with whose care she was chiefly intrusted, might have soothed and interested her; but she lived among them two years, and not one was sorry that she went away. The gentle tender-hearted Amelia Sedley was the only person to whom she could attach herself in the least; and who could help attaching herself to Amelia?

The happiness—the superior advantages of the young women round about her, gave Rebecca inexpressible pangs of envy. "What airs that girl gives herself, because she is an Earl's grand-daughter," she said of one. "How they cringe and bow to that Creole, because of her hundred thousand pounds! I am a thousand times cleverer and more charming than that creature, for all her wealth. I am as well bred as the Earl's grand-daughter, for all her fine pedigree; and yet every one passes me by here. And yet, when I was at my father's, did not the men give up their gayest balls and parties in order to pass the evening with me?" She determined at any rate to get free from the prison in which she found herself, and now began to act for herself, and for the first time to make connected plans for the future.

She took advantage, therefore, of the means of study the place offered her; and as she was already a musician and a good linguist, she speedily went through the little course of study which was considered necessary for ladies in those days. Her music she practised incessantly, and one day, when the girls were out, and she had remained at home, she was overheard to play a piece so well, that Minerva thought wisely, she could spare herself the expense of a master for the juniors, and intimated to Miss Sharp that she was to instruct them in music for the future.

The girl refused; and for the first time, and to the astonishment of the majestic mistress of the school. "I am here to speak French with the children," Rebecca said abruptly, "not to teach them music, and save money for you. Give me money, and I will teach them."

Minerva was obliged to yield, and, of course, disliked her from that day. "For five-and-thirty years," she said, and with great justice, "I never have seen the individual who has dared in my own house to question my authority. I have nourished a viper in my bosom."

"A viper—a fiddlestick," said Miss Sharp to the old lady, almost fainting with astonishment. "You took me because I was useful. There is no question of gratitude between us. I hate this place, and want to leave it. I will do nothing here but what I am obliged to do."

It was in vain that the old lady asked her if she was aware she was speaking to Miss Pinkerton? Rebecca laughed in her face, with a horrid sarcastic demoniacal laughter, that almost sent the schoolmistress into fits. "Give me a sum of money," said the girl, "and get rid of me—or, if you like better, get me a good place as governess in a nobleman's family—you can do so if you please." And in their further disputes she always returned to this point, "Get me a situation—we hate each other, and I am ready to go."

Worthy Miss Pinkerton, although she had a Roman nose and a turban, and was as tall as a grenadier, and had been up to this time an irresistible princess, had no will or strength like that of her little apprentice, and in vain did battle against her, and tried to overawe her. Attempting once to scold her in public, Rebecca hit upon the before-mentioned plan of answering her in French, which quite routed the old woman. In order to maintain authority in her school, it became necessary to remove this rebel, this monster, this serpent, this firebrand; and hearing about this time that Sir Pitt Crawley's family was in want of a governess, she actually recommended Miss Sharp for the situation, firebrand and servant as she was. "I cannot, certainly," she said, "find fault with Miss Sharp's conduct, except to myself; and must allow that her talents and accomplishments are of a high order. As far as the head goes, at least, she does credit to the educational system pursued at my establishment."

And so the schoolmistress reconciled the recommendation to her conscience, and the indentures were cancelled, and the apprentice was free. The battle here described in a few lines, of course, lasted for some months. And as Miss Sedley, being now in her seventeenth year, was about to leave school, and had a friendship for Miss Sharp, ("'tis the only point in Amelia's behaviour," said Minerva, "which has not been satisfactory to her mistress,") Miss Sharp was invited by her friend to pass a week with her at home, before she entered upon her duties as governess in a private family.

Thus the world began for these two young ladies. For Amelia it was quite a new, fresh, brilliant world, with all the bloom upon it. It was not quite a new one for Rebecca—(indeed, if the truth must be told with respect to the Crisp affair, the tart-woman hinted to somebody, who took an affidavit of the fact to somebody else, that there was a great deal more than was made public regarding Mr. Crisp and Miss Sharp, and that his letter was *in answer* to another letter). But who can tell you the real truth of the matter? At all events, if Rebecca was not beginning the world, she was beginning it over again.

By the time the young ladies reached Kensington turn-pike, Amelia had not forgotten her companions, but had dried her tears, and had blushed very much and been delighted at a young officer of the Life Guards, who spied her as he was riding by and said, "A dem fine gal, egad!" and before the carriage arrived in Russell Square, a great deal of conversation had taken place about the Drawing-room, and whether or not young ladies wore powder as well as hoops when presented, and whether she was to have that honour: to the Lord Mayor's ball she knew she was to go. And when at length home was reached, Miss Amelia Sedley skipped out on Sambo's arm, as happy and as handsome a girl as any in the whole big city of London. Both he and coachman agreed on this point, and so did her father and mother, and so did every one of the servants in the house, as they stood bobbing and curtseying, and smiling, in the hall to welcome their young mistress.

You may be sure that she showed Rebecca over every room of the house, and everything in every one of her drawers; and her books, and her piano, and her dresses, and all her necklaces, brooches, laces, and gimcracks. She insisted upon Rebecca accepting the white cornelian and the turquoise rings, and a sweet sprigged muslin, which was too small for her, though it would fit her friend to a nicety; and she determined in her heart to ask her mother's permission to present her white Cashmere shawl to her friend. Could she not spare it? and had not her brother Joseph just brought her two from India?

When Rebecca saw the two magnificent Cashmere shawls which Joseph Sedley had brought home to his sister, she said, with perfect truth, "that it must be delightful to have a brother," and easily got the pity of the tender-hearted Amelia, for being alone in the world, an orphan without friends or kindred.

"Not alone," said Amelia; "you know, Rebecca, I shall always be your friend, and love you as a sister—indeed I will."

"Ah, but to have parents, as you have—kind, rich, affectionate parents, who give you everything you ask for; and their love, which is more precious than all! My poor papa could give me nothing, and I had but two frocks in all the world! And then, to have a brother, a dear brother! Oh, how you must love him!"

Amelia laughed.

"What! *don't* you love him? you, who say you love everybody?"

"Yes, of course, I do—only—"

"Only what?"

"Only Joseph doesn't seem to care much whether I love him or not. He gave me two fingers to shake when he arrived after ten years' absence! He is very kind and good, but he scarcely ever speaks to me; I think he loves his pipe a great deal better than his" . . . but here Amelia checked herself, for why should she speak ill of her brother? "He was very kind to me as a child," she added; "I was but five years old when he went away."

"Isn't he very rich?" said Rebecca. "They say all Indian nabobs are enormously rich."

"I believe he has a very large income."

"And is your sister-in-law a nice pretty woman?"

"La! Joseph is not married," said Amelia, laughing again.

Perhaps she had mentioned the fact already to Rebecca, but that young lady did not appear to have remembered it; indeed, vowed and protested that she expected to see a number of Amelia's nephews and nieces. She was quite disappointed that Mr. Sedley was not married; she was sure Amelia had said he was, and she doted so on little children.

"I think you must have had enough of them at Chiswick," said Amelia, rather wondering at the sudden tenderness on her friend's part; and indeed in later days Miss Sharp would never have committed herself so far as to advance opinions, the untruth of which would have been so easily detected. But we must remember that she is but nineteen as yet, unused to the art of deceiving, poor innocent creature! and making her own experience in her own person. The meaning of the above series of queries, as translated in the heart of this ingenious young woman, was simply this:—"If Mr. Joseph Sedley is rich and unmarried, why should I not marry him? I have only a fort-

night, to be sure, but there is no harm in trying." And
she determined within herself to make this laudable attempt. She redoubled her caresses to Amelia; she kissed
the white cornelian necklace as she put it on; and vowed
she would never, never part with it. When the dinner-bell
rang she went down stairs with her arm round her friend's
waist, as is the habit of young ladies. She was so agitated
at the drawing-room door, that she could hardly find courage to enter. "Feel my heart, how it beats, dear!" said
she to her friend.

"No, it doesn't," said Amelia. "Come in, don't be frightened. Papa won't do you any harm."'

CHAPTER III

REBECCA IS IN PRESENCE OF THE ENEMY

A VERY stout, puffy man, in buckskins and Hessian boots, with several immense neckcloths, that rose almost to his nose, with a red striped waistcoat and an apple green coat with steel buttons almost as large as crown pieces, (it was the morning costume of a dandy or blood of those days) was reading the paper by the fire when the two girls entered, and bounced off his arm-chair, and blushed excessively, and hid his entire face almost in his neckcloths at this apparition.

"It's only your sister, Joseph," said Amelia, laughing and shaking the two fingers which he held out. "I've come home *for good*, you know; and this is my friend, Miss Sharp, whom you have heard me mention."

"No, never, upon my word," said the head under the neckcloth, shaking very much,—"that is, yes,—what abominably cold weather, Miss;"—and herewith he fell to poking the fire with all his might, although it was in the middle of June.

"He's very handsome," whispered Rebecca to Amelia, rather loud.

"Do you think so?" said the latter. "I'll tell him."

"Darling! not for worlds," said Miss Sharp, starting back as timid as a fawn. She had previously made a respectful virgin-like curtsey to the gentleman, and her modest eyes gazed so perseveringly on the carpet that it was a wonder how she should have found an opportunity to see him.

"Thank you for the beautiful shawls, brother," said Amelia to the fire poker. "Are they not beautiful, Rebecca?"

"O heavenly!" said Miss Sharp, and her eyes went from the carpet straight to the chandelier.

Joseph still continued a huge clattering at the poker and tongs, puffing and blowing the while, and turning as red as his yellow face would allow him. "I can't make you such

20

handsome presents, Joseph," continued his sister, "but while I was at school, I have embroidered for you a very beautiful pair of braces."

"Good Gad! Amelia," cried the brother, in serious alarm, "what do you mean?" and plunging with all his might at the bell-rope, that article of furniture came away in his hand, and increased the honest fellow's confusion. "For heaven's sake see if my buggy's at the door. I *can't* wait. I must go. D— that groom of mine. I must go."

At this minute the father of the family walked in, rattling his seals like a true British merchant. "What's the matter, Emmy?" says he.

"Joseph wants me to see if his—his *buggy* is at the door. What is a buggy, papa?"

"It is a one-horse palanquin," said the old gentleman, who was a wag in his way.

Joseph at this burst out into a wild fit of laughter; in which, encountering the eye of Miss Sharp, he stopped all of a sudden, as if he had been shot.

"This young lady is your friend? Miss Sharp, I am very happy to see you. Have you and Emmy been quarrelling already with Joseph, that he wants to be off?"

"I promised Bonamy of our service, sir," said Joseph, "to dine with him."

"O fie! didn't you tell your mother you would dine here?"

"But in this dress it's impossible."

"Look at him, isn't he handsome enough to dine anywhere, Miss Sharp?"

On which, of course, Miss Sharp looked at her friend, and they both set off in a fit of laughter, highly agreeable to the old gentleman.

"Did you ever see a pair of buckskins like those at Miss Pinkerton's?" continued he, following up his advantage.

"Gracious heavens! Father," cried Joseph.

"There now, I have hurt his feelings. Mrs. Sedley, my dear, I have hurt your son's feelings. I have alluded to his buckskins. Ask Miss Sharp if I haven't? Come, Joseph, be friends with Miss Sharp, and let us all go to dinner."

"There's a pillau, Joseph, just as you like it, and Papa has brought home the best turbot in Billingsgate."

"Come, come, sir, walk down stairs with Miss Sharp, and I will follow with these two young women," said the father, and he took an arm of wife and daughter and walked merrily off.

If Miss Rebecca Sharp had determined in her heart upon making the conquest of this big beau, I don't think, ladies, we have any right to blame her; for though the task of husband-hunting is generally, and with becoming modesty, entrusted by young persons to their mammas, recollect that Miss Sharp had no kind parent to arrange these delicate matters for her, and that if she did not get a husband for herself, there was no one else in the wide world who would take the trouble off her hands. What causes young people to "come *out*," but the noble ambition of matrimony? What sends them trooping to watering-places? What keeps them dancing till five o'clock in the morning through a whole mortal season? What causes them to labour at piano-forte sonatas, and to learn four songs from a fashionable master at a guinea a lesson, and to play the harp if they have handsome arms and neat elbows, and to wear Lincoln Green toxophilite hats and feathers, but that they may bring down some "desirable" young man with those killing bows and arrows of theirs? What causes respectable parents to take up their carpets, set their houses topsy-turvy, and spend a fifth of their year's income in ball suppers and iced champagne? Is it sheer love of their species, an unadulterated wish to see young people happy and dancing? Psha! they want to marry their daughters; and, as honest Mrs. Sedley has, in the depths of her kind heart, already arranged a score of little schemes for the settlement of her Amelia, so also had our beloved but unprotected Rebecca determined to do her very best to secure the husband, who was even more necessary for her than for her friend. She had a vivid imagination; she had, besides, read the *Arabian Nights* and *Guthrie's Geography;* and it is a fact, that while she was dressing for dinner, and after she had asked Amelia whether her brother was very rich, she had built for herself a most magnificent castle in the air, of which she was mistress, with a husband somewhere in the background (she had not seen him as yet, and his figure would not therefore be very distinct); she had arrayed herself in an infinity of shawls, turbans, and diamond necklaces, and had mounted upon an elephant to the sound of the march in Bluebeard, in order to pay a visit of ceremony to the Grand Mogul. Charming Alnaschar visions! it is the happy privilege of youth to construct you, and many a fanciful young creature besides Rebecca Sharp has indulged in these delightful day-dreams ere now!

Joseph Sedley was twelve years older than his sister Amelia. He was in the East India Company's Civil Service, and his name appeared, at the period of which we write, in the Bengal division of the East India Register, as collector of Boggley Wollah, an honourable and lucrative post, as everybody knows: in order to know to what higher posts Joseph rose in the service, the reader is referred to the same periodical.

Boggley Wollah is situated in a fine, lonely, marshy, jungly district, famous for snipe-shooting, and where not unfrequently you may flush a tiger. Ramgunge, where there is a magistrate, is only forty miles off, and there is a cavalry station about thirty miles farther; so Joseph wrote home to his parents, when he took possession of his collectorship. He had lived for about eight years of his life, quite alone, at this charming place, scarcely seeing a Christian face except twice a year, when the detachment arrived to carry off the revenues which he had collected, to Calcutta.

Luckily, at this time he caught a liver complaint, for the cure of which he returned to Europe, and which was the source of great comfort and amusement to him in his native country. He did not live with his family while in London, but had lodgings of his own, like a gay young bachelor. Before he went to India he was too young to partake of the delightful pleasures of a man about town, and plunged into them on his return with considerable assiduity. He drove his horses in the Park; he dined at the fashionable taverns (for the Oriental Club was not as yet invented); he frequented the theatres, as the mode was in those days, or made his appearance at the opera, laboriously attired in tights and a cocked hat.

On returning to India, and ever after, he used to talk of the pleasure of this period of his existence with great enthusiasm, and give you to understand that he and Brummel were the leading bucks of the day. But he was as lonely here as in his jungle at Boggley Wollah. He scarcely knew a single soul in the metropolis: and were it not for his doctor, and the society of his blue-pill, and his liver complaint, he must have died of loneliness. He was lazy, peevish, and a *bon-vivant;* the appearance of a lady frightened him beyond measure; hence it was but seldom that he joined the paternal circle in Russell Square, where there was plenty of gaiety, and where the jokes of his good natured old father frightened his *amour-propre.* His bulk caused Joseph much anxious thought and alarm; now and then he would make a desperate attempt to get rid of his superabundant fat; but his indolence and love of good living speedily got the better of these endeavours at reform, and he found himself again at his three meals a day. He never was well dressed; but he took the hugest pains to adorn his big person, and passed many hours daily in that occupation. His valet made a fortune out of his wardrobe: his toilet-table was covered with as many pomatums and essences as ever were employed by an old beauty: he had tried, in order to give himself a waist, every girth, stay, and waistband then invented. Like most fat men, he *would* have his clothes made too tight, and took care they should be of the most brilliant colours and youthful cut. When dressed at length, in the afternoon, he would issue forth to take a drive with nobody in the Park; and then would come back in order to dress again and go and dine with nobody at the Piazza Coffee-House. He was as vain as a girl; and perhaps his extreme shyness was one of the results of his extreme vanity. If Miss Rebecca can get the better of *him,* and at her first entrance into life, she is a young person of no ordinary cleverness.

The first move showed considerable skill. When she called Sedley a very handsome man, she knew that Amelia would tell her mother, who would probably tell Joseph, or who, at any rate, would be pleased by the compliment paid to her son. All mothers are. If you had told Sycorax that her son Caliban was as handsome as Apollo, she would have been pleased, witch as she was. Perhaps, too, Joseph Sedley would overhear the compliment—Rebecca spoke loud enough—and he *did* hear, and (thinking in his heart that he was a very fine man), the praise thrilled through every fibre of his big body, and made it tingle with pleasure.

Then, however, came a recoil. "Is the girl making fun of me?" he thought, and straightway he bounced towards the bell, and was for retreating, as we have seen, when his father's jokes and his mother's entreaties caused him to pause and stay where he was. He conducted the young lady down to dinner in a dubious and agitated frame of mind. "Does she really think I am handsome?" thought he, "or is she only making game of me?" We have talked of Joseph Sedley being as vain as a girl. Heaven help us! the girls have only to turn the tables, and say of one of their own sex, "She is as vain as a man," and they will have perfect reason. The bearded creatures are quite as eager for praise, quite as finikin over their toilets, quite as proud of their personal advantages, quite as conscious of their powers of fascination, as any coquette in the world.

Down stairs, then, they went, Joseph very red and blushing, Rebecca very modest, and holding her green eyes downwards. She was dressed in white, with bare shoulders as white as snow—the picture of youth, unprotected innocence, and humble virgin simplicity. "I must be very quiet," thought Rebecca, "and very much interested about India."

Now we have heard how Mrs. Sedley had prepared a fine curry for her son, just as he liked it, and in the course of dinner a portion of this dish was offered to Rebecca. "What is it?" said she, turning an appealing look to Mr. Joseph.

"Capital," said he. His mouth was full of it; his face quite red with the delightful exercise of gobbling. "Mother, it's as good as my own curries in India."

"Oh, I must try some, if it is an Indian dish," said Miss Rebecca. "I am sure everything must be good that comes from there."

"Give Miss Sharp some curry, my dear," said Mr. Sedley, laughing.

Rebecca had never tasted the dish before.

"Do you find it as good as everything else from India?" said Mr. Sedley.

"Oh, excellent!" said Rebecca, who was suffering tortures with the cayenne pepper.

"Try a chili with it, Miss Sharp," said Joseph, really interested.

"A chili," said Rebecca, gasping. "Oh, yes!" She thought a chili was something cool, as its name imported, and was served with some. "How fresh and green they look," she said, and put one into her mouth. It was hotter than the curry; flesh and blood could bear it no longer. She laid down her fork. "Water, for Heaven's sake, water!" she cried. Mr. Sedley burst out laughing (he was a coarse man, from the Stock Exchange, where they love all sorts of practical jokes). "They are real Indian, I assure you," said he. "Sambo, give Miss Sharp some water."

The paternal laugh was echoed by Joseph, who thought the joke capital. The ladies only smiled a little. They thought poor Rebecca suffered too much. She would have liked to choke old Sedley, but she swallowed her mortification as well as she had the abominable curry before it, and as soon as she could speak, said, with a comical, good-humoured air—

"I ought to have remembered the pepper which the Princess of Persia puts in the cream-tarts in the *Arabian Nights*. Do you put cayenne into your cream-tarts in India, sir?"

Old Sedley began to laugh, and thought Rebecca was a good-humoured girl. Joseph simply said—"Cream-tarts, Miss? Our cream is very bad in Bengal. We generally use goats' milk; and, 'gad, do you know, I've got to prefer it!"

"You won't like *everything* from India now, Miss Sharp," said the old gentleman; but when the ladies had retired after dinner, the wily old fellow said to his son, "Have a care, Joe; that girl is setting her cap at you."

"Pooh! nonsense!" said Joe, highly flattered. "I recollect, sir, there was a girl at Dumdum, a daughter of Cutler of the Artillery, and afterwards married to Lance, the surgeon, who made a dead set at me in the year '4—at me and Mulligatawney, whom I mentioned to you before dinner —a devilish good fellow, Mulligatawney—he's a magistrate at Budgebudge, and sure to be in council in five years. Well, sir, the Artillery gave a ball, and Quintin, of the King's 14th, said to me, 'Sedley,' said he, 'I bet you thirteen to ten that Sophy Cutler hooks either you or Mulligatawney before the rains.' 'Done,' says I; and egad, sir—this claret's very good. Adamson's or Carbonell's?" . . .

A slight snore was the only reply: the honest stock-broker was asleep, and so the rest of Joseph's story was lost for that day. But he was always exceedingly communicative in a man's party, and has told this delightful tale many scores of times to his apothecary, Dr. Gollop, when he came to inquire about the liver and the blue-pill.

Being an invalid, Joseph Sedley contented himself with a bottle of claret besides his Madeira at dinner, and he managed a couple of plates full of strawberries and cream, and twenty-four little rout cakes, that were lying neglected in a plate near him, and certainly (for novelists have the privilege of knowing everything), he thought a great deal about the girl upstairs. "A nice, gay, merry young creature," thought he to himself. "How she looked at me when I picked up her handkerchief at dinner! She dropped it twice. Who's that singing in the drawing-room? 'Gad! shall I go up and see?"

But his modesty came rushing upon him with uncontrollable force. His father was asleep: his hat was in the hall: there was a hackney-coach stand hard by in Southampton Row. "I'll go and see the *Forty Thieves*," said he, "and Miss Decamp's dance;" and he slipped gently away on the pointed toes of his boots, and disappeared, without waking his worthy parent.

"There goes Joseph," said Amelia, who was looking from the open windows of the drawing-room, while Rebecca was singing at the piano.

"Miss Sharp has frightened him away," said Mrs. Sedley. "Poor Joe, why *will* he be so shy?"

CHAPTER IV

The Green Silk Purse

POOR Joe's panic lasted for two or three days; during which he did not visit the house, nor during that period did Miss Rebecca ever mention his name. She was all respectful gratitude to Mrs. Sedley; delighted beyond measure at the Bazaars; and in a whirl of wonder at the theatre, whither the good-natured lady took her. One day, Amelia had a head-ache, and could not go upon some party of pleasure to which the two young people were invited; nothing could induce her friend to go without her. "What! you who have shown the poor orphan what happiness and love are for the first time in her life—quit *you?* never!" and the green eyes looked up to Heaven and filled with tears; and Mrs. Sedley could not but own that her daughter's friend had a charming kind heart of her own.

As for Mr. Sedley's jokes, Rebecca laughed at them with a cordiality and perseverance which not a little pleased and softened that good-natured gentleman. Nor was it with the chiefs of the family alone that Miss Sharp found favour. She interested Mrs. Blenkinsop by evincing the deepest sympathy in the raspberry-jam preserving, which operation was then going on in the Housekeeper's room; she persisted in calling Sambo "Sir," and "Mr. Sambo," to the delight of that attendant; and she apologised to the lady's maid for giving her trouble in venturing to ring the bell, with such sweetness and humility, that the Servants' Hall was almost as charmed with her as the Drawing Room.

Once, in looking over some drawings which Amelia had sent from school, Rebecca suddenly came upon one which caused her to burst into tears and leave the room. It was on the day when Joe Sedley made his second appearance.

Amelia hastened after her friend to know the cause of this display of feeling and the good-natured girl came back without her companion, rather affected too. "You know, her father was our drawing-master, Mamma, at Chiswick, and used to do all the best parts of our drawings."

"My love! I'm sure I always heard Miss Pinkerton say that he did not touch them—he only *mounted* them."

"It was called mounting, Mamma. Rebecca remembers the drawing, and her father working at it, and the thought of it came upon her rather suddenly—and so, you know, she——"

"The poor child is all heart," said Mrs. Sedley.

"I wish she could stay with us another week," said Amelia.

"She's devilish like Miss Cutler that I used to meet at Dumdum, only fairer. She's married now to Lance, the Artillery Surgeon. Do you know, Ma'am, that once Quintin, of the 14th, bet me——"

"O Joseph we know that story," said Amelia, laughing. "Never mind about telling that, but persuade Mamma to write to Sir Something Crawley for leave of absence for poor dear Rebecca:—here she comes, her eyes red with weeping."

"I'm better, now," said the girl, with the sweetest smile possible, taking good-natured Mrs. Sedley's extended hand and kissing it respectfully. "How kind you all are to me! All," she added, with a laugh, "except you, Mr. Joseph."

"Me!" said Joseph, meditating an instant departure. "Gracious Heavens! Good Gad! Miss Sharp!"

"Yes; how could you be so cruel as to make me eat that horrid pepper-dish at dinner, the first day I ever saw you? You are not so good to me as dear Amelia."

"He doesn't know you so well," cried Amelia.

"I defy anybody not to be good to you, my dear," said her mother.

"The curry was capital; indeed it was," said Joe, quite gravely. "Perhaps there was *not* enough citron juice in it; no, there was *not*."

"And the chilis?"

"By Jove, how they made you cry out!" said Joe, caught by the ridicule of the circumstance, and exploding in a fit of laughter which ended quite suddenly, as usual.

"I shall take care how I let *you* choose for me another time," said Rebecca, as they went down again to dinner. "I didn't think men were fond of putting poor harmless girls to pain."

"By Gad, Miss Rebecca, I wouldn't hurt you for the world."

"No," said she, "I *know* you wouldn't;" and then she gave him ever so gentle a pressure with her little hand, and drew it back quite frightened, and looked first for one instant in his face, and then down at the carpet-rods; and I am not prepared to say that Joe's heart did not thump at this little involuntary, timid, gentle motion of regard on the part of the simple girl.

It was an advance, and as such, perhaps, some ladies of indisputable correctness and gentility will condemn the action as immodest; but, you see, poor dear Rebecca had all this work to do for herself. If a person is too poor to keep a servant, though ever so elegant, he must sweep his own rooms: if a dear girl has no dear Mamma to settle matters with the young man, she must do it for herself. And oh, what a mercy it is that these women do not exercise their powers oftener! We can't resist them, if they do. Let them show ever so little inclination, and men go down on their knees at once: old or ugly, it is all the same. And this I set down as a positive truth. A woman with fair opportunities, and without an absolute hump, may marry WHOM SHE LIKES. Only let us be thankful that the darlings are like the beasts of the field, and don't know their own power. They would overcome us entirely if they did.

"Egad!" thought Joseph, entering the dining-room, "I exactly begin to feel as I did at Dumdum with Miss Cutler." Many sweet little appeals, half tender, half jocular, did Miss Sharp make to him about the dishes at dinner; for by this time she was on a footing of considerable familiarity with the family, and as for the girls, they loved each other like sisters. Young unmarried girls always do, if they are in a house together for ten days.

As if bent upon advancing Rebecca's plans in every way— what must Amelia do, but remind her brother of a promise made last Easter holidays—"When I was a girl at school," said she, laughing—a promise that he, Joseph, would take her to Vauxhall. "Now," she said, "that Rebecca is with us, will be the very time."

"O, delightful!" said Rebecca, going to clap her hands; but she recollected herself, and paused, like a modest creature, as she was.

"To-night is not the night," said Joe.

"Well, to-morrow."

"To-morrow your Papa and I dine out," said Mrs. Sedley.

"You don't suppose that *I'm* going, Mrs. Sed.?" said her husband, "and that a woman of your years and size is to catch cold, in such an abominable damp place?"

"The children must have some one with them," cried Mrs. Sedley.

"Let Joe go," said his father, laughing. "He's *big* enough." At which speech even Mr. Sambo at the sideboard burst out laughing, and poor fat Joe felt inclined to become a parricide almost.

"Undo his stays!" continued the pitiless old gentleman. "Fling some water in his face, Miss Sharp, or carry him upstairs: the dear creature's fainting. Poor victim! carry him up; he's as light as a feather!"

"If I stand this, I'm d——!" roared Joseph.

"Order Mr. Jos's elephant, Sambo!" cried the father. "Send to Exeter 'Change, Sambo;" but seeing Jos ready almost to cry with vexation, the old joker stopped his laughter, and said, holding out his hand to his son, "It's all fair on the Stock Exchange, Jos,—and, Sambo, never mind the elephant, but give me and Mr. Jos a glass of Champagne. Boney himself hasn't got such in his cellar, my boy!"

A goblet of Champagne restored Joseph's equanimity, and before the bottle was emptied, of which as an invalid he took two-thirds, he had agreed to take the young ladies to Vauxhall.

"The girls must have a gentleman apiece," said the old gentleman. "Jos will be sure to leave Emmy in the crowd, he will be so taken up with Miss Sharp here. Send to 96, and ask George Osborne if he'll come."

At this, I don't know in the least for what reason, Mrs. Sedley looked at her husband and laughed. Mr. Sedley's eyes twinkled in a manner indescribably roguish, and he looked at Amelia; and Amelia, hanging down her head, blushed as only young ladies of seventeen know how to blush, and as Miss Rebecca Sharp never blushed in her life —at least not since she was eight years old, and when she was caught stealing jam out of a cupboard by her godmother. "Amelia had better write a note," said her father; "and let George Osborne see what a beautiful hand-writing we have brought back from Miss Pinkerton's. Do you remember when you wrote to him to come on Twelfth-night, Emmy, and spelt twelfth without the f?"

"That was years ago," said Amelia.

"It seems like yesterday, don't it, John?" said Mrs. Sedley to her husband; and that night in a conversation which took place in a front room in the second-floor, in a sort of tent, hung round with chintz of a rich and fantastic India pattern, and *doublé* with calico of a tender rose-colour; in the interior of which species of marquee was a feather-bed, on which were two pillows, on which were two round red faces, one in a laced nightcap, and one in a simple cotton one, ending in a tassel:—in *a curtain lecture,* I say, Mrs. Sedley took her husband to task for his cruel conduct to poor Joe.

"It was quite wicked of you, Mr. Sedley," said she, "to torment the poor boy so."

"My dear," said the cotton-tassel in defence of his conduct, "Jos is a great deal vainer than you ever were in your life, and that's saying a good deal. Though, some thirty years ago, in the year seventeen hundred and eighty —what was it?—perhaps you had a right to be vain.—I don't say no.

"But I've no patience with Jos and his dandified modesty. It is out-Josephing Joseph, my dear, and all the while the boy is only thinking of himself. and what a fine fellow he is. I doubt, Ma'am, we shall have some trouble with him yet. Here is Emmy's little friend making love to him as hard as she can; that's quite clear; and if she does not catch him some other will. That man is destined to be a prey to woman, as I am to go on 'Change every day. It's a mercy he did not bring us over a black daughter-in-law, my dear. But, mark my words, the first woman who fishes for him, hooks him."

"She shall go off to-morrow, the little artful creature," said Mrs. Sedley, with great energy.

"Why not she as well as another, Mrs. Sedley? The girl's a white face at any rate. *I* don't care who marries him. Let Joe please himself."

And presently the voices of the two speakers were hushed, or were replaced by the gentle but unromantic music of the nose; and save when the church bells tolled the hour and the watchman called it, all was silent at the house of John Sedley, Esquire, of Russell Square, and the Stock Exchange.

When morning came, the good-natured Mrs. Sedley no longer thought of executing her threats with regard to Miss Sharp; for though nothing is more keen, nor more common, nor more justifiable, than maternal jealousy, yet she could not bring herself to suppose that the little, humble, grateful, gentle governess, would dare to look up to such a magnificent personage as the Collector of Boggley Wollah. The petition, too, for an extension of the young lady's leave of absence had already been despatched, and it would be difficult to find a pretext for abruptly dismissing her.

And as if all things conspired in favour of the gentle Rebecca, the very elements (although she was not inclined at first to acknowledge their action in her behalf) interposed to aid her. For on the evening appointed for the Vauxhall party, George Osborne having come to dinner, and the elders of the house having departed, according to invitation, to dine with Alderman Balls, at Highbury Barn, there came on such a thunder-storm as only happens on Vauxhall nights, and as obliged the young people, perforce, to remain at home. Mr. Osborne did not seem in the least disappointed at this occurrence. He and Joseph Sedley drank a fitting quantity of port-wine, *tête-à-tête,* in the dining-room,—during the drinking of which Sedley told a number of his best Indian stories; for he was extremely talkative in man's society;—and afterwards Miss Amelia Sedley did the honours of the drawing-room; and these four young persons passed such a comfortable evening together, that they declared they were rather glad of the thunder-storm than otherwise, which had caused them to put off their visit to Vauxhall.

Osborne was Sedley's godson, and had been one of the family any time these three-and-twenty years. At six weeks old, he had received from John Sedley a present of a silver cup; at six months old, a coral with gold whistle and bells; from his youth, upwards, he was "tipped" regularly by the old gentleman at Christmas: and on going back to school, he remembered perfectly well being thrashed by Joseph Sedley, when the latter was a big, swaggering, hobbadyhoy, and George an impudent urchin of ten years old. In a word George was as familiar with the family as such daily acts of kindness and intercourse could make him.

"Do you remember, Sedley, what a fury you were in when I cut off the tassels of your Hessian boots, and how Miss—hem—how Amelia rescued me from a beating, by falling down on her knees and crying out to her brother Jos, not to beat little George?"

Jos remembered this remarkable circumstance perfectly well, but vowed that he had totally forgotten it.

"Well, do you remember coming down in a gig to Dr. Swishtail's to see me, before you went to India, and giving me half a guinea and a pat on the head? I always had an idea that you were at least seven feet high, and was quite astonished at your return from India to find you no taller than myself."

"How good of Mr. Sedley to go to your school and give you the money!" exclaimed Rebecca, in accents of extreme delight.

"Yes, and after I had cut the tassels of his boots too. Boys never forget those tips at school, nor the givers."

"I delight in Hessian boots," said Rebecca. Jos Sedley, who admired his own legs prodigiously, and always wore this ornamental *chaussure,* was extremely pleased at this remark, though he drew his legs under his chair as it was made.

"Miss Sharp!" said George Osborne, "you who are so clever an artist, you must make a grand historical picture of the scene of the boots. Sedley shall be represented in buckskins, and holding one of the injured boots in one hand; by the other he shall have hold of my shirt-frill. Amelia shall be kneeling near him, with her little hands up, and the picture shall have a grand allegorical title, as the frontispieces have in the Medulla and the spelling-book."

"I shan't have time to do it here," said Rebecca. "I'll do it when—when I'm gone." And she dropped her voice, and looked so sad and piteous, that everybody felt how cruel her lot was, and how sorry they would be to part with her.

"O that you could stay longer, dear Rebecca," said Amelia.

"Why?" answered the other, still more sadly. "That I may be only the more unhap—unwilling to lose you?" And she turned away her head. Amelia began to give way to that natural infirmity of tears which, we have said, was one of the defects of this silly little thing. George Osborne looked at the two young women with a touched curiosity; and Joseph Sedley heaved something very like a sigh out of his big chest, as he cast his eyes down towards his favourite Hessian boots.

"Let us have some music, Miss Sedley—Amelia," said George, who felt at that moment an extraordinary, almost irresistible impulse to seize the above-mentioned young woman in his arms, and to kiss her in the face of the company; and she looked at him for a moment, and if I should say that they fell in love with each other at that single instant of time, I should perhaps be telling an untruth, for the fact is, that these two young people had been bred up by their parents for this very purpose, and their banns had, as it were, been read in their respective families any time these ten years. They went off to the piano, which was situated, as pianos usually are, in the back drawing-room; and as it was rather dark, Miss Amelia, in the most unaffected way in the world, put her hand into Mr. Osborne's, who, of course, could see the way among the chairs and ottomans a great deal better than she could. But this arrangement left Mr. Joseph Sedley *tête-à-tête* with Rebecca. at the drawing-room table, where the latter was occupied in knitting a green silk purse.

"There is no need to ask family secrets," said Miss Sharp. "Those two have told theirs."

"As soon as he gets his company," said Joseph, "I believe the affair is settled. George Osborne is a capital fellow."

"And your sister the dearest creature in the world," said Rebecca. "Happy the man who wins her!" With this Miss Sharp gave a great sigh.

When two unmarried persons get together, and talk upon such delicate subjects as the present, a great deal of confidence and intimacy is presently established between them. There is no need of giving a special report of the conversation, which now took place between Mr. Sedley and the young lady; for the conversation, as may be judged from the foregoing specimen, was not especially witty or eloquent; it seldom is in private societies, or anywhere except in very high-flown and ingenious novels. As there was music in the next room, the talk was carried on, of course, in a low and becoming tone, though, for the matter of that, the couple in the next apartment would not have been disturbed had the talking been so loud, so occupied were they with their own pursuits.

Almost for the first time in his life, Mr. Sedley found himself talking, without the least timidity or hesitation, to a person of the other sex. Miss Rebecca asked him a great number of questions about India, which gave him an opportunity of narrating many interesting anecdotes about that country and himself. He described the balls at Government House, and the manner in which they kept themselves cool in the hot weather, with punkahs, tatties, and other contrivances; and he was very witty regarding the number of Scotchmen whom Lord Minto, the Governor-General, patronised; and then he described a tiger-hunt; and the manner in which the mahout of his elephant had been pulled off his seat by one of the infuriated animals. How delighted Miss Rebecca was at the Government balls, and how she laughed at the stories of the Scotch *aides-de-camp*, and called Mr. Sedley a sad wicked satirical creature; and how frightened she was at the story of the elephant! "For your mother's sake, dear Mr. Sedley," she said, "for the sake of all your friends, promise *never* to go on one of those horrid expeditions."

"Pooh, pooh, Miss Sharp," said he pulling up his shirt-collars; "the danger makes the sport only the pleasanter." He had never been but once at a tiger-hunt, when the accident in question occurred, and when he was half killed—not by the tiger, but by the fright. And as he talked on, he grew quite bold, and actually had the audacity to ask Miss Rebecca for whom she was knitting the green silk purse? He was quite surprised and delighted at his own graceful familiar manner.

"For any one who wants a purse," replied Miss Rebecca, looking at him in the most gentle winning way. Sedley was going to make one of the most eloquent speeches possible, and had begun—"O Miss Sharp, how——" when some song which was performed in the other room came to an end, and caused him to hear his own voice so distinctly that he stopped, blushed, and blew his nose in great agitation.

"Did you ever hear anything like your brother's eloquence?" whispered Mr. Osborne to Amelia. "Why, your friend has worked miracles."

"The more the better," said Miss Amelia; who, like almost all women who are worth a pin, was a match-maker in her heart, and would have been delighted that Joseph should carry back a wife to India. She had, too, in the course of this few days' constant intercourse, warmed into a most tender friendship for Rebecca, and discovered a million of virtues and amiable qualities in her which she had not perceived when they were at Chiswick together. For the affection of young ladies is of as rapid growth as Jack's beanstalk, and reaches up to the sky in a night. It is no blame to them that after marriage this *Sehnsucht nach der Liebe* subsides. It is what sentimentalists, who deal in *very* big words, call a yearning after the Ideal, and simply means that women are commonly not satisfied until they have husbands and children on whom they may centre affections, which are spent elsewhere, as it were, in small change.

Having expended her little store of songs, or having stayed long enough in the back drawing-room, it now appeared proper to Miss Amelia to ask her friend to sing. "You would not have listened to me," she said to Mr. Osborne (though she knew she was telling a fib), "had you heard Rebecca first."

"I give Miss Sharp warning, though," said Osborne, "that, right or wrong, I consider Miss Amelia Sedley the first singer in the world."

"You shall hear," said Amelia; and Joseph Sedley was actually polite enough to carry the candles to the piano. Osborne hinted that he should like quite as well to sit in the dark; but Miss Sedley, laughing, declined to bear him company any farther, and the two accordingly followed Mr. Joseph. Rebecca sang far better than her friend (though of course Osborne was free to keep his opinion) and exerted herself to the utmost, and, indeed, to the wonder of Amelia, who had never known her perform so well. She sang a French song, which Joseph did not understand in the least, and which George confessed he did not understand, and then a number of those simple ballads which were the fashion forty years ago, and in which British tars, our King, poor Susan, blue-eyed Mary, and the like, were the principal themes. They are not, it is said, very brilliant, in a musical point of view, but contain numberless good-natured, simple appeals to the affections, which people understood better than the milk-and-water *lagrime, sospiri,* and *felicità* of the eternal Donizettian music with which we are favoured now-a-days.

Conversation of a sentimental sort, befitting the subject, was carried on between the songs, to which Sambo, after he had brought the tea, the delighted cook, and even Mrs. Blenkinsop, the housekeeper, condescended to listen on the landing-place.

Among these ditties was one, the last of the concert, and to the following effect:—

Ah ! bleak and barren was the moor,
　Ah ! loud and piercing was the storm,
The cottage roof was shelter'd sure,
　The cottage hearth was bright and warm.
An orphan boy the lattice pass'd,
　And, as he mark'd its cheerful glow,
Felt doubly keen the midnight blast,
　And doubly cold the fallen snow.

They mark'd him as he onward prest,
　With fainting heart and weary limb;
Kind voices bade him turn and rest,
　And gentle faces welcomed him.
The dawn is up—the guest is gone,
　The cottage hearth is blazing still;
Heaven pity all poor wanderers lone !
　Hark to the wind upon the hill !

It was the sentiment of the before-mentioned words,
"When I'm gone," over again. As she came to the last
words, Miss Sharp's "deep-toned voice faltered." Everybody
felt the allusion to her departure, and to her hapless orphan
state. Joseph Sedley, who was fond of music, and soft-
hearted, was in a state of ravishment during the performance
of the song, and profoundly touched at its conclusion. If he
had had the courage; if George and Miss Sedley had remained, according to the former's proposal, in the farther
room, Joseph Sedley's bachelorhood would have been at an
end, and this work would never have been written. But at
the close of the ditty, Rebecca quitted the piano, and giving
her hand to Amelia, walked away into the front drawing-
room twilight; and, at this moment, Mr. Sambo made his
appearance with a tray, containing sandwiches, jellies, and
some glittering glasses and decanters, on which Joseph Sedley's attention was immediately fixed. When the parents of
the house of Sedley returned from their dinner-party, they
found the young people so busy in talking, that they had not
heard the arrival of the carriage, and Mr. Joseph was in the
act of saying, "My dear Miss Sharp, one little teaspoonful of
jelly to recruit you after your immense—your—your *delightful* exertions."

"Bravo, Jos !" said Mr. Sedley; on hearing the bantering
of which well-known voice, Jos instantly relapsed into an

alarmed silence, and quickly took his departure. He did not lie awake all night thinking whether or not he was in love with Miss Sharp; the passion of love never interfered with the appetite or the slumber of Mr. Joseph Sedley; but he thought to himself how delightful it would be to hear such songs as those after Cutcherry—what a *distinguée* girl she was—how she could speak French better than the Governor-General's lady herself—and what a sensation she would make at the Calcutta balls. "It's evident the poor devil's in love with me," thought he. "She is just as rich as most of the girls who come out to India. I might go farther, and fare worse, egad!" And in these meditations he fell asleep.

How Miss Sharp lay awake, thinking, will he come or not to-morrow? need not be told here. To-morrow came, and, as sure as fate, Mr. Joseph Sedley made his appearance before luncheon. He had never been known to confer such an honour on Russell Square. George Osborne was somehow there already (sadly "putting out" Amelia, who was writing to her twelve dearest friends at Chiswick Mall), and Rebecca was employed upon her yesterday's work. As Joe's buggy drove up, and while, after his usual thundering knock and pompous bustle at the door, the ex-Collector of Boggley Wollah laboured upstairs to the drawing-room, knowing glances were telegraphed between Osborne and Miss Sedley, and the pair, smiling archly, looked at Rebecca, who actually blushed as she bent her fair ringlets over her knitting. How her heart beat as Joseph appeared,—Joseph, puffing from the staircase, in shining creaking boots,—Joseph, in a new waistcoat, red with heat and nervousness, and blushing behind his wadded neck-cloth. It was a nervous moment for all; and as for Amelia, I think she was more frightened than even the people most concerned.

Sambo, who flung open the door and announced Mr. Joseph, followed grinning, in the Collector's rear, and bearing two handsome nosegays of flowers, which the monster had actually had the gallantry to purchase in Covent Garden Market that morning—they were not as big as the haystacks which ladies carry about with them now-a-days, in cones of filigree paper; but the young women were delighted with the gift, as Joseph presented one to each, with an exceedingly solemn bow.

"Bravo, Jos!" cried Osborne.

"Thank you, dear Joseph," said Amelia, quite ready to kiss her brother, if he were so minded. (And I think for a kiss from such a dear creature as Amelia, I would purchase all Mr. Lee's conservatories out of hand.)

"O heavenly, heavenly flowers!" exclaimed Miss Sharp, and smelt them delicately, and held them to her bosom, and cast up her eyes to the ceiling, in an ecstasy of admiration. Perhaps she just looked first into the bouquet, to see whether there was a *billet-doux* hidden among the flowers; but there was no letter.

"Do they talk the language of flowers at Boggley Wollah, Sedley?" asked Osborne, laughing.

"Pooh, nonsense!" replied the sentimental youth. "Bought 'em at Nathan's; very glad you like 'em; and eh, Amelia, my dear, I bought a pine-apple at the same time, which I gave to Sambo. Let's have it for tiffin; very cool and nice this hot weather." Rebecca said she had never tasted a pine, and longed beyond everything to taste one.

So the conversation went on. I don't know on what pretext Osborne left the room, or why, presently, Amelia went away, perhaps to superintend the slicing of the pine-apple; but Jos was left alone with Rebecca, who had resumed her work, and the green silk and the shining needles were quivering rapidly under her white slender fingers.

"What a beautiful, *byoo-ootiful* song that was you sang last night, dear Miss Sharp," said the Collector. "It made me cry almost; 'pon my honour it did."

"Because you have a kind heart, Mr. Joseph; all the Sedleys have, I think."

"It kept me awake last night, and I was trying to hum it this morning, in bed; I was, upon my honour. Gollop, my doctor, came in at eleven (for I'm a sad invalid, you know, and see Gollop every day), and, 'gad! there I was, singing away like—a robbin."

"O you droll creature! Do let me hear you sing it."

"Me? No, you, Miss Sharp; my dear Miss Sharp, do sing it."

"Not now, Mr. Sedley," said Rebecca, with a sigh. "My spirits are not equal to it; besides, I must finish the purse. Will you help me, Mr. Sedley?" And before he had time to ask how, Mr. Joseph Sedley, of the East India Company's service, was actually seated *tête-à-tête* with a young lady, looking at her with a most killing expression; his arms stretched out before her in an imploring attitude, and his hands bound in a web of green silk, which she was unwinding.

. . . . . .

In this romantic position Osborne and Amelia found the interesting pair, when they entered to announce that tiffin was ready. The skein of silk was just wound round the card; but Mr. Jos had never spoken.

"I am sure he will to-night, dear," Amelia said, as she pressed Rebecca's hand; and Sedley, too, had communed with his soul, and said to himself, " 'Gad, I'll pop the question at Vauxhall."

CHAPTER V

Dobbin of Ours

CUFF'S fight with Dobbin, and the unexpected issue of that contest, will long be remembered by every man who was educated at Dr. Swishtail's famous school. The latter youth (who used to be called Heigh-ho Dobbin, Gee-ho Dobbin, and by many other names indicative of puerile contempt) was the quietest, the clumsiest, and, as it seemed, the dullest of all Dr. Swishtail's young gentlemen. His parent was a grocer in the city: and it was bruited abroad that he was admitted into Dr. Swishtail's academy upon what are called "mutual principles"—that is to say, the expenses of his board and schooling were defrayed by his father in goods, not money; and he stood there—almost at the bottom of the school—in his scraggy corduroys and jacket, through the seams of which his great big bones were bursting—as the representative of so many pounds of tea, candles, sugar, mottled-soap, plums (of which a very mild proportion was supplied for the puddings of the establishment), and other commodities. A dreadful day it was for young Dobbin when one of the youngsters of the school, having run into the town upon a poaching excursion for hardbake and polonies, espied the cart of Dobbin & Rudge, Grocers and Oilmen, Thames Street, London, at the Doctor's door, discharging a cargo of the wares in which the firm dealt.

Young Dobbin had no peace after that. The jokes were frightful, and merciless against him. "Hullo, Dobbin," one wag would say, "here's good news in the paper. Sugars is ris', my boy." Another would set a sum—"If a pound of mutton-candles cost sevenpence-halfpenny, how much must Dobbin cost?" and a roar would follow from all the circle of young knaves, usher and all, who rightly considered that the selling of goods by retail is a shameful and in-

43

famous practice, meriting the contempt and scorn of all real gentlemen.

"Your father's only a merchant, Osborne," Dobbin said in private to the little boy who had brought down the storm upon him. At which the latter replied haughtily, "My father's a gentleman, and keeps his carriage;" and Mr. William Dobbin retreated to a remote outhouse in the playground, where he passed a half-holiday in the bitterest sadness and woe. Who amongst us is there that does not recollect similar hours of bitter, bitter childish grief? Who feels injustice; who shrinks before a slight; who has a sense of wrong so acute, and so glowing a gratitude for kindness, as a generous boy? and how many of those gentle souls do you degrade, estrange, torture, for the sake of a little loose arithmetic, and miserable dog-latin?

Now, William Dobbin, from an incapacity to acquire the rudiments of the above language, as they are propounded in that wonderful book the Eton Latin Grammar, was compelled to remain among the very last of Doctor Swishtail's scholars, and was "taken down" continually by little fellows with pink faces and pinafores when he marched up with the lower form, a giant amongst them, with his downcast, stupefied look, his dog's-eared primer, and his tight corduroys. High and low, all made fun of him. They sewed up those corduroys, tight as they were. They cut his bed-strings. They upset buckets and benches, so that he might break his shins over them, which he never failed to do. They sent him parcels, which, when opened, were found to contain the paternal soap and candles. There was no little fellow but had his jeer and joke at Dobbin; and he bore everything quite patiently, and was entirely dumb and miserable.

Cuff, on the contrary, was the great chief and dandy of the Swishtail Seminary. He smuggled wine in. He fought the town-boys. Ponies used to come for him to ride home on Saturdays. He had his top-boots in his room, in which he used to hunt in the holidays. He had a gold repeater: and took snuff like the doctor. He had been to the Opera, and knew the merits of the principal actors, preferring Mr. Kean to Mr. Kemble. He could knock you off forty Latin

verses in an hour. He could make French poetry. What
else didn't he know, or couldn't he do? They said even the
Doctor himself was afraid of him.

Cuff, the unquestioned king of the school, ruled over his
subjects, and bullied them, with splendid superiority. This
one blacked his shoes: that toasted his bread, others would
fag out, and give him balls at cricket during whole summer
afternoons. "Figs" was the fellow whom he despised most,
and with whom, though always abusing him, and sneering at
him, he scarcely ever condescended to hold personal communication.

One day in private, the two young gentlemen had had
a difference. Figs, alone in the school-room, was blundering over a home letter; when Cuff, entering, bade him
go upon some message, of which tarts were probably the
subject.

"I can't," says Dobbin; "I want to finish my letter."

"You *can't?*" says Mr. Cuff, laying hold of that document (in which many words were scratched out, many were
mis-spelt, on which had been spent I don't know how much
thought, and labour, and tears; for the poor fellow was
writing to his mother, who was fond of him, although she
was a grocer's wife, and lived in a back parlour in Thames
Street). "You *can't?*" says Mr. Cuff: "I should like to
know why, pray? Can't you write to old Mother Figs to-
morrow?"

"Don't call names," Dobbin said, getting off the bench
very nervous.

"Well, sir, will you go?" crowed the cock of the school.

"Put down the letter," Dobbin replied; "no gentleman
readth letterth."

"Well, *now* will you go?" says the other.

"No, I won't. Don't strike, or I'll *thmash* you," roars
out Dobbin, springing to a leaden inkstand, and looking so
wicked, that Mr. Cuff paused, turned down his coat sleeves
again, put his hands into his pockets, and walked away
with a sneer. But he never meddled personally with the
grocer's boy after that; though we must do him the justice
to say he always spoke of Mr. Dobbin with contempt behind
his back.

Some time after this interview, it happened that **Mr.** Cuff, on a sunshiny afternoon, was in the neighbourhood of poor William Dobbin, who was lying under a tree in the play-ground, spelling over a favourite copy of the *Arabian Nights* which he had—apart from the rest of the school, who were pursuing their various sports—quite lonely, and almost happy. If people would but leave children to themselves; if teachers would cease to bully them; if parents would not insist upon directing their thoughts, and dominating their feelings—those feelings and thoughts which are a mystery to all (for how much do you and I know of each other, of our children, of our fathers, of our neighbour, and how far more beautiful and sacred are the thoughts of the poor lad or girl whom you govern likely to be, than those of the dull and world-corrupted person who rules him?)—if, I say, parents and masters would leave their children alone a little more,—small harm would accrue, although a less quantity of *as in præsenti* might be acquired.

Well, William Dobbin had for once forgotten the world, and was away with Sinbad the Sailor in the Valley of Diamonds, or with Prince Ahmed and the Fairy Peribanou in that delightful cavern where the Prince found her, and whither we should all like to make a tour; when shrill cries, as of a little fellow weeping, woke up his pleasant reverie; and looking up, he saw Cuff before him, belabouring a little boy.

It was the lad who had peached upon him about the grocer's cart; but he bore little malice, not at least towards the young and small. "How dare you, sir, break the bottle?" says Cuff to the little urchin, swinging a yellow cricket-stump over him.

The boy had been instructed to get over the play-ground wall (at a selected spot where the broken glass had been removed from the top, and niches made convenient in the brick); to run a quarter of a mile; to purchase a pint of rum-shrub on credit; to brave all the Doctor's outlying spies, and to clamber back into the playground again; during the performance of which feat, his foot had slipt, and the bottle was broken, and the shrub had been spilt, and his pantaloons had been damaged, and he appeared before his employer a perfectly guilty and trembling, though harmless, wretch.

"How dare you, sir, break it?" says Cuff; "you blundering little thief. You drank the shrub, and now you pretend to have broken the bottle. Hold out your hand, sir."

Down came the stump with a great heavy thump on the child's hand. A moan followed. Dobbin looked up. The Fairy Peribanou had fled into the inmost cavern with Prince Ahmed: the Roc had whisked away Sinbad the Sailor out of the Valley of Diamonds out of sight, far into the clouds: and there was every-day life before honest William; and a big boy beating a little one without cause.

"Hold out your other hand, sir," roars Cuff to his little school-fellow, whose face was distorted with pain. Dobbin quivered, and gathered himself up in his narrow old clothes.

"Take that, you little devil!" cried Mr. Cuff, and down came the wicket again on the child's hand.—Don't be horrified, ladies, every boy at a public school has done it. Your children will so do and be done by, in all probability. Down came the wicket again; and Dobbin started up.

I can't tell what his motive was. Torture in a public school is as much licensed as the knout in Russia. It would me ungentlemanlike (in a manner) to resist it. Perhaps Dobbin's foolish soul revolted against that exercise of tyranny; or perhaps he had a hankering feeling of revenge in his mind, and longed to measure himself against that splendid bully and tyrant, who had all the glory, pride, pomp, circumstance, banners flying, drums beating, guards saluting in the place. Whatever may have been his incentive, however, up he sprang, and screamed out, "Hold off, Cuff; don't bully that child any more; or I'll——"

"Or you'll what?" Cuff asked in amazement at this interruption. "Hold out your hand, you little beast."

"I'll give you the worst thrashing you ever had in your life," Dobbin said, in reply to the first part of Cuff's sentence; and little Osborne, gasping and in tears, looked up with wonder and incredulity at seeing this amazing champion put up suddenly to defend him: while Cuff's astonishment was scarcely less. Fancy our late monarch George III. when

he heard of the revolt of the North American colonies:
fancy brazen Goliath when little David stepped forward and
claimed a meeting; and you have the feelings of Mr. Reginald
Cuff when this rencontre was proposed to him.

"After school," says he, of course; after a pause and a
look, as much as to say, "Make your will, and communicate your last wishes to your friends between this time and
that."

"As you please," Dobbin said. "You must be my bottle-
holder, Osborne."

"Well, if you like," little Osborne replied; for you see
his papa kept a carriage, and he was rather ashamed of
his champion.

Yes, when the hour of battle came, he was almost ashamed
to say, "Go it, Figs;" and not a single other boy in the place
uttered that cry for the first two or three rounds of this
famous combat; at the commencement of which the scientific
Cuff, with a contemptuous smile on his face, and as light
and as gay as if he was at a ball, planted his blows upon his
adversary, and floored that unlucky champion three times
running. At each fall there was a cheer; and everybody was
anxious to have the honour of offering the conqueror a knee.

"What a licking I shall get when it's over," young Osborne
thought, picking up his man. "You'd best give in," he said
to Dobbin; "it's only a thrashing, Figs, and you know I'm
used to it." But Figs, all whose limbs were in a quiver, and
whose nostrils were breathing rage, put his little bottle-
holder aside, and went in for a fourth time.

As he did not in the least know how to parry the blows
that were aimed at himself, and Cuff had begun the attack
on the three preceding occasions, without ever allowing his
enemy to strike, Figs now determined that he would commence the engagement by a charge on his own part; and
accordingly, being a left-handed man, brought that arm
into action, and hit out a couple of times with all his might
—once at Mr. Cuff's left eye, and once on his beautiful
Roman nose.

Cuff went down this time, to the astonishment of the
assembly. "Well hit, by Jove," says little Osborne, with the

air of a connoisseur, clapping his man on the back. "Give it him with the left, Figs my boy."

Figs's left made terrific play during all the rest of the combat. Cuff went down every time. At the sixth round, there were almost as many fellows shouting out, "Go it, Figs," as there were youth exclaiming, "Go it, Cuff." At the twelfth round the latter champion was all aboard, as the saying is, and had lost all presence of mind and power of attack or defence. Figs, on the contrary, was as calm as a Quaker. His face being quite pale, his eyes shining open, and a great cut on his under lip bleeding profusely, gave this young fellow a fierce and ghastly air, which perhaps struck terror into many spectators. Nevertheless, his intrepid adversary prepared to close for the thirteenth time.

If I had the pen of a Napier, or a Bell's Life, I should like to describe this combat properly. It was the last charge of the Guard—(that is, *it would* have been, only Waterloo had not yet taken place)—it was Ney's column breasting the hill of La Haye Sainte, bristling with ten thousand bayonets, and crowned with twenty eagles—it was the shout of the beef-eating British, as leaping down the hill they rushed to hug the enemy in the savage arms of battle—in other words, Cuff, coming up full of pluck, but quite reeling and groggy, the Fig-merchant put in his left as usual on his adversary's nose, and sent him down for the last time.

"I think *that* will do for him," Figs said, as his opponent dropped as neatly on the green as I have seen Jack Spot's ball plump into the pocket at billiards; and the fact is, when time was called, Mr. Reginald Cuff was not able, or did not choose, to stand up again.

And now all the boys set up such a shout for Figs as would have made you think he had been their darling champion through the whole battle; and as absolutely brought Dr. Swishtail out of his study, curious to know the cause of the uproar. He threatened to flog Figs violently, of course; but Cuff, who had come to himself by this time, and was washing his wounds, stood up and said, "It's my fault, sir—not Figs'—not Dobbin's. I was bullying a little boy; and he served me right." By which magnanimous speech he not only saved his conqueror a whipping, but got back all his ascendency over the boys which his defeat had nearly cost him.

Young Osborne wrote home to his parents an account of the transaction.

> *"Sugarcane House, Richmond, March,* 18—
>
> "DEAR MAMA,—I hope you are quite well. I should be much obliged to you to send me a cake and five shillings. There has been a fight here between Cuff & Dobbin. Cuff, you know, was the Cock of the School. They fought thirteen rounds, and Dobbin Licked. So Cuff is now only Second Cock. The fight was about me. Cuff was licking me for breaking a bottle of milk, and Figs wouldn't stand it. We call him Figs because his father is a Grocer—Figs & Rudge, Thames St., City—I think as he fought for me you ought to buy your tea and sugar at his father's. Cuff goes home every Saturday, but can't this, because he has 2 Black Eyes. He has a white Pony to come and fetch him, and a groom in livery on a bay mare. I wish my Papa would let me have a Pony, and I am
>
> "Your dutiful Son,
>
>   "GEORGE SEDLEY OSBORNE.
>
> "P.S.—Give my love to little Emmy. I am cutting her out a Coach in cardboard. Please not a seed-cake, but a plum-cake."

In consequence of Dobbin's victory, his character rose prodigiously in the estimation of all his schoolfellows, and the name of Figs, which had been a byword of reproach, became as respectable and popular a nickname as any other in use in the school. "After all, it's not his fault that his father's a grocer," George Osborne said, who, though a little chap, had a very high popularity among the Swishtail youth; and his opinion was received with great applause. It was voted low to sneer at Dobbin about this accident of birth. "Old Figs" grew to be a name of kindness and endearment; and the sneak of an usher jeered at him no longer.

And Dobbin's spirit rose with his altered circumstances. He made wonderful advances in scholastic learning. The superb Cuff himself, at whose condescension Dobbin could only blush and wonder, helped him on with his Latin verses; "coached" him in play-hours: carried him triumphantly out of the little-boy class into the middle-sized form; and even there got a fair place for him. It was discovered, that although dull at classical learning, at mathematics he was uncommonly quick. To the contentment of all he passed third in algebra, and got a French prize-book at the public Mid-

summer examination. You should have seen his mother's
face when Télémaque (that delicious romance) was presented to him by the Doctor in the face of the whole school
and the parents and company, with an inscription to Gulielmo
Dobbin. All the boys clapped hands in token of applause and
sympathy. His blushes, his stumbles, his awkwardness, and
the number of feet which he crushed as he went back to his
place, who shall describe or calculate?

Old Dobbin, his father, who now respected him for the
first time, gave him two guineas publicly; most of which he
spent in a general tuck-out for the school: and he came back
in a tail-coat after the holidays.

Dobbin was much too modest a young fellow to suppose
that this happy change in all his circumstances arose from
his own generous and manly disposition: he chose, from
some perverseness, to attribute his good fortune to the sole
agency and benevolence of little George Osborne, to whom
henceforth he vowed such a love and affection as is only
felt by children—such an affection, as we read in the charming fairy-book, uncouth Orson had for splendid young
Valentine his conqueror. He flung himself down at little
Osborne's feet, and loved him. Even before they were acquainted, he had admired Osborne in secret. Now he was
his valet, his dog, his man Friday. He believed Osborne
to be the possessor of every perfection, to be the handsomest,
the bravest, the most active, the cleverest, the most generous
of created boys. He shared his money with him: bought
him uncountable presents of knives, pencil-cases, gold seals,
toffee, Little Warblers, and romantic books, with large
coloured pictures of knights and robbers, in many of which
latter you might read inscriptions to George Sedley Osborne,
Esquire, from his attached friend William Dobbin—the which
tokens of homage George received very graciously, as became his superior merit.

So that Lieutenant Osborne, when coming to Russell
Square on the day of the Vauxhall party, said to the ladies,
"Mrs. Sedley, Ma'am, I hope you have room; I've asked
Dobbin of ours to come and dine here, and go with us to
Vauxhall. He's almost as modest as Jos."

"Modesty! pooh," said the stout gentleman, casting a *vainqueur* look at Miss Sharp.

"He is—but you are incomparably more graceful, Sedley," Osborne added, laughing. "I met him at the Bedford, when I went to look for you; and I told him that Miss Amelia was come home, and that we were all bent on going out for a night's pleasuring; and that Mrs. Sedley had forgiven his breaking the punch-bowl at the child's party. Don't you remember the catastrophe, Ma'am, seven years ago?"

"Over Mrs. Flamingo's crimson silk gown," said goodnatured Mrs. Sedley. "What a gawky it was! And his sisters are not much more graceful. Lady Dobbin was at Highbury last night with three of them. Such figures! my dears."

"The Alderman's very rich, isn't he?" Osborne said archly. "Don't you think one of the daughters would be a good spec for me, Ma'am?"

"You foolish creature! Who would take *you,* I should like to know, with your yellow face?"

"Mine a yellow face? Stop till you see Dobbin. Why, he had the yellow fever three times; twice at Nassau, and once at St. Kitts."

"Well, well; yours is quite yellow enough for us. Isn't it, Emmy?" Mrs. Sedley said: at which speech Miss Amelia only made a smile and a blush; and looking at Mr. George Osborne's pale interesting countenance, and those beautiful black, curling, shining whiskers, which the young gentleman himself regarded with no ordinary complacency, she thought in her little heart, that in His Majesty's army, or in the wide world, there never was such a face or such a hero. "I don't care about Captain Dobbin's complexion," she said, "or about his awkwardness. *I* shall always like him, I know;" her little reason being, that he was the friend and champion of George.

"There's not a finer fellow in the service," Osborne said, "nor a better officer, though he is not an Adonis, certainly." And he looked towards the glass himself with much *naïveté;* and in so doing, caught Miss Sharp's eye fixed keenly upon him, at which he blushed a little, and Rebecca thought in her

heart, *"Ah, mon beau Monsieur!* I think I have *your* gauge,"
—the little artful minx!

That evening, when Amelia came tripping into the drawing-room in a white muslin frock, prepared for conquest at
Vauxhall, singing like a lark, and as fresh as a rose—a
very tall ungainly gentleman, with large hands and feet,
and large ears, set off by a closely cropped head of black
hair, and in the hideous military frogged coat and cocked-
hat of those times, advanced to meet her, and made her one
of the clumsiest bows that was ever performed by a mortal.

This was no other than Captain William Dobbin, of His
Majesty's —— Regiment of Foot, returned from yellow
fever, in the West Indies, to which the fortune of the service
had ordered his regiment, whilst so many of his gallant
comrades were reaping glory in the Peninsula.

He had arrived with a knock so very timid and quiet,
that it was inaudible to the ladies upstairs: otherwise, you
may be sure Miss Amelia would never have been so bold as
to come singing into the room. As it was, the sweet fresh
little voice went right into the Captain's heart, and nestled
there. When she held out her hand for him to shake, before he enveloped it in his own, he paused, and thought—
"Well, is it possible—are you the little maid I remember
in the pink frock, such a short time ago—the night I upset
the punch-bowl, just after I was gazetted? Are you the
little girl that George Osborne said should marry him?
What a blooming young creature you seem, and what a
prize the rogue has got!" All this he thought, before he
took Amelia's hand into his own, and as he let his cocked-
hat fall.

His history since he left school, until the very moment
when we have the pleasure of meeting him again, although
not fully narrated, has yet, I think, been indicated sufficiently for an ingenious reader by the conversation in the
last page. Dobbin, the despised grocer, was Alderman
Dobbin—Alderman Dobbin was Colonel of the City Light
Horse, then burning with military ardour to resist the
French Invasion. Colonel Dobbin's corps, in which old Mr.
Osborne himself was but an indifferent corporal, had been
reviewed by the Sovereign and the Duke of York; and the

colonel and alderman had been knighted. His son had entered the army: and young Osborne followed presently in the same regiment. They had served in the West Indies and in Canada. Their regiment had just come home, and the attachment of Dobbin to George Osborne was as warm and generous now as it had been when the two were schoolboys.

So these worthy people sat down to dinner presently. They talked about war and glory, and Boney and Lord Wellington, and the last Gazette. In those famous days every gazette had a victory in it, and the two gallant young men longed to see their own names in the glorious list, and cursed their unlucky fate to belong to a regiment which had been away from the chances of honour. Miss Sharp kindled with this exciting talk, but Miss Sedley trembled and grew quite faint as she heard it. Mr. Jos told several of his tiger-hunting stories, finished the one about Miss Cutler and Lance the surgeon; helped Rebecca to everything on the table, and himself gobbled and drank a great deal.

He sprang to open the door for the ladies, when they retired, with the most killing grace—and coming back to the table, filled himself bumper after bumper of claret, which he swallowed with nervous rapidity.

"He's priming himself," Osborne whispered to Dobbin, and at length the hour and the carriage arrived for Vauxhall.

CHAPTER VI

Vauxhall

I KNOW that the tune I am piping is a very mild one (although there are some terrific chapters coming presently), and must beg the good-natured reader to remember, that we are only discoursing at present about a stock-broker's family in Russell Square, who are taking walks, or luncheon, or dinner, or talking and making love as people do in common life, and without a single passionate and wonderful incident to mark the progress of their loves. The argument stands thus—Osborne, in love with Amelia, has asked an old friend to dinner and to Vauxhall—Jos Sedley is in love with Rebecca. Will he marry her? That is the great subject now in hand.

We might have treated this subject in the genteel, or in the romantic, or in the facetious manner. Suppose we had laid the scene in Grosvenor Square, with the very same adventures would not some people have listened? Suppose we had shown how Lord Joseph Sedley fell in love, and the Marquis of Osborne became attached to Lady Amelia, with the full consent of the Duke, her noble father: or instead of the supremely genteel, suppose we had resorted to the entirely low, and described what was going on in Mr. Sedley's kitchen;—how black Sambo was in love with the cook (as indeed he was), and how he fought a battle with the coachman in her behalf; how the knife-boy was caught stealing a cold shoulder of mutton, and Miss Sedley's new *femme de chambre* refused to go to bed without a wax candle; such incidents might be made to provoke much delightful laughter, and be supposed to represent scenes of "life." Or if, on the contrary, we had taken a fancy for the terrible, and made the lover of the new *femme de chambre* a professional burglar, who bursts into the house with his band, slaughters black Sambo at the feet of his master, and carries off Amelia in her night-dress, not to be let loose again till the third volume, we should easily have constructed a tale of thrilling interest, through the fiery chapters of which the reader should hurry, panting. But my readers must hope for no such romance, only a homely story, and must be content with a chapter about Vauxhall, which is so short that it scarce deserves to be called a chapter at all. And yet it is a chapter, and a very important one too. Are not there little chapters in everybody's life, that seem to be nothing, and yet affect all the rest of the history?

Let us then step into the coach with the Russell Square party, and be off to the Gardens. There is barely room between Jos and Miss Sharp, who are on the front seat. Mr. Osborne sitting bodkin opposite, between Captain Dobbin and Amelia.

Every soul in the coach agreed, that on that night, Jos would propose to make Rebecca Sharp Mrs. Sedley. The parents at home had acquiesced in the arrangement, though, between ourselves, old Mr. Sedley had a feeling very much akin to contempt for his son. He said he was vain, selfish, lazy, and effeminate. He could not endure his airs as a man of fashion, and laughed heartily at his pompous braggadocio stories. "I shall leave the fellow half my property," he said; "and he will have, besides, plenty of his own; but as I am perfectly sure that if you, and I, and his sister were to die to-morrow, he would say 'Good Gad!' and eat his dinner just as well as usual, I am not going to make myself anxious about him. Let him marry whom he likes. It's no affair of mine."

Amelia, on the other hand, as became a young woman of her prudence and temperament, was quite enthusiastic for the match. Once or twice Jos had been on the point of saying something very important to her, to which she was most willing to lend an ear, but the fat fellow could not be brought to unbosom himself of his great secret, and very much to his sister's disappointment he only rid himself of a large sigh and turned away.

This mystery served to keep Amelia's gentle bosom in a perpetual flutter of excitement. If she did not speak with Rebecca on the tender subject, she compensated herself with long and intimate conversations with Mrs. Blenkinsop, the housekeeper, who dropped some hints to the lady's-maid, who may have cursorily mentioned the matter to the cook, who carried the news, I have no doubt, to all the tradesmen, so that Mr. Jos's marriage was now talked of by a very considerable number of persons in the Russell Square world.

It was, of course, Mrs. Sedley's opinion that her son would demean himself by a marriage with an artist's daughter. "But, lor', Ma'am," ejaculated Mrs. Blenkinsop, "we was only grocers when we married Mr. S., who was a stock-broker's clerk, and we hadn't five hundred pounds among us, and we're rich enough now." And Amelia was entirely of this opinion, to which, gradually, the good-natured Mrs. Sedley was brought.

Mr. Sedley was neutral. "Let Jos marry whom he likes," he said; "it's no affair of mine. This girl has no fortune; no more had Mrs. Sedley. She seems good-humoured and clever, and will keep him in order, perhaps. Better she, my dear, than a black Mrs. Sedley, and a dozen of mahogany grandchildren."

So that everything seemed to smile upon Rebecca's fortunes. She took Jos's arm, as a matter of course, on going to dinner; she had sate by him on the box of his open carriage (a most tremendous "buck" he was, as he sat there, serene, in state, driving his greys), and though nobody said a word on the subject of the marriage, everybody seemed to understand it. All she wanted was the proposal, and ah! how Rebecca now felt the want of a mother!—a dear, tender mother, who would have managed the business in ten minutes, and, in the course of a little delicate confidential conversation, would have extracted the interesting avowal from the bashful lips of the young man!

Such was the state of affairs as the carriage crossed West-minster-bridge.

The party was landed at the Royal Gardens in due time. As the majestic Jos stepped out of the creaking vehicle the crowd gave a cheer for the fat gentleman, who blushed and looked very big and mighty, as he walked away with Rebecca under his arm. George, of course, took charge of Amelia. She looked as happy as a rosetree in sunshine.

"I say, Dobbin," says George, "just look to the shawls and things, there's a good fellow." And so while he paired off with Miss Sedley, and Jos squeezed through the gate into the gardens with Rebecca at his side, honest Dobbin contented himself by giving an arm to the shawls, and by paying at the door for the whole party.

He walked very modestly behind them. He was not willing to spoil sport. About Rebecca and Jos he did not care a fig. But he thought Amelia worthy even of the brilliant George Osborne, and as he saw that good-looking couple threading the walks to the girl's delight and wonder, he watched her artless happiness with a sort of fatherly pleasure. Perhaps he felt that he would have liked to have something on his own arm besides a shawl (the people laughed at seeing the gawky young officer carrying this female burthen): but William Dobbin was very little addicted to selfish calculation at all; and so long as his friend was enjoying himself, how should he be discontented? And the truth is, that of all the delights of the Gardens; of the hundred thousand *extra* lamps, which were always lighted; the fiddlers in cocked hats, who played ravishing melodies under the gilded cockle-shell in the midst of the gardens; the singers, both of comic and sentimental ballads, who charmed the ears there; the country dances, formed by bouncing cockneys and cockneyesses, and executed amidst jumping, thumping, and laughter; the signal which announced that Madame Saqui was about to mount skyward on a slack-rope ascending to the stars; the hermit that always sat in the illuminated hermitage; the dark walks, so favourable to the interviews of young lovers; the pots of stout handed about by the people in the shabby old liveries; and the twinkling boxes, in which the happy feasters made-believe to eat slices of almost invisible ham;—of all these things, and of the gentle Simpson, that kind smiling idiot, who, I daresay, presided even then over the place— Captain William Dobbin did not take the silghtest notice.

He carried about Amelia's white cashmere shawl, and having attended under the gilt cockle-shell, while Mrs. Salmon performed the Battle of Borodino (a savage cantata against the Corsican upstart, who had lately met with his Russian reverses)—Mr. Dobbin tried to hum it as he walked

away, and found he was humming—the tune which Amelia
Sedley sang on the stairs, as she came down to dinner.

He burst out laughing at himself; for the truth is, he
could sing no better than an owl.

It is to be understood, as a matter of course, that our
young people, being in parties of two and two, made the
most solemn promises to keep together during the evening,
and separated in ten minutes afterwards. Parties at Vauxhall always did separate, but 'twas only to meet again at
supper-time, when they could talk of their mutual adventures
in the interval.

What were the adventures of Mr. Osborne and Miss
Amelia? That is a secret. But be sure of this—they were
perfectly happy, and correct in their behaviour; and as
they had been in the habit of being together any time these
fifteen years, their *tête-à-tête* offered no particular novelty.

But when Miss Rebecca Sharp and her stout companion
lost themselves in a solitary walk, in which there were not
above five score more of couples similarly straying, they
both felt that the situation was extremely tender and critical,
and now or never was the moment, Miss Sharp thought, to
provoke that declaration which was trembling on the timid
lips of Mr. Sedley. They had previously been to the pano-
rama of Moscow, where a rude fellow, treading on Miss
Sharp's foot, caused her to fall back with a little shriek into
the arms of Mr. Sedley, and this little incident increased the
tenderness and confidence of that gentleman to such a degree,
that he told her several of his favourite Indian stories over
again for, at least, the sixth time.

"How I should like to see India!" said Rebecca.

"*Should* you?" said Joseph, with a most killing tenderness; and was no doubt about to follow up this artful in-
terrogatory by a question still more tender (for he puffed
and panted a great deal, and Rebecca's hand, which was
placed near his heart, could count the feverish pulsations
of that organ), when, oh, provoking! the bell rang for the
fireworks, and, a great scuffling and running taking place,
these interesting lovers were obliged to follow in the stream
of people.

Captain Dobbin had some thoughts of joining the party at supper: as, in truth, he found the Vauxhall amusements not particularly lively—but he paraded twice before the box where the now united couples were met, and nobody took any notice of him. Covers were laid for four. The mated pairs were prattling away quite happily, and Dobbin knew he was as clean forgotten as if he had never existed in this world.

"I should only be *de trop*," said the Captain, looking at them rather wistfully. "I'd best go and talk to the hermit," —and so he strolled off out of the hum of men, and noise, and clatter of the banquet, into the dark walk, at the end of which lived that well-known pasteboard Solitary. It wasn't very good fun for Dobbin—and, indeed, to be alone at Vauxhall, I have found, from my own experience, to be one of the most dismal sports ever entered into by a bachelor.

The two couples were perfectly happy then in their box: where the most delightful and intimate conversation took place. Jos was in his glory, ordering about the waiters with great majesty. He made the salad; and uncorked the Champagne; and carved the chickens; and ate and drank the greater part of the refreshments on the tables. Finally, he insisted upon having a bowl of rack punch; everybody had rack punch at Vauxhall. "Waiter, rack punch."

That bowl of rack punch was the cause of all this history. And why not a bowl of rack punch as well as any other cause? Was not a bowl of prussic acid the cause of Fair Rosamond's retiring from the world? Was not a bowl of wine the cause of the demise of Alexander the Great, or, at least, does not Dr. Lempriere say so?—so did this bowl of rack punch influence the fates of all the principal characters in this "Novel without a Hero," which we are now relating. It influenced their life, although most of them did not taste a drop of it.

The young ladies did not drink it; Osborne did not like it; and the consequence was that Jos, that fat *gourmand*, drank up the whole contents of the bowl; and the consequence of his drinking up the whole contents of the bowl was, a liveliness which at first was astonishing, and then became almost painful; for he talked and laughed so loud as to bring scores of listeners round the box, much to the confusion of the innocent party within it; and, volunteering to sing a song (which he did in that maudlin high key peculiar to gentlemen in an inebriated state), he almost drew away the audience who were gathered round the musicians in the gilt scollop-shell, and received from his hearers a great deal of applause.

"Brayvo, Fat un!" said one; "Angcore, Daniel Lambert!" said another; "What a figure for the tight-rope!" exclaimed another wag, to the inexpressible alarm of the ladies, and the great anger of Mr. Osborne.

"For Heaven's sake, Jos, let us get up and go," cried that gentleman, and the young women rose.

"Stop, my dearest diddle-diddle-darling," shouted Jos, now as bold as a lion, and clasping Miss Rebecca round the waist. Rebecca started, but she could not get away her hand. The laughter outside redoubled. Jos continued to drink, to make love, and to sing; and, winking and waving his glass gracefully to his audience, challenged all or any to come in and take a share of his punch.

Mr. Osborne was just on the point of knocking down a gentleman in top-boots, who proposed to take advantage of this invitation, and a commotion seemed to be inevitable, when by the greatest good luck a gentleman of the name of Dobbin, who had been walking about the gardens, stepped up to the box. "Be off, you fools!" said this gentleman—shouldering off a great number of the crowd, who vanished presently before his cocked hat and fierce appearance—and he entered the box in a most agitated state.

"Good Heavens! Dobbin, where *have* you been?" Osborne said, seizing the white cashmere shawl from his friend's arm, and huddling up Amelia in it.—"Make yourself useful, take charge of Jos here, whilst I take the ladies to the carriage."

Jos was for rising to interfere—but a single push from Osborne's finger sent him puffing back into his seat again, and the lieutenant was enabled to remove the ladies in safety. Jos kissed his hand to them as they retreated, and hiccupped out "Bless you! Bless you!" Then, seizing Captain Dobbin's hand, and weeping in the most pitiful way, he confided to that gentleman the secret of his loves. He adored that girl

who had just gone out; he had broken her heart, he knew
he had, by his conduct; he would marry her next morning
at St. George's, Hanover Square; he'd knock up the Archbishop of Canterbury at Lambeth: he would, by Jove! and
have him in readiness; and, acting on this hint, Captain
Dobbin shrewdly induced him to leave the gardens and hasten
to Lambeth Palace, and, when once out of the gates, easily
conveyed Mr. Jos Sedley into a hackney-coach, which de-
posited him safely at his lodgings.

George Osborne conducted the girls home in safety: and
when the door was closed upon him, and as he walked
across Russell Square, laughed so as to astonish the watchman. Amelia looked very ruefully at her friend, as they
went up stairs, and kissed her, and went to bed without any
more talking.

"He must propose to-morrow," thought Rebecca. "He
called me his soul's darling, four times; he squeezed my
hand in Amelia's presence. He must propose to-morrow."
And so thought Amelia, too. And I dare say she thought
of the dress she was to wear as bridesmaid, and of the presents which she should make to her nice little sister-in-law,
and of a subsequent ceremony in which she herself might
play a principal part, &c., and &c., and &c., and &c.
Oh, ignorant young creatures! How little do you know
the effect of rack punch! What is the rack in the punch,
at night, to the rack in the head of a morning? To this
truth I can vouch as a man; there is no headache in the
world like that caused by Vauxhall punch. Through the
lapse of twenty years, I can remember the consequence of two
glasses!—two wine-glasses!—but two, upon the honour of a
gentleman; and Joseph Sedley, who had a liver complaint,
had swallowed at least a quart of the abominable mixture.
That next morning, which Rebecca thought was to dawn
upon her fortune, found Sedley groaning in agonies which
the pen refuses to describe. Soda-water was not invented
yet. Small beer—will it be believed—was the only drink
with which unhappy gentlemen soothed the fever of their
previous night's potation. With this mild beverage before

him, George Osborne found the ex-collector of Boggley Wollah groaning on the sofa at his lodgings. Dobbin was already in the room, good-naturedly tending his patient of the night before. The two officers, looking at the prostrate Bacchanalian, and askance at each other, exchanged the most frightful sympathetic grins. Even Sedley's valet, the most solemn and correct of gentlemen, with the muteness and gravity of an undertaker, could hardly keep his countenance in order, as he looked at his unfortunate master.

"Mr. Sedley was uncommon wild last night, sir," he whispered in confidence to Osborne, as the latter mounted the stair. "He wanted to fight the 'ackney-coachman, sir. The Capting was obliged to bring him up stairs in his harms like a babby." A momentary smile flickered over Mr. Brush's features as he spoke; instantly, however, they relapsed into their usual unfathomable calm, as he flung open the drawing-room door, and announced "Mr. Hosbin."

"How are you, Sedley?" that young wag began, after surveying his victim. "No bones broke? There's a hackney-coachman down stairs with a black eye, and a tied-up head, vowing he'll have the law of you."

"What do you mean,—law?" Sedley faintly asked.

"For thrashing him last night—didn't he, Dobbin? You hit out, sir, like Molyneux. The watchman says he never saw a fellow go down so straight. Ask Dobbin."

"You *did* have a round with the coachman," Captain Dobbin said, "and showed plenty of fight too."

"And that fellow with the white coat at Vauxhall! How Jos drove at him! How the women screamed! By Jove, sir, it did my heart good to see you. I thought you civilians had no pluck; but *I'll* never get in your way when you are in your cups, Jos."

"I believe I'm very terrible, when I'm roused," ejaculated Jos from the sofa, and made a grimace so dreary and ludicrous, that the Captain's politeness could restrain him no longer and he and Osborne fired off a ringing volley of laughter.

Osborne pursued his advantage pitilessly. He thought Jos a milk-sop. He had been revolving in his mind the marriage-question pending between Jos and Rebecca, and was not over well pleased that a member of a family into which he, George Osborne, of the —th, was going to marry, should make a *mésalliance* with a little nobody—a little upstart governess. "You hit, you poor old fellow!" said Osborne. "You were terrible! Why, man, you couldn't stand —you made everybody laugh in the Gardens, though you were crying yourself. You were maudlin, Jos. Don't you remember singing a song?"

"A what?" Jos asked.

"A sentimental song, and calling Rosa, Rebecca, what's her name, Amelia's little friend—your dearest diddle-diddle-darling?" And this ruthless young fellow, seizing hold of Dobbin's hand, acted over the scene, to the horror of the original performer, and in spite of Dobbin's good-natured entreaties to him to have mercy.

"Why should I spare him?" Osborne said to his friend's remonstrances, when they quitted the invalid, leaving him under the hands of Doctor Gollop. "What the deuce right has he to give himself his patronizing airs, and make fools of us at Vauxhall? Who's this little school-girl that is ogling and making love to him? Hang it, the family's low enough already, without *her*. A governess is all very well, but I'd rather have a lady for my sister-in-law. I'm a liberal man; but I've proper pride, and know my own station: let her know hers. And I'll take down that great hectoring Nabob, and prevent him from being made a greater fool than he is. That's why I told him to look out, lest she brought an action against him."

"I suppose you know best," Dobbin said, though rather dubiously. "You always were a Tory, and your family's one of the oldest in England. But——"

"Come and see the girls, and make love to Miss Sharp yourself," the lieutenant here interrupted his friend; but Captain Dobbin declined to join Osborne in his daily visit to the young ladies in Russell Square.

As George walked down Southampton Row, from Holborn, he laughed as he saw, at the Sedley Mansion, in two different stories, two heads on the look-out.

The fact is, Miss Amelia, in the drawing-room balcony, was looking very eagerly towards the opposite side of the square, where Mr. Osborne dwelt, on the watch for the lieutenant himself; and Miss Sharp, from her little bedroom on the second floor, was in observation until Mr. Joseph's great form should heave in sight.

"Sister Anne is on the watch-tower," said he to Amelia, "but there's nobody coming;" and laughing and enjoying the joke hugely, he described in the most ludicrous terms to Miss Sedley, the dismal condition of her brother.

"I think it's very cruel of you to laugh, George," she said, looking particularly unhappy; but George only laughed the more at her piteous and discomfited mien, persisted in thinking the joke a most diverting one, and when Miss Sharp came down stairs, bantered her with a great deal of liveliness upon the effect of her charms on the fat civilian."

"O Miss Sharp! if you could but see him this morning," he said—"moaning in his flowered dressing-gown—writhing on his sofa; if you could but have seen him lolling out his tongue to Gollop the apothecary."

"See whom?" said Miss Sharp.

"Whom? O whom? Captain Dobbin, of course, to whom we were all so attentive, by the way, last night."

"We were very unkind to him," Emmy said, blushing very much. "I—I quite forgot him."

"Of course you did," cried Osborne, still on the laugh. "One can't be *always* thinking about Dobbin, you know, Amelia. Can one, Miss Sharp?"

"Except when he overset the glass of wine at dinner," Miss Sharp said, with a haughty air and a toss of the head, "I never gave the existence of Captain Dobbin one single moment's consideration."

"Very good, Miss Sharp, I'll tell him," Osborne said; and as he spoke Miss Sharp began to have a feeling of distrust and hatred towards this young officer, which he was quite unconscious of having inspired. "*He* is to make fun of me, is he?" thought Rebecca. "Has he been laughing about me to Joseph? Has he frightened him? Perhaps he won't come."—A film passed over her eyes, and her heart beat quite quick.

"You're always joking," said she, smiling as innocently as she could. "Joke away, Mr. George; there's nobody to

defend *me*." And George Osborne, as she walked away—
and Amelia looked reprovingly at him—felt some little
manly compunction for having inflicted any unnecessary
unkindness upon this helpless creature. "My dearest Amelia,"
said he, "you are too good—too kind. You don't know the
world. I do. And your little friend Miss Sharp must learn
her station."

"Don't you think Jos will——"

"Upon my word, my dear, I don't know. He may, or
may not. I'm not his master. I only know he is a very
foolish vain fellow, and put my dear little girl into a very
painful and awkward position last night. My dearest diddle-
diddle-darling!" He was off laughing again; and he did
it so drolly that Emmy laughed too.

All that day Jos never came. But Amelia had no fear
about this; for the little schemer had actually sent away
the page, Mr. Sambo's aid-de-camp, to Mr. Joseph's lodgings, to ask for some book he had promised, and how he
was; and the reply through Jos's man, Mr. Brush, was,
that his master was ill in bed and had just had the doctor
with him. He must come to-morrow, she thought, but she
never had the courage to speak a word on the subject to
Rebecca; nor did that young woman herself allude to it in
any way during the whole evening after the night at Vauxhall.

The next day, however, as the two young ladies sate on
the sofa, pretending to work, or to write letters, or to read
novels, Sambo came into the room with his usual engaging
grin, with a packet under his arm, and a note on a tray.
"Note from Mr. Jos, Miss," says Sambo.

How Amelia trembled as she opened it!

So it ran—

"DEAR AMELIA,—I send you the 'Orphan of the Forest.' I was
too ill to come yesterday. I leave town to-day for Cheltenham.
Pray excuse me, if you can, to the amiable Miss Sharp, for my
conduct at Vauxhall, and entreat her to pardon and forget every
word I may have uttered when excited by that fatal supper. As
soon as I have recovered, for my health is very much shaken, I
shall go to Scotland for some months, and am
                                "Truly yours,
                                        "JOS. SEDLEY."

It was the death-warrant. All was over. Amelia did not dare to look at Rebecca's pale face and burning eyes, but she dropt the letter into her friend's lap; and got up, and went up stairs to her room, and cried her little heart out.

Blenkinsop, the housekeeper, there sought her presently with consolation, on whose shoulder Amelia wept confidentially, and relieved herself a good deal. "Don't take on, Miss. I didn't like to tell you. But none of us in the house have liked her except at fust. I sor her with my own eyes reading your Ma's letters. Pinner says she's always about your trinket-box and drawers, and everybody's drawers, and she's sure she's put your white ribbing into her box."

"I gave it her, I gave it her," Amelia said.

But this did not alter Mrs. Blenkinsop's opinion of Miss Sharp. "I don't trust them governesses, Pinner," she remarked to the maid. "They give themselves the hairs and hupstarts of ladies, and their wages is no better than you nor me."

It now became clear to every soul in the house, except poor Amelia, that Rebecca should take her departure, and high and low (always with the one exception) agreed that that event should take place as speedily as possible. Our good child ransacked all her drawers, cupboards, reticules, and gimcrack boxes—passed in review all her gowns, fichus, tags, bobbins, laces, silk stockings, and fallals—selecting this thing and that and the other, to make a little heap for Rebecca. And going to her Papa, that generous British merchant, who had promised to give her as many guineas as she was years old—she begged the old gentleman to give the money to dear Rebecca, who must want it, while she lacked for nothing.

She even made George Osborne contribute, and nothing loth (for he was as free-handed a young fellow as any in the army), he went to Bond Street, and bought the best hat and spenser that money could buy.

"That's George's present to you, Rebecca, dear," said Amelia, quite proud of the bandbox conveying these gifts. "What a taste he has! There's nobody like him."

"Nobody," Rebecca answered. "How thankful I am to him!" She was thinking in her heart, "It was George

Osborne who prevented my marriage."—And she loved George Osborne accordingly.

She made her preparations for departure with great equanimity; and accepted all the kind little Amelia's presents, after just the proper degree of hesitation and reluctance. She vowed eternal gratitude to Mrs. Sedley, of course; but did not intrude herself upon that good lady too much, who was embarrassed, and evidently wishing to avoid her. She kissed Mr. Sedley's hand, when he presented her with the purse; and asked permission to consider him for the future as her kind, kind friend and protector. Her behaviour was so affecting that he was going to write her a cheque for twenty pounds more; but he restrained his feelings: the carriage was in waiting to take him to dinner, so he tripped away with a "God bless you, my dear, always come here when you come to town, you know.—Drive to the Mansion House, James."

Finally came the parting with Miss Amelia, over which picture I intend to throw a veil. But after a scene in which one person was in earnest and the other a perfect performer—after the tenderest caresses, the most pathetic tears, the smelling-bottle, and some of the very best feelings of the heart, had been called into requisition—Rebecca and Amelia parted, the former vowing to love her friend for ever and ever and ever.

CHAPTER VII

CRAWLEY OF QUEEN'S CRAWLEY

AMONG the most respected of the names beginning in C, which the *Court-Guide* contained, in the year 18—, was that of Crawley, Sir Pitt, Baronet, Great Gaunt Street, and Queen's Crawley, Hants. This honourable name had figured constantly also in the parliamentary list for many years, in conjunction with that of a number of other worthy gentlemen who sat in turns for the borough.

It is related, with regard to the borough of Queen's Crawley, that Queen Elizabeth in one of her progresses, stopping at Crawley to breakfast, was so delighted with some remarkably fine Hampshire beer which was then presented to her by the Crawley of the day (a handsome gentleman with a trim beard and a good leg), that she forthwith erected Crawley into a borough to send two members to Parliament; and the place, from the day of that illustrious visit, took the name of Queen's Crawley, which it holds up to the present moment. And though, by the lapse of time, and those mutations which age produces in empires, cities, and boroughs, Queen's Crawley was no longer so populous a place as it had been in Queen Bess's time—nay, was come down to that condition of borough which used to be denominated rotten—yet, as Sir Pitt Crawley would say with perfect justice in his elegant way, "Rotten! be hanged—it produces me a good fifteen hundred a year."

Sir Pitt Crawley (named after that great Commoner) was the son of Walpole Crawley, first Baronet, of the Tape and Sealing-Wax Office in the reign of George II., when he was impeached for peculation, as were a great number of other honest gentlemen of those days; and Walpole Crawley was, as need scarcely be said, son of John Churchill Crawley, named after the celebrated military commander of the reign of Queen Anne. The family tree (which hangs up at

Queen's Crawley,) furthermore mentions Charles Stuart, afterwards called Barebones Crawley, son of the Crawley of James the First's time; and finally, Queen Elizabeth's Crawley, who is represented as the foreground of the picture in his forked beard and armour. Out of his waistcoat, as usual, grows a tree, on the main branches of which the above illustrious names are inscribed. Close by the name of Sir Pitt Crawley, Baronet (the subject of the present memoir), are written that of his brother, the Reverend Bute Crawley (the great Commoner was in disgrace when the reverend gentleman was born), rector of Crawley-cum-Snailby, and of various other male and female members of the Crawley family.

Sir Pitt was first married to Grizzel, sixth daughter of Mungo Binkie, Lord Binkie, and cousin, in consequence, of Mr. Dundas. She brought him two sons: Pitt, named not so much after his father as after the heaven-born minister; and Rawdon Crawley, from the Prince of Wales's friend, whom his Majesty George IV. forgot so completely. Many years after her ladyship's demise, Sir Pitt led to the altar Rosa, daughter of Mr. G. Dawson, of Mudbury, by whom he had two daughters, for whose benefit Miss Rebecca Sharp was now engaged as governess. It will be seen that the young lady was come into a family of very genteel connexions, and was about to move in a much more distinguished circle than that humble one which she had just quitted in Russell Square.

She had received her orders to join her pupils, in a note which was written upon an old envelope, and which contained the following words:—

"Sir Pitt Crawley begs Miss Sharp and baggidge may be hear on Tuesday, as I leaf for Queen's Crawley to-morrow morning *erly*.
"Great Gaunt Street."

Rebecca had never seen a Baronet, as far as she knew, and as soon as she had taken leave of Amelia, and counted the guineas which good-natured Mr. Sedley had put into a purse for her, and as soon as she had done wiping her eyes with her handkerchief (which operation she concluded the very moment the carriage had turned the corner of the street), she began to depict in her own mind what a baronet must be. "I wonder, does he wear a star?" thought she, "or is it only lords that wear stars? But he will be very handsomely dressed in a court suit, with ruffles, and his hair a little powdered, like Mr. Wroughton at Covent Garden. I suppose he will be awfully proud, and that I shall be treated most contemptuously. Still I must bear my hard lot as well as I can—at least, I shall be amongst *gentlefolks,* and not with vulgar city people:" and she fell to thinking of her Russell Square friends with that very same philosophical bitterness with which, in a certain apologue, the fox is represented as speaking of the grapes.

Having passed through Gaunt Square into Great Gaunt Street, the carriage at length stopped at a tall gloomy house between two other tall gloomy houses, each with a hatchment over the middle drawing-room window; as is the custom of houses in Great Gaunt Street, in which gloomy locality death seems to reign perpetual. The shutters of the first-floor windows of Sir Pitt's mansion were closed —those of the dining-room were partially open, and the blinds neatly covered up in old newspapers.

John, the groom, who had driven the carriage alone, did not care to descend to ring the bell; and so prayed a passing milk-boy to perform that office for him. When the bell was rung, a head appeared between the interstices of the dining-room shutters, and the door was opened by a man in drab breeches and gaiters, with a dirty old coat, a foul old neckcloth lashed round his bristly neck, a shining bald head, a leering red face, a pair of twinkling grey eyes, and a mouth perpetually on the grin.

"This Sir Pitt Crawley's?" says John, from the box.

"Ees," says the man at the door, with a nod.

"Hand down these 'ere trunks, then," said John.

"Hand 'n down yourself," said the porter.

"Don't you see I can't leave my hosses? Come, bear a hand, my fine feller, and Miss will give you some beer," said John, with a horse-laugh, for he was no longer respectful to Miss Sharp, as her connexion with the family was broken off, and as she had given nothing to the servants on coming away.

The bald-headed man, taking his hands out of his breeches pockets, advanced on this summons, and throwing Miss Sharp's trunk over his shoulder, carried it into the house.

"Take this basket and shawl, if you please, and open the door," said Miss Sharp, and descended from the carriage in much indignation. "I shall write to Mr. Sedley and inform him of your conduct," said she to the groom.

"Don't," replied that functionary. "I hope you've forgot nothink? Miss 'Melia's gownds—have you got them—as the lady's maid was to have 'ad? I hope they'll fit you. Shut the door, Jim, you'll get no good out of '*er*," continued John, pointing with his thumb towards Miss Sharp; "a bad lot, I tell you, a bad lot," and so saying, Mr. Sedley's groom drove away. The truth is, he was attached to the lady's maid in question, and indignant that she should have been robbed of her perquisites.

On entering the dining-room, by the orders of the individual in gaiters, Rebecca found that apartment not more cheerful than such rooms usually are, when genteel families are out of town. The faithful chambers seem, as it were, to mourn the absence of their masters. The turkey carpet has rolled itself up, and retired sulkily under the sideboard: the pictures have hidden their faces behind old sheets of brown paper: the ceiling lamp is muffled up in a dismal sack of brown holland: the window-curtains have disappeared under all sorts of shabby envelopes: the marble bust of Sir Walpole Crawley is looking from its black corner at the bare boards and the oiled fire-irons, and the empty card-racks over the mantel-piece: the cellaret has lurked away behind the carpet: the chairs are turned up heads and tails along the walls: and in the dark corner opposite the statue, is an old-fashioned crabbed knife-box locked and sitting on a dumb waiter.

Two kitchen chairs, and a round table, and an attenuated old poker and tongs were, however, gathered round the fire-place, as was a saucepan over a feeble sputtering fire. There was a bit of cheese and bread, and a tin candlestick on the table, and a little black porter in a pint-pot.

"Had your dinner, I suppose? It is not too warm for you? Like a drop of beer?"

"Where is Sir Pitt Crawley?" said Miss Sharp majestically.

"He, he! *I'm* Sir Pitt Crawley. Reklect you owe me a pint for bringing down your luggage. He, he! Ask Tinker if I aynt. Mrs. Tinker, Miss Sharp; Miss Governess, Mrs. Charwoman. Ho, ho!"

The lady addressed as Mrs. Tinker, at this moment made her appearance with a pipe and a paper of tobacco, for which she had been despatched a minute before Miss Sharp's arrival; and she handed the articles over to Sir Pitt, who had taken his seat by the fire.

"Where's the farden?" said he. "I gave you three halfpence. Where's the change, old Tinker?"

"There!" replied Mrs. Tinker, flinging down the coin; "it's only baronets as cares about farthings."

"A farthing a day is seven shillings a year," answered the M.P.; "seven shillings a year is the interest of seven guineas. Take care of your farthings, old Tinker, and your guineas will come quite nat'ral."

"You may be sure it's Sir Pitt Crawley, young woman," said Mrs. Tinker, surlily; "because he looks to his farthings. You'll know him better afore long."

"And like me none the worse, Miss Sharp," said the old gentleman, with an air almost of politeness. "I must be just before I'm generous."

"He never gave away a farthing in his life," growled Tinker.

"Never, and never will: it's against my principle. Go and get another chair from the kitchen, Tinker, if you want to sit down; and then we'll have a bit of supper."

Presently the baronet plunged a fork into the saucepan on the fire and withdrew from the pot a piece of tripe and an onion, which he divided into pretty equal portions, and of which he partook with Mrs. Tinker. "You see, Miss Sharp, when I'm not here Tinker's on board wages: when I'm in town she dines with the family. Haw, haw! I'm glad Miss Sharp's not hungry, ain't you, Tink?" And they fell to upon their frugal supper.

After supper Sir Pitt Crawley began to smoke his pipe; and when it became quite dark, he lighted the rushlight in the tin candlestick, and producing from an interminable pocket a huge mass of papers, began reading them, and putting them in order.

"I'm here on law business, my dear, and that's how it happens that I shall have the pleasure of such a pretty travelling companion to-morrow."

"He's always at law business," said Mrs. Tinker, taking up the pot of porter.

"Drink and drink about," said the baronet. "Yes, my dear, Tinker is quite right: I've lost and won more lawsuits than any man in England. Look here at Crawley, Bart, v. Snaffle. I'll throw him over, or my name's not Pitt Crawley. Podder and another versus Crawley, Bart. Overseers of Snailey parish against Crawley, Bart. They can't prove it's common: I'll defy 'em; the land's mine. It no more belongs to the parish than it does to you or Tinker here. I'll beat 'em, if it costs me a thousand guineas. Look over the papers; you may if you like, my dear. Do you write a good hand? I'll make you useful when we're at Queen's Crawley, depend on it, Miss Sharp. Now the dowager's dead I want some one."

"She was as bad as he," said Tinker. "She took the law of every one of her tradesmen; and turned away forty-eight footmen in four year."

"She was close—very close," said the baronet, simply; "but she was a valyble woman to me, and saved me a steward."—And in this confidential strain, and much to the amusement of the new-comer, the conversation continued for a considerable time. Whatever Sir Pitt Crawley's qualities might be, good or bad, he did not make the least disguise of them. He talked of himself incessantly, sometimes in the coarsest and vulgarest Hampshire accent; sometimes adopting the tone of a man of the world. And so, with injunctions to Miss Sharp to be ready at five in the morning, he bade her good night. "You'll sleep with Tinker to-night," he said; "it's a big bed, and there's room for two. Lady Crawley died in it. Good night."

Sir Pitt went off after this benediction, and the solemn Tinker, rushlight in hand, led the way up the great bleak stone stairs, past the great dreary drawing-room doors, with the handles muffled up in paper, into the great front bed-room, where Lady Crawley had slept her last. The bed and chamber were so funereal and gloomy, you might have fancied, not only that Lady Crawley died in the room, but that her ghost inhabited it. Rebecca sprang about the apartment, however, with the greatest liveliness, and had peeped into the huge wardrobes, and the closets, and the cupboards, and tried the drawers which were locked, and examined the dreary pictures and toilette appointments, while the old charwoman was saying her prayers. "I shouldn't like to sleep in this yeer bed without a good conscience, Miss," said the old woman. "There's room for us and a half-dozen of ghosts in it," says Rebecca. "Tell me all about Lady Crawley and Sir Pitt Crawley, and everybody, my *dear* Mrs. Tinker."

But old Tinker was not to be pumped by this little cross-questioner; and signifying to her that bed was a place for sleeping, not conversation, set up in her corner of the bed such a snore as only the nose of innocence can produce. Rebecca lay awake for a long, long time, thinking of the morrow, and of the new world into which she was going, and of her chances of success there. The rushlight flickered in the basin. The mantel-piece cast up a great black shadow, over half of a mouldy old sampler, which her defunct ladyship had worked, no doubt, and over two little family pictures of young lads, one in a college gown, and the other in a red jacket like a soldier. When she went to sleep, Rebecca chose that one to dream about.

At four o'clock, on such a roseate summer's morning as even made Great Gaunt Street look cheerful, the faithful Tinker, having wakened her bedfellow, and bid her prepare for departure, unbarred and unbolted the great hall door (the clanging and clapping whereof startled the sleeping echoes in the street), and taking her way into Oxford Street, summoned a coach from a stand there. It is needless to particularize the number of the vehicle, or to state that the driver was stationed thus early in the neighbourhood of Swallow Street, in hopes that some young buck, reeling homeward from the tavern, might need the aid of his vehicle, and pay him with the generosity of intoxication.

It is likewise needless to say, that the driver, if he had any such hopes as those above stated, was grossly disappointed; and that the worthy Baronet whom he drove to the City did not give him one single penny more than his fare. It was in vain that Jehu appealed and stormed; that he flung down Miss Sharp's bandboxes in the gutter at the 'Necks, and swore he would take the law of his fare.

"You'd better not," said one of the hostlers; "it's Sir Pitt Crawley."

"So it is, Joe," cried the Baronet, approvingly; "and I'd like to see the man can do me."

"So should oi," said Joe, grinning sulkily, and mounting the Baronet's baggage on the roof of the coach.

"Keep the box for me, Leader," exclaims the Member of Parliament to the coachman; who replied, "Yes, Sir Pitt," with a touch of his hat, and rage in his soul (for he had promised the box to a young gentleman from Cambridge, who would have given a crown to a certainty), and Miss Sharp was accommodated with a back seat inside the carriage, which might be said to be carrying her into the wide world.

How the young man from Cambridge sulkily put his five great coats in front; but was reconciled when little Miss Sharp was made to quit the carriage, and mount up beside him—when he covered her up in one of his Benjamins, and became perfectly good-humoured—how the asthmatic gentleman, the prim lady, who declared upon her sacred honour she had never travelled in a public carriage before (there is always such a lady in a coach,—Alas! was; for the coaches, where are they?), and the fat widow with the brandy-bottle, took their places inside—how the porter asked them all for money, and got sixpence from the gentleman and five greasy halfpence from the fat widow—and how the carriage at length drove away—now, threading the dark lanes of Aldersgate, anon clattering by the Blue Cupola of St. Paul's, jingling rapidly by the strangers' entry of Fleet-Market, which, with Exeter 'Change, has now departed to the world of shadows—how they passed the White Bear in Piccadilly, and saw the dew rising up from the market-gardens of Knightsbridge—how Turnham-green, Brentford,

Bagshot, were passed—need not be told here. But the writer of these pages, who has pursued in former days, and in the same bright weather, the same remarkable journey, cannot but think of it with a sweet and tender regret. Where is the road now, and its merry incidents of life? Is there no Chelsea or Greenwich for the old honest pimple-nosed coachmen? I wonder where are they, those good fellows? Is old Weller alive or dead? and the waiters, yea, and the inns at which they waited, and the cold rounds of beef inside, and the stunted ostler, with his blue nose and clinking pail, where is he, and where is his generation? To those great geniuses now in petticoats, who shall write novels for the beloved reader's children, these men and things will be as much legend and history as Nineveh, or Cœur de Lion, or Jack Sheppard. For them stage-coaches will have become romances—a team of four bays as fabulous as Bucephalus or Black Bess. Ah, how their coats shone, as the stable-men pulled their clothes off, and away they went—ah, how their tails shook, as with smoking sides at the stage's end they demurely walked away into the inn-yard. Alas! we shall never hear the horn sing at midnight, or see the pike-gates fly open any more. Whither, however, is the light four-inside Trafalgar coach carrying us? Let us be set down at Queen's Crawley without further divagation, and see how Miss Rebecca Sharp speeds there.

CHAPTER VIII

PRIVATE AND CONFIDENTIAL

Miss Rebecca Sharp to Miss Amelia Sedley, Russell Square, London.
(Free.—Pitt Crawley.)

"MY DEAREST, SWEETEST AMELIA,

WITH what mingled joy and sorrow do I take up the pen to write to my dearest friend! Oh, what a change between to-day and yesterday! *Now* I am friendless and alone; yesterday I was at home, in the sweet company of a sister, whom I shall ever, *ever* cherish!

"I will not tell you in what tears and sadness I passed the fatal night in which I separated from you. *You* went on Tuesday to joy and happiness, with your mother and *your devoted young soldier* by your side; and I thought of you all night, dancing at the Perkins's, the prettiest, I am sure, of all the young ladies at the Ball. I was brought by the groom in the old carriage to Sir Pitt Crawley's town house, where, after John the groom had behaved most rudely and insolently to me (alas! 'twas safe to insult poverty and misfortune!), I was given over to Sir P.'s care, and made to pass the night in an old gloomy bed, and by the side of a horrid gloomy old charwoman, who keeps the house. I did not sleep one single wink the whole night.

"Sir Pitt is not what we silly girls, when we used to read Cecilia at Chiswick, imagined a baronet must have been. Anything, indeed, less like Lord Orville cannot be imagined. Fancy an old, stumpy, short, vulgar, and very dirty man, in old clothes and shabby old gaiters, who smokes a horrid pipe, and cooks his own horrid supper in a saucepan. He speaks with a country accent, and swore a great deal at the old charwoman, at the hackney coachman who drove us to the inn where the coach went from, and on which I made the journey *outside for the greater part of the way.*

"I was awakened at daybreak by the charwoman, and having arrived at the inn, was at first placed inside the coach. But, when we got to a place called Leakington, where the rain began to fall very heavily—will you believe it?—I was forced to come outside; for Sir Pitt is a proprietor of the coach, and as a passenger came at Mudbury, who wanted an inside place, I was obliged to go outside in the rain, where, however, a young gentleman from Cambridge College sheltered me very kindly in one of his *several* great coats.

"This gentleman and the guard seemed to know Sir Pitt very well, and laughed at him a great deal. They both agreed in calling him an *old screw;* which means a very stingy, avaricious person. He

78

never gives any money to anybody, they said (and this meanness I hate) ; and the young gentleman made me remark that we drove very slow for the last two stages on the road, because Sir Pitt was on the box, and because he is proprietor of the horses for this part of the journey. 'But won't I flog 'em on to Squashmore, when I take the ribbons?' said the young *Cantab.* 'And sarve 'em right, Master Jack,' said the guard. When I comprehended the meaning of this phrase, and that Master Jack intended to drive the rest of the way, and revenge himself on Sir Pitt's horses, of course I laughed too.

"A carriage and four splendid horses, covered with armorial bearings, however, awaited us at Mudbury, four miles from Queen's Crawley, and we made our entrance to the baronet's park in state. There is a fine avenue of a mile long leading to the house, and the woman at the lodge-gate (over the pillars of which are a serpent and a dove, the supporters of the Crawley arms), made us a number of curtsies as she flung open the old iron carved doors, which are something like those at odious Chiswick.

" 'There's an avenue,' said Sir Pitt, 'a mile long. There's six thousand pound of timber in them there trees. Do you call that nothing?' He pronounced avenue—*evenue,* and nothing—*nothink,* so droll; and he had a Mr. Hodson, his hind from Mudbury, into the carriage with him, and they talked about distraining, and selling up, and draining and subsoiling, and a great deal about tenants and farming—much more than I could understand. Sam Miles had been caught poaching, and Peter Bailey had gone to the workhouse at last. 'Serve him right,' said Sir Pitt; 'him and his family has been cheating me on that farm these hundred and fifty years.' Some old tenant, I suppose, who could not pay his rent. Sir Pitt might have said '*he* and his family,' to be sure; but rich baronets do not need to be careful about grammar, as poor governesses must be.

"As we passed, I remarked a beautiful church-spire rising above some old elms in the park; and before them, in the midst of a lawn, and some outhouses, an old red house with tall chimneys covered with ivy, and the windows shining in the sun. 'Is that your church, sir?' I said.

" 'Yes, hang it,' (said Sir Pitt, only he used, dear, *a much wickeder word*) ; 'how's Buty, Hodson? Buty's my brother Bute, my dear—my brother the parson. Buty and the Beast I call him, ha, ha !'

"Hodson laughed too, and then looking more grave and nodding his head, said, 'I'm afraid he's better, Sir Pitt. He was out on his pony yesterday, looking at our corn.'

" 'Looking after his tithes, hang 'un (only he used the same wicked word). Will brandy and water never kill him? He's as tough as old whatdyecallum—old Methusalem.'

"Mr. Hodson laughed again. 'The young men is home from college. They've whopped John Scroggins till he's well nigh dead.'

" 'Whop my second keeper !' roared out Sir Pitt.

" 'He was on the parson's ground, sir,' replied Mr. Hodson ; and Sir Pitt in a fury swore that if he ever caught 'em poaching on his ground, he'd transport 'em, by the lord he would. However, he said, 'I've sold the presentation of the living, Hodson; none of that breed shall get it, I war'nt;' and Mr. Hodson said he was quite right: and I have no doubt from this that the two brothers are at variance—as brothers often are, and sisters too. Don't you remember the two Miss Scratchleys at Chiswick, how they used always to fight and quarrel—and Mary Box, how she was always thumping Louisa?

"Presently, seeing two little boys gathering sticks in the wood, Mr. Hodson jumped out of the carriage, at Sir Pitt's order, and rushed upon them with his whip. 'Pitch into 'em, Hodson,' roared the baronet; 'flog their little souls out, and bring 'em up to the house, the vagabonds; I'll commit 'em as sure as my name's Pitt.' And presently we heard Mr. Hodson's whip cracking on the shoulders of the poor little blubbering wretches, and Sir Pitt, seeing that the malefactors were in custody, drove on to the hall.

"All the servants were ready to meet us, and

.　　　.　　　.　　　.　　　.　　　.　　　.

"Here, my dear, I was interrupted last night by a dreadful thumping at my door: and who do you think it was? Sir Pitt Crawley in his night-cap and dressing-gown, such a figure! As I shrank away from such a visitor, he came forward and seized my candle. 'No candles after eleven o'clock, Miss Becky,' said he. 'Go to bed in the dark, you pretty little hussey' (that is what he called me), 'and unless you wish me to come for the candle every night, mind and be in bed at eleven.' And with this, he and Mr. Horrocks the butler went off laughing. You may be sure I shall not encourage any more of their visits. They let loose two immense blood-hounds at night, which all last night were yelling and howling at the moon. 'I call the dog Gorer,' said Sir Pitt; 'he's killed a man that dog has, and is master of a bull, and the mother I used to call Flora; but now I calls her Aroarer, for she's too old to bite. Haw, haw!'

"Before the house of Queen's Crawley, which is an odious old-fashioned red brick mansion, with tall chimneys and gables of the style of Queen Bess, there is a terrace flanked by the family dove and serpent, and on which the great hall-door opens. And oh, my dear, the great hall I am sure is as big and as glum as the great hall in the dear castle of Udolpho. It has a large fire-place, in which we might put half Miss Pinkerton's school, and the grate is big enough to roast an ox at the very least. Round the room hang I don't know how many generations of Crawleys, some with beards and ruffs, some with huge wigs and toes turned out, some dressed in long straight stays and gowns that look as stiff as towers, and some with long ringlets, and oh, my dear! scarcely any stays at all. At one end of the hall is the great staircase all in black oak, as dismal as may be, and on either side are tall doors with stags' heads over them, leading to the billiard-room and the library, and the great yellow saloon and the morning-rooms. I think there are at least twenty bed-rooms on the first-floor; one of them has the bed in which Queen Elizabeth slept; and I have been taken by my new pupils through all these fine apartments this morning. They are not rendered less gloomy, I promise you, by having the shutters always shut; and there is scarce one of the apartments, but when the light was let into it, I expected to see a ghost in the room. We have a school-room on the second floor, with my bed-room leading into it on one side, and that of the young ladies on the other. Then there are Mr. Pitt's apartments—Mr. Crawley, he is called—the eldest son, and Mr. Rawdon Crawley's rooms—he is an officer like *somebody*, and away with his regiment. There is no want of room I assure you. You might lodge all the people in Russell Square in the house, I think, and have space to spare.

"Half an hour after our arrival, the great dinner-bell was rung, and I came down with my two pupils (they are very thin insignificant little chits of ten and eight years old). I came down in your *dear* muslin gown (about which that odious Mrs. Pinner was so rude, because you gave it me); for I am to be treated as one of the family, except on company days, when the young ladies and I are to dine upstairs.

"Well, the great dinner-bell rang, and we all assembled in the little drawing-room where my Lady Crawley sits. She is the second Lady Crawley, and mother of the young ladies. She was an iron-monger's daughter, and her marriage was thought a great match. She looks as if she had been handsome once, and her eyes are always weeping for the loss of her beauty. She is pale and meagre and high-shouldered; and has not a word to say for herself, evidently. Her step-son, Mr. Crawley, was likewise in the room. He was in full dress, as pompous as an undertaker. He is pale, thin, ugly, silent; he has thin legs, no chest, hay-coloured whiskers, and straw-coloured hair. He is the very picture of his sainted mother over the mantel-piece—Griselda of the noble house of Binkie.

" 'This is the new governess, Mr. Crawley,' said Lady Crawley, coming forward and taking my hand. 'Miss Sharp.'

" 'O !' said Mr. Crawley, and pushed his head once forward and began again to read a great pamphlet with which he was busy.

" 'I hope you will be kind to my girls,' said Lady Crawley, with her pink eyes always full of tears.

" 'La, Ma, of course she will,' said the eldest: and I saw at a glance that I need not be afraid of *that* woman.

" 'My lady is served,' says the Butler in black, in an immense white shirt-frill, that looked as if it had been one of the Queen Elizabeth's ruffs depicted in the hall; and so, taking Mr. Crawley's arm, she led the way to the dining-room, whither I followed with my little pupils in each hand.

"Sir Pitt was already in the room with a silver jug. He had just been to the cellar, and was in full dress too; that is, he had taken his gaiters off, and showed his little dumpy legs in black worsted stockings. The sideboard was covered with glistening old plate—old cups, both gold and silver; old salvers and cruet-stands, like Rundell and Bridge's shop. Everything on the table was in silver too, and two footmen, with red hair and canary-coloured liveries, stood on either side of the side-board.

"Mr. Crawley said a long grace, and Sir Pitt said amen, and the great silver dish-covers were removed.

" 'What have we for dinner, Betsy?' said the Baronet.

" 'Mutton broth, I believe, Sir Pitt,' answered Lady Crawley.

" '*Mouton aux navets,*' added the butler gravely (pronounce, if you please, moutongonavvy) ; 'and the soup is *pottage de mouton à l'Ecossaise.* The side-dishes contain *pommes de terre au naturel,* and *choufleur à l'eau.*'

" 'Mutton's mutton,' said the Baronet, 'and a devilish good thing. What *ship* was it, Horrocks, and when did you kill?'

" 'One of the black-faced Scotch, Sir Pitt: we killed on Thursday.'

" 'Who took any?'

" 'Steel, of Mudbury, took the saddle and two legs, Sir Pitt; but he says the last was too young and confounded woolly, Sir Pitt.'

" 'Will you take some *potage*, Miss ah—Miss Blunt?' said Mr. Crawley.

" 'Capital Scotch broth, my dear,' said Sir Pitt, 'though they call it by a French name.'

" 'I believe it is the custom, sir, in decent society,' said Mr. Crawley, haughtily, 'to call the dish as I have called it;' and it was served to us on silver soup-plates by the footmen in the canary coats, with the *mouton aux navets.* Then 'ale and water' were brought, and served to us young ladies in wine-glasses. I am not a judge of ale, but I can say with a clear conscience I prefer water.

"While we were enjoying our repast, Sir Pitt took occasion to ask what had become of the shoulders of the mutton.

" 'I believe they were eaten in the servants' hall,' said my lady, humbly.

" 'They was, my lady,' said Horrocks, 'and precious little else we get there neither.'

"Sir Pitt burst into a horse-laugh, and continued his conversation with Mr. Horrocks. 'That there little black pig of the Kent sow's breed must be uncommon fat now.'

" 'It's not quite busting, Sir Pitt,' said the Butler with the gravest air, at which Sir Pitt, and with him the young ladies, this time, began to laugh violently.

" 'Miss Crawley, Miss Rose Crawley,' said Mr. Crawley, 'your laughter strikes me as being ·exceedingly out of place.'

" 'Never mind, my lord,' said the Baronet, 'we'll try the porker on Saturday. Kill un on Saturday morning, John Horrocks. Miss Sharp adores pork, don't you, Miss Sharp?'

"And I think this is all the conversation that I remember at dinner. When the repast was concluded a jug of hot water was placed before Sir Pitt, with a case-bottle containing, I believe, rum. Mr. Horrocks served myself and my pupils with three little glasses of wine, and a bumper was poured out for my lady. When we retired, she took from her work-drawer an enormous interminable piece of knitting; the young ladies began to play at cribbage with a dirty pack of cards. We had but one candle lighted, but it was in a magnificent old silver candlestick, and after a very few questions from my lady, I had my choice of amusement between a volume of sermons, and a pamphlet on the corn-laws, which Mr. Crawley had been reading before dinner.

"So we sat for an hour until steps were heard.

" 'Put away the cards, girls,' cried my lady, in a great tremor; 'put down Mr. Crawley's books, Miss Sharp:' and these orders had been scarcely obeyed, when Mr. Crawley entered the room.

" 'We will resume yesterday's discourse, young ladies,' said he, 'and you shall each read a page by turns; so that Miss a—Miss Short may have an opportunity of hearing you;' and the poor girls began to spell a long dismal sermon delivered at Bethesda Chapel, Liverpool, on behalf of the mission for the Chickasaw Indians. Was it not a charming evening?

"At ten the servants were told to call Sir Pitt and the household to prayers. Sir Pitt came in first, very much flushed, and rather unsteady in his gait; and after him the butler, the canaries, Mr. Crawley's man, three other men, smelling very much of the stable, and four women, one of whom, I remarked, was very much over-dressed, and who flung me a look of great scorn as she plumped down on her knees.

"After Mr. Crawley had done haranguing and expounding, we received our candles, and then we went to bed; and then I was disturbed in my writing, as I have described to my dearest sweetest Amelia.

"Good night. A thousand, thousand, thousand kisses!

"*Saturday.*—This morning, at five, I heard the shrieking of the little black pig. Rose and Violet introduced me to it yesterday; and to the stables, and to the kennel, and to the gardener, who was picking fruit to send to market, and from whom they begged hard a bunch of hot-house grapes; but he said that Sir Pitt had numbered every 'Man Jack' of them, and it would be as much as his place was worth to give any away. The darling girls caught a colt in a paddock, and asked me if I would ride, and began to ride themselves, when the groom, coming with horrid oaths, drove them away.

"Lady Crawley is always knitting the worsted. Sir Pitt is always tipsy, every night; and I believe, sits with Horrocks, the butler. Mr. Crawley always reads sermons in the evening, and in the morning is locked up in his study, or else rides to Mudbury, on county business, or to Squashmore, where he preaches, on Wednesdays and Fridays, to the tenants there.

"A hundred thousand grateful loves to your dear papa and mamma. Is your poor brother recovered of his rack-punch? Oh, dear! Oh, dear! How men should beware of wicked punch!

"Ever and ever thine own
"REBECCA."

Everything considered, I think it is quite as well for our dear Amelia Sedley, in Russell Square, that Miss Sharp and she are parted. Rebecca is a droll funny creature, to

be sure; and those descriptions of the poor lady weeping
for the loss of her beauty, and the gentleman "with hay-
coloured whiskers and straw-coloured hair," are very smart,
doubtless, and show a great knowledge of the world. That
she might, when on her knees, have been thinking of something better than Miss Horrock's ribbons, has possibly
struck both of us. But my kind reader will please to remember that this history has "Vanity Fair" for a title,
and that Vanity Fair is a very vain, wicked, foolish place,
full of all sorts of humbugs and falseness and pretensions.
And while the moralist, who is holding forth on the cover[1]
(an accurate portrait of your humble servant), professes
to wear neither gown nor bands, but only the very same
long-eared livery in which his congregation is arrayed: yet,
look you, one is bound to speak the truth as far as one
knows it, whether one mounts a cap and bells or a shovel-
hat; and a deal of disagreeable matter must come out in
the course of such an undertaking.

I have heard a brother of the story-telling trade, at
Naples, preaching to a pack of good-for-nothing honest
lazy fellows by the sea-shore, work himself up into such a
rage and passion with some of the villains whose wicked
deeds he was describing and inventing, that the audience
could not resist it; and they and the poet together would
burst out into a roar of oaths and execrations against the
fictitious monster of the tale, so that the hat went round,
and the bajocchi tumbled into it, in the midst of a perfect
storm of sympathy.

At the little Paris theatres, on the other hand, you will
not only hear the people yelling out: *"Ah gredin! Ah
monstre!"* and cursing the tyrant of the play from the
boxes; but the actors themselves positively refuse to play
the wicked parts, such as those of *infâmes Anglais*, brutal
Cossacks, and what not, and prefer to appear at a smaller
salary, in their real characters as loyal Frenchmen. I set
the two stories one against the other, so that you may see
that it is not from mere mercenary motives that the present
performer is desirous to show up and trounce his villains;
but because he has a sincere hatred of them, which he can-

---

[1] A reference to a woodcut on the cover of the original edition.

not keep down, and which must find a vent in suitable abuse and bad language.

I warn my "kyind friends," then, that I am going to tell a story of harrowing villany and complicated—but, as I trust, intensely interesting—crime. My rascals are not milk-and-water rascals, I promise you. When we come to the proper places we won't spare fine language—No. no! But when we are going over the quiet country we must perforce be calm. A tempest in a slop-basin is absurd. We will reserve that sort of thing for the mighty ocean and the lonely midnight. The present Chapter is very mild. Others——But we will not anticipate *those*.

And, as we bring our characters forward, I will ask leave, as a man and a brother, not only to introduce, but occasionally to step down from the platform, and talk about them: if they are good and kindly, to love them and shake them by the hand: if they are silly, to laugh at them confidentially in the reader's sleeve: if they are wicked and heartless, to abuse them in the strongest terms which politeness admits of.

Otherwise you might fancy it was I who was sneering at the practice of devotion, which Miss Sharp finds so ridiculous; that it was I who laughed good-humouredly at the reeling old Silenus of a baronet—whereas the laughter comes from one who has no reverence except for prosperity, and no eye for anything beyond success. Such people there are living and flourishing in the world—Faithless, Hopeless, Charityless: let us have at them, dear friends, with might and main. Some there are, and very successful too, mere quacks and fools: and it was to combat and expose such as those, no doubt, that Laughter was made.

CHAPTER IX

FAMILY PORTRAITS

SIR PITT CRAWLEY was a philosopher with a taste for what is called low life. His first marriage with the daughter of the noble Binkie had been made under the auspices of his parents; and as he often told Lady Crawley in her life-time she was such a confounded quarrelsome high-bred jade that when she died he was hanged if he would ever take another of her sort, at her ladyship's demise he kept his promise, and selected for a second wife Miss Rose Dawson, daughter of Mr. John Thomas Dawson, ironmonger, of Mudbury. What a happy woman was Rose to be my Lady Crawley!

Let us set down the items of her happiness. In the first place, she gave up Peter Butt, a young man who kept company with her, and in consequence of his disappointment in love, took to smuggling, poaching, and a thousand other bad courses. Then she quarrelled, as in duty bound, with all the friends and intimates of her youth, who, of course, could not be received by my Lady at Queen's Crawley—nor did she find in her new rank and abode many persons who were willing to welcome her. Who ever did? Sir Huddleston Fuddleston had three daughters who all hoped to be Lady Crawley. Sir Giles Wapshot's family were insulted that one of the Wapshot girls had not the preference in the marriage, and the remaining baronets of the county were indignant at their comrade's misalliance.

Never mind the commoners, whom we will leave to grumble anonymously.

Sir Pitt did not care, as he said, a brass farden for any one of them. He had his pretty Rose, and what more need a man require than to please himself? So he used to get **drunk every night:** to beat his pretty Rose sometimes: to

86

leave her in Hampshire when he went to London for the
parliamentary session, without a single friend in the wide
world. Even Mrs. Bute Crawley, the Rector's wife, refused to visit her, as she said she would never give the *pas*
to a tradesman's daughter.

As the only endowments with which Nature had gifted
Lady Crawley were those of pink cheeks and a white
skin, and as she had no sort of character, nor talents, nor
opinions, nor occupations, nor amusements, nor that vigour
of soul and ferocity of temper which often falls to the lot
of entirely foolish women, her hold upon Sir Pitt's affections was not very great. Her roses faded out of her
cheeks, and the pretty freshness left her figure after the
birth of a couple of children, and she became a mere
machine in her husband's house, of no more use than the
late Lady Crawley's grand piano. Being a light-com-
plexioned woman, she wore light clothes, as most blondes
will, and appeared, in preference, in draggled sea-green, or
slatternly sky-blue. She worked that worsted day and night,
or other pieces like it. She had counterpanes in the
course of a few years to all the beds in Crawley. She
had a small flower-garden, for which she had rather an
affection, but beyond this no other like or disliking. When
her husband was rude to her she was apathetic. whenever
he struck her she cried. She had not character enough
to take to drinking, and moaned about, slip-shod and in
curl-papers all day. O Vanity Fair—Vanity Fair! This
might have been, but for you, a cheery lass:—Peter Butt
and Rose a happy man and wife, in a snug farm, with a
hearty family; and an honest portion of pleasures, cares,
hopes and struggles:—but a title and a coach and four are
toys more precious than happiness in Vanity Fair: and if
Harry the Eighth or Bluebeard were alive now, and wanted
a tenth wife, do you suppose he could not get the prettiest
girl that shall be presented this season?

The languid dulness of their mamma did not, as it may
be supposed, awaken much affection in her little daughters,
but they were very happy in the servants' hall and in the
stables; and the Scotch gardener having luckily a good wife
and some good children, they got a little wholesome society

and instruction in his lodge, which was the only education bestowed upon them until Miss Sharp came.

Her engagement was owing to the remonstrances of Mr. Pitt Crawley, the only friend or protector Lady Crawley ever had, and the only person, besides her children, for whom she entertained a little feeble attachment. Mr. Pitt took after the noble Binkies, from whom he was descended, and was a very polite and proper gentleman. When he grew to man's estate, and came back from Christchurch, he began to reform the slackened discipline of the hall, in spite of his father, who stood in awe of him. He was a man of such rigid refinement, that he would have starved rather than have dined without a white neck-cloth. Once, when just from college, and when Horrocks the butler brought him a letter without placing it previously on a tray, he gave that domestic a look, and administered to him a speech so cutting, that Horrocks ever after trembled before him; the whole household bowed to him: Lady Crawley's curl-papers came off earlier when he was at home: Sir Pitt's muddy gaiters disappeared; and if that incorrigible old man still adhered to other old habits, he never fuddled himself with rum-and-water in his son's presence, and only talked to his servants in a very reserved and polite manner; and those persons remarked that Sir Pitt never swore at Lady Crawley while his son was in the room.

It was he who taught the butler to say, "My lady is served," and who insisted on handing her ladyship in to dinner. He seldom spoke to her, but when he did it was with the most powerful respect; and he never let her quit the apartment, without rising in the most stately manner to open the door, and making an elegant bow at her egress.

At Eton he was called Miss Crawley; and there, I am sorry to say, his younger brother Rawdon used to lick him violently. But though his parts were not brilliant, he made up for his lack of talent by meritorious industry, and was never known, during eight years at school, to be subject to that punishment which it is generally thought none but a cherub can escape.

At college his career was of course highly creditable. And here he prepared himself for public life, into which he was to be introduced by the patronage of his grandfather, Lord Binkie, by studying the ancient and modern orators with great assiduity, and by speaking unceasingly at the debating societies. But though he had a fine flux of words, and delivered his little voice with great pomposity and pleasure to himself, and never advanced any sentiment or opinion which was not perfectly trite and stale, and supported by a Latin quotation; yet he failed somehow, in spite of a mediocrity which ought to have insured any man a success. He did not even get the prize poem, which all his friends said he was sure of.

After leaving college he became Private Secretary to Lord Binkie, and was then appointed Attaché to the Legation at Pumpernickel, which post he filled with perfect honour, and brough home despatches, consisting of Strasburg pie, to the Foreign Minister of the day. After remaining ten years Attaché (several years after the lamented Lord Binkie's demise), and finding the advancement slow, he at length gave up the diplomatic service in some disgust, and began to turn country gentleman.

He wrote a pamphlet on Malt on returning to England (for he was an ambitious man, and always liked to be before the public), and took a strong part in the Negro Emancipation question. Then he became a friend of Mr. Wilberforce's, whose politics he admired, and had that famous correspondence with the Reverend Silas Hornblower, on the Ashantee Mission. He was in London, if not for the Parliament session, at least in May, for the religious meetings. In the country he was a magistrate, and an active visitor and speaker among those destitute of religious instruction. He was said to be paying his addresses to Lady Jane Sheepshanks, Lord Southdown's third daughter, and whose sister, Lady Emily, wrote those sweet tracts, "The Sailor's True Binnacle," and "The Applewoman of Finchley Common."

Miss Sharp's accounts of his employment at Queen's Crawley were not caricatures. He subjected the servants there to the devotional exercises before mentioned, in which (and so much the better) he brought his father to join. He patronised an Independent meeting-house in Crawley parish, much to the indignation of his uncle the Rector, and to the consequent delight of Sir Pitt, who was induced to go himself once or twice, which occasioned some violent sermons at Crawley parish church, directed point-blank at the Baronet's old gothic pew there. Honest Sir Pitt, however, did not feel the force of these discourses, as he always took his nap during sermon-time.

Mr. Crawley was very earnest, for the good of the nation and of the Christian world, that the old gentleman should yield him up his place in Parliament; but this the elder constantly refused to do. Both were of course too prudent to give up the fifteen hundred a year which was brought in by the second seat (at this period filled by Mr. Quadroon, with carte-blanche on the Slave question); indeed the family estate was much embarrassed, and the income drawn from the borough was of great use to the house of Queen's Crawley.

It had never recovered the heavy fine imposed upon Walpole Crawley, first baronet, for peculation in the Tape and Sealing Wax Office. Sir Walpole was a jolly fellow, eager to seize and to spend money ("alieni appetens, sui profusus," as Mr. Crawley would remark with a sigh), and in his day beloved by all the county for the constant drunkenness and hospitality which was maintained at Queen's Crawley.

The cellars were filled with burgundy then, the kennels with hounds, and the stables with gallant hunters; now, such horses as Queen's Crawley possessed went to plough, or ran in the Trafalgar Coach; and it was with a team of these very horses, on an off-day, that Miss Sharp was brought to the Hall; for boor as he was, Sir Pitt was a stickler for his dignity while at home, and seldom drove out but with four horses, and though he dined off boiled mutton, had always three footmen to serve it.

If mere parsimony could have made a man rich, Sir Pitt Crawley might have become very wealthy—if he had been an attorney in a country town, with no capital but his brains, it is very possible that he would have turned them to good account, and might have achieved for himself a very considerable influence and competency. But he was unluckily endowed with a good name and a large though encumbered estate, both of which went rather to injure than to advance him. He had a taste for law, which cost him many thousands yearly; and being a great deal too clever to be robbed, as he said, by any single agent, allowed his affairs to be mismanaged by a dozen, whom he all equally mistrusted. He was such a sharp landlord, that he could hardly find any but bankrupt tenants; and such a close farmer, as to grudge almost the seed to the ground, where-upon revengeful Nature grudged him the crops which she granted to more liberal husbandmen. He speculated in every possible way; he worked mines; bought canal-shares; horsed coaches; took government contracts, and was the busiest man and magistrate of his county. As he would not pay honest agents at his granite quarry, he had the satisfaction of finding that four overseers ran away, and took fortunes with them to America. For want of proper precautions, his coal-mines filled with water; the govern-ment flung his contract of damaged beef upon his hands: and for his coach-horses, every mail proprietor in the king-dom knew that he lost more horses than any man in the country, from underfeeding and buying cheap. In disposi-tion he was sociable, and far from being proud; nay, he rather preferred the society of a farmer or a horse-dealer to that of a gentleman, like my lord, his son: he was fond of drink, of swearing, of joking with the farmers' daughters: he was never known to give away a shilling or to do a good action, but was of a pleasant, sly, laughing mood, and would cut his joke and drink his glass with a tenant and sell him up the next day; or have his laugh with the poacher he was transporting with equal good humour. His politeness for the fair sex has already been hinted at by Miss Rebecca Sharp—in a word, the whole baronetage, peerage, commonage of England, did not contain a more cunning, mean, selfish, foolish, disreputable old man. That blood-red hand of Sir Pitt Crawley's would be in anybody's pocket except his own; and it is with grief and pain, that, as admirers of the British aristocracy, we find ourselves obliged to admit the existence of so many ill qualities in a person whose name is in Debrett.

One great cause why Mr. Crawley had such a hold over the affections of his father, resulted from money arrangements. The Baronet owed his son a sum of money out of the jointure of his mother, which he did not find it convenient to pay; indeed he had an almost invincible repugnance to paying anybody, and could only be brought by force to discharge his debts. Miss Sharp calculated (for she became, as we shall hear speedily, inducted into most of the secrets of the family) that the mere payment of his creditors cost the honourable Baronet several hundreds yearly; but this was a delight he could not forego; he had a savage pleasure in making the poor wretches wait, and in shifting from court to court and from term to term the period of satisfaction. What's the good of being in Parliament, he said, if you must pay your debts? Hence, indeed, his position as a senator was not a little useful to him.

Vanity Fair—Vanity Fair! Here was a man, who could not spell, and did not care to read—who had the habits and the cunning of a boor: whose aim in life was pettifogging: who never had a taste, or emotion, or enjoyment, but what was sordid and foul; and yet he had rank, and honours, and power, somehow: and was a dignitary of the land, and a pillar of the state. He was high sheriff, and rode in a golden coach. Great ministers and statesmen courted him; and in Vanity Fair he had a higher place than the most brilliant genius or spotless virtue.

Sir Pitt had an unmarried half-sister who inherited her mother's large fortune, and though the Baronet proposed to borrow this money of her on mortgage, Miss Crawley declined the offer, and preferred the security of the funds. She had signified, however, her intention of leaving her inheritance between Sir Pitt's second son and the family at the Rectory, and had once or twice paid the debts of Rawdon Crawley in his career at college and in the army. Miss Crawley was, in consequence, an object of great respect when she came to Queen's Crawley, for she had a balance at her banker's which would have made her beloved anywhere.

What a dignity it gives an old lady, that balance at the banker's! How tenderly we look at her faults if she is a relative (and may every reader have a score of such), what a kind good-natured old creature we find her! How the junior partner of Hobbs and Dobbs leads her smiling to the carriage with the lozenge upon it, and the fat wheezy coachman! How, when she comes to pay us a visit, we generally find an opportunity to let our friends know her station in the world! We say (and with perfect truth) I wish I had Miss MacWhirter's signature to a cheque for five thousand pounds. She wouldn't miss it, says your wife. She is my aunt, say you, in an easy careless way, when your friend asks if Miss MacWhirter is any relative. Your wife is perpetually sending her little testimonies of affection, your little girls work endless worsted baskets, cushions, and footstools for her. What a good fire there is in her room when she comes to pay you a visit, although your wife laces her stays without one! The house during her stay assumes a festive, neat, warm, jovial, snug appearance not visible at other seasons. You yourself, dear sir, forget to go to sleep after dinner, and find yourself all of a sudden (though you invariably lose) very fond of a rubber. What good dinners you have—game every day, Malmsey-Madeira, and no end of fish from London. Even the servants in the kitchen share in the general prosperity; and, somehow, during the stay of Miss MacWhirter's fat coachman, the beer is grown much stronger, and the consumption of tea and sugar in the nursery (where her maid takes her meals) is not regarded in the least. Is it so, or is it not so? I appeal to the middle classes. Ah, gracious powers! I wish you would send me an old aunt—a maiden aunt—an aunt with a lozenge on her carriage, and a front of light coffee-coloured hair—how my children should work workbags for her, and my Julia and I would make her comfortable! Sweet —sweet vision! Foolish—foolish dream!

CHAPTER X

Miss Sharp Begins to Make Friends

AND now, being received as a member of the amiable family whose portraits we have sketched in the foregoing pages, it became naturally Rebecca's duty to make herself, as she said, agreeable to her benefactors, and to gain their confidence to the utmost of her power. Who can but admire this quality of gratitude in an unprotected orphan; and, if there entered some degree of selfishness into her calculations, who can say but that her prudence was perfectly justifiable! "I am alone in the world," said the friendless girl. "I have nothing to look for but what my own labour can bring me; and while that little pink-faced chit Amelia, with not half my sense, has ten thousand pounds and an establishment secure, poor Rebecca (and my figure is far better than hers) has only herself and her own wits to trust to. Well, let us see if my wits cannot provide me with an honourable maintenance, and if some day or the other I cannot show Miss Amelia my real superiority over her. Not that I dislike poor Amelia: who can dislike such a harmless, good-natured creature?—only it will be a fine day when I can take my place above her in the world, as why, indeed, should I not?" Thus it was that our little romantic friend formed visions of the future for herself,—nor must we be scandalised that, in all her castles in the air, a husband was the principal inhabitant. Of what else have young ladies to think, but husbands? Of what else do their dear mammas think? "I must be my own mamma," said Rebecca; not without a tingling consciousness of defeat, as she thought over her little misadventure with Jos Sedley.

So she wisely determined to render her position with the Queen's Crawley family comfortable and secure, and to this end resolved to make friends of every one around her who could at all interfere with her comfort.

As my Lady Crawley was not one of these personages, and a woman, moreover, so indolent and void of character as not to be of the least consequence in her own house, Rebecca soon found that it was not at all necessary to cultivate her good will—indeed, impossible to gain it. She used to talk to her pupils about their "poor mamma;" and, though she treated that lady with every demonstration of cool respect, it was to the rest of the family that she wisely directed the chief part of her attentions.

With the young people, whose applause she thoroughly gained, her method was pretty simple. She did not pester their young brains with too much learning, but, on the contrary, let them have their own way in regard to educating themselves; for what instruction is more effectual than self-instruction? The eldest was rather fond of books, and as there was in the old library at Queens Crawley a considerable provision of works of light literature of the last century, both in the French and English languages (they had been purchased by the Secretary of the Tape and Sealing Wax Office at the period of his disgrace), and as nobody ever troubled the bookshelves but herself, Rebecca was enabled agreeably, and, as it were, in playing, to impart a great deal of instruction to Miss Rose Crawley.

She and Miss Rose thus read together many delightful French and English works, among which may be mentioned those of the learned Dr. Smollett, of the ingenious Mr. Henry Fielding, of the graceful and fantastic Monsieur Crébillon the younger, whom our immortal poet Gray so much admired, and of the universal Monsieur de Voltaire. Once, when Mr. Crawley asked what the young people were reading, the governess replied "Smollett." "Oh, Smollett," said Mr. Crawley, quite satisfied. "His history is more dull, but by no means so dangerous as that of Mr. Hume. It is history you are reading?" "Yes," said Miss Rose; without, however, adding that it was the history of Mr. Humphrey Clinker. On another occasion he was rather scandalised at finding his sister with a book of French plays; but as the governess remarked that it was for the purpose of acquiring the French idiom in conversation, he was fain to be content. Mr. Crawley, as a diplomatist, was exceedingly proud of his own skill in speaking the French language (for he was of the world still), and not a little pleased with the compliments which the governess continually paid him upon his proficiency.

Miss Violet's tastes were, on the contrary, more rude and boisterous than those of her sister. She knew the sequestered spots where the hens laid their eggs. She could climb a tree to rob the nests of the feathered songsters of their speckled spoils. And her pleasure was to ride the young colts, and to scour the plains like Camilla. She was the favourite of her father and of the stable-men. She was the darling, and withal the terror of the cook; for she discovered the haunt of the jam-pots and would attack them when they were within her reach. She and her sister were engaged in constant battles. Any of which peccadilloes, if Miss Sharp discovered, she did not tell them to Lady Crawley, who would have told them to the father, or worse, to Mr. Crawley; but promised not to tell if Miss Violet would be a good girl and love her governess.

With Mr. Crawley Miss Sharp was respectful and obedient. She used to consult him on passages of French which she could not understand, though her mother was a French-woman, and which he would construe to her satisfaction: and, besides giving her his aid in profane literature, he was kind enough to select for her books of a more serious tendency, and address to her much of his conversation. She admired, beyond measure, his speech at the Quashimaboo-Aid Society; took an interest in his pamphlet on malt; was often affected, even to tears, by his discourses of an evening, and would say—"Oh, thank you, sir," with a sigh, and a look up to heaven, that made him occasionally condescend to shake hands with her. "Blood is everything, after all," would that aristocratic religionist say. "How Miss Sharp is awakened by my words, when not one of the people here is touched. I am too fine for them—too delicate. I must familiarise my style—but she understands it. Her mother was a Montmorency."

Indeed it was from this famous family, as it appears, that Miss Sharp, by the mother's side, was descended. Of course she did not say that her mother had been on the stage; it would have shocked Mr. Crawley's religious scruples. How many noble *émigrées* had this horrid revolution plunged in poverty! She had several stories about her ancestors ere she had been many months in the house; some of which Mr. Crawley happened to find in D'Hozier's dictionary, which was in the library, and which strengthened his belief in their truth, and in the high-breeding of Rebecca. Are we to suppose from this curiosity and prying into dictionaries, could our heroine suppose, that Mr. Crawley was interested in her? —no, only in a friendly way. Have we not stated that he was attached to Lady Jane Sheepshanks?

He took Rebecca to task once or twice about the propriety of playing at backgammon with Sir Pitt, saying that it was a godless amusement, and that she would be much better engaged in reading "Thrump's Legacy," or "The Blind Washerwoman of Moorfields," or any work of a more serious nature; but Miss Sharp said her dear mother used often to play the same game with the old Count de Trictrac and the venerable Abbé du Cornet, and so found an excuse for this and other worldly amusements.

But it was not only by playing at backgammon with the Baronet, that the little governess rendered herself agreeable to her employer. She found many different ways of being useful to him. She read over, with indefatigable patience, all those law papers, with which, before she came to Queen's Crawley, he had promised to entertain her. She volunteered to copy many of his letters, and adroitly altered the spelling of them so as to suit the usages of the present day. She became interested in everything appertaining to the estate, to the farm, the park, the garden, and the stables; and so delightful a companion was she, that the Baronet would seldom take his after-breakfast walk without her (and the children of course), when she would give her advice as to the trees which were to be lopped in the shrubberies, the garden-beds to be dug, the crops which were to be cut, the horses which were to go to cart or plough. Before she had been a year at Queen's Crawley she had quite won the Baronet's confidence; and the conversation at the dinner-table, which before used to be held between him and Mr. Horrocks the butler, was now almost exclusively between Sir Pitt and Miss Sharp. She was almost mistress of the house when Mr. Crawley was absent, but conducted herself in her new and exalted situation with such circumspection and modesty as not to offend the authorities of the kitchen and stable, among whom her behaviour was always exceedingly modest and affable. She was quite a different person from the haughty, shy, dissatisfied little girl whom we have known previously, and this change of temper proved great prudence, a sincere desire of amendment, or at any rate great moral courage on her part. Whether it was the heart which dictated this new system of complaisance and humility adopted by our Rebecca, is to be proved by her after-history. A system of hypocrisy, which lasts through whole years, is one seldom satisfactorily practised by a person of one-and-twenty; however, our readers will recollect, that, though young in years, our heroine was old in life and experience, and we have written to no purpose if they have not discovered that she was a very clever woman.

The elder and younger son of the house of Crawley were, like the gentleman and lady in the weather-box, never at home together—they hated each other cordially: indeed, Rawdon Crawley, the dragoon, had a great contempt for the establishment altogether, and seldom come thither except when his aunt paid her annual visit.

The great good quality of this old lady has been mentioned. She possessed seventy thousand pounds, and had almost adopted Rawdon. She disliked her elder nephew exceedingly, and despised him as a milksop. In return he did not hesitate to state that her soul was irretrievably lost, and was of opinion that his brother's chance in the next world was not a whit better. "She is a godless woman of the world," would Mr. Crawley say; "she lives with atheists and Frenchmen. My mind shudders when I think of her awful, awful situation, and that, near as she is to the grave, she should be so given up to vanity, licentiousness, profaneness, and folly." In fact, the old lady declined altogether to hear his hour's lecture of an evening; and when she came to Queen's Crawley alone, he was obliged to pretermit his usual devotional exercises.

"Shut up your sarmons, Pitt, when Miss Crawley comes down," said his father; "she has written to say that she won't stand the preachifying."

"O, sir! consider the servants."

"The servants be hanged," said Sir Pitt; and his son thought even worse would happen were they deprived of the benefit of his instruction.

"Why, hang it, Pitt!" said the father to his remonstrance. "You wouldn't be such a flat as to let three thousand a year go out of the family?"

"What is money compared to our souls, sir?" continued Mr. Crawley.

"You mean that the old lady won't leave the money to you?"—and who knows but it *was* Mr. Crawley's meaning?

Old Miss Crawley was certainly one of the reprobates. She had a snug little house in Park Lane, and, as she ate and drank a great deal too much during the season in London, she went to Harrowgate or Cheltenham for the summer. She was the most hospitable and jovial of old vestals, and had been a beauty in her day, she said. (All old women were beauties once, we very well know.) She was a *bel esprit,* and a dreadful Radical for those days. She had been in France (where St. Just, they say, inspired her with an unfortunate passion), and loved, ever after, French novels, French cookery, and French wines. She read Voltaire, and had Rousseau by heart; talked very lightly about divorce, and most energetically of the rights of women. She had pictures of Mr. Fox in every room in the house: when that statesman was in opposition. I am not sure that she had not flung a main with him; and when he came into office, she took great credit for bringing over to him Sir Pitt and his colleague for Queen's Crawley, although Sir Pitt would have come over himself, without any trouble on the honest lady's part. It is needless to say that Sir Pitt was brought to change his views after the death of the great Whig statesman.

This worthy old lady took a fancy to Rawdon Crawley when a boy, sent him to Cambridge (in opposition to his brother at Oxford), and, when the young man was requested by the authorities of the first-named University to quit after a residence of two years, she bought him his commission in the Life Guards Green.

A perfect and celebrated "blood," or dandy about town, was this young officer. Boxing, rat-hunting, the fives court, and four-in-hand driving were then the fashion of our British aristocracy; and he was an adept in all these noble sciences. And though he belonged to the household troops, who, as it was their duty to rally round the Prince Regent, had not shown their valour in foreign service yet, Rawdon Crawley had already (*àpropos* of play, of which he was immoderately fond) fought three bloody duels, in which he gave ample proofs of his contempt for death.

"And for what follows after death," would Mr. Crawley observe, throwing his gooseberry-coloured eyes up to the ceiling. He was always thinking of his brother's soul, or of the souls of those who differed with him in opinion: it is a sort of comfort which many of the serious give themselves.

Silly, romantic Miss Crawley, far from being horrified at the courage of her favourite, always used to pay his debts after his duels; and would not listen to a word that was whispered against his morality. "He will sow his wild-oats," she would say, "and is worth far more than that puling hypocrite of a brother of his."

CHAPTER XI

ARCADIAN SIMPLICITY

BESIDES these honest folks at the Hall (whose simplicity and sweet rural purity surely show the advantage of a country life over a town one), we must introduce the reader to their relatives and neighbours at the Rectory, Bute Crawley and his wife.

The Reverend Bute Crawley was a tall, stately, jolly, shovel-hatted man, far more popular in his county than the Baronet his brother. At college he pulled stroke-oar in the Christchurch boat, and had thrashed all the best bruisers of the "town." He carried his taste for boxing and athletic exercises into private life; there was not a fight within twenty miles at which he was not present, nor a race, nor a coursing match, nor a regatta, nor a ball, nor an election, nor a visitation dinner, nor indeed a good dinner in the whole county, but he found means to attend it. You might see his bay-mare and gig-lamps a score of miles away from his Rectory House, whenever there was any dinner-party at Fuddleston, or at Roxby, or at Wapshot Hall, or at the great lords of the county, with all of whom he was intimate. He had a fine voice; sang "A southerly wind and a cloudy sky;" and gave the "whoop" in chorus with general applause. He rode to hounds in a pepper-and-salt frock, and was one of the best fishermen in the county.

Mrs. Crawley, the rector's wife, was a smart little body, who wrote this worthy divine's sermons. Being of a domestic turn, and keeping the house a great deal with her daughters, she ruled absolutely within the rectory, wisely giving her husband full liberty without. He was welcome to come and go, and dine abroad as many days as his fancy dictated, for Mrs. Crawley was a saving woman and knew the price of port wine. Ever since Mrs. Bute carried off the young Rector of Queen's Crawley (she was of a good family, daughter of the late Lieut.-Colonel Hector MacTavish, and she and her mother played for Bute and won him at Harrowgate), she had been a prudent and thrifty wife to him. In spite of her care, however, he was always in debt. It took him at least ten years to pay off his college bills contracted during his father's lifetime. In the year 179—, when he was just clear of these incumbrances, he gave the odds of 100 to 1 (in twenties) against Kangaroo, who won the Derby. The Rector was obliged to take up the money at a ruinous interest, and had been struggling ever since. His sister helped him with a hundred now and then, but of course his great hope was in her death—when "hang it" (as he would say), "Matilda *must* leave me half her money."

So that the Baronet and his brother had every reason which two brothers possibly can have for being by the ears. Sir Pitt had had the better of Bute in innumerable family transactions. Young Pitt not only did not hunt, but set up a meeting house under his uncle's very nose. Rawdon, it was known, was to come in for the bulk of Miss Crawley's property. These money transactions—these speculations in life and death—these silent battles for reversionary spoil—make brothers very loving towards each other in Vanity Fair. I, for my part, have known a five-pound note to interpose and knock up a half century's attachment between two brethren; and can't but admire, as I think what a fine and durable thing Love is among worldly people.

It cannot be supposed that the arrival of such a personage as Rebecca at Queen's Crawley, and her gradual establishment in the good graces of all people there, could be unremarked by Mrs. Bute Crawley. Mrs. Bute, who knew how many days the sirloin of beef lasted at the Hall; how much linen was got ready at the great wash; how many peaches were on the south wall; how many doses her ladyship took when she was ill—for such points are matters of intense interest to certain persons in the country—Mrs. Bute, I say, could not pass over the Hall governess without making every inquiry respecting her history and character. There was always the best understanding between the servants at the Rectory and the Hall. There was always a good glass of ale in the kitchen of the former place for the

Hall people, whose ordinary drink was very small—and, indeed, the Rector's lady knew exactly how much malt went to every barrel of Hall beer—ties of relationship existed between the Hall and Rectory domestics, as between their masters; and through these channels each family was perfectly well acquainted with the doings of the other. That, by the way, may be set down as a general remark. When you and your brother are friends, his doings are indifferent to you. When you have quarrelled, all his outgoings and incomings you know, as if you were his spy.

Very soon after her arrival, Rebecca began to take a regular place in Mrs. Crawley's bulletin from the Hall. It was to this effect:—"The black porker's killed—weighed x stone—salted the sides—pig's pudding and leg of pork for dinner. Mr. Cramp from Mudbury, over with Sir Pitt about putting John Blackmore in gaol—Mr. Pitt at meeting (with all the names of the people who attended)—my lady as usual—the young ladies with the governess."

Then the report would come—the new governess be a rare manager—Sir Pitt be very sweet on her—Mr. Crawley too—He be reading tracts to her—"What an abandoned wretch!" said little, eager, active, black-faced Mrs. Bute Crawley.

Finally, the reports were that the governess had "come round" everybody, wrote Sir Pitt's letters, did his business, managed his accounts—had the upper hand of the whole house, my lady, Mr. Crawley, the girls and all—at which Mrs. Crawley declared she was an artful hussey, and had some dreadful designs in view. Thus the doings at the Hall were the great food for conversation at the Rectory, and Mrs. Bute's bright eyes spied out everything that took place in the enemy's camp—everything and a great deal besides.

"MRS. BUTE CRAWLEY TO MISS PINKERTON, THE MALL, CHISWICK.

"Rectory, Queen's Crawley, December—.

"MY DEAR MADAM,—Although it is so many *years* since I profited by your *delightful* and *invaluable* instructions, yet I have *ever* retained the *fondest* and *most reverential* regard for Miss Pinkerton, and *dear* Chiswick. I hope your health is *good.* The world and *the cause of education* cannot afford to lose Miss Pinkerton for *many many years.* When my friend, Lady Fuddleston, mentioned that her dear girls required an instructress (I am *too poor* to engage a governess for mine, but was I not educated at Chiswick?)

—'Who,' I exclaimed, 'can we consult but the excellent, the incomparable Miss Pinkerton?' In a word, have you, dear madam, any ladies on your list, whose services might be made available to my kind friend and neighbour? I assure you she will take no governess *but of your choosing*.

"My dear husband is pleased to say that he likes *everything which comes from Miss Pinkerton's school*. How I wish I could present him and my beloved girls to the friend of my youth, and the *admired* of the great lexicographer of our country! If you ever travel into Hampshire, Mr. Crawley begs me to say, he hopes you will adorn our *rural rectory* with your presence. 'Tis the humble but happy home of

"Your affectionate

"MARTHA CRAWLEY.

"P. S.—Mr. Crawley's brother, the baronet, with whom we are not, alas! upon those terms of *unity* in which it *becomes brethern to dwell*, has a governess for his little girls, who, I am told, had the good fortune to be educated at Chiswick. I hear various reports of her; and as I have the tenderest interest in my dearest little nieces, whom I wish, in spite of family differences, to see among my own children—and as I long to be attentive to *any pupil of yours*—do, my dear Miss Pinkerton, tell me *the history* of this young lady, whom, for *your sake* I am most anxious to befriend.—M. C."

"MISS PINKERTON TO MRS. BUTE CRAWLEY,

"*Johnson House, Chiswick, Dec.* 18—.

"DEAR MADAM,—I have the honour to acknowledge your polite communication, to which I promptly reply. 'Tis most gratifying to one in any most arduous position to find that my maternal cares have elicited a responsive affection; and to recognize in the amiable Mrs. Bute Crawley my excellent pupil of former years, *sprightly and accomplished* Miss Martha MacTavish. I am happy to have under my charge now the daughters of many of those who were your contemporaries at my establishment—what pleasure it would give me if your own beloved young ladies had need of my instructive superintendence!

"Presenting my respectful compliments to Lady Fuddleston, I have the honour (epistolarily) to introduce to her ladyship my two friends, Miss Tuffin and Miss Hawky.

"Either of these young ladies is *perfectly qualified* to instruct in Greek, Latin, and the rudiments of Hebrew; in mathematics and history; in Spanish, French, Italian, and geography; in music, vocal and instrumental; in dancing, without the aid of a master; and in the elements of natural sciences. In the use of the globes both are proficients. In addition to these Miss Tuffin, who is the daughter of the late Reverend Thomas Tuffin (Fellow of Corpus College, Cambridge), can instruct in the Syriac language, and the elements of Constitutional law. But as she is only eighteen years of age, and of exceedingly pleasing personal appearance, perhaps this young lady may be objectionable in Sir Huddleston Fuddleston's family. "Miss Letitia Hawky, on the other hand, is not personally well-favoured. She is twenty-nine; her face is much pitted with the small-pox. She has a halt in her gait, red hair, and a trifling obliquity of vision. Both ladies are endowed with *every moral and religious virtue*. Their terms, of course, are such as their accomplishments merit. With my most grateful respects to the Reverend Bute Crawley, I have the honour to be,

"Dear Madam,

"Your most faithful and obedient servant,

"Barbara Pinkerton.

"P.S. The Miss Sharp, whom you mention as governess to Sir Pitt Crawley, Bart., M.P., was a pupil of mine, and I have nothing to say in her disfavour. Though her appearance is disagreeable, we cannot control the operations of nature; and though her parents were disreputable (her father being a painter, several times bankrupt, and her mother, as I have since learned, with horror, a dancer at the Opera); yet her talents are considerable, and I cannot regret that I received her *out of charity*. My dread is, lest the principles of the mother—who was represented to me as a French Countess, forced to emigrate in the late revolutionary horrors; but who, as I have since found, was a person of the *very lowest order and morals*—should at any time prove to be *hereditary* in the unhappy young woman whom I took as *an outcast*. But her principles have *hitherto* been correct (I believe), and I am sure nothing will ever in the future stem in the elegant and polished circle of the eminent Sir Pitt Crawley.'

"Miss Rebecca Sharp to Miss Amelia Sedley.

"I have not written to my beloved Amelia for these many weeks past, for what news was there to tell of the sayings and doings at Humdrum Hall, as I have christened it; and what do you care whether the turnip crop is good or bad; whether the fat pig weighed thirteen stone or fourteen; and whether the beasts thrive well upon manglewurzel? Every day since I last wrote has been like its neighbour. Before breakfast, a walk with Sir Pitt and his spud; after breakfast studies (such as they are) in the school-room; after school-room, reading and writing about lawyers, leases, coal-mines, canals, with Sir Pitt (whose secretary I am become); after dinner Mr. Crawley's discourses or the baronet's back-gammon; during both of which amusements my lady looks on with equal placidity. She has become rather more interesting by being ailing of late, which has brought a new visitor to the Hall, in the person of a young doctor. Well, my dear, young women need never despair. The young doctor gave a certain friend of yours to understand that, if she chose to be Mrs. Glauber, she was welcome to ornament the surgery! I told his impudence that the gilt pestle and mortar was quite ornament enough; as if I was born, indeed, to be a country surgeon's wife! Mr. Glauber went home seriously indisposed at his rebuff, took a cooling draught, and is now quite cured. Sir Pitt applauded my resolution highly; he would be sorry to lose his little secretary, I think; and I believe the old wretch likes me as much as it is in his nature to like any one. Marry, indeed! and with a country apothecary, after——No, no, one cannot so soon forget old associations, about which I will talk no more. Let us return to Humdrum Hall.

"For some time past it is Humdrum Hall no longer. My dear, Miss Crawley has arrived with her fat horses, fat servants, fat spaniel—the great rich Miss Crawley, with seventy thousand pounds in the five per cents., whom, or I had better say *which*, her two brothers adore. She looks very apoplectic, the dear soul; no wonder her brothers are anxious about her. You should see them struggling to settle her cushions, or to hand her coffee! 'When I come into the country,' she says (for she has a great deal of humour), 'I leave my toady, Miss Briggs, at home. My brothers are my toadies here, my dear, and a pretty pair they are!'

"When she comes into the country our hall is thrown open, and for a month, at least, you would fancy old Sir Walpole was come to life again. We have dinner-parties, and drive out in the coach-and-four—the footmen put on their newest canary-coloured liveries; we drink claret and champagne as if we were accustomed to it every day. We have wax candles in the schoolroom, and fires to warm ourselves with. Lady Crawley is made to put on the brightest pea-green in her wardrobe, and my pupils leave off their thick shoes and tight old tartan pelisses, and wear silk stockings and muslin frocks, as fashionable baronets' daughters should. Rose came in yesterday in a sad plight—the Wiltshire sow (an enormous pet of hers) ran her down, and destroyed a most lovely flowered lilac silk dress by dancing over it—had this happened a week ago, Sir Pitt would have sworn frightfully, have boxed the poor wretch's ears, and put her upon bread and water for a month. All he said was, 'I'll serve you out, Miss, when your aunt's gone,' and laughed off the accident as quite trivial. Let us hope his wrath will have passed away before Miss Crawley's departure. I hope so, for Miss Rose's sake, I am sure. What a charming reconciler and peace-maker money is!

"Another admirable effect of Miss Crawley and her seventy thousand pounds is to be seen in the conduct of the two brothers Crawley. I mean the baronet and the rector, not *our* brothers— but the former, who hate each other all the year round, become quite loving at Christmas. I wrote to you last year how the abominable horse-racing rector was in the habit of preaching clumsy sermons at us at church, and how Sir Pitt snored in answer. When Miss Crawley arrives there is no such thing as quarrelling heard of—the Hall visits the Rectory, and *vice-versa*—the parson and the baronet talk about the pigs and the poachers, and the county business, in the most affable manner, and without quarrelling in their cups, I believe—indeed Miss Crawley won't hear of their quarrelling, and vows that she will leave her money to the Shropshire Crawleys if they offend her. If they were clever people, those Shropshire Crawleys, they might have it all, I think; but the Shropshire Crawley is a clergyman like his Hampshire cousin, and mortally offended Miss Crawley (who had fled thither in a fit of rage against her impracticable brethren) by some strait-laced notions of morality. He would have prayers in the house, I believe.

"Our sermon books are shut up when Miss Crawley arrives, and Mr. Pitt, whom she abominates, finds it convenient to go to town. On the other hand, the young dandy—'blood,' I believe, is the term—Captain Crawley makes his appearance, and I suppose you will like to know what sort of a person he is.

"Well, he is a very large young dandy. He is six feet high, and speaks with a great voice; and swears a great deal; and orders about the servants, who all adore him nevertheless; for he is very generous of his money, and the domestics will do anything for him. Last week the keepers almost killed a bailiff and his man who came down from London to arrest the Captain, and who were found lurking about the Park wall—they beat them, ducked them, and were going to shoot them for poachers, but the baronet interfered.

"The Captain has a hearty contempt for his father, I can see, and calls him an old *put,* an old *snob,* an old *chawbacon,* and numberless other pretty names. He has a *dreadful reputation* among the ladies. He brings his hunters home with him, lives with the Squires of the county, asks whom he pleases to dinner, and Sir Pitt dares not say no, for fear of offending Miss Crawley, and missing his legacy when she dies of her apoplexy. Shall I tell you a compliment the Captain paid me? I must, it is so pretty. One evening we actually had a dance; there was Sir Huddleston Fuddleston and his family, Sir Giles Wapshot and his young ladies, and I don't know how many more. Well, I heard him say—'By jove, she's a neat little filly!' meaning your humble servant; and he did me the honour to dance two country-dances with me. He gets on pretty gaily with the young Squires, with whom he drinks, bets, rides, and talks about hunting and shooting; but he says the country girls are *bores;* indeed, I don't think he is far wrong. You should see the contempt with which they look down on poor me! When they dance I sit and play the piano very demurely; but the other night, coming in rather flushed from the dining-room, and seeing me employed in this way, he swore out loud that I was the best dancer in the room, and took a great oath that he would have the fiddlers from Mudbury.

" 'I'll go and play a country-dance,' said Mrs. Bute Crawley, very readily (she is a little, black-faced old woman in a turban, rather crooked, and with very twinkling eyes) ; and after the Captain and your poor little Rebecca had performed a dance together, do you know she actually did me the honour to compliment me upon my steps! Such a thing was never heard of before; the proud Mrs. Bute Crawley, first cousin to the Earl of Tiptoff, who won't con-

descend to visit Lady Crawley, except when her sister is in the country. Poor Lady Crawley! during most part of these gaieties, she is
upstairs taking pills.

"Mrs. Bute has all of a sudden taken a great fancy to me. 'My
dear Miss Sharp,' she says, 'why not bring over your girls to the
Rectory?—their cousins will be so happy to see them.' I know
what she means. Signor Clementi did not teach us the piano for
nothing; at which price Mrs. Bute hopes to get a professor for her
children. I can see through her schemes, as though she told them
to me; but I shall go, as I am determined to make myself agreeable
—is it not a poor governess's duty, who has not a friend or protector in the world? The Rector's wife paid me a score of compliments about the progress my pupils made, and thought, no doubt,
to touch my heart—poor, simple, country soul!—as if I cared a fig
about pupils!

"Your India muslin and your pink silk, dearest Amelia, are said
to become me very well. They are a good deal worn now; but,
you know, we poor girls can't afford *des fraiches toilettes*. Happy,
happy you! who have but to drive to St. James's Street, and a dear
mother who will give you any thing you ask. Farewell, dearest girl,
                                          "Your affectionate
                                                    "REBECCA.

"P. S.—I wish you could have seen the faces of the Miss Blackbrooks (Admiral Blackbrooks' daughters, my dear), fine young ladies,
with dresses from London, when Captain Rawdon selected poor me
for a partner!"

When Mrs. Bute Crawley (whose artifices our ingenious
Rebecca had so soon discovered) had procured from Miss
Sharp the promise of a visit, she induced the all-powerful
Miss Crawley to make the necessary application to Sir Pitt,
and the good-natured old lady, who loved to be gay herself,
and to see every one gay and happy round about her, was
quite charmed, and ready to establish a reconcilation and intimacy between her two brothers. It was therefore agreed
that the young people of both families should visit each other
frequently for the future, and the friendship of course lasted
as long as the jovial old mediatrix was there to keep the
peace.

"Why did you ask that scoundrel, Rawdon Crawley, to
dine?" said the Rector to his lady, as they were walking
home through the park. "*I* don't want the fellow. He looks
down upon us country people as so many blackamoors.
He's never content unless he gets my yellow-sealed wine,
which costs me ten shillings a bottle, hang him! Besides,

he's such an infernal character—he's a gambler—he's a drunkard—he's a profligate in every way. He shot a man in a duel—he's over head and ears in debt, and he's robbed me and mine of the best part of Miss Crawley's fortune. Waxy says she has him"—here the Rector shook his fist at the moon, with something very like an oath, and added, in a melancholious tone—"——, down in her will for fifty thousand; and there won't be above thirty to divide."

"I think she's going," said the Rector's wife. "She was very red in the face when we left dinner. I was obliged to unlace her."

"She drank seven glasses of champagne, said the reverend gentleman, in a low voice; "and filthy champagne it is, too, that my brother poisons us with—but you women never know what's what."

"We know nothing," said Mrs. Bute Crawley.

"She drank cherry-brandy after dinner," continued his Reverence, "and took curaçoa with her coffee. *I* wouldn't take a glass for a five-pound note: it kills me with heartburn. She can't stand it, Mrs. Crawley—she must go—flesh and blood won't bear it! and I lay five to two, Matilda drops in a year."

Indulging in these solemn speculations, and thinking about his debts, and his son Jim at College, and Frank at Woolwich, and the four girls, who were not beauties, poor things, and would not have a penny but what they got from the aunt's expected legacy, the Rector and his lady walked on for a while.

"Pitt can't be such an infernal villain as to sell the reversion of the living. And that Methodist milksop of an eldest son looks to Parliament," continued Mr. Crawley, after a pause.

"Sir Pitt Crawley will do anything," said the Rector's wife. "We must get Miss Crawley to make him promise it to James."

"Pitt will promise anything," replied the brother. "He promised he'd pay my college bills, when my father died; he promised he'd built the new wing to the Rectory; he promised he'd let me have Jibbs field and the Six-acre Meadow—and much he executed his promises! And it's to this man's

son—this scoundrel, gambler, swindler, murderer of a Rawdon Crawley, that Matilda leaves the bulk of her money. I
say it's un-christian. By Jove, it is. The infamous dog has
got every vice except hypocrisy, and that belongs to his
brother."

"Hush, my dearest love! we're in Sir Pitt's grounds," interposed his wife.

"I say he *has* got every vice, Mrs. Crawley. Don't, Ma'am,
bully *me*. Didn't he shoot Captain Marker? Didn't he rob
young Lord Dovedale at the Cocoa-Tree? Didn't he cross
the fight between Bill Soames and the Cheshire Trump, by
which I lost forty pound? You know he did; and as for the
women, why, you heard that before me, in my own magistrate's room——"

"For heaven's sake, Mr. Crawley," said the lady, "spare me
the details."

"And you ask this villain into your house!" continued the
exasperated Rector. "You, the mother of a young family—
the wife of a clergyman of the Church of England. By
Jove!"

"Bute Crawley, you are a fool," said the Rector's wife
scornfully.

"Well, Ma'am, fool or not—and I don't say, Martha, I'm
so clever as *you* are, I never did. But I won't meet Rawdon
Crawley, that's flat. I'll go over to Huddleston, that I will,
and see his black greyhound, Mrs. Crawley; and I'll run
Lancelot against him for fifty. By Jove, I will; or against
any dog in England. But I won't meet that beast Rawdon
Crawley."

"Mr. Crawley, you are intoxicated, as usual," replied his
wife. And the next morning, when the Rector woke, and
called for small beer, she put him in mind of his promise to
visit Sir Huddleston Fuddleston on Saturday, and as he knew
he should have a *wet night*, it was agreed that he might gal-
lop back again in time for church on Sunday morning. Thus
it will be seen that the parishioners of Crawley were equally
happy in their Squire and in their Rector.

Miss Crawley had not long been established at the Hall
before Rebecca's fascinations had won the heart of that
good-natured London rake, as they had of the country inno-

cents whom we have been describing. Taking her accustomed drive, one day, she thought fit to order that "that little
governess" should accompany her to Mudbury. Before they
had returned Rebecca had made a conquest of her; having
made her laugh four times, and amused her during the whole
of the little journey.

"Not let Miss Sharp dine at table!" said she to Sir Pitt,
who had arranged a dinner of ceremony, and asked all the
neighbouring baronets. "My dear creature, do you suppose
I can talk about the nursery with Lady Fuddleston, or discuss
justices' business with that goose, old Sir Giles Wapshot?
I insist upon Miss Sharp appearing. Let Lady Crawley remain upstairs, if there is no room. But little Miss Sharp!
Why, she's the only person fit to talk to in the country."

Of course, after such a peremptory order as this, Miss
Sharp, the governess, received commands to dine with the
illustrious company below stairs. And when Sir Huddleston
had, with great pomp and ceremony, handed Miss Crawley in
to dinner, and was preparing to take his place by her side,
the old lady cried out, in a shrill voice, "Becky Sharp! Miss
Sharp! Come you and sit by me and amuse me; and let Sir
Huddleston sit by Lady Wapshot."

When the parties were over, and the carriages had rolled
away, the insatiable Miss Crawley would say, "Come to my
dressing-room, Becky, and let us abuse the company,"—
which, between them, this pair of friends did perfectly. Old
Sir Huddleston wheezed a great deal at dinner; Sir Giles
Wapshot had a particularly noisy manner of imbibing his
soup, and her ladyship a wink of the left eye; all of which
Becky caricatured to admiration; as well as the particulars
of the night's conversation; the politics; the war; the quarter-
sessions; the famous run with the H.H., and those heavy and
dreary themes, about which country gentlemen converse. As
for the Misses Wapshot's toilets and Lady Fuddleston's
famous yellow hat, Miss Sharp tore them to tatters, to the
infinite amusement of her audience.

"My dear, you are a perfect *trouvaille,*" Miss Crawley
would say. "I wish you could come to me in London, but I
couldn't make a butt of you as I do of poor Briggs—no, no,
you little sly creature; you are too clever—Isn't she, Firkin?"

Mrs. Firkin (who was dressing the very small remnant of hair which remained on Miss Crawley's pate), flung up her head and said, "I think Miss *is* very clever," with the most killing sarcastic air. In fact, Mrs. Firkin had that natural jealousy which is one of the main principles of every honest woman.

After rebuffing Sir Huddleston Fuddleston, Miss Crawley ordered that Rawdon Crawley should lead her in to dinner every day, and that Becky should follow with her cushion— or else she would have Becky's arm and Rawdon with the pillow. "We must sit together," she said. "We're the only three Christians in the county, my love"—in which case, it must be confessed, that religion was at a very low ebb in the county of Hants.

Besides being such a fine religionist, Miss Crawley was, as we have said, an Ultra-liberal in opinions, and always took occasion to express these in the most candid manner.

"What is birth, my dear?" she would say to Rebecca— "Look at my brother Pitt; look at the Huddlestons, who have been here since Henry II.; look at poor Bute at the parsonage;—is any one of them equal to you in intelligence or breeding? Equal to *you*—they are not even equal to poor dear Riggs, my companion, or Bowls, my butler. You, my love, are a little paragon—positively a little jewel—You have more brains than half the shire—if merit had its reward you ought to be a Duchess—no, there ought to be no duchesses at all—but you ought to have no superior, and I consider you, my love, as my equal in every respect; and—will you put some coals on the fire, my dear; and will you pick this dress of mine, and alter it, you who can do it so well?" So this old philanthropist used to make her equal run her errands, execute her millinery, and read her to sleep with French novels, every night.

At this time, as some old readers may recollect, the genteel world had been thrown into a considerable state of excitement by two events, which, as the papers say, might give employment to the gentlemen of the long robe. Ensign Shafton had run away with Lady Barbara Fitzurse, the Earl of Bruin's daughter and heiress; and poor Vere Vane, a gentleman who, up to forty, had maintained a most respectable

character and reared a numerous family, suddenly and out-
rageously left his home, for the sake of Mrs. Rougemont, the
actress, who was sixty-five years of age.

"That was the most beautiful part of dear Lord Nelson's
character," Miss Crawley said. "He went to the deuce for a
woman. There *must* be good in a man who will do that.
I adore all imprudent matches—What I like best, is for a
nobleman to marry a miller's daughter, as Lord Flowerdale
did—it makes all the women so angry—I wish some great
man would run away with *you*, my dear; I'm sure you're
pretty enough."

"Two post-boys!—Oh, it would be delightful!" Rebecca
owned.

"And what I like next best, is, for a poor fellow to run
away with a rich girl. I have set my heart on Rawdon running away with some one."

"A rich some one, or a poor some one?"

"Why, you goose! Rawdon has not a shilling but what
I give him. He is *criblé de dettes*—he must repair his fortunes, and succeed in the world."

"Is he very clever?" Rebecca asked.

"Clever, my love?—not an idea in the world beyond his
horses, and his regiment, and his hunting, and his play; but
he must succeed he's so delightfully wicked. Don't you
know he has hit a man, and shot an injured father through
the hat only? He's adored in his regiment; and all the young
men at Wattier's and the Cocoa-Tree swear by him."

When Miss Rebecca Sharp wrote to her beloved friend
the account of the little ball at Queen's Crawley, and the
manner in which, for the first time, Captain Crawley had
distinguished her, she did not, strange to relate, give an
altogether accurate account of the transaction. The Captain had distinguished her a great number of times before.
The Captain had met her in a half score of walks. The
Captain had lighted upon her in a half-hundred of corridors
and passages. The Captain had hung over her piano twenty
times of an evening (my Lady was now upstairs, being ill,
and nobody heeded her) as Miss Sharp sang. The Captain
had written her notes (the best that the great blundering
dragoon could devise and spell; but dulness gets on as well

as any other quality with women). But when he put the
first of the notes into the leaves of the song she was singing, the little governess, rising and looking him steadily in
the face, took up the triangular missive daintily, and waved
it about as if it were a cocked hat, and she, advancing to
the enemy, popped the note into the fire, and made him a
very low curtsey, and went back to her place, and began to
sing away again more merrily than ever.

"What's that?" said Miss Crawley, interrupted in her
after-dinner doze by the stoppage of the music.

"It's a false note," Miss Sharp said with a laugh; and
Rawdon Crawley fumed with rage and mortification.

Seeing the evident partiality of Miss Crawley for the new
governess, how good it was of Mrs. Bute Crawley not to be
jealous, and to welcome the young lady to the Rectory, and
not only her, but Rawdon Crawley, her husband's rival in
the old Maid's five per cents! They became very fond of
each other's society, Miss Crawley and her nephew. He
gave up hunting; he declined entertainments at Fuddleston: he would not dine with the mess of the depôt at
Mudbury: his great pleasure was to stroll over to Crawley
parsonage—whither Miss Crawley came too; and as their
mamma was ill, why not the children with Miss Sharp?
So the children (little dears!) came with Miss Sharp; and
of an evening some of the party would walk back together.
Not Miss Crawley—she preferred her carriage—but the
walk over the Rectory fields, and in at the little park
wicket, and through the dark plantation, and up the check-
ered avenue to Queen's Crawley, was charming in the moonlight to two such lovers of the picturesque as the Captain
and Miss Rebecca.

"O those stars, those stars!" Miss Rebecca would say,
turning her twinkling green eyes up towards them. "I
feel myself almost a spirit when I gaze upon them."

"O—ah—Gad—yes, so do I exactly, Miss Sharp," the
other enthusiast replied. "You don't mind my cigar, do
you, Miss Sharp?" Miss Sharp loved the smell of a cigar
out of doors beyond everything in the world—and she just
tasted one too, in the prettiest way possible, and gave a
little puff, and a little scream, and a little giggle, and re-

stored the delicacy to the Captain, who twirled his moustache, and straightway puffed it into a blaze that glowed
quite red in the dark plantation, and swore—"Jove—aw—
Gad—aw—it's the finest segaw I ever smoked in the world
aw," for his intellect and conversation were alike brilliant
and becoming to a heavy young dragoon.

Old Sir Pitt, who was taking his pipe and beer, and
talking to John Horrocks about a "ship" that was to be
killed, espied the pair so occupied from his study-window,
and with dreadful oaths swore that if it wasn't for Miss
Crawley, he'd take Rawdon and bundle un out of doors,
like a rogue as he was.

"He *be* a bad'n, sure enough," Mr. Horrocks remarked;
"and his man Flethers is wuss, and have made such a row
in the housekeeper's room about the dinners and hale, as
no lord would make—but I think Miss Sharp's a match
for'n, Sir Pitt," he added, after a pause.

And so, in truth, she was—for father and son too.

CHAPTER XII

QUITE A SENTIMENTAL CHAPTER

WE must now take leave of Arcadia, and those amiable people practising the rural virtues there, and travel back to London, to inquire what has become of Miss Amelia. "We don't care a fig for her," writes some unknown correspondent with a pretty little handwriting and a pink seal to her note. "She is *fade* and insipid," and adds some more kind remarks in this strain, which I should never have repeated at all, but that they are in truth prodigiously complimentary to the young lady whom they concern.

Has the beloved reader, in his experience of society, never heard similar remarks by good-natured female friends; who always wonder what you *can* see in Miss Smith that is so fascinating; or what *could* induce Major Jones to propose for that silly insignificant simpering Miss Thompson, who has nothing but her wax-doll face to recommend her? What is there in a pair of pink cheeks and blue eyes forsooth? these dear Moralists ask, and hint wisely that the gifts of genius, the accomplishments of the mind, the mastery of Mangnall's Questions, and a ladylike knowledge of botany and geology, the knack of making poetry, the power of rattling sonatas in the Herz-manner, and so forth, are far more valuable endowments for a female, than those fugitive charms which a few years will inevitably tarnish. It is quite edifying to hear women speculate upon the worthlessness and the duration of beauty.

But though virtue is a much finer thing, and those hapless creatures who suffer under the misfortune of good looks ought to be continually put in mind of the fate which awaits them; and though, very likely, the heroic female character which ladies admire is a more glorious and beautiful object than the kind, fresh, smiling, artless, tender

116

little domestic goddess, whom men are inclined to worship
—yet the latter and inferior sort of women must have this
consolation—that the men *do* admire them after all; and
that, in spite of all our kind friends' warnings and protests, we go on in our desperate error and folly, and shall
to the end of the chapter. Indeed, for my own part,
though I have been repeatedly told by persons for whom I
have the greatest respect, that Miss Brown is an insignificant chit, and Mrs. White has nothing but her *petit minois
chiffonné,* and Mrs. Black has not a word to say for herself; yet I know that I have had the most delightful conversations with Mrs. Black (of course, my dear Madam,
they are inviolable): I see all the men in a cluster round
Mrs. White's chair: all the young fellows battling to dance
with Miss Brown; and so I am tempted to think that to be
despised by her sex is a very great compliment to a woman.

The young ladies in Amelia's society did this for her
very satisfactorily. For instance, there was scarcely any
point upon which the Misses Osborne, George's sisters, and
the Mesdemoiselles Dobbin agreed so well as in their esti-
mate of her very trifling merits: and their wonder that
their brothers could find any charms in her. "We are kind
to her," the Misses Osborne said, a pair of fine black-
browed young ladies who had had the best of governesses,
masters, and milliners; and they treated her with such extreme kindness and condescension, and patronised her so
insufferably, that the poor little thing *was* in fact perfectly
dumb in their presence, and to all outward appearance as
stupid as they thought her. She made efforts to like them,
as in duty bound, and as sisters of her future husband.
She passed "long mornings" with them—the most dreary
and serious of forenoons. She drove out solemnly in their
great family coach with them, and Miss Wirt their governess, that raw-boned Vestal. They took her to the ancient
concerts by way of a treat, and to the oratorio, and to St.
Paul's to see the charity children, where in such terror was
she of her friends, she almost did not dare be affected by
the hymn the children sang. Their house was comfortable;
their papa's table rich and handsome! their society solemn
and genteel; their self-respect prodigious; they had the

best pew at the Foundling: all their habits were pompous and orderly, and all their amusements intolerably dull and decorous. After every one of her visits (and oh how glad she was when they were over!) Miss Osborne and Miss Maria Osborne, and Miss Wirt, the vestal governess, asked each other with increased wonder, "What *could* George find in that creature?"

How is this? some carping reader exclaims. How is it that Amelia, who had such a number of friends at school, and was so beloved there, comes out into the world and is spurned by her discriminating sex? My dear sir, there was no man at Miss Pinkerton's establishment except the old dancing-master; and you would not have had the girls fall out about *him?* When George, their handsome brother, ran off directly after breakfast, and dined from home half-a-dozen times a-week, no wonder the neglected sisters felt a little vexation. When young Bullock (of the firm of Hulker, Bullock & Co., Bankers, Lombard Street), who had been making up to Miss Maria the last two seasons, actually asked Amelia to dance the cotillon, could you expect that the former young lady should be pleased? And yet she said she was, like an artless forgiving creature. "I'm so delighted you like dear Amelia," she said quite eagerly to Mr. Bullock after the dance. "She's engaged to my brother George; there's not much in her, but she's the best-natured and most unaffected young creature: at home we're all *so* fond of her." Dear girl! who can calculate the depth of affection expressed in that enthusiastic *so?*

Miss Wirt and these two affectionate young women so earnestly and frequently impressed upon George Osborne's mind the enormity of the sacrifice he was making, and his romantic generosity in throwing himself away upon Amelia, that I'm not sure but that he really thought he was one of the most deserving characters in the British army, and gave himself up to be loved with a good deal of easy resignation.

Somehow, although he left home every morning, as was stated, and dined abroad six days in the week, when his sisters believed the infatuated youth to be at Miss Sedley's apron-strings: he was *not* always with Amelia, whilst the world supposed him at her feet. Certain it is that on more

occasions than one, when Captain Dobbin called to look
for his friend, Miss Osborne (who was very attentive to the
Captain, and anxious to hear his military stories, and to
know about the health of his dear Mamma,) would laughingly point to the opposite side of the square, and say,
"Oh, you must go to the Sedleys to ask for George; *we*
never see him from morning till night." At which kind of
speech the Captain would laugh in rather an absurd con-
strained manner, and turn off the conversation, like a consummate man of the world, to some topic of general interest, such as the Opera, the Prince's last ball at Carlton
House, or the weather—that blessing to society.

"What an innocent it is, that pet of yours," Miss Maria
would then say to Miss Jane, upon the Captain's departure:
"Did you see how he blushed at the mention of poor George
on duty?"

"It's a pity Frederick Bulloch hadn't some of his modesty,
Maria," replies the elder sister, with a toss of her head.

"Modesty! Awkwardness you mean, Jane. I don't want
Frederick to trample a hole in my muslin frock, as Captain
Dobbin did in yours at Mrs. Perkins'."

"In *your* frock, he, he! How could he? Wasn't he
dancing with Amelia?"

The fact is, when Captain Dobbin blushed so, and looked
so awkward, he remembered a circumstance of which he
did not think it was necessary to inform the young ladies,
viz., that he had been calling at Mr. Sedley's house already,
on the pretence of seeing George, of course, and George
wasn't there, only poor little Amelia, with rather a sad
wistful face, seated near the drawing-room window, who,
after some very trifling stupid talk, ventured to ask, was
there any truth in the report that the regiment was soon
to be ordered abroad; and had Captain Dobbin seen Mr.
Osborne that day?

The regiment was not ordered abroad as yet; and Captain
Dobbin had not seen George. "He was with his sister,
most likely," the Captain said. "Should he go and fetch
the truant?" So she gave him her hand kindly and grate-
fully: and he crossed the square; and she waited and waited,
but George never came.

Poor little tender heart! and so it goes on hoping and beating, and longing and trusting. You see it is not much of a life to describe. There is not much of what you call incident in it. Only one feeling all day—when will he come? only one thought to sleep and wake upon. I believe George was playing billiards with Captain Cannon in Swallow Street at the time when Amelia was asking Captain Dobbin about him; for George was a jolly sociable fellow, and excellent in all games of skill.

Once, after three days of absence, Miss Amelia put on her bonnet, and actually invaded the Osborne house. "What! leave our brother to come to us?" said the young ladies. "Have you had a quarrel, Amelia? Do tell us!" No, indeed, there had been no quarrel. "Who could quarrel with him?" says she, with her eyes filled with tears. She only came over to—to see her dear friends; they had not met for so long. And this day she was so perfectly stupid and awkward, that the Misses Osborne and their governess, who stared after her as she went sadly away, wondered more than ever what George could see in poor little Amelia.

Of course they did. How was she to bare that timid little heart for the inspection of those young ladies with their bold black eyes? It was best that it should shrink and hide itself. I know the Misses Osborne were excellent critics of a Cashmere shawl, or a pink satin slip; and when Miss Turner had hers dyed purple, and made into a spencer; and when Miss Pickford had her ermine tippet twisted into a muff and trimmings, I warrant you the changes did not escape the two intelligent young women before mentioned. But there are things, look you, of a finer texture than fur or satin, and all Solomon's glories, and all the wardrobe of the Queen of Sheba;—things whereof the beauty escapes the eyes of many connoisseurs. And there are sweet modest little souls on which you light, fragrant and blooming tenderly in quiet shady places; and there are garden-ornaments, as big as brass warming-pans, that are fit to stare the sun itself out of countenance. Miss Sedley was not of the sunflower sort; and I say it is out of the rules of all proportion to draw a violet of the size of a double dahlia.

No, indeed; the life of a good young girl who is in the paternal nest as yet, can't have many of those thrilling incidents to which the heroine of romance commonly lays claim. Snares or shot may take off the old birds foraging without —hawks may be abroad, from which they escape or by whom they suffer; but the young ones in the nest have a pretty comfortable unromantic sort of existence in the down and the straw, till it comes to their turn, too, to get on the wing. While Becky Sharp was on her own wing in the country, hopping on all sorts of twigs, and amid a multiplicity of traps, and pecking up her food quite harmless and successful, Amelia lay snug in her home of Russell Square; if she went into the world, it was under the guidance of the elders; nor did it seem that any evil could befall her or that opulent cheery comfortable home in which she was affectionately sheltered. Mamma had her morning duties, and her daily drive, and the delightful round of visits and shopping which forms the amusement, or the profession as you may call it, of the rich London lady. Papa conducted his mysterious operations in the City—a stirring place in those days, when war was raging all over Europe, and empires were being staked; when the "Courier" newspaper had tens of thousands of subscribers; when one day brought you a battle of Vittoria, another a burning of Moscow, or a newsman's horn blowing down Russell Square about dinnertime, announced such a fact as—"Battle of Leipsic—six hundred thousand men engaged—total defeat of the French —two hundred thousand killed." Old Sedley once or twice came home with a very grave face; and no wonder, when such news as this was agitating all the hearts and all the Stocks of Europe.

Meanwhile matters went on in Russell Square, Bloomsbury, just as if matters in Europe were not in the least disorganised. The retreat from Leipsic made no difference in the number of meals Mr. Sambo took in the servants' hall; the allies poured into France, and the dinner-bell rang at five o'clock just as usual. I don't think poor Amelia cared anything about Brienne and Montmirail, or was fairly interested in the war until the abdication of the Emperor; when she clapped her hands and said prayers,—

oh, how grateful! and flung herself into George Osborne's arms with all her soul, to the astonishment of everybody who witnessed that ebullition of sentiment. The fact is, peace was declared, Europe was going to be at rest; the Corsican was overthrown, and Lieutenant Osborne's regiment would not be ordered on service. That was the way in which Miss Amelia reasoned. The fate of Europe was Lieutenant George Osborne to her. His dangers being over, she sang Te Deum. He was her Europe; her emperor: her allied monarchs and august prince regent. He was her sun and moon; and I believe she thought the grand illumination and ball at the Mansion House, given to the sovereigns, were especially in honour of George Osborne.

We have talked of shift, self, and poverty, as those dismal instructors under whom poor Miss Becky Sharp got her education. Now, love was Miss Amelia Sedley's last tutoress, and it was amazing what progress our young lady made under that popular teacher. In the course of fifteen or eighteen months' daily and constant attention to this eminent finishing governess, what a deal of secrets Amelia learned, which Miss Wirt and the black-eyed young ladies over the way, which old Miss Pinkerton of Chiswick herself, had no cognizance of! As, indeed, how should any of those prim and reputable virgins? With Misses P. and W. the tender passion is out of the question: I would not dare to breathe such an idea regarding them. Miss Maria Osborne, it is true, was "attached" to Mr. Frederick Augustus Bullock, of the firm of Hulker, Bullock & Bullock; but hers was a most respectable attachment, and she would have taken Bullock Senior just the same, her mind being fixed,—as that of a well-bred young woman should be,— upon a house in Park Lane, a country house at Wimbledon, a handsome chariot, and two prodigious tall horses and footmen, and a fourth of the annual profits of the eminent firm of Hulker & Bullock, all of which advantages were represented in the person of Frederick Augustus. Had orange blossoms been invented then (those touching emblems of female purity imported by us from France, where people's daughters are universally sold in marriage), Miss Maria, I say, would have assumed the spotless wreath, and stepped into the travelling carriage by the side of gouty, old, bald-headed, bottle-nosed Bullock Senior; and devoted her beautiful existence to his happiness with perfect modesty,—only the old gentleman was married already; so she bestowed her young affections on the junior partner. Sweet, blooming, orange flowers! The other day I saw Miss Trotter (that was), arrayed in them, trip into the travelling carriage at St. George's, Hanover Square, and Lord Methuselah hobbled in after. With what an engaging modesty she pulled down the blinds of the chariot—the dear innocent! There were half the carriages of Vanity Fair at the wedding.

This was not the sort of love that finished Amelia's education; and in the course of a year turned a good young girl into a good young woman—to be a good wife presently, when the happy time should come. This young person (perhaps it was very imprudent in her parents to encourage her, and abet her in such idolatry and silly romantic ideas) loved, with all her heart, the young officer in his Majesty's service with whom we have made a brief acquaintance. She thought about him the very first moment on waking; and his was the very last name mentioned in her prayers. She never had seen a man so beautiful or so clever: such a figure on horseback: such a dancer: such a hero in general. Talk of the Prince's bow! what was it to George's? She had seen Mr. Brummell, whom everybody praised so. Compare such a person as that to her George! Not amongst all the beaux at the Opera (and there were beaux in those days with actual opera hats) was there any one to equal him. He was only good enough to be a fairy prince; and oh, what magnanimity to stoop to such a humble Cinderella! Miss Pinkerton would have tried to check this blind devotion very likely, had she been Amelia's confidante; but not with much success, depend upon it. It is in the nature and instinct of some women. Some are made to scheme, and some to love; and I wish any respected bachelor that reads this may take the sort that best likes him.

While under this overpowering impression, Miss Amelia neglected her twelve dear friends at Chiswick most cruelly, as such selfish people commonly will do. She had but this subject, of course, to think about; and Miss Saltire was too cold for a confidante, and she couldn't bring her mind to tell Miss Swartz, the woolly-haired young heiress from St. Kitt's. She had little Laura Martin home for the holidays; and my belief is, she made a confidante of her, and promised that Laura should come and live with her when she was married, and gave Laura a great deal of information regarding the passion of love, which must have been singularly useful and novel to that little person. Alas, alas! I fear poor Emmy had not a well-regulated mind.

What were her parents doing, not to keep this little heart from beating so fast? Old Sedley did not seem much to notice matters. He was graver of late, and his City affairs absorbed him. Mrs. Sedley was of so easy and uninquisitive a nature, that she wasn't even jealous. Mr. Jos was away, being besieged by an Irish widow at Cheltenham. Amelia had the house to herself—ah! too much to herself sometimes—not that she ever doubted; for, to be sure, George must be at the Horse-Guards; and he can't always get leave from Chatham; and he must see his friends and sisters, and mingle in society when in town (he, such an ornament to every society!); and when he is with the regiment, he is too tired to write long letters. I know where she kept that packet she had—and can steal in and out of her chamber like Iachimo—like Iachimo? No—that is a bad part. I will only act Moonshine, and peep harmless into the bed where faith and beauty and innocence lie dreaming.

But if Osborne's were short and soldierlike letters, it must be confessed, that were Miss Sedley's letters to Mr. Osborne to be published, we should have to extend this novel to such a multiplicity of volumes as not the most sentimental reader could support; that she not only filled sheets of large paper, but crossed them with the most astonishing perverseness; that she wrote whole pages out of poetry-books without the least pity; that she underlined words and passages with quite a frantic emphasis; and, in fine, gave the usual tokens of her condition. She wasn't a heroine. Her letters *were* full of repetition. She wrote rather doubtful grammar sometimes, and in her verses took all sorts of liberties with the metre. But oh, mesdames, if you are not allowed to touch the heart sometimes in spite of syntax, and are not to be loved until you all know the difference between trimeter and tetrameter, may all Poetry go to the deuce, and every schoolmaster perish miserably!

CHAPTER XIII

SENTIMENTAL AND OTHERWISE

I FEAR the gentleman to whom Miss Amelia's letters were addressed was rather an obdurate critic. Such a number of notes followed Lieutenant Osborne about the country, that he became almost ashamed of the jokes of his mess-room companions regarding them, and ordered his servant never to deliver them except at his private apartment. He was seen lighting his cigar with one, to the horror of Captain Dobbin, who, it is my belief, would have given a bank-note for the document.

For some time George strove to keep the liaison a secret. There *was* a woman in the case, that he admitted. "And not the first either," said Ensign Spooney to Ensign Stubble. "That Osborne's a devil of a fellow. There was a judge's daughter at Demerara went almost mad about him; then there was that beautiful quadroon girl, Miss Pye, at St. Vincent's, you know; and since he's been home, they say he's a regular Don Giovanni, by Jove."

Stubble and Spooney thought that to be a "regular Don Giovanni, by Jove" was one of the finest qualities a man could possess; and Osborne's reputation was prodigious amongst the young men of the regiment. He was famous in field-sports, famous at a song, famous on parade; free with his money, which was bountifully supplied by his father. His coats were better made than any man's in the regiment, and he had more of them. He was adored by the men. He could drink more than any officer of the whole mess, including old Heavytop, the colonel. He could spar better than Knuckles, the private (who would have been a corporal but for his drunkenness, and who had been in the prize-ring); and was the best batter and bowler, out and out, of the regimental club. He rode his own horse, Greased Lightning, and won the Garrison cup at Quebec races. There were other people besides Amelia who worshipped him. Stubble and Spooney thought him a sort of Apollo; Dobbin took him to be an Admirable Crichton; and Mrs. Major O'Dowd acknowledged he was an elegant young fellow, and put her in mind of Fitzjurld Fogarty, Lord Castlefogarty's second son.

Well, Stubble and Spooney and the rest indulged in most romantic conjectures regarding this female correspondent of Osborne's,—opining that it was a Duchess in London who was in love with him,—or that it was a General's daughter, who was engaged to somebody else, and madly attached to him,—or that it was a Member of Parliament's lady, who proposed four horses and an elopement,—or that it was some other victim of a passion delightfully exciting, romantic, and disgraceful to all parties, on none of which conjectures would Osborne throw the least light, leaving his young admirers and friends to invent and arrange their whole history.

And the real state of the case would never have been known at all in the regiment but for Captain Dobbin's indiscretion. The Captain was eating his breakfast one day in the mess-room, while Cackle, the assistant-surgeon, and the two above-named worthies were speculating upon Osborne's intrigue—Stubble holding out that the lady was a Duchess about Queen Charlotte's court, and Cackle vowing she was an opera-singer of the worst reputation. At this idea Dobbin became so moved, that though his mouth was full of eggs and bread-and-butter at the time, and though he ought not to have spoken at all, yet he couldn't help blurting out, "Cackle, you're a stupid fool. You're always talking nonsense and scandal. Osborne is not going to run off with a Duchess or ruin a milliner. Miss Sedley is one of the most charming young women that ever lived. He's been engaged to her ever so long; and the man who calls her names had better not do so in my hearing." With which, turning exceedingly red, Dobbin ceased speaking, and almost choked himself with a cup of tea. The story was over the regiment in half-an-hour; and that very evening Mrs. Major O'Dowd wrote off to her sister Glorvina at O'Dowdstown not to hurry from Dublin,—young Osborne being prematurely engaged already.

She complimented the Lieutenant in an appropriate speech over a glass of whisky-toddy that evening, and he went home perfectly furious to quarrel with Dobbin, (who had declined Mrs. Major O'Dowd's party, and sat in his own room playing the flute, and, I believe, writing poetry in a very melancholy manner)—to quarrel with Dobbin for betraying his secret.

"Who the deuce asked you to talk about my affairs?" Osborne shouted indignantly. "Why the devil is all the regiment to know that I am going to be married? Why is that tattling old harridan, Peggy O'Dowd, to make free with my name at her d—d supper-table, and advertise my engagement over the three kingdoms? After all, what right have you to say I *am* engaged, or to meddle in my business at all, Dobbin?"

"It seems to me,"—Captain Dobbin began.

"Seems be hanged, Dobbin," his junior interrupted him. "I am under obligations to you, I know it, a d—d deal too well too; but I won't be always sermonised by you because you're five years my senior. I'm hanged if I'll stand your airs of superiority and infernal pity and patronage. Pity and patronage! I should like to know in what I'm your inferior?"

"Are you engaged?" Captain Dobbin interposed.

"What the devil's that to you or any one here if I am?"

"Are you ashamed of it?" Dobbin resumed.

"What right have you to ask me that question, sir? I should like to know," George said.

"Good God, you don't mean to say you want to break off?" asked Dobbin, starting up.

"In other words, you ask me if I'm a man of honour," said Osborne, fiercely; "is that what you mean? You've adopted such a tone regarding me lately that I'm —— if I'll bear it any more."

"What have I done? I've told you you were neglecting a sweet girl, George. I've told you that when you go to town you ought to go to her, and not to the gambling-houses about St. James's."

"You want your money back, I suppose," said George, with a sneer.

"Of course I do—I always did, didn't I?" says Dobbin. "You speak like a generous fellow."

"No, hang it, William, I beg your pardon"—here George interposed in a fit of remorse; "you *have* been my friend in a hundred ways, Heaven knows. You've got me out of a score of scrapes. When Crawley of the Guards won that sum of money of me I should have been done but for you: I know I should. But you shouldn't deal so hardly with me; you shouldn't be always catechising me. I *am* very fond of Amelia; I adore her, and that sort of thing. Don't look angry. She's faultless; I know she is. But you see there's no fun in winning a thing unless you play for it. Hang it: the regiment's just back from the West Indies, I must have a little fling, and then when I'm married I'll reform; I will upon my honour, now. And—I say—Dob—don't be angry with me, and I'll give you a hundred next month, when I know my father will stand something handsome; and I'll ask Heavytop for leave, and I'll go to town, and see Amelia to-morrow—there now, will *that* satisfy you?"

"It is impossible to be long angry with you, George," said the good-natured Captain; "and as for the money, old boy, you know if I wanted it you'd share your last shilling with me."

"That I would, by Jove, Dobbin," George said, with the greatest generosity, though by the way he never had any money to spare.

"Only I wish you had sown those wild oats of yours, George. If you could have seen poor little Miss Emmy's face when she asked me about you the other day, you would have pitched those billiard-balls to the deuce. Go and comfort her, you rascal. Go and write her a long letter. Do something to make her happy; a very little will."

"I believe she's d—d fond of me," the lieutenant said, with a self-satisfied air; and went off to finish the evening with some jolly fellows in the mess room.

Amelia meanwhile, in Russell Square, was looking at the moon, which was shining upon that peaceful spot, as well as upon the square of the Chatham barracks, where Lieutenant Osborne was quartered, and thinking to herself how her hero was employed. Perhaps he is visiting the sentries, thought she; perhaps he is bivouacking; perhaps he is attending the couch of a wounded comrade, or studying the art of war up in his own desolate chamber. And her kind thoughts sped away as if they were angels and had wings, and flying down the river to Chatham and Rochester, strove to peep into the barracks where George was. . . . . All things considered, I think it was as well the gates were shut, and the sentry allowed no one to pass; so that the poor little white-robed angel could not hear the songs those young fellows were roaring over the whisky-punch.

The day after the little conversation at Chatham barracks, young Osborne, to show that he would be as good as his word, prepared to go to town, thereby incurring Captain Dobbin's applause. "I should have liked to make her a little present," Osborne said to his friend in confidence, "only I am quite out of cash until my father tips up." But Dobbin would not allow this good nature and generosity to be balked, and so accommodated Mr. Osborne with a few pound notes, which the latter took after a little faint scruple.

And I dare say he would have bought something very handsome for Amelia; only, getting off the coach in Fleet Street, he was attracted by a handsome shirt-pin in a jeweller's window, which he could not resist; and having paid for that, had very little money to spare for indulging in any further exercise of kindness. Never mind: you may be sure it was not his presents Amelia wanted. When he came to Russell Square, her face lighted up as if he had been sunshine. The little cares, fears, tears, timid misgivings, sleepless fancies of I don't know how many days and nights, were forgotten, under one moment's influence of that familiar, irresistible smile. He beamed on her from the drawing-room door—magnificent, with ambrosial whiskers, like a god. Sambo, whose face as he announced Captain Osbin (having conferred a brevet rank on that young officer) blazed with a sympathetic grin, saw the little girl start, and flush, and jump up from her watching-place in the window; and Sambo retreated: and as soon as the door was shut, she went fluttering to Lieutenant George

Osborne's heart as if it was the only natural home for her
to nestle in. Oh, thou poor panting little soul! The very
finest tree in the whole forest, with the straightest stem,
and the strongest arms, and the thickest foliage, wherein
you choose to build and coo, may be marked, for what you
know, and may be down with a crash ere long. What an
old, old simile that is, between man and timber.

In the meanwhile, George kissed her very kindly on her
forehead and glistening eyes, and was very gracious and
good; and she thought his diamond shirt-pin (which she
had not known him to wear before) the prettiest ornament
ever seen.

The observant reader, who has marked our young Lieutenant's previous behaviour, and has preserved our report
of the brief conversation which he has just had with
Captain Dobbin, has possibly come to certain conclusions
regarding the character of Mr. Osborne. Some cynical
Frenchman has said that there are two parties to a love-
transaction: the one who loves and the other who condescends to be so treated. Perhaps the love is occasionally
on the man's side; perhaps on the lady's. Perhaps some
infatuated swain has ere this mistaken insensibility for
modesty, dulness for maiden reserve, mere vacuity for sweet
bashfulness, and a goose, in a word, for a swan. Perhaps
some beloved female subscriber has arrayed an ass in the
splendour and glory of her imagination; admired his dulness
as manly simplicity; worshipped his selfishness as manly
superiority; treated his stupidity as majestic gravity, and
used him as the brilliant fairy Titania did a certain weaver
at Athens. I think I have seen such comedies of errors
going on in the world. But this is certain, that Amelia believed her lover to be one of the most gallant and brilliant
men in the empire; and it is possible Lieutenant Osborne
thought so too.

He was a little wild: how many young men are; and
don't girls like a rake better than a milksop? He hadn't
sown his wild oats as yet, but he would soon: and quit the
army now that peace was proclaimed; the Corsican monster
locked up at Elba; promotion by consequence over; and no

chance left for the display of his undoubted military talents and valour: and his allowance, with Amelia's settlement, would enable them to take a snug place in the country somewhere, in a good sporting neighbourhood; and he would hunt a little, and farm a little; and they would be very happy. As for remaining in the army as a married man, that was impossible. Fancy Mrs. George Osborne in lodgings in a county town; or, worse still, in the East or West Indies, with a society of officers, and patronised by Mrs. Major O'Dowd! Amelia died with laughing at Osborne's stories about Mrs. Major O'Dowd. He loved her much too fondly to subject her to that horrid woman and her vulgarities, and the rough treatment of a soldier's wife. He didn't care for himself—not he; but his dear little girl should take the place in society to which, as his wife, she was entitled: and to these proposals you may be sure she acceded, as she would to any other from the same author.

Holding this kind of conversation, and building number-less castles in the air (which Amelia adorned with all sorts of flower-gardens, rustic walks, country churches, Sunday schools, and the like; while George had his mind's eye directed to the stables, the kennel, and the cellar), this young pair passed away a couple of hours very pleasantly; and as the Lieutenant had only that single day in town, and a great deal of most important business to transact, it was proposed that Miss Emmy should dine with her future sisters-in-law. This invitation was accepted joyfully. He conducted her to his sisters; where he left her talking and prattling in a way that astonished those ladies, who thought that George might make something of her; and he then went off to transact his business.

In a word, he went out and ate ices at a pastry-cook's shop in Charing Cross; tried a new coat in Pall Mall; dropped in at the Old Slaughters', and called for Captain Cannon; played eleven games at billiards with the Captain, of which he won eight, and returned to Russell Square half-an-hour late for dinner, but in very good humour.

It was not so with old Mr. Osborne. When that gentleman came from the City, and was welcomed in the drawing-

room by his daughters and the elegant Miss Wirt, they
saw at once by his face—which was puffy, solemn, and yellow at the best of times—and by the scowl and twitching
of his black eye-brows, that the heart within his large
white waistcoat was disturbed and uneasy. When Amelia
stepped forward to salute him, which she always did with
great trembling and timidity, he gave a surly grunt of
recognition, and dropped the little hand out of his great
hirsute paw without any attempt to hold it there. He
looked round gloomily at his eldest daughter; who, com-
prehending the meaning of his look, which asked unmis-
takably, "Why the devil is *she* here?" said at once:—

"George is in town, Papa; and has gone to the Horse
Guards, and will be back to dinner."

"O he is, is he? I won't have the dinner kept waiting
for *him*, Jane;" with which this worthy man lapsed into
his particular chair, and then the utter silence in his genteel, well-furnished drawing-room was only interrupted by
the alarmed ticking of the great French clock.

When that chronometer, which was surmounted by a
cheerful brass group of the sacrifice of Iphigenia, tolled
five in a heavy cathedral tone, Mr. Osborne pulled the bell
at his right hand violently, and the butler rushed up.

"Dinner!" roared Mr. Osborne.

"Mr. George isn't come in, sir," interposed the man.

"Damn Mr. George, sir. Am I master of the house?
DINNER!" Mr. Osborne scowled. Amelia trembled. A
telegraphic communication of eyes passed between the other
three ladies. The obedient bell in the lower regions began
ringing the announcement of the meal. The tolling over,
the head of the family thrust his hands into the great tail-
pockets of his great blue coat and brass buttons, and without waiting for a further announcement, strode down stairs
alone, scowling over his shoulder at the four females.

"What's the matter now, my dear?" asked one of the
other, as they rose and tripped gingerly behind the sire.

"I suppose the funds are falling," whispered Miss Wirt;
and so, trembling and in silence, this hushed female company followed their dark leader. They took their places
in silence. He growled out a blessing, which sounded as

gruffly as a curse. The great silver dish-covers were removed. Amelia trembled in her place, for she was next to the awful Osborne, and alone on her side of the table—the gap being occasioned by the absence of George.

"Soup?" says Mr. Osborne, clutching the ladle, fixing his eyes on her, in a sepulchral tone; and having helped her and the rest, did not speak for a while.

"Take Miss Sedley's plate away," at last he said. "She can't eat the soup—no more can I. It's beastly. Take away the soup, Hicks, and to-morrow turn the cook out of the house, Jane."

Having concluded his observations upon the soup, Mr. Osborne made a few curt remarks respecting the fish, also of a savage and satirical tendency, and cursed Billingsgate with an emphasis quite worthy of the place. Then he lapsed into silence, and swallowed sundry glasses of wine, looking more and more terrible, till a brisk knock at the door told of George's arrival, when everybody began to rally.

"He could not come before. General Daguilet had kept him waiting at the Horse Guards. Never mind soup or fish. Give him anything—he didn't care what. Capital mutton—capital everything." His good humour contrasted with his father's severity; and he rattled on unceasingly during dinner, to the delight of all—of one especially, who need not be mentioned.

As soon as the young ladies had discussed the orange and the glass of wine which formed the ordinary conclusion of the dismal banquets at Mr. Osborne's house, the signal to make sail for the drawing-room was given, and they all arose and departed. Amelia hoped George would soon join them there. She began playing some of his favourite waltzes (then newly imported) at the great carved-legged, leather-cased grand piano in the drawing-room overhead. This little artifice did not bring him. He was deaf to the waltzes; they grew fainter and fainter; the discomfited performer left the huge instrument presently; and though her three friends performed some of the loudest and most brilliant new pieces of their *répertoire,* she did not hear a single note, but sate thinking, and boding evil. Old Osborne's

scowl, terrific always, had never before looked so deadly
to her. His eyes followed her out of the room, as if she had
been guilty of something. When they brought her coffee,
she started as though it were a cup of poison which Mr.
Hicks, the butler, wished to propose to her. What mystery
was there lurking? Oh, those women. They nurse and
cuddle their presentiments, and make darlings of their
ugliest thoughts, as they do of their deformed children.

The gloom on the paternal countenance had also impressed George Osborne with anxiety. With such eyebrows, and a look so decidedly bilious, how was he to ex-
tract that money from the governor, of which George was
consumedly in want? He began praising his father's wine.

That was generally a successful means of cajoling the
old gentleman.

"We never got such Madeira in the West Indies, sir, as
yours. Colonel Heavytop took off three bottles of that you
sent me down, under his belt the other day."

"Did he?" said the old gentleman. "It stands me in
eight shillings a bottle."

"Will you take six guineas a dozen for it, sir?" said
George, with a laugh. "There's one of the greatest men
in the kingdom wants come."

"Does he?" growled the senior. "Wish he may get it."

"When General Daguilet was at Chatham, sir, Heavytop
gave him a breakfast, and asked me for some of the wine.
The General liked it just as well—wanted a pipe for the
Commander-in-Chief. He's his Royal Highness' right-
hand man."

"It *is* devilish fine wine," said the Eyebrows, and they
looked more good-humoured; and George was going to take
advantage of this complacency, and bring the supply question on the mahogany, when the father, relapsing into
solemnity, though rather cordial in manner, bade him ring
the bell for claret. "And we'll see if that's as good as the
Madeira, George, to which his Royal Highness is welcome,
I'm sure. And as we are drinking it, I'll talk to you about
a matter of importance."

Amelia heard the claret bell ringing as she sat nervously
upstairs. She thought, somehow, it was a mysterious and

presentimental bell. Of the presentiments which some people are always having, *some* surely must come right.

"What I want to know, George," the old gentleman said,
after slowly smacking his first bumper—"What I want to
know is, how you and—ah—that little thing upstairs, are
carrying on?"

"I think, sir, it's not hard to see," George said, with a
self-satisfied grin. "Pretty clear, sir.—What capital wine!"

"What d'you mean, pretty clear, sir?"

"Why, hang it, sir, don't push me too hard. I'm a
modest man. I—ah—I don't set up to be a lady-killer;
but I do own that she's as devilish fond of me as she can
be. Anybody can see that with half an eye."

"And you yourself?"

"Why, sir, didn't you order me to marry her, and ain't
I a good boy? Haven't our Papas settled it ever so long?"

"A pretty boy, indeed. Haven't I heard of your doings,
sir, with Lord Tarquin, Captain Crawley of the guards, the
Honourable Mr. Deuceace and that set. Have a care, sir,
have a care."

The old gentleman pronounced these aristocratic names
with the greatest gusto. Whenever he met a great man he
grovelled before him, and my-lorded him as only a free-
born Briton can do. He came home and looked out his
history in the Peerage; he introduced his name into his
daily conversation; he bragged about his Lordship to his
daughters. He fell down prostrate and basked in him as a
Neapolitan beggar does in the sun. George was alarmed
when he heard the names. He feared his father might
have been informed of certain transactions at play. But
the old moralist eased him by saying serenely:—

"Well, well, young men will be young men. And the
comfort to me is, George, that living in the best society in
England, as I hope you do; as I think you do; as my
means will allow you to do—"

"Thank you, sir," says George, making his point at
once. "One can't live with these great folks for nothing;
and my purse, sir, look at it;" and he held up a little token
which had been netted by Amelia, and contained the very
last of Dobbin's pound notes.

"You shan't want, sir. The British merchant's son shan't want, sir. My guineas are as good as theirs, George, my boy; and I don't grudge 'em. Call on Mr. Chopper as you go through the City to-morrow; he'll have something for you. I don't grudge money when I know you're in good society, because I know that good society can never go wrong. There's no pride in me. I was a humbly born man—but you have had advantages. Make a good use of 'em. Mix with the young nobility. There's many of 'em who can't spend a dollar to your guinea, my boy. And as for the pink bonnets (here from under the heavy eyebrows there came a knowing and not very pleasing leer)—why boys will be boys. Only there's one thing I order you to avoid, which, if you do not, I'll cut you off with a shilling, by Jove; and that's gambling, sir."

"Oh, of course, sir," said George.

"But to return to the other business about Amelia: why shouldn't you marry higher than a stockbroker's daughter, George—that's what I want to know?"

"It's a family business, sir," says George, cracking filberts. "You and Mr. Sedley made the match a hundred years ago."

"I don't deny it; but people's positions alter, sir. I don't deny that Sedley made my fortune, or rather put me in the way of acquiring, by my own talents and genius, that proud position, which, I may say, I occupy in the tallow trade and the City of London. I've shown my gratitude to Sedley; and he's tried it of late, sir, as my cheque-book can show. George! I tell you in confidence I don't like the looks of Mr. Sedley's affairs. My chief clerk, Mr. Chopper, does not like the looks of 'em, and he's an old file, and knows 'Change as well as any man in London. Hulker & Bullock are looking shy at him. He's been dabbling on his own account I fear. They say the Jeune Amélie was his, which was taken by the Yankee privateer Molasses. And that's flat,—unless I see Amelia's ten thousand down you don't marry her. I'll have no lame duck's daughter in my family. Pass the wine, sir—or ring for coffee."

With which Mr. Osborne spread out the evening paper, and George knew from this signal that the colloquy was ended, and that his Papa was about to take a nap.

He hurried upstairs to Amelia in the highest spirits.
What was it that made him more attentive to her on that
night than he had been for a long time—more eager to
amuse her, more tender, more brilliant in talk? Was it
that his generous heart warmed to her at the prospect of
misfortune; or that the idea of losing the dear little prize
made him value it more?

She lived upon the recollections of that happy evening
for many days afterwards, remembering his words; his
looks; the song he sang; his attitude, as he leant over her
or looked at her from a distance. As it seemed to her, no
night ever passed so quickly at Mr. Osborne's house before;
and for once this young person was almost provoked to be
angry by the premature arrival of Mr. Sambo with her
shawl.

George came and took a tender leave of her the next
morning; and then hurried off to the City, where he visited
Mr. Chopper, his father's head man, and received from
that gentleman a document which he exchanged at Hulker
& Bullock's for a whole pocket-full of money. As George
entered the house, old John Sedley was passing out of the
banker's parlour, looking very dismal. But his godson
was much too elated to mark the worthy stockbroker's depression, or the dreary eyes which the kind old gentleman
cast upon him. Young Bullock did not come grinning out
of the parlour with him as had been his wont in former
years.

And as the swinging doors of Hulker, Bullock & Co.
closed upon Mr. Sedley, Mr. Quill, the cashier (whose
benevolent occupation it is to hand out crisp bank-notes
from a drawer and dispense sovereigns out of a copper
shovel), winked at Mr. Driver, the clerk at the desk on
his right. Mr. Driver winked again.

"No go," Mr. D. whispered.

"Not at no price," Mr. Q. said. "Mr. George Osborne,
sir, how will you take it?" George crammed eagerly a
quantity of notes into his pockets, and paid Dobbin fifty
pounds that very evening at mess.

The very evening Amelia wrote him the tenderest of
long letters. Her heart was overflowing with tenderness,

but it still foreboded evil. What was the cause of Mr. Osborne's dark looks? she asked. Had any difference arisen between him and her papa? Her poor papa returned so melancholy from the City, that all were alarmed about him at home—in fine, there were four pages of loves and fears and hopes and forebodings.

"Poor little Emmy—dear little Emmy. How fond she is of me," George said, as he perused the missive—"and Gad, what a head-ache that mixed punch has given me!" Poor little Emmy, indeed.

CHAPTER XIV

Miss Crawley at Home

ABOUT this time there drove up to an exceedingly snug and well appointed house in Park Lane, a travelling chariot with a lozenge on the panels, a discontented female in a green veil and crimped curls on the rumble, and a large and confidential man on the box. It was the equipage of our friend Miss Crawley, returning from Hants. The carriage windows were shut; the fat spaniel, whose head and tongue ordinarily lolled out of one of them, reposed on the lap of the discontented female. When the vehicle stopped, a large round bundle of shawls was taken out of the carriage by the aid of various domestics and a young lady who accompanied the heap of cloaks. That bundle contained Miss Crawley, who was conveyed upstairs forthwith, and put into a bed and chamber warmed properly as for the reception of an invalid. Messengers went off for her physician and medical man. They came, consulted, prescribed, vanished. The young companion of Miss Crawley, at the conclusion of their interview, came in to receive their instructions, and administered those antiphlogistic medicines which the eminent men ordered.

Captain Crawley of the Life Guards rode up from Knightsbridge Barracks the next day; his black charger pawed the straw before his invalid aunt's door. He was most affectionate in his inquiries regarding that amiable relative. There seemed to be much source of apprehension. He found Miss Crawley's maid (the discontented female) unusually sulky and despondent; he found Miss Briggs, her dame de còmpagnie, in tears alone in the drawing-room. She had hastened home, hearing of her beloved friend's illness. She wished to fly to her couch, that couch which she, Briggs, had so often smoothed in the hour of sickness. She was denied admission to Miss Crawley's

apartment. A stranger was administering her medicines—
a stranger from the country—an odious Miss . . .—tears
choked the utterance of the dame de compagnie, and she
buried her crushed affections and her poor old red nose in
her pocket handkerchief.

Rawdon Crawley sent up his name by the sulky femme
de chambre, and Miss Crawley's new companion, coming
tripping down from the sick-room, put a little hand into his
as he stepped forward eagerly to meet her, gave a glance
of great scorn at the bewildered Briggs, and beckoning the
young Guardsman out of the back drawing-room, led him
downstairs into that now desolate dining-parlour, where so
many a good dinner had been celebrated.

Here these two talked for ten minutes, discussing, no
doubt, the symptoms of the old invalid above stairs; at the
end of which period the parlour bell was rung briskly, and
answered on that instant by Mr. Bowls, Miss Crawley's
large confidential butler. (who, indeed, happened to be at
the keyhole during the most part of the interview); and
the Captain coming out, curling his moustachios, mounted
the black charger pawing among the straw, to the admiration of the little blackguard boys collected in the street.
He looked in at the dining-room window, managing his
horse, which curvetted and capered beautifully—for one
instant the young person might be seen at the window,
when her figure vanished, and, doubtless, she went upstairs
again to resume the affecting duties of benevolence.

Who could this young woman be, I wonder? That evening a little dinner for two persons was laid in the dining-
room—when Mrs. Firkin, the lady's maid, pushed into her
mistress's apartment, and bustled about there during the
vacancy occasioned by the departure of the new nurse—and
the latter and Miss Briggs sat down to the neat little meal.

Briggs was so much choked by emotion that she could
hardly take a morsel of meat. The young person carved a
fowl with the utmost delicacy, and asked so distinctly for
egg-sauce, that poor Briggs, before whom that delicious
condiment was placed, started, made a great clattering with
the ladle, and once more fell back in the most gushing
hysterical state.

"Had you not better give Miss Briggs a glass of wine?" said the person to Mr. Bowls, the large confidential man. He did so. Briggs seized it mechanically, gasped it down convulsively, moaned a little, and began to play with the chicken on her plate.

"I think we shall be able to help each other," said the person with great suavity: "and shall have no need of Mr. Bowls's kind services. Mr. Bowls, if you please, we will ring when we want you." He went downstairs, where, by the way, he vented the most horrid curses upon the unoffending footman, his subordinate.

"It is a pity you take on so, Miss Briggs," the young lady said, with a cool, slightly sarcastic, air.

"My dearest friend is so ill, and wo—o—o—on't see me," gurgled out Briggs in an agony of renewed grief.

"She's not very ill any more. Console yourself, dear Miss Briggs. She has only overeaten herself—that is all. She is greatly better. She will soon be quite restored again. She is weak from being cupped and from medical treatment, but she will rally immediately. Pray console yourself, and take a little more wine."

"But why, why won't she see me again?" Miss Briggs bleated out. "Oh, Matilda, Matilda, after three-and-twenty years' tenderness! is this the return to your poor, poor Arabella?"

"Don't cry too much, poor Arabella," the other said (with ever so little of a grin); "she only won't see you, because she says you don't nurse her as well as I do. It's no pleasure to me to sit up all night. I wish you might do it instead."

"Have I not tended that dear couch for years?" Arabella said, "and now——"

"Now she prefers somebody else. Well, sick people have these fancies, and must be humoured. When she's well I shall go."

"Never, never," Arabella exclaimed, madly inhaling her salts-bottle.

"Never be well or never go, Miss Briggs?" the other said, with the same provoking good-nature. "Pooh—she will be well in a fortnight, when I shall go back to my little pupils at Queen's Crawley, and to their mother, who is a great deal more sick than our friend. You need not be jealous about me, my dear Miss Briggs. I am a poor little girl without any friends, or any harm in me. I don't want to supplant you in Miss Crawley's good graces. She will forget me a week after I am gone: and her affection for you has been the work of years. Give me a little wine if you please, my dear Miss Briggs, and let us be friends. I'm sure I want friends."

The placable and soft-hearted Briggs speechlessly pushed out her hand at this appeal; but she felt the desertion most keenly for all that, and bitterly, bitterly moaned the fickleness of her Matilda. At the end of half an hour, the meal over, Miss Rebecca Sharp (for such, astonishing to state, is the name of her who has been described ingeniously as "the person" hitherto), went upstairs again to her patient's rooms, from which, with the most engaging politeness, she eliminated poor Firkin. "Thank you, Mrs. Firkin, that will quite do; how nicely you make it! I will ring when anything is wanted." "Thank you;" and Firkin came downstairs in a tempest of jealousy, only the more dangerous because she was forced to confine it in her own bosom.

Could it be the tempest which, as she passed the landing of the first floor, blew open the drawing-room door? No; it was stealthily opened by the hand of Briggs. Briggs had been on the watch. Briggs too well heard the creaking Firkin descend the stairs, and the clink of the spoon and gruel-basin the neglected female carried.

"Well, Firkin?" says she, as the other entered the apartment. "Well, Jane?"

"Wuss and wuss, Miss B.," Firkin said, wagging her head.

"Is she not better then?"

"She never spoke but once, and I asked her if she felt a little more easy, and she told me to hold my stupid tongue. Oh, Miss B., I never thought to have seen *this* day!" And the water-works again began to play.

"What sort of a person is this Miss Sharp, Firkin? I little thought, while enjoying my Christmas revels in the elegant home of my firm friends, the Reverend Lionel

Delamere and his amiable lady, to find a stranger had taken my place in the affections of my dearest, my still dearest Matilda!" Miss Briggs, it will be seen by her language, was of a literary and sentimental turn, and had once published a volume of poems—"Trills of the Nightingale"—by subscription.

"Miss B., they are all infatyated about that young woman," Firkin replied. "Sir Pitt wouldn't have let her go, but he daredn't refuse Miss Crawley anything. Mrs. Bute at the Rectory jist as bad—never happy out of her sight. The Capting quite wild about her. Mr. Crawley mortial jealous. Since Miss C. was took ill, she won't have nobody near her but Miss Sharp, I can't tell for where nor for why; and I think somethink has bewidged everybody."

Rebecca passed that night in constant watching upon Miss Crawley; the next night the old lady slept so comfortably, that Rebecca had time for several hours' comfortable repose herself on the sofa, at the foot of her patroness's bed; very soon, Miss Crawley was so well that she sat up and laughed heartily at a perfect imitation of Miss Briggs and her grief, which Rebecca described to her. Briggs' weeping snuffle, and her manner of using the handkerchief, were so completely rendered, that Miss Crawley became quite cheerful, to the admiration of the doctors when they visited her, who usually found this worthy woman of the world, when the least sickness attacked her, under the most abject depression and terror of death.

Captain Crawley came every day, and received bulletins from Miss Rebecca respecting his aunt's health. This improved so rapidly, that poor Briggs was allowed to see her patroness; and persons with tender hearts may imagine the smothered emotions of that sentimental female, and the affecting nature of the interview.

Miss Crawley liked to have Briggs in a good deal soon. Rebecca used to mimic her to her face with the most admirable gravity, thereby rendering the imitation doubly piquant to her worthy patroness.

The causes which had led to the deplorable illness of Miss Crawley, and her departure from her brother's house in the country, were of such an unromantic nature that they are hardly fit to be explained in this genteel and sentimental novel. For how is it possible to hint of a delicate female, living in good society, that she ate and drank too much, and that a hot supper of lobsters profusely enjoyed at the Rectory was the reason of an indisposition which Miss Crawley herself persisted was solely attributable to the dampness of the weather? The attack was so sharp that Matilda—as his Reverence expressed it—was very nearly "off the hooks;" all the family were in a fever of expectation regarding the will, and Rawdon Crawley was making sure of at least forty thousand pounds before the commencement of the London season. Mr. Crawley sent over a choice parcel of tracts, to prepare her for the change from Vanity Fair and Park Lane for another world; but a good doctor from Southampton being called in in time, vanquished the lobster which was no nearly fatal to her, and gave her sufficient strength to enable her to return to London. The Baronet did not disguise his exceeding mortification at the turn which affairs took.

While everybody was attending on Miss Crawley, and messengers every hour from the Rectory were carrying news of her health to the affectionate folks there, there was a lady in another part of the house, being exceedingly ill, of whom no one took any notice at all; and this was the lady of Crawley herself. The good doctor shook his head after seeing her; to which visit Sir Pitt consented, as it could be paid without a fee; and she was left fading away in her lonely chamber, with no more heed paid to her than to a weed in the park.

The young ladies, too, lost much of the inestimable benefit of their governess's instruction. So affectionate a nurse was Miss Sharp, that Miss Crawley would take her medicines from no other hand. Firkin had been deposed long before her mistress's departure from the country. That faithful attendant found a gloomy consolation on returning to London, in seeing Miss Briggs suffer the same pangs of jealousy and undergo the same faithless treatment to which she herself had been subject.

Captain Rawdon got an extension of leave on his aunt's illness, and remained dutifully at home. He was always in her antechamber. (She lay sick in the state bed-room, into which you entered by the little blue saloon.) His father was always meeting him there; or if he came down the corridor ever so quietly his father's door was sure to open, and the hyæna face of the old gentleman to glare out. What was it set one to watch the other so? A generous rivalry, no doubt, as to which should be most attentive to the dear sufferer in the state bed-room. Rebecca used to come out and comfort both of them; or one or the other of them rather. Both of these worthy gentlemen were most anxious to have news of the invalid from her little confidential messenger.

At dinner—to which meal she descended for half an hour —she kept the peace between them: after which she disappeared for the night; when Rawdon would ride over to the depôt of the 150th at Mudbury, leaving his Papa to the society of Mr. Horrocks and his rum and water. She passed as weary a fortnight as ever mortal spent in Miss Crawley's sick-room; but her little nerves seemed to be of iron, as she was quite unshaken by the duty and the tedium of the sick-chamber.

She never told until long afterwards how painful that duty was; how peevish a patient was the jovial old lady; how angry; how sleepless; in what horrors of death; during what long nights she lay moaning, and in almost delirious agonies respecting that future world which she quite ignored when she was in good health.—Picture to yourself, oh fair young reader, a worldly, selfish, graceless, thankless, religionless old woman, writhing in pain and fear, and without her wig. Picture her to yourself, and ere you be old, learn to love and pray!

Sharp watched this graceless bedside with indomitable patience. Nothing escaped her; and, like a prudent steward, she found a use for everything. She told many a good story about Miss Crawley's illness in after days,— stories which made the lady blush through her artificial carnations. During the illness she was never out of temper; always alert; she slept light, having a perfectly clear conscience; and could take that refreshment at almost any minute's warning. And so you saw very few traces of fatigue in her appearance. Her face might be a trifle paler, and the circles round her eyes a little blacker than usual; but whenever she came out from the sick-room she was always smiling, fresh, and neat, and looked as trim in her little dressing-gown and cap, as in her smartest evening suit.

The Captain thought so, and raved about her in uncouth convulsions. The barbed shaft of love had penetrated his dull hide. Six weeks—appropinquity—opportunity—had victimised him completely. He made a confidante of his aunt at the Rectory, of all persons in the world. She rallied him about it; she had preceived his folly; she warned him; she finished by owning that little Sharp was the most clever, droll, odd, good-natured, simple, kindly creature in England. Rawdon must not trifle with her affections, though—dear Miss Crawley would never pardon him for that; for she, too, was quite overcome by the little governess, and loved Sharp like a daughter. Rawdon must go away—go back to his regiment and naughty London and not play with a poor artless girl's feelings.

Many and many a time this good-natured lady, compassionating the forlorn life-guardsman's condition, gave him an opportunity of seeing Miss Sharp at the Rectory, and of walking home with her, as we have seen. When men of a certain sort, ladies, are in love, though they see the hook and the string, and the whole apparatus with which they are to be taken, they gorge the bait nevertheless—they must come to it—they must swallow it—and are presently struck and landed gasping. Rawdon saw there was a manifest intention on Mrs. Bute's part to captivate him with Rebecca. He was not very wise; but he was a man about town, and had seen several seasons. A light dawned upon his dusky soul, as he thought, through a speech of Mrs. Bute's.

"Mark my words, Rawdon," she said. "You will have Miss Sharp one day for your relation."

"What relation,—my cousin, hey, Mrs. Bute? James sweet on her, hey?" inquired the waggish officer.

"More than that," Mrs. Bute said, with a flash from her black eyes.

"Not Pitt?—He shan't have her. The sneak a'n't worthy of her. He's booked to Lady Jane Sheepshanks."

"You men perceive nothing. You silly, blind creature—if anything happens to Lady Crawley, Miss Sharp will be your mother-in-law; and *that's* what will happen."

Rawdon Crawley, Esquire, gave vent to a prodigious whistle, in token of astonishment at this announcement. He couldn't deny it. His father's evident liking for Miss Sharp had not escaped him. He knew the old gentleman's character well; and a more unscrupulous old—whyou—he did not conclude the sentence, but walked home, curling his mustachios, and convinced he had found a clue to Mrs. Bute's mystery.

"By Jove, it's too bad," thought Rawdon, "too bad, by Jove! I do believe the woman wants the poor girl to be ruined, in order that she shouldn't come into the family as Lady Crawley."

When he saw Rebecca alone, he rallied her about his father's attachment in his graceful way. She flung up her head scornfully, looked him full in the face, and said,—

"Well, suppose he *is* fond of me. I know he is, and others too. You don't think I'm afraid of him, Captain Crawley? You don't suppose I can't defend my own honour," said the little woman, looking as stately as a queen.

"O, ah, why—give you fair warning—look out, you know—that's all," said the mustachio-twiddler.

"You hint at something not honourable, then?" said she, flashing out.

"O—Gad—really—Miss Rebecca," the heavy dragoon interposed.

"Do you suppose I have no feeling of self-respect, because I am poor and friendless, and because rich people have none? Do you think, because I am a governess, I have not as much sense, and feeling, and good breeding as you gentlefolks in Hampshire? I'm a Montmorency. Do you suppose a Montmorency is not as good as a Crawley?"

When Miss Sharp was agitated, and alluded to her maternal relatives, she spoke with ever so slight a foreign accent, which gave a great charm to her clear ringing voice. "No," she continued, kindling as she spoke to the Captain;

"I can endure poverty, but not shame—neglect, but not insult; and insult from—from *you*."

Her feelings gave way, and she burst into tears.

"Hang it, Miss Sharp—Rebecca—by Jove—upon my soul, I wouldn't for a thousand pounds. Stop, Rebecca!"

She was gone. She drove out with Miss Crawley that day. It was before the latter's illness. At dinner she was unusually brilliant and lively; but she would take no notice of the hints, or the nods, or the clumsy expostulations of the humiliated, infatuated guardsman. Skirmishes of this sort passed perpetually during the little campaign—tedious to relate, and similar in result. The Crawley heavy cavalry was maddened by defeat, and routed every day.

If the Baronet of Queen's Crawley had not had the fear of losing his sister's legacy before his eyes, he never would have permitted his dear girls to lose the educational blessings which their invaluable governess was conferring upon them. The old house at home seemed a desert without her, so useful and pleasant had Rebecca made herself there. Sir Pitt's letters were not copied and corrected; his books not made up; his household business and manifold schemes neglected, now that his little secretary was away. And it was easy to see how necessary such an amanuensis was to him, by the tenor and spelling of the numerous letters which he sent to her, entreating her and commanding her to return. Almost every day brought a frank from the Baronet, enclosing the most urgent prayers to Becky for her return, or conveying pathetic statements to Miss Crawley, regarding the neglected state of his daughters' education; of which documents Miss Crawley took very little heed.

Miss Briggs was not formally dismissed, but her place as companion was a sinecure and a derision; and her company was the fat spaniel in the drawing-room, or occasionally the discontented Firkin in the housekeeper's closet. Nor though the old lady would by no means hear of Rebecca's departure, was the latter regularly installed in office in Park Lane. Like many wealthy people, it was Miss Crawley's habit to accept as much service as she could get from her inferiors; and good-naturedly to take leave of them when she no longer found them useful. Gratitude among certain rich folks is scarcely natural or to be thought of. They take needy people's services as their due. Nor have you, O poor parasite and humble hanger-on, much reason to complain! Your friendship for Dives is about as sincere as the return which it usually gets. It is money you love, and not the man; and were Crœsus and his footman to change places you know, you poor rogue, who would have the benefit of your allegiance.

And I am not sure, that, in spite of Rebecca's simplicity and activity, and gentleness and untiring good humour, the shrewd old London lady, upon whom these treasures of friendship were lavished, had not a lurking suspicion all the while of her affectionate nurse and friend. It must have often crossed Miss Crawley's mind that nobody does anything for nothing. If she measured her own feeling towards the world, she must have been pretty well able to gauge those of the world, towards herself; and perhaps she reflected, that it is the ordinary lot of people to have no friends if they themselves care for nobody.

Well, meanwhile Becky was the greatest comfort and convenience to her, and she gave her a couple of new gowns, and an old necklace and shawl, and showed her friendship by abusing all her intimate acquaintances to her new confidante (than which there can't be a more touching proof of regard), and meditated vaguely some great future benefit—to marry her perhaps to Clump, the apothecary, or to settle her in some advantageous way of life; or at any rate, to send her back to Queen's Crawley when she had done with her, and the full London season had begun.

When Miss Crawley was convalescent and descended to the drawing-room, Becky sang to her, and otherwise amused her; when she was well enough to drive out, Becky accompanied her. And amongst the drives which they took, whither, of all places in the world, did Miss Crawley's admirable good-nature and friendship actually induce her to penetrate, but to Russell Square, Bloomsbury, and the house of John Sedley, Esquire.

Ere that event, many notes had passed, as may be imagined, between the two dear friends. During the months of Rebecca's stay in Hampshire, the eternal friendship had (must it be owned?) suffered considerable diminution, and grown so decrepit and feeble with old age as to threaten demise altogether. The fact is, both girls had their own real affairs to think of: Rebecca her advance with her employers—Amelia her own absorbing topic. When the two girls met, and flew into each other's arms with that impetuosity which distinguishes the behaviour of young ladies towards each other, Rebecca performed her part of the embrace with the most perfect briskness and energy. Poor little Amelia blushed as she kissed her friend, and thought she had been guilty of something very like coldness towards her.

Their first interview was but a very short one. Amelia was just ready to go out for a walk. Miss Crawley was waiting in her carriage below, her people wondering at the locality in which they found themselves, and gazing upon honest Sambo, the black footman of Bloomsbury, as one of the queer natives of the place. But when Amelia came down with her kind smiling looks (Rebecca must introduce her to her friend, Miss Crawley was longing to see her, and was too ill to leave her carriage)—when, I say, Amelia came down, the Park Lane shoulder-knot aristocracy wondered more and more that such a thing could come out of Bloomsbury; and Miss Crawley was fairly captivated by the sweet blushing face of the young lady who came forward so timidly and so gracefully to pay her respects to the protector of her friend.

"What a complexion, my dear! What a sweet voice!" Miss Crawley said, as they drove away westward after the little interview. "My dear Sharp, your young friend is charming. Send for her to Park Lane, do you hear?" Miss Crawley had a good taste. She liked natural manners—a little timidity only set them off. She liked pretty faces near her; as she liked pretty pictures and nice china. She talked of Amelia with rapture half-a-dozen times that day. She mentioned her to Rawdon Crawley, who came dutifully to partake of his aunt's chicken.

Of course, on this Rebecca instantly stated, that Amelia was engaged to be married—to a Lieutenant Osborne—a very old flame.

"Is he a man in a line-regiment?" Captain Crawley asked, remembering after an effort, as became a guardsman, the number of the regiment, the —th.

Rebecca thought that was the regiment. "The Captain's name," she said, "was Captain Dobbin."

"A lanky gawky fellow," said Crawley, "tumbles over everybody. I know him; and Osborne's a goodish-looking fellow, with large black whiskers?"

"Enormous," Miss Rebecca Sharp said, "and enormously proud of them, I assure you."

Captain Rawdon Crawley burst into a horse-laugh by way of reply; and being pressed by the ladies to explain, did so when the explosion of hilarity was over. "He fancies he can play at billiards," said he. "I won two hundred of him at the Cocoa-Tree. *He* play, the young flat! He'd have played for anything that day, but his friend Captain Dobbin carried him off, hang him!"

"Rawdon, Rawdon, don't be so wicked," Miss Crawley remarked, highly pleased.

"Why, ma'am, of all the young fellows I've seen out of the line, I think this fellow's the greenest. Tarquin and Deuceace get what money they like out of him. He'd go to the deuce to be seen with a lord. He pays their dinners at Greenwich, and they invite the company."

"And very pretty company too, I dare say."

"Quite right, Miss Sharp. Right, as usual, Miss Sharp. Uncommon pretty company,—haw, haw!" and the Captain laughed more and more, thinking he had made a good joke.

"Rawdon, don't be naughty!" his aunt exclaimed.

"Well, his father's a City man—immensely rich, they say. Hang those City fellows, they must bleed; and I've not done with him yet, I can tell you. Haw, haw!"

"Fie, Captain Crawley; I shall warn Amelia. A gambling husband!"

"Horrid, ain't he, hey?" the Captain said with great solemnity; and then added, a sudden thought having struck him:— "Gad, I say, ma'am, we'll have him here."

"Is he a presentable sort of person?" the aunt inquired.

"Presentable?—oh, very well. You wouldn't see any difference," Captain Crawley answered. "Do let's have him,

when you begin to see a few people; and his whatdyecallem
—his inamorata—eh, Miss Sharp; that's what you call it—
comes. Gad, I'll write him a note, and have him; and I'll
try if he can play piquet as well as billiards. Where does
he live, Miss Sharp?"

Miss Sharp told Crawley the Lieutenant's town address;
and a few days after this conversation, Lieutenant Osborne
received a letter, in Captain Rawdon's school-boy hand,
and enclosing a note of invitation from Miss Crawley.

Rebecca despatched also an invitation to her darling
Amelia, who, you may be sure, was ready enough to accept
it when she heard that George was to be of the party. It
was arranged that Amelia was to spend the morning with
the ladies of Park Lane, where all were very kind to her.
Rebecca patronised her with calm superiority: she was so
much the cleverer of the two, and her friend so gentle and
unassuming, that she always yielded, when anybody chose
to command, and so took Rebecca's orders with perfect
meekness and good humour. Miss Crawley's graciousness
was also remarkable. She continued her raptures about
little Amelia, talked about her before her face as if she
were a doll, or a servant, or a picture, and admired her
with the most benevolent wonder possible. I admire that
admiration which the genteel world sometimes extends to
the commonalty. There is no more agreeable object in life
than to see May Fair folks condescending. Miss Crawley's
prodigious benevolence rather fatigued poor little Amelia.
and I am not sure that of the three ladies in Park Lane
she did not find honest Miss Briggs the most agreeable.
She sympathised with Briggs as with all neglected or gentle
people: she wasn't what you call a woman of spirit.

George came to dinner—a repast *en garçon* with Captain
Crawley.

The great family coach of the Osbornes transported him
to Park Lane from Russell Square; where the young ladies,
who were not themselves invited, and professed the greatest
indifference at that slight, nevertheless looked at Sir Pitt
Crawley's name in the baronetage; and learned everything
which that work had to teach about the Crawley family and
their pedigree, and the Binkies, their relatives, &c., &c.

Rawdon Crawley received George Osborne with great frankness and graciousness: praised his play at billiards: asked him when he would have his revenge: was interested about Osborne's regiment: and would have proposed piquet to him that very evening, but Miss Crawley absolutely forbade any gambling in her house; so that the young Lieutenant's purse was not lightened by his gallant patron, for that day at least. However, they made an engagement for the next, somewhere: to look at a horse that Crawley had to sell, and to try him in the Park; and to dine together, and to pass the evening with some jolly fellows. "That is, if you're not on duty to that pretty Miss Sedley," Crawley said, with a knowing wink. "Monstrous nice girl, 'pon my honour, though, Osborne," he was good enough to add, "Lots of tin, I suppose, eh?"

Osborne wasn't on duty; he would join Crawley with pleasure: and the latter, when they met the next day, praised his new friend's horsemanship—as he might with perfect honesty—and introduced him to three or four young men of the first fashion, whose acquaintance immensely elated the simple young officer.

"How's little Miss Sharp, by-the-bye?" Osborne inquired of his friend over their wine, with a dandified air. "Good-natured little girl that. Does she suit you well at Queen's Crawley? Miss Sedley liked her a good deal last year."

Captain Crawley looked savagely at the Lieutenant out of his little blue eyes, and watched him when he went up to resume his acquaintanceship with the fair governess. Her conduct must have relieved Crawley if there was any jealousy in the bosom of that life-guardsman.

When the young men went upstairs, and after Osborne's introduction to Miss Crawley, he walked up to Rebecca with a patronising, easy swagger. He was going to be kind to her and protect her. He would even shake hands with her, as a friend of Amelia's; and saying, "Ah, Miss Sharp! how-dy-doo?" held out his left hand towards her, expecting that she would be quite confounded at the honour.

Miss Sharp put out her right fore-finger, and gave him a little nod, so cool and killing, that Rawdon Crawley, watching the operations from the other room, could hardly restrain his laughter as he saw the Lieutenant's entire discomfiture; the start he gave, the pause, and the perfect clumsiness with which he at length condescended to take the finger which was offered for his embrace.

"She'd beat the devil, by Jove!" the Captain said, in a rapture; and the Lieutenant, by way of beginning the conversation, agreeably asked Rebecca how she liked her new place.

"My place?" said Miss Sharp, coolly, "how kind of you to remind me of it! It's a tolerably good place: the wages are pretty good—not so good as Miss Wirt's, I believe, with your sisters in Russell Square. How are those young ladies?—not that I ought to ask."

"Why not?" Mr. Osborne said, amazed.

"Why, they never condescended to speak to me, or to ask me into their house, whilst I was staying with Amelia; but we poor governesses, you know, are used to slights of this sort."

"My dear Miss Sharp!" Osborne ejaculated.

"At least in some families," Rebecca continued. "You can't think what a difference there is though, We are not so wealthy in Hampshire as you lucky folks of the City. But then I am in a gentleman's family—good old English stock. I suppose you know Sir Pitt's father refused a peerage. And you see how I am treated. I am pretty comfortable. Indeed it is rather a good place. But how *very* good of you to inquire!"

Osborne was quite savage The little governess patronised him and *persifléd* him until this young British Lion felt quite uneasy; nor could he muster sufficient presence of mind to find a pretext for backing out of this most delectable conversation.

"I thought you liked the City families pretty well," he said, haughtily.

"Last year you mean, when I was fresh from that horrid vulgar school? Of course I did. Doesn't every girl like to come home for the holidays? And how was I to know any better? But oh, Mr. Osborne, what a difference eighteen months' experience makes!—eighteen months spent, pardon me for saying so, with gentlemen. As for dear Amelia, she,

I grant you, is a pearl, and would be charming anywhere. There now, I see you are beginning to be in a good humour; but oh these queer odd City people! And Mr. Jos—how is that wonderful Mr. Joseph?"

"It seems to me you didn't dislike that wonderful Mr. Joseph last year," Osborne said kindly.

"How severe of you! Well, *entre nous,* I didn't break my heart about him; yet if he had asked me to do what you mean by your looks (and very expressive and kind they are, too), I wouldn't have said no."

Mr. Osborne gave a look as much as to say, "Indeed, how very obliging!"

"What an honour to have had you for a brother-in-law, you are thinking? To be sister-in-law to George Osborne, Esquire, son of John Osborne, Esquire, son of—what was your grandpapa, Mr. Osborne? Well, don't be angry. You can't help your pedigree, and I quite agree with you that I would have married Mr. Joe Sedley; for could a poor penniless girl do better? Now you know the whole secret. *I'm* frank and open; considering all things, it was very kind of you to allude to the circumstance—very kind and polite. Amelia, dear, Mr. Osborne and I were talking about your brother Joseph. How is he?"

Thus was George utterly routed. Not that Rebecca was in the right; but she had managed most successfully to put him in the wrong. And he now shamefully fled, feeling, if he stayed another minute, that he would have been made to look foolish in the presence of Amelia.

Though Rebecca had had the better of him, George was above the meanness of tale-bearing or revenge upon a lady, —only he could not help cleverly confiding to Captain Crawley, next day, some notions of his regarding Miss Rebecca—that she was a sharp one, a dangerous one, a desperate flirt, &c.; in all of which opinions Crawley agreed laughingly, and with every one of which Miss Rebecca was made acquainted before twenty-four hours were over. They added to her original regard for Mr. Osborne. Her woman's instinct had told her, that it was George who had interrupted the success of her first love-passage, and she esteemed him accordingly.

"I only just warn you," he said to Rawdon Crawley, with a knowing look—he had bought the horse, and lost some score of guineas after dinner, "I just warn you—I know women, and counsel you to be on the look-out."

"Thank you, my boy," said Crawley, with a look of peculiar gratitude. "You're wide awake, I see." And George went off, thinking Crawley was quite right.

He told Amelia of what he had done, and how he had counselled Rawdon Crawley—a devilish good, straight-forward fellow—to be on his guard against that little sly, scheming Rebecca.

"Against *whom?*" Amelia cried.

"Your friend the governess.—Don't look so astonished."

"O George, what *have* you done?" Amelia said. For her woman's eyes, which Love had made sharp-sighted, had in one instant discovered a secret which was invisible to Miss Crawley, to poor virgin Briggs, and above all, to the stupid peepers of that young whiskered prig, Lieutenant Osborne.

For as Rebecca was shawling her in an upper apartment, where these two friends had an opportunity for a little of that secret talking and conspiring which forms the delight of female life, Amelia, coming up to Rebecca, and taking her two little hands in hers, said, "Rebecca, I see it all."

Rebecca kissed her.

And regarding this delightful secret, not one syllable more was said by either of the young women. But it was destined to come out before long.

Some short period after the above events, and Miss Rebecca Sharp still remaining at her patroness's house in Park Lane, one more hatchment might have been seen in Great Gaunt Street, figuring amongst the many which usually ornament that dismal quarter. It was over Sir Pitt Crawley's house; but it did not indicate the worthy baronet's demise. It was a feminine hatchment, and indeed a few years back had served as a funeral compliment to Sir Pitt's old mother, the late dowager Lady Crawley. Its period of service over, the hatchment had come down from the front of the house, and lived in retirement somewhere in the back premises of Sir Pitt's mansion. It re-

appeared now for poor Rose Dawson.   Sir Pitt was a wid-
ower again.   The arms quartered on the shield along with
his own were not, to be sure, poor Rose's.   She had no
arms.   But the cherubs painted on the scutcheon answered
as well for her as for Sir Pitt's mother, and *Resurgam* was
written under the coat, flanked by the Crawley Dove and
Serpent.   Arms and Hatchments, Resurgam.—Here is an
opportunity for moralising!

Mr. Crawley had tended that otherwise friendless bed-
side.   She went out of the world strengthened by such
words and comfort as he could give her.   For many years his
was the only kindness she ever knew; the only friendship
that solaced in any way that feeble, lonely soul.   Her heart
was dead long before her body.   She had sold it to become
Sir Pitt Crawley's wife.   Mothers and daughters are making
the same bargain every day in Vanity Fair.

When the demise took place, her husband was in London
attending to some of his innumerable schemes, and busy
with his endless lawyers.   He had found time, nevertheless,
to call often in Park Lane, and to despatch many notes to
Rebecca, entreating her, enjoining her, commanding her to
return to her young pupils in the country, who were now
utterly without companionship during their mother's illness.
But Miss Crawley would not hear of her departure; for
though there was no lady of fashion in London who would
desert her friends more complacently as soon as she was
tired of their society, and though few tired of them sooner,
yet as long as her *engoûment* lasted her attachment was
prodigious, and she clung still with the greatest energy to
Rebecca.

The news of Lady Crawley's death provoked no more
grief or comment than might have been expected in Miss
Crawley's family circle.   "I suppose I must put off my party
for the 3rd," Miss Crawley said; and added, after a pause,
"I hope my brother will have the decency not to marry
again."   "What a confounded rage Pitt will be in if he does,"
Rawdon remarked, with his usual regard for his elder
brother.   Rebecca said nothing.   She seemed by far the
gravest and most impressed of the family.   She left the
room before Rawdon went away that day; but they met by

chance below, as he was going away after taking leave, **and** had a parley together.

On the morrow, as Rebecca was gazing from the window, she startled Miss Crawley, who was placidly occupied with a French novel, by crying out in an alarmed tone, "Here's Sir Pitt, Ma'am!" and the Baronet's knock followed this announcement.

"My dear, I can't see him. I won't see him. Tell Bowls not at home, or go downstairs and say I'm too ill to receive any one. My nerves really won't bear my brother at this moment;" cried out Miss Crawley, and resumed the novel.

"She's too ill to see you, sir," Rebecca said, tripping down to Sir Pitt, who was preparing to ascend.

"So much the better," Sir Pitt answered. "I want to see *you*, Miss Becky. Come along a me into the parlour," and they entered that apartment together.

"I wawnt you back at Queen's Crawley, Miss," the baronet said, fixing his eyes upon her, and taking off his black gloves and his hat with its great crape hat-band. His eyes had such a strange look, and fixed upon her so steadfastly, that Rebecca Sharp began almost to tremble.

"I hope to come soon," she said in a low voice, "as soon as Miss Crawley is better—and return to—to the dear children."

"You've said so these three months, Becky," replied Sir Pitt, "and still you go hanging on to my sister, who'll fling you off like an old shoe, when she's wore you out. I tell you I *want* you. I'm going back to the Vuneral. Will you come back? Yes or no?"

"I daren't—I don't think—it would be right—to be alone —with you, sir," Becky said, seemingly in great agitation.

"I say agin, I want you," Sir Pitt said, thumping the table. "I can't git on without you. I didn't see what it was till you went away. The house all goes wrong. It's not the same place. All my accounts has got muddled agin. You *must* come back. Do come back. Dear Becky, do come back."

"Come—as what, sir?" Rebecca gasped out.

"Come as Lady Crawley, if you like," the Baronet said, grasping his crape hat. "There! will that zatusfy you? Come back and be my wife. You're vit vor't. Birth be hanged. You're as good a lady as ever I see. You've got more brains in your little vinger than any baronet's wife in the county. Will you come? Yes or no?"

"Oh, Sir Pitt!" Rebecca said, very much moved.

"Say yes, Becky," Sir Pitt continued. "I'm an old man, but a good'n. I'm good for twenty years. I'll make you happy, zee if I don't. You shall do what you like; spend what you like; and 'av it all your own way. I'll make you a zettlement. I'll do everything reglar. Look year!" and the old man fell down on his knees and leered at her like a satyr.

Rebecca started back a picture of consternation. In the course of this history we have never seen her lose her presence of mind; but she did now, and wept some of the most genuine tears that ever fell from her eyes.

"Oh, Sir Pitt!" she said. "Oh, sir—I—I'm *married already*."

CHAPTER XV

EVERY reader of a sentimental turn (and we desire no other) must have been pleased with the *tableau* with which the last act of our little drama concluded; for what can be prettier than an image of Love on his knees before Beauty?

But when Love heard that awful confession from Beauty that she was married already, he bounced up from his attitude of humility on the carpet, uttering exclamations which caused poor little Beauty to be more frightened than she was when she made her avowal. "Married; you're joking" the Baronet cried, after the first explosion of rage and wonder. "You're making vun of me, Becky. Who'd ever go to marry you without a shilling to your vortune?"

"Married! married!" Rebecca said, in an agony of tears —her voice choking with emotion, her handkerchief up to her ready eyes, fainting against the mantel-piece—a figure of woe fit to melt the most obdurate heart. "O Sir Pitt, dear Sir Pitt, do not think me ungrateful for all your goodness to me. It is only your generosity that has extorted my secret."

"Generosity be hanged!" Sir Pitt roared out. "Who is it tu, then, you're married? Where was it?"

"Let me come back with you to the country, sir! Let me watch over you as faithfully as ever! Don't, don't separate me from dear Queen's Crawley!"

"The feller has left you, has he?" the Baronet said, beginning, as he fancied, to comprehend. "Well, Becky—come back if you like. You can't eat your cake and have it. Any ways I made you a vair offer. Coom back as governess—you shall have it all your own way." She held out one hand. She cried fit to break her heart; her ringlets fell over her face, and over the marble mantel-piece where she laid it.

"So the rascal ran off, eh?" Sir Pitt said, with a hideous attempt at consolation. "Never mind, Becky, *I'll* take care of 'ee."

"O sir! it would be the pride of my life to go back to Queen's Crawley and take care of the children, and of you as formerly, when you said you were pleased with the services of your little Rebecca. When I think of what you have just offered me, my heart fills with gratitude—indeed it does. I can't be your wife, sir; let me—let me be your daughter!"

Saying which, Rebecca went down on *her* knees in a most tragical way, and, taking Sir Pitt's horny black hand between her own two (which were very pretty and white, and as soft as satin), looked up in his face with an expression of exquisite pathos and confidence, when—when the door opened, and Miss Crawley sailed in.

Mrs. Firkin and Miss Briggs, who happened by chance to be at the parlour door soon after the Baronet and Rebecca entered the apartment, had also seen accidentally, through the key-hole, the old gentleman prostrate before the governess, and had heard the generous proposal which he made her. It was scarcely out of his mouth when Mrs. Firkin and Miss Briggs had streamed up the stairs, had rushed into the drawing-room where Miss Crawley was reading the French novel, and had given that old lady the astounding intelligence that Sir Pitt was on his knees, proposing to Miss Sharp. And if you calculate the time for the above dialogue to take place—the time for Briggs and Firkin to fly to the drawing-room—the time for Miss Crawley to be astonished, and to drop her volume of Pigault le Brun—and the time for her to come downstairs—you will see how exactly accurate this history is, and how Miss Crawley *must* have appeared at the very instant when Rebecca had assumed the attitude of humility.

"It is the lady on the ground, and not the gentleman," Miss Crawley said, with a look and voice of great scorn. "They told me that *you* were on your knees, Sir Pitt: do kneel once more, and let me see this pretty couple!"

"I have thanked Sir Pitt Crawley Ma'am," Rebecca said, rising, "and have told him that—that I never can become Lady Crawley."

"Refused him!" Miss Crawley said more bewildered than ever.

Briggs and Firkin at the door opened the eyes of astonishment and the lips of wonder.

"Yes—refused," Rebecca continued, with a sad, tearful voice.

"And am I to credit my ears that you absolutely proposed to her, Sir Pitt?" the old lady asked.

"Ees," said the Baronet, "I did."

"And she refused you as she says?"

"Ees," Sir Pitt said, his features on a broad grin.

"It does not seem to break your heart at any rate," Miss Crawley remarked.

"Nawt a bit," answered Sir Pitt, with a coolness and good-humour which set Miss Crawley almost mad with bewilderment. That an old gentleman of station should fall on his knees to a penniless governess, and burst out laughing because she refused to marry him,—that a penniless governess should refuse a Baronet with four thousand a year,—these were mysteries which Miss Crawley could never comprehend. It surpassed any complications of intrigue in her favourite Pigault le Brun.

"I'm glad you think it good sport, brother," she continued, groping wildly through this amazement.

"Vamous," said Sir Pitt. "Who'd ha' thought it! what a sly little devil! what a little fox it was!" he muttered to himself, chuckling with pleasure.

"Who'd have thought what?" cries Miss Crawley, stamping her foot. "Pray, Miss Sharp, are you waiting for the Prince Regent's divorce, that you don't think our family good enough for you?"

"My attitude," Rebecca said, "when you came in Ma'am, did not look as if I despised such an honour as this good —this noble man has deigned to offer me. Do you think I have no heart? Have you all loved me, and been so kind to the poor orphan—deserted—girl, and am *I* to feel nothing? O my friends! O my benefactors may not love, my life, my duty, try to repay the confidence you have shown me? Do you grudge me even gratitude, Miss Crawley? It is too much—my heart is too full;" and she sank

down in a chair so pathetically, that most of the audience
present were perfectly melted with her sadness.

"Whether you marry me or not, you're a good little
girl, Becky, and I'm your vriend, mind," said Sir Pitt, and
putting on his crape-bound hat, he walked away—greatly
to Rebecca's relief; for it was evident that her secret was
unrevealed to Miss Crawley, and she had the advantage of
a brief reprieve.

Putting her handkerchief to her eyes, and nodding away
honest Briggs, who would have followed her upstairs, she
went up to her apartment; while Briggs and Miss Crawley,
in a high state of excitement, remained to discuss the
strange event, and Firkin, no less moved, dived down into
the kitchen regions, and talked of it with all the male and
female company there.   And so impressed was Mrs. Firkin
with the news, that she thought proper to write off by that
very night's post, "with her humble duty to Mrs. Bute
Crawley and the family at the Rectory, and Sir Pitt has
been and proposed for to marry Miss Sharp, wherein she
has refused him, to the wonder of all."

The two ladies in the dining-room (where worthy Miss
Briggs was delighted to be admitted once more to a confidential conversation with her patroness) wondered to their
hearts' content at Sir Pitt's offer, and Rebecca's refusal;
Briggs very acutely suggesting that there must have been
some obstacle in the shape of a previous attachment, otherwise no young woman in her senses would ever have refused
so advantageous a proposal.

"You would have accepted it yourself, wouldn't you,
Briggs?" Miss Crawley said, kindly.

"Would it not be a privilege to be Miss Crawley's sister?" Briggs replied, with meek evasion.

"Well, Becky would have made a good Lady Crawley,
after all," Miss Crawley remarked (who was mollified by
the girl's refusal, and very liberal and generous now there
was no call for her sacrifices).   "She has brains in plenty
(much more wit in her little finger than you have, my poor
dear Briggs, in all your head).   Her manners are excellent,
now I have formed her.   She is a Montmorency, Briggs,
and blood *is* something, though I despise it for my part;

and she would have held her own amongst those pompous stupid Hampshire people much better than that unfortunate ironmonger's daughter."

Briggs coincided as usual, and the "previous attachment" was then discussed in conjectures. "You poor friendless creatures are always having some foolish *tendre*," Miss Crawley said. "You yourself, you know, were in love with a writing-master (don't cry, Briggs—you're always crying, and it won't bring him to life again), and I suppose this unfortunate Becky has been silly and sentimental too—some apothecary, or house-steward, or painter, or young curate, or something of that sort."

"Poor thing, poor thing!" says Briggs (who was thinking of twenty-four years back, and that hectic young writing-master whose lock of yellow hair, and whose letters, beautiful in their illegibility, she cherished in her old desk upstairs). "Poor thing, poor thing!" says Briggs. Once more she was a fresh-cheeked lass of eighteen; she was at evening church, and the hectic writing-master and she were quavering out of the same psalm-book.

"After such conduct on Rebecca's part," Miss Crawley said enthusiastically, "our family should do something. Find out who is the *objet*, Briggs. I'll set him up in a shop; or order my portrait of him, you know; or speak to my cousin, the Bishop—and I'll *doter* Becky, and we'll have a wedding, Briggs, and you shall make the breakfast, and be a bridesmaid."

Briggs declared that it would be delightful, and vowed that her dear Miss Crawley was always kind and generous, and went up to Rebecca's bed-room to console her and prattle about the offer, and the refusal, and the cause thereof; and to hint at the generous intentions of Miss Crawley, and to find out who was the gentleman that had the mastery of Miss Sharp's heart.

Rebecca was very kind, very affectionate and affected—responded to Brigg's offer of tenderness with grateful fervour—owned there was a secret attachment—a delicious mystery—what a pity Miss Briggs had not remained half a minute longer at the key-hole! Rebecca might, perhaps, have told more: but five minutes after Miss Briggs's arrival in Rebecca's apartment, Miss Crawley actually made her appearance there—an unheard-of honour;—her impatience had overcome her; she could not wait for the tardy operations of her ambassadress: so she came in person, and ordered Briggs out of the room. And expressing her approval of Rebecca's conduct, she asked particulars of the interview, and the previous transactions which had brought about the astonishing offer of Sir Pitt.

Rebecca said she had long had some notion of the partiality with which Sir Pitt honoured her, (for he was in the habit of making his feelings known in a very frank and unreserved manner,) but, not to mention private reasons with which she would not for the present trouble Miss Crawley, Sir Pitt's age, station, and habits were such as to render a marriage quite impossible; and could a woman with any feeling of self-respect and any decency listen to proposals at such a moment, when the funeral of the lover's deceased wife had not actually taken place?

"Nonsense, my dear, you would never have refused him had there not been some one else in the case," Miss Crawley said, coming to her point at once. "Tell me the private reasons; what are the private reasons? There *is* some one; who is it that has touched your heart?"

Rebecca cast down her eyes, and owned there was. "You have guessed right, dear lady," she said, with a sweet simple faltering voice. "You wonder at one so poor and friendless having an attachment, don't you? I have never heard that poverty was any safeguard against it. I wish it were."

"My poor dear child," cried Miss Crawley, who was always quite ready to be sentimental, "is our passion unrequited, then? Are we pining in secret? Tell me all, and let me console you."

"I wish you could, dear Madam," Rebecca said in the same tearful tone. "Indeed, indeed, I need it." And she laid her head upon Miss Crawley's shoulder and wept there so naturally that the old lady, surprised into sympathy, embraced her with an almost maternal kindness, uttered many soothing protests of regard and affection for her, vowed that she loved her as a daughter, and would do everything in her power to serve her. "And now, who is it, my dear? Is it that pretty Miss Sedley's brother? You said something about an affair with him. I'll ask him here, my dear. And you shall have him: indeed you shall."

"Don't ask me now," Rebecca said. "You shall know all soon. Indeed you shall. Dear kind Miss Crawley— Dear friend, may I say so?"

"That you may, my child," the old lady replied, kissing her.

"I can't tell you now," sobbed out Rebecca, "I am very miserable. But O! love me always—promise you will love me always." And in the midst of mutual tears—for the emotions of the younger woman had awakened the sympathies of the elder—this promise was solemnly given by Miss Crawley, who left her little *protégée*, blessing and admiring her as a dear, artless, tender-hearted, affectionate, incomprehensible creature.

And now she was left alone to think over the sudden and wonderful events of the day, and of what had been and what might have been. What think you were the private feelings of Miss, no (begging her pardon) of Mrs. Rebecca? If, a few pages back, the present writer claimed the privilege of peeping into Miss Amelia Sedley's bedroom, and understanding with the omniscience of the novelist all the gentle pains and passions which were tossing upon that innocent pillow, why should he not declare himself to be Rebecca's confidante too, master of her secrets, and seal-keeper of that young woman's conscience?

Well, then, in the first place, Rebecca gave way to some very sincere and touching regrets that a piece of marvellous good fortune should have been so near her, and she actually obliged to decline it. In this natural emotion every properly regulated mind will certainly share. What good mother is there that would not commiserate a penniless spinster, who might have been my lady, and have shared four thousand a year? What well-bred young person is there in all Vanity Fair, who will not feel for a hard working, ingenious, meritorious girl, who gets such an honourable, advantageous, provoking offer, just at the very moment when it is out of her power to accept it? I am sure our friend Becky's disappointment deserves and will command every sympathy.

I remember one night being in the Fair myself, at an evening party. I observed old Miss Toady there also present, single out for her special attentions and flattery little Mrs. Briefless, the barrister's wife, who is of a good family certainly, but, as we all know, is as poor as poor can be.

What, I asked in my own mind, can cause this obsequiousness on the part of Miss Toady; has Briefless got a county court, or his wife had a fortune left her? Miss Toady explained presently, with that simplicity which distinguishes all her conduct. "You know," she said, "Mrs. Briefless is granddaughter of Sir John Redhand, who is so ill at Cheltenham that he can't last six months. Mrs. Briefless's papa succeeds; so you see she *will* be a baronet's daughter." And Toady asked Briefless and his wife to dinner the very next week.

If the mere chance of becoming a baronet's daughter can procure a lady such homage in the world, surely, surely we may respect the agonies of a young woman who has lost the opportunity of becoming a baronet's wife. Who would have dreamed of Lady Crawley dying so soon? She was one of those sickly women that might have lasted these ten years—Rebecca thought to herself, in all the woes of repentance—and I might have been my lady! I might have led that old man whither I would. I might have thanked Mrs. Bute for her patronage, and Mr. Pitt for his insufferable condescension. I would have had the town-house newly furnished and decorated. I would have had the handsomest carriage in London, and a box at the opera; and I would have been presented next season. All this *might* have been; and now—now all was doubt and mystery.

But Rebecca was a young lady of too much resolution and energy of character to permit herself much useless and unseemly sorrow for the irrevocable past; so, having devoted only the proper portion of regret to it, she wisely turned her whole attention towards the future, which was now vastly more important to her. And she surveyed her position, and its hopes, doubts, and chances.

In the first place, she was *married;*—that was a great fact. Sir Pitt knew it. She was not so much surprised into the avowal, as induced to make it by a sudden calculation. It must have come some day: and why not now as at a later period? He who would have married her himself must at least be silent with regard to her marriage. How Miss Crawley would bear the news—was the great question. Misgivings Rebecca had; but she remembered all Miss Crawley had said; the old lady's avowed contempt for birth; her daring liberal opinions; her general romantic propensities; her almost doting attachment to her nephew, and her repeatedly-expressed fondness for Rebecca herself. She is so fond of him, Rebecca thought, that she will forgive him anything: she is so used to me that I don't think she could be comfortable without me: when the *éclaircissement* comes there will be a scene, and hysterics, and a great quarrel, and then a great reconciliation. At all events, what use was there in delaying? the die was thrown, and now or to-morrow the issue must be the same. And so, resolved that Miss Crawley should have the news, the young person debated in her mind as to the best means of conveying it to her; and whether she should face the storm that must come, or fly and avoid it until its first fury was blown over. In this state of meditation she wrote the following letter :—

Dearest Friend,—The great crisis which we have debated about so often is *come.* Half of my secret is known, and I have thought and thought, until I am quite sure that now is the time to reveal *the whole of the mystery.* Sir Pitt came to me this morning, and made —what do you think?—*a declaration in form.* Think of that! Poor little me. I might have been Lady Crawley. How pleased Mrs. Bute would have been and *ma tante* if I had taken precedence of her. I might have been somebody's mamma, instead of—O, I tremble, I tremble, when I think how soon we must tell all!—

Sir Pitt knows I am married, and not knowing to whom, is not very much displeased as yet. *Ma tante is actually angry* that I should have refused him. But she is all kindness and graciousness. She condescends to say I would have made him a good wife; and vows that she will be a mother to your little Rebecca. She will be shaken when she first hears the news. But need we fear anything beyond a momentary anger? I think not: *I am sure* not. She dotes upon you so (you naughty, good-for-nothing man), that she would pardon you *anything:* and, indeed, I believe, the next place in her heart is mine : and that she would be miserable without me.   Dearest ! something *tells me* we shall conquer.   You shall leave that odious regiment : quit gaming, racing, and *be a good boy;* and we shall all live in Park Lane, and *ma tante* shall leave us all her money.

I shall try and walk to-morrow at 3 in the usual place.   If Miss B. accompanies me, you must come to dinner, and bring an answer, and put it in the third volume of Porteus's Sermons.   But, at all events, come to your own

R.

To Miss Eliza Styles,
     At Mr. Barnet's, Saddler, Knightsbridge.

And I trust there is no reader of this little story who has not discernment enough to perceive that the Miss Eliza Styles (an old schoolfellow, Rebecca said, with whom she had resumed an active correspondence of late, and who used to fetch these letters from the saddler's), wore brass spurs, and large curling mustachios, and was indeed no other than Captain Rawdon Crawley.

CHAPTER XVI

The Letter on the Pincushion

HOW they were married is not of the slightest consequence to anybody. What is to hinder a Captain who is a major, and a young lady who is of age, from purchasing a license, and uniting themselves at any church in this town? Who needs to be told, that if a woman has a will, she will assuredly find a way?—My belief is, that one day, when Miss Sharp had gone to pass the forenoon with her dear friend Miss Amelia Sedley in Russell Square, a lady very like her might have been seen entering a church in the City, in company with a gentleman with dyed mustachios, who, after a quarter of an hour's interval, escorted her back to the hackney-coach in waiting, and that this was a quiet bridal party.

And who on earth, after the daily experience we have, can question the probability of a gentleman marrying anybody? How many of the wise and learned have married their cooks? Did not Lord Eldon himself, the most prudent of men, make a run-away match? Were not Achilles and Ajax both in love with their servant maids? And are we to expect a heavy dragoon with strong desires and small brains, who had never controlled a passion in his life, to become prudent all of a sudden, and to refuse to pay any price for an indulgence to which he had a mind? If people only made prudent marriages, what a stop to population there would be!

It seems to me, for my part, that Mr. Rawdon's marriage was one of the honestest actions which we shall have to record in any portion of that gentleman's biography which has to do with the present history. No one will say it is unmanly to be captivated by a woman, or, being captivated, to marry her; and the admiration, the delight, the passion, the wonder, the unbounded confidence, and frantic adoration with which, by degrees, this big warrior got to regard the little Rebecca, were feelings which the ladies at least will pronounce were not altogether discreditable to him. When she sang, every note thrilled in his dull soul, and tingled through his huge frame. When she spoke, he brought all the force of his brains to listen and wonder. If she was jocular, he used to revolve her jokes in his mind, and explode over them half an hour afterwards in the street, to the surprise of the groom in the tilbury by his side, or the comrade riding with him in Rotten Row. Her words were oracles to him, her smallest actions marked by an infallible grace and wisdom. "How she sings,—how she paints," thought he. "How she rode that kicking mare at Queen's Crawley!" And he would say to her in confidential moments, "By Jove, Beck, you're fit to be Commander-in-Chief, or Archbishop of Canterbury, by Jove." Is his case a rare one? and don't we see every day in the world many an honest Hercules at the apron-strings of Omphale and great whiskered Samsons prostrate in Delilah's lap?

When, then, Becky told him that the great crisis was near, and the time for action had arrived, Rawdon expressed himself as ready to act under her orders, as he would be to charge with his troop at the command of his colonel. There was no need for him to put his letter into the third volume of Porteus. Rebecca easily found a means to get rid of Briggs, her companion, and met her faithful friend in "the usual place" on the next day. She had thought over matters at night, and communicated to Rawdon the result of her determinations. He agreed, of course, to everything; was quite sure that it was all right; that what she proposed was best; that Miss Crawley would infallibly relent, or "come round," as he said, after a time. Had Rebecca's resolutions been entirely different, he would have followed them as implicitly. "You have head enough for both of us, Beck," said he. "You're sure to get us out of the scrape. I never saw your equal, and I've met with some clippers in my time too." And with this simple confession of faith, the love-stricken dragoon left her to execute his part of the project which she had formed for the pair.

It consisted simply in the hiring of quiet lodgings at Brompton, or in the neighbourhood of the barracks, for Captain and Mrs. Crawley. For Rebecca had determined, and very prudently, we think, to fly. Rawdon was only too happy at her resolve; he had been entreating her to take this measure any time for weeks past. He pranced off to engage the lodgings with all the impetuosity of love. He agreed to pay two guineas a week so readily, that the landlady regretted she had asked him so little. He ordered in a piano, and half a nursery-house full of flowers: and a heap of good things. As for shawls, kid gloves, silk stockings, gold French watches, bracelets and perfumery, he sent them in with the profusion of blind love and unbounded credit. And having relieved his mind by this outpouring of generosity, he went and dined nervously at the club, waiting until the great moment of his life should come.

The occurrences of the previous day; the admirable conduct of Rebecca in refusing an offer so advantageous to her, the secret unhappiness preying upon her, the sweetness and silence with which she bore her affliction, made Miss Crawley much more tender than usual. An event of this nature, a marriage, or a refusal, or a proposal, thrills through a whole household of women, and sets all their hysterical sympathies at work. As an observer of human nature, I regularly frequent St. George's, Hanover Square, during the genteel marriage season; and though I have never seen the bridegroom's male friends give way to tears, or the beadles and officiating clergy any way affected, yet it is not at all uncommon to see women who are not in the least concerned in the operations going on—old ladies who are long past marrying, stout middle-aged females with plenty of sons and daughters, let alone pretty young creatures in pink bonnets, who are on their promotion, and may naturally take an interest in the ceremony,—I say it is quite common to see the women present piping, sobbing, sniffling; hiding their little faces in their little useless pocket-handkerchiefs; and heaving, old and young, with emotion. When my friend, the fashionable John Pimlico, married the lovely Lady

Belgravia Green Parker, the excitement was so general, that even the little snuffy old pew-opener who let me into the seat was in tears. And wherefore? I inquired of my own soul: *she* was not going to be married.

Miss Crawley and Briggs in a word, after the affair of Sir Pitt, indulged in the utmost luxury of sentiment, and Rebecca became an object of the most tender interest to them. In her absence Miss Crawley solaced herself with the most sentimental of the novels in her library. Little Sharp, with her secret griefs, was the heroine of the day.

That night Rebecca sang more sweetly and talked more pleasantly than she had ever been heard to do in Park Lane. She twined herself round the heart of Miss Crawley. She spoke lightly and laughingly of Sir Pitt's proposal, ridiculed it as the foolish fancy of an old man; and her eyes filled with tears, and Briggs's heart with unutterable pangs of defeat, as she said she desired no other lot than to remain for ever with her dear benefactress. "My dear little creature," the old lady said, "I don't intend to let you stir for years, that you may depend upon it. As for going back to that odious brother of mine after what has passed, it is out of the question. Here you stay with me and Briggs. Briggs wants to go to see her relations very often. Briggs, you may go when you like. But as for you, my dear, you must stay and take care of the old woman."

If Rawdon Crawley had been then and there present, instead of being at the club nervously drinking claret, the pair might have gone down on their knees before the old spinster, avowed all, and been forgiven in a twinkling. But that good chance was denied to the young couple, doubtless in order that this story might be written, in which numbers of their wonderful adventures are narrated—adventures which could never have occurred to them if they had been housed and sheltered under the comfortable uninteresting forgiveness of Miss Crawley.

Under Mrs. Firkin's orders, in the Park Lane establishment, was a young woman from Hampshire, whose business it was, among other duties, to knock at Miss Sharp's door with that jug of hot water, which Firkin would rather have perished than have presented to the intruder. This girl, bred on the family estate, had a brother in Captain Crawley's troop, and if the truth were known, I dare say it would come out that she was aware of certain arrangements, which have a great deal to do with this history. At any rate she purchased a yellow shawl, a pair of green boots, and a light blue hat with a red feather with three guineas which Rebecca gave her, and as little Sharp was by no means too liberal with her money, no doubt it was for services rendered that Betty Martin was so bribed.

On the second day after Sir Pitt Crawley's offer to Miss Sharp, the sun rose as usual, and at the usual hour Betty Martin, the upstairs maid, knocked at the door of the governess's bed-chamber.

No answer was returned, and she knocked again. Silence was still uninterrupted; and Betty, with the hot water, opened the door and entered the chamber.

The little white dimity bed was as smooth and trim as on the day previous, when Betty's own hands had helped to make it. Two little trunks were corded in one end of the room; and on the table before the window—on the pincushion—the great fat pincushion lined with pink inside, and twilled like a lady's nightcap—lay a letter. It had been reposing there probably all night.

Betty advanced towards it on tiptoe, as if she were afraid to awake it—looked at it, and round the room, with an air of great wonder and satisfaction; took up the letter, and grinned intensely as she turned it round and over, and finally carried it into Miss Briggs's room below.

How could Betty tell that the letter was for Miss Briggs, I should like to know? All the schooling Betty had was at Mrs. Bute Crawley's Sunday School, and she could no more read writing than Hebrew.

"La, Miss Briggs," the girl exclaimed, "O, Miss, something must have happened—there's nobody in Miss Sharp's room; the bed ain't been slep in, and she've run away, and left this letter for you, Miss."

"*What!*" cries Briggs, dropping her comb, the thin wisp of faded hair falling over her shoulders; "an elopement! Miss Sharp a fugitive! What, what is this?" and she eagerly broke the neat seal, and, as they say, "devoured the contents" of the letter addressed to her.

"Dear Miss Briggs," the refugee wrote, "the kindest heart in the world, as yours is, will pity and sympathise with me and excuse me. With tears, and prayers, and blessings, I leave the home where the poor orphan has ever met with kindness and affection. Claims even superior to those of my benefactress call me hence. I go to my duty —to my *husband*. Yes, I am married. My husband *commands* me to seek the *humble home* which we call ours. Dearest Miss Briggs, break the news as your delicate sympathy will know how to do it —to my dear, my beloved friend and benefactress. Tell her, ere I went, I shed tears on her dear pillow—that pillow that I have so often soothed in sickness—that I long *again* to watch —Oh, with what joy shall I return to dear Park Lane! How I tremble for the answer which is to *seal my fate!* When Sir Pitt deigned to offer me his hand, an honour of which my beloved Miss Crawley said I was *deserving* (my blessings go with her for judging the poor orphan worthy to be *her sister!*) I told Sir Pitt that I was *already a wife*. Even he forgave me. But my courage failed me, when I should have told him all—that I could not be his wife, for I *was his daughter!* I am wedded to the best and most generous of men —Miss Crawley's Rawdon is *my* Rawdon. At his *command* I open my lips, and follow him to our humble home, as I would *through the world*. O, my excellent and kind friend, intercede with my Rawdon's beloved aunt for him and the poor girl to whom all *his noble race* have shown such *unparalleled affection*. Ask Miss Crawley to receive *her children*. I can say no more, but blessings, blessings on all in the dear house I leave, prays

"Your affectionate and *grateful*
"REBECCA CRAWLEY.

"Midnight."

Just as Briggs had finished reading this affecting and interesting document, which reinstated her in her position as first confidante of Miss Crawley, Mrs. Firkin entered the room. "Here's Mrs. Bute Crawley just arrived by the mail from Hampshire, and wants some tea; will you come down and make breakfast, Miss?"

And to the surprise of Firkin, clasping her dressing-gown around her, the wisp of hair floating dishevelled behind her, the little curl-papers still sticking in bunches round her forehead, Briggs sailed down to Mrs. Bute with the letter in her hand containing the wonderful news.

"Oh, Mrs. Firkin," gasped Betty, "sech a business. Miss Sharp have a gone and run away with the Capting, and they're off to Gretney Green!" We would devote a chapter to describe the emotions of Mrs. Firkin, did not the passions of her mistresses occupy our genteeler muse.

When Mrs. Bute Crawley, numbed with midnight travelling, and warming herself at the newly crackling parlour fire, heard from Miss Briggs the intelligence of the clandestine marriage, she declared it was quite providential that she should have arrived at such a time to assist poor dear Miss Crawley in supporting the shock—that Rebecca was an artful little hussy of whom she had always had her suspicions; and that as for Rawdon Crawley, she never could account for his aunt's infatuation regarding him, and had long considered him a profligate, lost, and abandoned being. And this awful conduct, Mrs. Bute said, will have at least *this* good effect, it will open poor dear Miss Crawley's eyes to the real character of this wicked man. Then Mrs. Bute had a comfortable hot toast and tea; and as there was a vacant room in the house now, there was no need for her to remain at the Gloster Coffee House where the Portsmouth mail had set her down, and whence she ordered Mr. Bowls's aide-de-camp the footman to bring away her trunks.

Miss Crawley, be it known, did not leave her room until near noon—taking chocolate in bed in the morning, while Becky Sharp read the *Morning Post* to her, or otherwise amusing herself or dawdling. The conspirators below agreed that they would spare the dear lady's feelings until she appeared in her drawing-room: meanwhile it was announced to her, that Mrs. Bute Crawley had come up from Hampshire by the mail, was staying at the Gloster, sent her love to Miss Crawley, and asked for breakfast with Miss Briggs. The arrival of Mrs. Bute, which would not have caused any extreme delight at another period, was hailed with pleasure now; Miss Crawley being pleased at the notion of a gossip with her sister-in-law regarding the late Lady Crawley, the funeral arrangements pending, and Sir Pitt's abrupt proposals to Rebecca.

It was not until the old lady was fairly ensconced in her usual arm-chair in the drawing-room, and the preliminary embraces and inquiries had taken place between the ladies, that the conspirators thought it advisable to submit her to the operation. Who has not admired the artifices and

delicate approaches with which women "prepare" their
friends for bad news? Miss Crawley's two friends made
such an apparatus of mystery before they broke the intelligence to her, that they worked her up to the necessary
degree of doubt and alarm.

"And she refused Sir Pitt, my dear, dear Miss Crawley,
prepare yourself for it," Mrs. Bute said, "because—because she couldn't help herself."

"Of course there was a reason," Miss Crawley answered.
"She liked somebody else. I told Briggs so yesterday."

"*Likes* somebody else!" Briggs gasped. "O my dear
friend, she is married already."

"Married already," Mrs. Bute chimed in; and both sate
with clasped hands looking from each other at their victim.

"Send her to me, the instant she comes in. The little
sly wretch: how dared she not tell me?" cried out Miss
Crawley.

"She won't come in soon. Prepare yourself, dear friend
—she's gone out for a long time—she's—she's gone altogether."

"Gracious goodness, and who's to make my chocolate?
Send for her and have her back; I desire that she come
back," the old lady said.

"She decamped last night, Ma'am," cried Mrs. Bute.

"She left a letter for me," Briggs exclaimed. "She's
married to—"

"Prepare her, for heaven's sake. Don't torture her, my
dear Miss Briggs."

"She's married to whom?" cries the spinster in a nervous
fury.

"To—to a relation of——"

"She refused Sir Pitt!" cried the victim. "Speak at
once. Don't drive me mad."

"O Ma'am—prepare her, Miss Briggs—she's married to
Rawdon Crawley."

"Rawdon married—Rebecca—governess—nobod—Get out
of my house, you fool, you idiot—you stupid old Briggs
—how dare you? You're in the plot—you made him marry,
thinking that I'd leave my money from him—you did,
Martha," the poor old lady screamed in hysteric sentences.

"I, Ma'am, ask a member of this family to marry a drawing-master's daughter?"

"Her mother was a Montmorency," cried out the old lady, pulling at the bell with all her might.

"Her mother was an opera girl, and she has been on the stage or worse herself," said Mrs. Bute.

Miss Crawley gave a final scream, and fell back in a faint. They were forced to take her back to the room which she had just quitted. One fit of hysterics succeeded another. The doctor was sent for—the apothecary arrived.

Mrs. Bute took up the post of nurse by her bedside. "Her relations ought to be round about her," that amiable woman said.

She had scarcely been carried up to her room, when a new person arrived to whom it was also necessary to break the news. This was Sir Pitt. "Where's Becky?" he said, coming in. "Where's her traps? She's coming with me to Queen's Crawley."

"Have you not heard the astonishing intelligence regarding her surreptitious union?" Briggs asked.

"What's that to me?" Sir Pitt asked. "I know she's married. That makes no odds. Tell her to come down at once, and not keep me."

"Are you not aware, sir," Miss Briggs asked, "that she has left our roof, to the dismay of Miss Crawley, who is nearly killed by the intelligence of Captain Rawdon's union with her?"

When Sir Pitt Crawley heard that Rebecca was married to his son, he broke out into a fury of language, which it would do no good to repeat in this place, as indeed it sent poor Briggs shuddering out of the room; and with her we will shut the door upon the figure of the frenzied old man, wild with hatred and insane with baffled desire.

One day after he went to Queen's Crawley, he burst like a madman into the room she had used when there—dashed open her boxes with his foot, and flung about her papers, clothes, and other relics. Miss Horrocks, the butler's daughter, took some of them. The children dressed themselves and acted plays in the others. It was but a few days after the poor mother had gone to her lonely burying-place; and was laid, unwept and disregarded, in a vault full of strangers.

"Suppose the old lady doesn't come to," Rawdon said to his little wife, as they sate together in the snug little Brompton lodgings. She had been trying the new piano all the morning. The new gloves fitted her to a nicety; the new shawls became her wonderfully; the new rings glittered on her little hands, and the new watch ticked at her waist; "suppose she don't come round, eh, Becky?"

"*I'll* make your fortune," she said; and Delilah patted Samson's cheek.

"You can do anything," he said, kissing the little hand. "By Jove, you can; and we'll drive down to the Star and Garter, and dine, by Jove."

CHAPTER XVII

How Captain Dobbin Bought a Piano

IF there is any exhibition in all Vanity Fair which Satire and Sentiment can visit arm in arm together; where you light on the strangest contrasts laughable and tearful: where you may be gentle and pathetic, or savage and cynical with perfect propriety: it is at one of those public assemblies, a crowd of which are advertised every day in the last page of the *Times* newspaper, and over which the late Mr. George Robins used to preside with so much dignity. There are very few London people, as I fancy, who have not attended at these meetings, and all with a taste for moralizing must have thought, with a sensation and interest not a little startling and queer, of the day when their turn shall come too, and Mr. Hammerdown will sell by the orders of Diogenes's assignees, or will be instructed by the executors, to offer to public competition, the library, furniture, plate, wardrobe, and choice cellar of wines of Epicurus deceased.

Even with the most selfish disposition, the Vanity-fairian, as he witnesses this sordid part of the obsequies of a departed friend, can't but feel some sympathies and regret. My Lord Dives's remains are in the family vault: the statuaries are cutting an inscription veraciously commemorating his virtues, and the sorrows of his heir, who is disposing of his goods. What guest at Dives's table can pass the familiar house without a sigh?—the familiar house of which the lights used to shine so cheerfully at seven o'clock, of which the hall-doors opened so readily, of which the obsequious servants, as you passed up the comfortable stair, sounded your name from landing to landing, until it reached the apartment where jolly old Dives welcomed his friends! What a number of them he had; and what a noble way of entertaining them. How witty people used to be here who were morose when they got out of the door;

and how courteous and friendly men who slandered and
hated each other everywhere else! He was pompous, but
with such a cook what would one not swallow? he was
rather dull, perhaps, but would not such wine make any
conversation pleasant? We must get some of his Burgundy
at any price, the mourners cry at his club. "I got this box
at old Dives's sale," Pincher says, handing it round, "one
of Louis XV.'s mistresses—pretty thing, is it not?—sweet
miniature," and they talk of the way in which young Dives
is dissipating his fortune.

How changed the house is, though! The front is patched
over with bills, setting forth the particulars of the furniture
in staring capitals. They have hung a shred of carpet out
of an upstairs window—a half dozen of porters are lounging
on the dirty steps—the hall swarms with dingy guests of
oriental countenance, who thrust printed cards into your
hand, and offer to bid. Old women and amateurs have invaded the upper apartments, pinching the bed-curtains,
poking into the feathers, shampooing the mattresses, and
clapping the wardrobe drawers to and fro. Enterprising
young housekeepers are measuring the looking-glasses and
hangings to see if they will suit the new *ménage*—(Snob
will brag for years that he has purchased this or that at
Dives's sale,) and Mr. Hammerdown is sitting on the great
mahogany dining-tables, in the dining-room below, waving
the ivory hammer, and employing all the artifices of eloquence, enthusiasm, entreaty, reason, despair; shouting to
his people; satirizing Mr. Davids for his sluggishness;
inspiriting Mr. Moss into action; imploring, commanding,
bellowing, until down comes the hammer like fate, and we
pass to the next lot. O Dives, who would ever have thought,
as we sat around the broad table sparkling with plate and
spotless linen, to have seen such a dish at the head of it
as that roaring auctioneer?

It was rather late in the sale. The excellent drawing-
room furniture by the best makers; the rare and famous
wines selected, regardless of cost, and with the well-known
taste of the purchaser; the rich and complete set of family
plate had been sold on the previous days. Certain of the
best wines (which all had a great character among amateurs

in the neighbourhood) had been purchased for his master, who knew them very well, by the butler of our friend John Osborne, Esquire, of Russell Square. A small portion of the most useful articles of the plate had been bought by some young stock-brokers from the City. And now the public being invited to the purchase of minor objects, it happened that the orator on the table was expatiating on the merits of a picture, which he sought to recommend to his audience: it was by no means so select or numerous a company as had attended the previous days of the auction.

"No. 369," roared Mr. Hammerdown. "Portrait of a gentleman on an elephant. Who'll bid for the gentleman on the elephant? Lift up the picture, Blowman, and let the company examine this lot." A long, pale, military-looking gentleman, seated demurely at the mahogany table, could not help grinning as this valuable lot was shown by Mr. Blowman. "Turn the elephant to the Captain, Blowman. What shall we say, sir, for the elephant?" but the Captain, blushing in a very hurried and discomfited manner, turned away his head.

"Shall we say twenty guineas for this work of art?—fifteen, five, name your own price. The gentleman without the elephant is worth five pound."

"I wonder it ain't come down with him," said a professional wag, "he's anyhow a precious big one;" at which (for the elephant-rider was represented as of a very stout figure) there was a general giggle in the room.

"Don't be trying to deprecate the value of the lot, Mr. Moss," Mr. Hammerdown said; "let the company examine it as a work of art—the attitude of the gallant animal quite according to natur'; the gentleman in a nankeen-jacket, his gun in his hand, is going to the chase; in the distance a banyhann-tree and a pagody, most likely resemblances of some interesting spot in our famous Eastern possessions. How much for this lot? Come, gentlemen, don't keep me here all day."

Some one bid five shillings, at which the military gentleman looked towards the quarter from which this splendid offer had come, and there saw another officer with a young lady on his arm, who both appeared to be highly amused with the scene, and to whom, finally, this lot was knocked down for half-a-guinea. He at the table looked more surprised and discomposed than ever when he spied this pair, and his head sank into his military collar, and he turned his back upon them, so as to avoid them altogether.

Of all the other articles which Mr. Hammerdown had the honour to offer for public competition that day it is not our purpose to make mention, save of one only, a little square piano, which came down from the upper regions of the house (the state grand piano having been disposed of previously); this the young lady tried with a rapid and skilful hand (making the officer blush and start again), and for it, when its turn came, her agent began to bid.

But there was an opposition here. The Hebrew aide-de-camp in the service of the officer at the table bid against the Hebrew gentleman employed by the elephant purchasers, and a brisk battle ensued over this little piano, the combatants being greatly encouraged by Mr. Hammerdown.

At last, when the competition had been prolonged for some time, the elephant captain and lady desisted from the race; and the hammer coming down, the auctioneer said:—"Mr. Lewis, twenty-five," and Mr. Lewis's chief thus became the proprietor of the little square piano. Having effected the purchase, he sate up as if he was greatly relieved, and the unsuccessful competitors catching a glimpse of him at this moment, the lady said to her friend,

"Why, Rawdon, it's Captain Dobbin."

I suppose Becky was discontented with the new piano her husband had hired for her, or perhaps the proprietors of that instrument had fetched it away, declining farther credit, or perhaps she had a particular attachment for the one which she had just tried to purchase, recollecting it in old days, when she used to play upon it, in the little sitting-room of our dear Amelia Sedley.

The sale was at the old house in Russell Square, where we passed some evenings together at the beginning of this story. Good old John Sedley was a ruined man. His name had been proclaimed as a defaulter on the Stock Exchange, and his bankruptcy and commercial extermination had followed. Mr. Osborne's butler came to buy some of the

famous port wine to transfer to the cellars over the way.
As for one dozen well-manufactured silver spoons and
forks at per oz., and one dozen dessert ditto ditto, there
were three young stockbrokers (Messrs. Dale, Spiggot, and
Dale, of Threadneedle-Street, indeed), who, having had
dealings with the old man, and kindnesses from him in days
when he was kind to everybody with whom he dealt, sent
this little spar out of the wreck with their love to good
Mrs. Sedley; and with respect to the piano, as it had been
Amelia's, and as she might miss it and want one now, and
as Captain William Dobbin could no more play upon it than
he could dance on the tight-rope, it is probable that he did
not purchase the instrument for his own use.

In a word, it arrived that evening at a wonderful small
cottage in a street leading from the Fulham Road—one of
those streets which have the finest romantic names—(this
was called St. Adelaide Villas, Anna-Maria Road, West),
where the houses look like baby-houses; where the people,
looking out of the first-floor windows, must infallibly, as
you think, sit with their feet in the parlours; where the
shrubs in the little gardens in front, bloom with a perennial
display of little children's pinafores, little red socks, caps,
&c. (polyandria polygynia); whence you hear the sound of
jingling spinets and women singing; where little porter
pots hang on the railings sunning themselves; whither of
evenings you see City clerks padding wearily: here it was
that Mr. Clapp, the clerk of Mr. Sedley, had his domicile,
and in this asylum the good old gentleman hid his head
with his wife and daughter when the crash came.

Jos Sedley had acted as a man of his disposition would,
when the announcement of the family misfortune reached
him. He did not come to London, but he wrote to his
mother to draw upon his agents for whatever money was
wanted, so that his kind broken-spirited old parents had no
present poverty to fear. This done, Jos went on at the
boarding-house at Cheltenham pretty much as before. He
drove his curricle; he drank his claret; he played his rubber; he told his Indian stories, and the Irish widow consoled and flattered him as usual. His present of money,
needful as it was, made little impression on his parents;

and I have heard Amelia say, that the first day on which she saw her father lift up his head after the failure, was on the receipt of the packet of forks and spoons with the young stockbrokers' love, over which he burst out crying like a child, being greatly more affected than even his wife, to whom the present was addressed. Edward Dale, the junior of the house, who purchased the spoons for the firm, was, in fact, very sweet upon Amelia, and offered for her in spite of all. He married Miss Louisa Cutts (daughter of Higham and Cutts, the eminent cornfactors) with a handsome fortune in 1820; and is now living in splendour, and with a numerous family, at his elegant villa, Muswell Hill. But we must not let the recollections of this good fellow cause us to diverge from the principal history.

I hope the reader has much too good an opinion of Captain and Mrs. Crawley to suppose that they ever would have dreamed of paying a visit to so remote a district as Bloomsbury, if they thought the family whom they proposed to honour with a visit were not merely out of fashion, but out of money, and could be serviceable to them in no possible manner. Rebecca was entirely surprised at the sight of the comfortable old house where she had met with no small kindness, ransacked by brokers and bargainers, and its quiet family treasures given up to public desecration and plunder. A month after her flight, she had bethought her of Amelia, and Rawdon, with a horse-laugh, had expressed a perfect willingness to see young George Osborne again. "He's a very agreeable acquaintance, Beck," the wag added. "I'd like to sell him another horse, Beck. I'd like to play a few more games at billiards with him. He'd be what I call *useful* just now, Mrs. C.—ha, ha!" by which sort of speech it is not to be supposed that Rawdon Crawley had a deliberate desire to cheat Mr. Osborne at play, but only wished to take that fair advantage of him which almost every sporting gentleman in Vanity Fair considers to be his due from his neighbour.

The old Aunt was long in "coming-to." A month had elapsed. Rawdon was denied the door by Mr. Bowls; his servants could not get a lodgment in the house at Park

Lane; his letters were sent back unopened. Miss Crawley never stirred out—she was unwell—and Mrs. Bute remained still and never left her. Crawley and his wife both of them augured evil from the continued presence of Mrs. Bute.

"Gad, I begin to perceive now why she was always bringing us together at Queen's Crawley," Rawdon said.

"What an artful little woman!" ejaculated Rebecca.

"Well, I don't regret it, if you don't," the Captain cried, still in an amorous rapture with his wife, who rewarded him with a kiss by way of reply, and was indeed not a little gratified by the generous confidence of her husband.

"If he had but a little more brains," she thought to herself, "I might make something of him;" but she never let him perceive the opinion she had of him; listened with indefatigable complacency to his stories of the stable and the mess; laughed at all his jokes; felt the greatest interest in Jack Spatterdash, whose cab-horse had come down, and Bob Martingale, who had been taken up in a gambling-house, and Tom Cinqbars, who was going to ride the steeple-chase. When he came home she was alert and happy: when he went out she pressed him to go: when he stayed at home, she played and sang for him, made him good drinks, superintended his dinner, warmed his slippers, and steeped his soul in comfort. The best of women (I have heard my grandmother say) are hypocrites. We don't know how much they hide from us: how watchful they are when they seem most artless and confidential: how often those frank smiles which they wear so easily, are traps to cajole or elude or disarm—I don't mean in your mere coquettes, but your domestic models, and paragons of female virtue. Who has not seen a woman hide the dulness of a stupid husband, or coax the fury of a savage one? We accept this amiable slavishness, and praise a woman for it: we call this pretty treachery truth. A good housewife is of necessity a humbug; and Cornelia's husband was hoodwinked, as Potiphar was—only in a different way.

By these attentions, that veteran rake, Rawdon Crawley, found himself converted into a very happy and submissive married man. His former haunts knew him not. They asked about him once or twice at his clubs, but did not miss

him much: in those booths of Vanity Fair people seldom
do miss each other. His secluded wife ever smiling and
cheerful, his little comfortable lodgings, snug meals, and
homely evenings, had all the charms of novelty and secrecy.
The marriage was not yet declared to the world, or published in the *Morning Post*. All his creditors would have
come rushing on him in a body, had they known that he
was united to a woman without fortune. "My relations
won't cry fie upon me," Becky said, with rather a bitter
laugh; and she was quite contented to wait until the old
aunt should be reconciled, before she claimed her place in
society. So she lived at Brompton, and meanwhile saw no
one, or only those few of her husband's male companions
who were admitted into her little dining-room. These were
all charmed with her. The little dinners, the laughing and
chatting, the music afterwards, delighted all who partici-
pated in these enjoyments. Major Martingale never thought
about asking to see the marriage licence. Captain Cinqbars
was perfectly enchanted with her skill in making punch.
And young Lieutenant Spatterdash (who was fond of piquet,
and whom Crawley would often invite) was evidently and
quickly smitten by Mrs. Crawley; but her own circumspection and modesty never forsook her for a moment, and
Crawley's reputation as a fire-eating and jealous warrior
was a further and complete defence to his little wife.

There are gentlemen of very good blood and fashion in
this city, who never have entered a lady's drawing-room;
so that though Rawdon Crawley's marriage might be talked
about in his county, where, of course, Mrs. Bute had spread
the news, in London it was doubted, or not heeded, or not
talked about at all. He lived comfortably on credit. He had
a large capital of debts, which laid out judiciously, will carry
a man along for many years, and on which certain men about
town contrive to live a hundred times better than even men
with ready money can do. Indeed who is there that walks
London streets, but can point out a half-dozen of men riding
by him splendidly, while he is on foot, courted by fashion,
bowed into their carriages by tradesmen, denying themselves
nothing, and living on who knows what? We see Jack
Thriftless prancing in the park, or darting in his brougham

down Pall Mall: we eat his dinners served on his miraculous plate. "How did this begin," we say, "or where will it end?" "My dear fellow," I heard Jack once say, "I owe money in every capital in Europe." The end must come some day, but in the meantime Jack thrives as much as ever; people are glad enough to shake him by the hand, ignore the little dark stories that are whispered every now and then against him, and pronounce him a good-natured, jovial, reckless fellow.

Truth obliges us to confess that Rebecca had married a gentleman of this order. Everything was plentiful in his house but ready money, of which their *ménage* pretty early felt the want; and reading the Gazette one day, and coming upon the announcement of "Lieutenant G. Osborne to be Captain by purchase, vice Smith, who exchanges," Rawdon uttered that sentiment regarding Amelia's lover, which ended in the visit to Russell Square.

When Rawdon and his wife wished to communicate with Captain Dobbin at the sale, and to know particulars of the catastrophe which had befallen Rebecca's old acquaintances, the Captain had vanished; and such information as they got was from a stray porter or broker at the auction.

"Look at them with their hooked beaks," Becky said, getting into the buggy, her picture under her arm, in great glee. "They're like vultures after a battle."

"Don't know. Never was in action, my dear. Ask Martingale; he was in Spain, aide-de-camp to General Blazes."

"He was a very kind old man, Mr. Sedley," Rebecca said; "I'm really sorry he's gone wrong."

"O stockbrokers—bankrupts—used to it, you know," Rawdon replied, cutting a fly off the horse's ear.

"I wish we could have afforded some of the plate, Rawdon," the wife continued sentimentally. "Five-and-twenty guineas was monstrously dear for that little piano. We chose it at Broadwood's for Amelia, when she came from school. It only cost five-and-thirty then."

"What d'ye-call 'em—'Osborne,' will cry off now, I suppose, since the family is smashed. How cut up your pretty little friend will be; hey, Becky?"

"I daresay she'll recover it;" Becky said with a smile—and they drove on and talked about something else.

CHAPTER XVIII

Who Played on the Piano Captain Dobbin Bought

OUR surprised story now finds itself for a moment among very famous events and personages, and hanging on to the skirts of history. When the eagles of Napoleon Bonaparte, the Corsican upstart, were flying from Provence, where they had perched after a brief sojourn in Elba, and from steeple to steeple until they reached the towers of Notre Dame, I wonder whether the Imperial birds had any eye for a little corner of the parish of Bloomsbury, London, which you might have thought so quiet, that even the whirring and flapping of those mighty wings would pass unobserved there?

"Napoleon has landed at Cannes." Such news might create a panic at Vienna, and cause Russia to drop his cards, and take Prussia into a corner, and Talleyrand and Metternich to wag their heads together, while Prince Hardenberg, and even the present Marquis of Londonderry, were puzzled; but how was this intelligence to affect a young lady in Russell Square, before whose door the watchman sang the hours when she was asleep: who, if she strolled in the square, was guarded there by the railings and the beadle: who, if she walked ever so short a distance to buy a ribbon in Southampton Row, was followed by Black Sambo with an enormous cane: who was always cared for, dressed, put to bed, and watched over by ever so many guardian angels, with and without wages? *Bon Dieu,* I say, is it not hard that the fateful rush of the great Imperial struggle can't take place without affecting a poor little harmless girl of eighteen, who is occupied in billing and cooing, or working muslin collars in Russell Square? You, too, kindly, homely flower!—is the great roaring war tempest coming to sweep you down, here, although cowering under the shelter of Holborn? Yes; Napoleon is flinging his last stake, and poor little Emmy Sedley's happiness forms, somehow, part of it.

190

In the first place, her father's fortune was swept down
with that fatal news. All his speculations had of late gone
wrong with the luckless old gentleman. Ventures had failed;
merchants had broken; funds had risen when he calculated
they would fall. What need to particularize? If success is
rare and slow, everybody knows how quick and easy ruin
is. Old Sedley had kept his own sad counsel. Everything
seemed to go on as usual in the quiet, opulent house; the
good-natured mistress pursuing, quite unsuspiciously, her
bustling idleness, and daily easy avocations; the daughter
absorbed still in one selfish, tender thought, and quite regardless of all the world besides, when that final crash came,
under which the worthy family fell.

One night Mrs. Sedley was writing cards for a party;
the Osbornes had given one, and she must not be behind-
hand; John Sedley, who had come home very late from
the City, sate silent at the chimney side, while his wife was
prattling to him; Emmy had gone up to her room ailing
and low-spirited. "She's not happy," the mother went on.
"George Osborne neglects her. I've no patience with the
airs of those people. The girls have not been in the house
these three weeks; and George has been twice in town without coming. Edward Dale saw him at the Opera. Edward
would marry her I'm sure: and there's Captain Dobbin who,
I think, would—only I hate all army men. Such a dandy
as George has become. With his military airs, indeed! We
must show some folks that we're as good as they. Only
give Edward Dale any encouragement, and you'll see. We
must have a party, Mr. S. Why don't you speak, John?
Shall I say Tuesday fortnight? Why don't you answer?
Good God, John, what has happened?"

John Sedley sprang up out of his chair to meet his wife,
who ran to him. He seized her in his arms, and said with
a hasty voice, "We're ruined, Mary. We've got the world
to begin over again, dear. It's best that you should know
all, and at once." As he spoke, he trembled in every limb,
and almost fell. He thought the news would have overpowered his wife—his wife, to whom he had never said a
hard word. But it was he that was the most moved, sudden as the shock was to her. When he sank back into his

seat, it was the wife that took the office of consoler. She took his trembling hand, and kissed it, and put it round her neck: she called him her John—her dear John—her old man—her kind old man; she poured out a hundred words of incoherent love and tenderness; her faithful voice and simple caresses wrought this sad heart up to an inexpressible delight and anguish, and cheered and solaced his over-burdened soul.

Only once in the course of the long night as they sate together, and poor Sedley opened his pent-up soul, and told the story of his losses and embarrassments—the treason of some of his oldest friends, the manly kindness of some, from whom he never could have expected it—in a general confession—only once did the faithful wife give way to emotion.

"My God, my God, it will break Emmy's heart," she said.

The father had forgotten the poor girl. She was lying, awake and unhappy, overhead. In the midst of friends, home, and kind parents, she was alone. To how many people can any one tell all? Who will be open where there is no sympathy, or has call to speak to those who never can understand? Our gentle Amelia was thus solitary. She had no confidante, so to speak, ever since she had anything to confide. She could not tell the old mother her doubts and cares; the would-be sisters seemed every day more strange to her. And she had misgivings and fears which she dared not acknowledge to herself, though she was always secretly brooding over them.

Her heart tried to persist in asserting that George Osborne was worthy and faithful to her, though she knew otherwise. How many a thing had she said, and got no echo from him. How many suspicions of selfishness and indifference had she to encounter and obstinately overcome. To whom could the poor litle martyr tell these daily struggles and tortures? Her hero himself only half understood her. She did not dare to own that the man she loved was her inferior; or to feel that she had given her heart away too soon. Given once, the pure bashful maiden was too modest, too tender, too trustful, too weak, too much woman to recall it. We are Turks with the affections of our women; and have made them subscribe to our doctrine too. We let their bodies go abroad liberally enough, with smiles and ringlets and pink bonnets to disguise them instead of veils and yakmaks. But their souls must be seen by only one man, and they obey not unwillingly, and consent to remain at home as our slaves— ministering to us and doing drudgery for us.

So imprisoned and tortured was this gentle little heart, when in the month of March, Anno Domini 1815, Napoleon landed at Cannes, and Louis XVIII. fled, and all Europe was in alarm, and the funds fell, and old John Sedley was ruined.

We are not going to follow the worthy old stockbroker through those last pangs and agonies of ruin through which he passed before his commercial demise befell. They declared him at the Stock Exchange; he was absent from his house of business: his bills were protested: his act of bankruptcy formal. The house and furniture of Russell Square were seized and sold up, and he and his family were thrust away, as we have seen, to hide their heads where they might.

John Sedley had not the heart to review the domestic establishment who have appeared now and anon in our pages, and of whom he was now forced by poverty to take leave.

The wages of those worthy people were discharged with that punctuality which men frequently show who only owe in great sums—they were sorry to leave good places— but they did not break their hearts at parting from their adored master and mistress. Amelia's maid was profuse in condolences, but went off quite resigned to better herself in a genteeler quarter of the town. Black Sambo, with the infatuation of his profession, determined on setting up a public-house. Honest old Mrs. Blenkinsop indeed, who had seen the birth of Jos and Amelia, and the wooing of John Sedley and his wife, was for staying by them without wages, having amassed a considerable sum in their service: and she accompanied the fallen people into their new and humble place of refuge, where she tended them and grumbled against them for a while.

Of all Sedley's opponents in his debates with his creditors which now ensued, and harassed the feelings of the humiliated old gentleman so severely, that in six weeks he oldened more than he had done for fifteen years before—the most determined and obstinate seemed to be John Osborne, his old friend and neighbour—John Osborne, whom he had set up in life—who was under a hundred obligations to him—and whose son was to marry Sedley's daughter. Any one of these circumstances would account for the bitterness of Osborne's opposition.

When one man has been under very remarkable obligations to another, with whom he subsequently quarrels, a common sense of decency, as it were, makes of the former a much severer enemy than a mere stranger would be. To account for your own hard-heartedness and ingratitude in such a case, you are bound to prove the other party's crime. It is not that you are selfish, brutal, and angry at the failure of a speculation—no, no—it is that your partner has led you into it by the basest treachery and with the most sinister motives.

From a mere sense of consistency, a persecutor is bound to show that the fallen man is a villain—otherwise he, the persecutor, is a wretch himself.

And as a general rule, which may make all creditors who are inclined to be severe pretty comfortable in their minds, no men embarrassed are altogether honest, very likely. They conceal something; they exaggerate chances of good luck; hide away the real state of affairs; say that things are flourishing when they are hopeless; keep a smiling face (a dreary smile it is) upon the verge of bankruptcy—are ready to lay hold of any pretext for delay or of any money, so as to stave off the inevitable ruin a few days longer. "Down with such dishonesty," says the creditor in triumph, and reviles his sinking enemy. "You fool, why do you catch at a straw?" calm good sense says to the man that is drowning. "You villain, why do you shrink from plunging into the irretrievable Gazette?" says prosperity to the poor devil battling in that black gulf. Who has not remarked the readiness with which the closest of friends and honestest of men suspect and accuse each other of cheating when they fall not on money matters? Everybody does it. Everybody is right, I suppose, and the world is a rogue.

Then Osborne had the intolerable sense of former benefits to goad and irritate him: these are always a cause of hostility aggravated. Finally, he had to break off the match between Sedley's daughter and his son; and as it had gone very far indeed, and as the poor girl's happiness and perhaps character were compromised, it was necessary to show the strongest reasons for the rupture, and for John Osborne to prove John Sedley to be a very bad character indeed.

At the meetings of creditors, then, he comported himself with a savageness and scorn towards Sedley, which almost succeeded in breaking the heart of that ruined bankrupt man. On George's intercourse with Amelia he put an instant veto—menacing the youth with maledictions if he broke his commands, and vilipending the poor innocent girl as the basest and most artful of vixens. One of the great conditions of anger and hatred is, that you must tell and believe lies against the hated object, in order, as we said, to be consistent.

When the great crash came—the announcement of ruin, and the departure from Russell Square, and the declaration that all was over between her and George—all over between her and love, her and happiness, her and faith in the world —a brutal letter from John Osborne told her in a few curt lines that her father's conduct had been of such a nature that all engagements between the families were at an end— when the final award came, it did not shock her so much as her parents, as her mother rather expected (for John Sedley himself was entirely prostrate in the ruins of his own affairs and shattered honour). Amelia took the news very palely and calmly. It was only the confirmation of the dark presages which had long gone before. It was the mere reading of the sentence—of the crime she had long ago been guilty—the crime of loving wrongly, too violently, against reason. She told no more of her thoughts now than she had before. She seemed scarcely more unhappy now when convinced all hope was over, than before when she felt but dared not confess that it was gone. So she changed from the large house to the small one without any mark or difference; remained in her little room for the most part; pined silently; and died away day by day. I do not mean to say that all females are so. My dear Miss Bullock, I do not think *your* heart would break in this way. You are a strong-minded young woman with proper principles. I do not venture to say that mine would; it has suffered, and, it must be confessed, survived. But there are some souls thus gently constituted, thus frail, and delicate, and tender.

Whenever old John Sedley thought of the affair between George and Amelia, or alluded to it, it was with bitterness almost as great as Mr. Osborne himself had shown. He cursed Osborne and his family as heartless, wicked, and ungrateful. No power on earth, he swore, would induce him to marry his daughter to the son of such a villain, and he ordered Emmy to banish George from her mind, and to return all the presents and letters which she had ever had from him.

She promised acquiescence, and tried to obey. She put up the two or three trinkets: and, as for the letters, she drew them out of the place where she kept them; and read them over—as if she did not know them by heart already; but she could not part with them. That effort was too much for her; she placed them back in her bosom again— as you have seen a woman nurse a child that is dead. Young Amelia felt that she would die or lose her senses outright, if torn away from this last consolation. How she used to blush and lighten up when those letters came! How she used to trip away with a beating heart, so that she might read unseen! If they were cold, yet how perversely this fond little soul interpreted them into warmth. If they were short or selfish, what excuses she found for the writer!

It was over these few worthless papers that she brooded and brooded. She lived in her past life—every letter seemed to recall some circumstance of it. How well she remembered them all! His looks and tones, his dress, what he said and how—these relics and remembrances of dead affection were all that were left her in the world. And the business of her life, was—to watch the corpse of Love.

To death she looked with inexpressible longing. Then, she thought, I shall always be able to follow him. I am not praising her conduct or setting her up as a model for Miss Bullock to imitate. Miss B. knows how to regulate her feelings better than this poor little creature. Miss B. would never have committed herself as that imprudent Amelia had done; pledged her love irretrievably; confessed her heart away, and got back nothing—only a brittle promise which was snapt and worthless in a moment. A long engagement is a partnership which one party is free to keep or to break, but which involves all the capital of the other.

Be cautious then, young ladies; be wary how you engage. Be shy of loving frankly; never tell all you feel, or (a better way still), feel very little. See the consequences of being prematurely honest and confiding, and mistrust yourselves and everybody. Get yourselves married as they do in France, where the lawyers are the bridesmaids and confidantes. At any rate, never have any feelings which may make you uncomfortable, or make any promises which you cannot at any required moment command and withdraw That is the way to get on, and be respected, and have a virtuous character in Vanity Fair.

If Amelia could have heard the comments regarding her which were made in the circle from which her father's ruin had just driven her, she would have seen what her own crimes were, and how entirely her character was jeopardised. Such criminal imprudence Mrs. Smith never knew of; such horrid familiarities Mrs. Brown had always condemned, and the end might be a warning to *her* daughters. "Captain Osborne, of course, could not marry a bankrupt's daughter," the Misses Dobbin said. "It was quite enough to have been swindled by the father. As for that little Amelia, her folly had really passed all—"

"All what?" Captain Dobbin roared out. "Haven't they been engaged ever since they were children? Wasn't it as good as a marriage? Dare any soul on earth breathe a word against the sweetest, the purest, the tenderest, the most angelical of young women?"

"La, William, don't be so highty tighty with *us*. We're not men. We can't fight you," Miss Jane said. "We've said nothing against Miss Sedley: but that her conduct throughout was *most imprudent,* not to call it by any worse name; and that her parents are people who certainly merit their misfortunes."

"Hadn't you better, now that Miss Sedley is free, propose for her yourself, William?" Miss Ann asked sarcastically. "It would be a most eligible family connection. He! he!"

"I marry her!" Dobbin said, blushing very much, and talking quick. "If you are so ready, young ladies, to chop and change, do you suppose that *she* is? Laugh and sneer at that angel. She can't hear it; and she's miserable and unfortunate, and deserves to be laughed at. Go on joking, Ann. You're the wit of the family, and the others like to hear it."

"I must tell you again we're not in a barrack, William," Miss Ann remarked.

"In a barrack, by Jove—I wish anybody in a barrack would say what you do," cried out this uproused British lion. "I should like to hear a man breathe a word against her, by Jupiter. But men don't talk in this way, Ann: it's only women, who get together and hiss, and shriek, and cackle. There, get away—don't begin to cry. I only said you were a couple of geese," Will Dobbin said, perceiving Miss Ann's pink eyes were beginning to moisten as usual. "Well, you're not geese, you're swans—anything you like, only do, do leave Miss Sedley alone."

Anything like William's infatuation about that silly little flirting, ogling thing was never known, the mamma and sisters agreed together in thinking: and they trembled lest, her engagement being off with Osborne, she should take up immediately her other admirer and Captain. In which forebodings these worthy young women no doubt judged according to the best of their experience; or rather (for as yet they had had no opportunities of marying or of jilting) according to their own notions of right and wrong.

"It is a mercy, Mamma, that the regiment is ordered abroad," the girls said. *"This* danger, at any rate, is spared our brother."

Such, indeed, was the fact; and so it is that the French Emperor comes in to perform a part in this domestic comedy of Vanity Fair which we are now playing, and which would never have been enacted without the intervention of this august mute personage. It was he that ruined the Bourbons and Mr. John Sedley. It was he whose arrival in his capital called up all France in arms to defend him there; and all Europe to oust him. While the French nation and army were swearing fidelity round the eagles in the Champ de Mars, four mighty European hosts were getting in motion for the great *chasse-à-l'aigle;* and one of these was a British army, of which two heroes of ours, Captain Dobbin and Captain Osborne, formed a portion.

The news of Napoleon's escape and landing was received by the gallant —th with a fiery delight and enthusiasm, which everybody can understand who knows that famous corps. From the colonel to the smallest drummer in the regiment, all were filled with hope and ambition and patriotic fury; and thanked the French Emperor as for a personal kindness in coming to disturb the peace of Europe. Now was the time the —th had so long panted for, to show their comrades in arms that they could fight as well as the Peninsular veterans, and that all the pluck and valour of the —th had not been killed by the West Indies and the yellow fever. Stubble and Spooney looked to get their companies without purchase. Before the end of the campaign (which she resolved to share), Mrs. Major O'Dowd hoped to write herself Mrs. Colonel O'Dowd, C.B. Our two friends (Dobbin and Osborne) were quite as much excited as the rest: and each in his way—Mr. Dobbin very quietly, Mr. Osborne very loudly and energetically—was bent upon doing his duty, and gaining his share of honour and distinction.

The agitation thrilling through the country and army in consequence of this news was so great, that private matters were little heeded: and hence probably George Osborne, just gazetted to his company, busy with preparations for the march, which must come inevitably, and panting for further promotion—was not so much affected by other incidents which would have interested him at a more quiet period. He was not, it must be confessed, very much cast down by good old Mr. Sedley's catastrophe. He tried his new uniform, which became him very handsomely, on the

day when the first meeting of the creditors of the unfortunate gentleman took place. His father told him of the
wicked, rascally, shameful conduct of the bankrupt, re-
minded him of what he had said about Amelia, and that
their connection was broken off for ever; and gave him that
evening a good sum of money to pay for the new clothes
and epaulets in which he looked so well. Money was always useful to this free-handed young fellow, and he took
it without many words. The bills were up in the Sedley
house, where he had passed so many, many happy hours.
He could see them as he walked from home that night (to
the Old Slaughters', where he put up when in town) shining white in the moon. That comfortable home was shut,
then, upon Amelia and her parents: where had they taken
refuge? The thought of their ruin affected him not a little.
He was very melancholy that night in the coffee-room at
the Slaughters'; and drank a good deal, as his comrades
remarked there.

Dobbin came in presently, cautioned him about the drink,
which he only took, he said, because he was deuced low;
but when his friend began to put to him clumsy inquiries,
and asked him for news in a significant manner, Osborne
declined entering into conversation with him; avowing,
however, that he was devilish disturbed and unhappy.

Three days afterwards, Dobbin found Osborne in his
room at the barracks:—his head on the table, a number of
papers about, the young Captain evidently in a state of
great despondency. "She—she's sent me back some things
I gave her—some damned trinkets. Look here!" There
was a little packet directed in the well-known hand to Captain George Osborne, and some things lying about—a ring,
a silver knife he had bought, as a boy, for her at a fair; a
gold chain, and a locket with hair in it. "It's all over,"
said he, with a groan of sickening remorse. "Look, Will,
you may read it if you like."

There was a little letter of a few lines, to which he pointed,
which said:—

"My papa has ordered me to return to you these presents, which
you made in happier days to me; and I am to write to you for the
last time. I think, I know you feel as much as I do the blow which

has come upon us. It is I that absolve you from an engagement
which is impossible in our present misery. I am sure you had no
share in it, or in the cruel suspicions of Mr. Osborne, which are the
hardest of all our griefs to bear. Farewell. Farewell. I pray God
to strengthen me to bear this and other calamities, and to bless
you always.
                                                            A.
"I shall often play upon the piano—your piano. It was like you
to send it."

Dobbin was very soft-hearted. The sight of women and
children in pain always used to melt him. The idea of
Amelia broken-hearted and lonely, tore that good-natured
soul with anguish. And he broke out into an emotion,
which anybody who likes may consider unmanly. He swore
that Amelia was an angel, to which Osborne said aye with
all his heart. He, too, had been reviewing the history of their
lives—and had seen her from her childhood to her present
age, so sweet, so innocent, so charmingly simple, and art-
lessly fond and tender.

What a pang it was to lose all that: to have had it and
not prized it! A thousand homely scenes and recollections
crowded on him—in which he always saw her good and
beautiful. And for himself, he blushed with remorse and
shame, as the remembrance of his own selfishness and indifference contrasted with that perfect purity. For a while,
glory, war, everything was forgotten, and the pair of friends
talked about her only.

"Where are they?" Osborne asked, after a long talk,
and a long pause,—and, in truth, with no little shame at
thinking that he had taken no steps to follow her. "Where
are they? There's no address to the note."

Dobbin knew. He had not merely sent the piano; but
had written a note to Mrs. Sedley, and asked permission to
come and see her,—and he had seen her, and Amelia too,
yesterday, before he came down to Chatham; and, what is
more, he had brought that farewell letter and packet which
had so moved them.

The good-natured fellow had found Mrs. Sedley only too
willing to receive him, and greatly agitated by the arrival
of the piano, which, as she conjectured, *must* have come
from George, and was a signal of amity on his part. Captain Dobbin did not correct this error of the worthy lady,

but listened to all her story of complaints and misfortunes with great sympathy—condoled with her losses and privations, and agreed in reprehending the cruel conduct of Mr. Osborne towards his first benefactor. When she had eased her overflowing bosom somewhat, and poured forth many of her sorrows, he had the courage to ask actually to see Amelia, who was above in her room as usual, and whom her mother led trembling downstairs.

Her appearance was so ghastly, and her look of despair so pathetic, that honest William Dobbin was frightened as he beheld it; and read the most fatal forebodings in that pale fixed face. After sitting in his company a minute or two, she put the packet into his hand, and said, "Take this to Captain Osborne, if you please, and—and I hope he's quite well—and it was very kind of you to come and see us —and we like our new house very much. And I—I think I'll go upstairs, Mamma, for I'm not very strong." And with this, and a curtsey and a smile, the poor child went her way. The mother, as she led her up, cast back looks of anguish towards Dobbin. The good fellow wanted no such appeal. He loved her himself too fondly for that. Inexpressible grief, and pity, and terror pursued him, and he came away as if he was a criminal after seeing her.

When Osborne heard that his friend had found her, he made hot and anxious inquiries regarding the poor child. How was she? How did she look? What did she say? His comrade took his hand, and looked him in the face.

"George, she's dying," William Dobbin said,—and could speak no more.

There was a buxom Irish servant-girl, who performed all the duties of the little house where the Sedley family had found refuge: and this girl had in vain, on many previous days, striven to give Amelia aid or consolation. Emmy was much too sad to answer, or even to be aware of the attempts the other was making in her favour.

Four hours after the talk between Dobbin and Osborne, this servant maid came into Amelia's room, where she sat as usual, brooding silently over her letters—her little treasures. The girl, smiling, and looking arch and happy, made many trials to attract poor Emmy's attention, who, however, took no heed of her.

"Miss Emmy," said the girl.

"I'm coming," Emmy said, not looking round.

"There's a message," the maid went on. "There's something—somebody—sure, here's a new letter for you—don't be reading them old ones any more." And she gave her a letter, which Emmy took, and read.

"I must see you," the letter said. "Dearest Emmy—dearest love—dearest wife, come to me."

George and her mother were outside, waiting until she had read the letter.

CHAPTER XIX

Miss Crawley at Nurse

WE have seen how Mrs. Firkin, the lady's maid, as soon as any event of importance to the Crawley family came to her knowledge, felt bound to communicate it to Mrs. Bute Crawley, at the Rectory; and have before mentioned how particularly kind and attentive that good-natured lady was to Miss Crawley's confidential servant. She had been a gracious friend to Miss Briggs, the companion, also; and had secured the latter's good-will by a number of those attentions and promises, which cost so little in the making, and are yet so valuable and agreeable to the recipient. Indeed every good economist and manager of a household must know how cheap and yet how amiable these professions are, and what a flavour they give to the most homely dish in life. Who was the blundering idiot who said that "fine words butter no parsnips"? Half the parsnips of society are served and rendered palatable with no other sauce. As the immortal Alexis Soyer can make more delicious soup for a halfpenny than an ignorant cook can concoct with pounds of vegetables and meat, so a skilful artist will make a few simple and pleasing phrases go farther than ever so much substantial benefit-stock in the hands of a mere bungler. Nay, we know that substantial benefits often sicken some stomachs; whereas, most will digest any amount of fine words, and be always eager for more of the same food. Mrs. Bute had told Briggs and Firkin so often of the depth of her affection for them; and what *she* would do, if she had Miss Crawley's fortune, for friends so excellent and attached, that the ladies in question had the deepest regard for her; and felt as much gratitude and confidence as if Mrs. Bute had loaded them with the most expensive favours.

Rawdon Crawley, on the other hand, like a selfish heavy dragoon as he was, never took the least trouble to conciliate

his aunt's aides-de-camp, showed his contempt for the pair
with entire frankness—made Firkin pull off his boots on one
occasion—sent her out in the rain on ignominious messages
—and if he gave her a guinea, flung it to her as if it were
a box on the ear. As his Aunt, too, made a butt of Briggs,
the Captain followed the example, and levelled his jokes at
her—jokes about as delicate as a kick from his charger.
Whereas, Mrs. Bute consulted her in matters of taste or
difficulty, admired her poetry, and by a thousand acts of
kindness and politeness, showed her appreciation of Briggs;
and if she made Firkin a twopenny-halfpenny present, accompanied it with so many compliments, that the twopence-
halfpenny was transmuted into gold in the heart of the
grateful waiting-maid, who, besides, was looking forwards
quite contentedly to some prodigious benefit which must
happen to her on the day when Mrs. Bute came into her
fortune.

The different conduct of these two people is pointed out
respectfully to the attention of persons commencing the
world. Praise everybody, I say to such: never be squeamish,
but speak out your compliment both point blank in a man's
face, and behind his back, when you know there is a reason-
able chance of his hearing it again. Never lose a chance of
saying a kind word. As Collingwood never saw a vacant
place in his estate but he took an acorn out of his pocket and
popped it in; so deal with your compliments through life.
An acorn costs nothing; but it may sprout into a prodigious
bit of timber.

In a word, during Rawdon Crawley's prosperity, he was
only obeyed with sulky acquiescence; when his disgrace
came, there was nobody to help or pity him. Whereas, when
Mrs. Bute took the command at Miss Crawley's house, the
garrison there were charmed to act under such a leader,
expecting all sorts of promotion from her promises, her
generosity, and her kind words.

That he would consider himself beaten, after one defeat,
and make no attempt to regain the position he had lost,
Mrs. Bute Crawley never allowed herself to suppose. She
knew Rebecca to be too clever and spirited, and desperate
a woman to submit without a struggle; and felt that she

must prepare for that combat, and be incessantly watchful against assault, or mine, or surprise.

In the first place, though she held the town, was she sure of the principal inhabitant? Would Miss Crawley herself hold out; and had she not a secret longing to welcome back the ousted adversary? The old lady liked Rawdon, and Rebecca, who amused her. Mrs. Bute could not disguise from herself the fact that none of her party could so contribute to the pleasures of the town-bred lady. "My girls' singing, after that little odious governess's, I know is unbearable," the candid Rector's wife owned to herself. "She always used to go to sleep when Martha and Louisa played their duets. Jim's stiff college manners and poor dear Bute's talk about his dogs and horses always annoyed her. If I took her to the Rectory, she would grow angry with us all, and fly, I know she would; and might fall into that horrid Rawdon's clutches again, and be the victim of that little viper of a Sharp. Meanwhile, it is clear to me that she is exceedingly unwell, and cannot move for some weeks, at any rate; during which we must think of some plan to protect her from the arts of those unprincipled people."

In the very best of moments, if anybody told Miss Crawley that she was, or looked ill, the trembling old lady sent off for her doctor; and I daresay she *was* very unwell after the sudden family event, which might serve to shake stronger nerves than hers. At least, Mrs. Bute thought it was her duty to inform the physician, and the apothecary, and the dame-de-compagnie, and the domestics, that Miss Crawley was in a most critical state, and that they were to act accordingly. She had the street laid knee-deep with straw; and the knocker put by with Mr. Bowls's plate. She insisted that the Doctor should call twice a day; and deluged her patient with draughts every two hours. When anybody entered the room, she uttered a *shshshsh* so sibilant and ominous, that it frightened the poor old lady in her bed, from which she could not look without seeing Mrs. Bute's beady eyes eagerly fixed on her, as the latter sate steadfast in the arm-chair by the bedside. They seemed to lighten in the dark (for she kept the curtains closed) as she moved

about the room on velvet paws like a cat. There Miss
Crawley lay for days—ever so many days—Mrs. Bute reading books of devotion to her: for nights, long nights, during
which she had to hear the watchman sing, the night-light
sputter; visited at midnight, the last thing, by the stealthy
apothecary; and then left to look at Mrs. Bute's twinkling
eyes, or the flicks of yellow that the rushlight threw on the
dreary darkened ceiling. Hygeia herself would have fallen
sick under such a regimen; and how much more this poor
old nervous victim? It has been said that when she was in
health and good spirits this venerable inhabitant of Vanity
Fair had as free notions about religion and morals as Monsieur de Voltaire himself could desire, but when illness over-
took her, it was aggravated by the most dreadful terrors of
death, and an utter cowardice took possession of the prostrate old sinner.

Sick-bed homilies and pious reflections are, to be sure,
out of place in mere story-books, and we are not going
(after the fashion of some novelists of the present day) to
cajole the public into a sermon, when it is only a comedy
that the reader pays his money to witness. But, without
preaching, the truth may surely be borne in mind, that the
bustle, and triumph, and laughter, and gaiety which Vanity-
Fair exhibits in public, do not always pursue the performer
into private life, and that the most dreary depression of
spirits and dismal repentances sometimes overcome him. Recollections of the best ordained banquets will scarcely cheer
sick epicures. Reminiscences of the most becoming dresses
and brilliant ball-triumphs will go very little way to console
faded beauties. Perhaps statesmen, at a particular period of
existence, are not much gratified at thinking over the most
triumphant divisions; and the success or the pleasure of
yesterday becomes of very small account when a certain
(albeit uncertain) morrow is in view, about which all of us
must some day or other be speculating. O brother wearers
of motley! Are there not moments when one grows sick of
grinning and tumbling, and the jingling of cap and bells?
This, dear friends and companions, is my amiable object—to
walk with you through the Fair, to examine the shops and the
shows there; and that we should all come home after the flare,

and the noise, and the gaiety, and be perfectly miserable in private.

"If that poor man of mine had a head on his shoulders," Mrs. Bute Crawley thought to herself, "how useful he might be, under present circumstances, to this unhappy old lady! He might make her repent of her shocking free-thinking ways; he might urge her to do her duty, and cast off that odious reprobate who has disgraced himself and his family; and he might induce her to do justice to my dear girls and the two boys, who require and deserve, I am sure, every assistance which their relatives can give them."

And, as the hatred of vice is always a progress towards virtue, Mrs. Bute Crawley endeavoured to instil into her sister-in-law a proper abhorrence for all Rawdon Crawley's manifold sins: of which his uncle's wife brought forward such a catalogue as indeed would have served to condemn a whole regiment of young officers. If a man has committed wrong in life, I don't know any moralist more anxious to point his errors out to the world than his own relations; so Mrs. Bute showed a perfect family interest and knowledge of Rawdon's history. She had all the particulars of that ugly quarrel with Captain Marker, in which Rawdon, wrong from the beginning, ended in shooting the Captain. She knew how the unhappy Lord Dovedale, whose mamma had taken a house at Oxford, so that he might be educated there, and who had never touched a card in his life till he came to London, was perverted by Rawdon at the Cocoa-Tree, made helplessly tipsy by this abominable seducer and perverter of youth, and fleeced of four thousand pounds. She described with the most vivid minuteness the agonies of the country families whom he had ruined—the sons whom he had plunged into dishonour and poverty—the daughters whom he had inveigled into perdition. She knew the poor tradesmen who were bankrupt by his extravagance —the mean shifts and rogueries with which he had ministered to it—the astounding falsehoods by which he had imposed upon the most generous of aunts, and the ingratitude by which he had repaid her sacrifices. She imparted these stories gradually to Miss Crawley; gave her the whole benefit

of them; felt it to be her bounden duty as a Christian woman
and mother of a family to do so; had not the smallest remorse or compunction for the victim whom her tongue was
immolating; nay, very likely thought her act was quite
meritorious, and plumed herself upon her resolute manner of
performing it. Yes, if a man's character is to be abused, say
what you will, there's nobody like a relation to do the business. And one is bound to own, regarding this unfortunate
wretch of a Rawdon Crawley, that the mere truth was
enough to condemn him, and that all inventions of scandal
were quite superfluous pains on his friends' parts.

Rebecca, too, being now a relative, came in for the fullest
share of Mrs. Bute's kind inquiries. This indefatigable
pursuer of truth (having given strict orders that the door
was to be denied to all emissaries or letters from Rawdon),
took Miss Crawley's carriage, and drove to her old friend
Miss Pinkerton, at Minerva House, Chiswick Mall, to whom
she announced the dreadful intelligence of Captain Rawdon's
seduction by Miss Sharp, and from whom she got sundry
strange particulars regarding the ex-governess's birth and
early history. The friend of the Lexicographer had plenty
of information to give. Miss Jemima was made to fetch the
drawing-master's receipts and letters. This one was from a
spunging-house: that entreated an advance: another was full
of gratitude for Rebecca's reception by the ladies of Chiswick: and the last document from the unlucky artist's pen
was that in which, from his dying bed, he recommended his
orphan child to Miss Pinkerton's protection. There were
juvenile letters and petitions from Rebecca, too, in the collection, imploring aid for her father or declaring her own
gratitude. Perhaps in Vanity Fair there are no better satires
than letters. Take a bundle of your dear friend's of ten
years back—your dear friend whom you hate now. Look at a
file of your sister's! how you clung to each other till you
quarrelled about the twenty-pound legacy! Get down the
round-hand scrawls of your son who has half broken your
heart with selfish undutifulness since; or a parcel of your
own, breathing endless ardour and love eternal, which were
sent back by your mistress when she married the Nabob—
your mistress for whom you now care no more than for

Queen Elizabeth. Vows, love, promises, confidences, gratitude; how queerly they read after a while! There ought to be a law in Vanity Fair ordering the destruction of every written document (except receipted tradesmen's bills) after a certain brief and proper interval. Those quacks and misanthropes who advertise indelible Japan ink should be made to perish along with their wicked discoveries. The best ink for Vanity Fair use would be one that faded utterly in a couple of days, and left the paper clean and blank, so that you might write on it to somebody else.

From Miss Pinkerton's the indefatigable Mrs. Bute followed the track of Sharp and his daughter back to the lodgings in Greek Street, which the defunct painter had occupied; and where portraits of the landlady in white satin, and of the husband in brass buttons, done by Sharp in lieu of a quarter's rent, still decorated the parlour walls. Mrs. Stokes was a communicative person, and quickly told all she knew about Mr. Sharp; how dissolute and poor he was; how good-natured and amusing: how he was always hunted by bailiffs and duns: how, to the landlady's horror, though she never could abide the woman, he did not marry his wife till a short time before her death: and what a queer little wild vixen his daughter was; how she kept them all laughing with her fun and mimicry; how she used to fetch the gin from the public-house, and was known in all the studios in the quarter—in brief, Mrs. Bute got such a full account of her new niece's parentage, education, and behaviour as would scarcely have pleased Rebecca, had the latter known that such inquiries were being made concerning her.

Of all these industrious researches Miss Crawley had the full benefit. Mrs. Rawdon Crawley was the daughter of an opera-girl. She had danced herself. She had been a model to the painters. She was brought up as became her mother's daughter. She drank gin with her father, &c., &c. It was a lost woman who was married to a lost man; and the moral to be inferred from Mrs. Bute's tale was, that the knavery of the pair was irremediable, and that no properly-conducted person should ever notice them again.

These were the materials which prudent Mrs. Bute gathered together in Park Lane, the provisions and ammunition as it

were with which she fortified the house against the siege
which she knew that Rawdon and his wife would lay to
Miss Crawley.

But if a fault may be found with her arrangements, it is
this, that she was too eager: she managed rather too well;
undoubtedly she made Miss Crawley more ill than was necessary; and though the old invalid succumbed to her authority,
it was so harassing and severe, that the victim would be
inclined to escape at the very first chance which fell in
her way. Managing women, the ornaments of their sex,—
women who order everything for everybody, and know so
much better than any person concerned what is good for their
neighbours, don't sometimes speculate upon the possibility
of a domestic revolt, or upon other extreme consequences
resulting from their overstrained authority.

Thus, for instance, Mrs. Bute, with the best intentions
no doubt in the world, and wearing herself to death as she
did by foregoing sleep, dinner, fresh air, for the sake of her
invalid sister-in-law, carried her conviction of the old lady's
illness so far that she almost managed her into her coffin.
She pointed out her sacrifices and their results one day to
the constant apothecary, Mr. Clump.

"I am sure, my dear Mr. Clump," she said, "no efforts of
mine have been wanting to restore our dear invalid, whom
the ingratitude of her nephew has laid on the bed of sickness.
I never shrink from personal discomfort; *I* never refuse to
sacrifice myself."

"Your devotion, it must be confessed, is admirable," Mr.
Clump says, with a low bow; "but—"

"I have scarcely closed my eyes since my arrival: I give
up sleep, health, every comfort, to my sense of duty. When
my poor James was in the small-pox, did I allow any hireling
to nurse him? No."

"You did what became on excellent mother, my dear
Madam—the best of mothers; but—"

"As the mother of a family and the wife of an English
clergyman, I humbly trust that my principles are good,"
Mrs. Bute said, with a happy solemnity of conviction; "and
as long as Nature supports me, never, never, Mr. Clump,

will I desert the post of duty. Others may bring that grey
head with sorrow to the bed of sickness (here Mrs. Bute,
waving her hand, pointed to one of old Miss Crawley's coffee-
coloured fronts, which was perched on a stand in the dressing-room), but *I* will never quit it. Ah, Mr. Clump! I fear,
I know, that that couch needs spiritual as well as medical
consolation."

"What I was going to observe, my dear Madam,"—here
the resolute Clump once more interposed with a bland air
—"what I was going to observe when you gave utterance
to sentiments which do you so much honour, was that I
think you alarm yourself needlessly about our kind friend,
and sacrifice your own health too prodigally in her favour."

"I would lay down my life for my duty, or for any member
of my husband's family," Mrs. Bute interposed.

"Yes, Madam, if need were; but we don't want Mrs.
Bute Crawley to be a martyr," Clump said gallantly. "Dr.
Squills and myself have both considered Miss Crawley's
case with every anxiety and care, as you may suppose.
We see her low-spirited and nervous; family events have
agitated her."

"Her nephew will come to perdition," Mrs. Crawley cried.

"Have agitated her: and you arrived like a guardian angel,
my dear Madam, a positive guardian angel, I assure you, to
soothe her under the pressure of calamity. But Dr. Squills
and I were thinking that our amiable friend is not in such a
state as renders confinement to her bed necessary. She is
depressed, but this confinement perhaps adds to her depression. She should have change, fresh air, gaiety; the most
delightful remedies in the pharmacopœia," Mr. Clump said,
grinning and showing his handsome teeth. "Persuade her
to rise, dear Madam; drag her from her couch and her low
spirits; insist upon her taking little drives. They will restore
the roses too to *your* cheeks, if I may so speak to Mrs. Bute
Crawley."

"The sight of her horrid nephew casually in the Park,
where I am told the wretch drives with the brazen partner
of his crimes," Mrs. Bute said (letting the cat of selfishness
out of the bag of secrecy), "would cause her such a shock,
that we should have to bring her back to bed again. She

must not go out, Mr. Clump. She shall not go out as long as I remain to watch over her. And as for *my* health, what matters it? I give it cheerfully, sir. I sacrifice it at the altar of my duty."

"Upon my word, Madam," Mr. Clump now said bluntly, "I won't answer for her life if she remains locked up in that dark room. She is so nervous that we may lose her any day; and if you wish Captain Crawley to be her heir, I warn you frankly, Madam, that you are doing your very best to serve him."

"Gracious mercy! is her life in danger?" Mrs. Bute cried. "Why, why, Mr. Clump, did you not inform me sooner?"

The night before, Mr. Clump and Dr. Squills had had a consultation (over a bottle of wine at the house of Sir Lapin Warren, whose lady was about to present him with a thirteenth blessing), regarding Miss Crawley and her case.

"What a little harpy that woman from Hampshire is, Clump," Squills remarked, "that has seized upon old Tilly Crawley. Devilish good Madeira."

"What a fool Rawdon Crawley has been," Clump replied, "to go and marry a governess! There was something about the girl, too."

"Green eyes, fair skin, pretty figure, famous frontal development," Squills remarked. "There is something about her; and Crawley *was* a fool, Squills."

"A d—— fool—always was," the apothecary replied.

"Of course the old girl will fling him over," said the physician, and after a pause added, "She'll cut up well, I suppose."

"Cut up," says Clump with a grin: "I wouldn't have her cut up for two hundred a year."

"That Hampshire woman will kill her in two months, Clump, my boy, if she stops about her," Dr. Squills said. "Old woman: full feeder; nervous subject; palpitation of the heart; pressure on the brain; apoplexy; off she goes. Get her up, Clump; get her out: or I wouldn't give many weeks' purchase for your two hundred a year." And it was acting upon this hint that the worthy apothecary spoke with so much candour to Mrs. Bute Crawley.

Having the old lady under her hand: in bed: with nobody near, Mrs. Bute had made more than one assault upon her, to induce her to alter her will. But Miss Crawley's usual terrors regarding death increased greatly when such dismal propositions were made to her, and Mrs. Bute saw that she must get her patient into cheerful spirits and health before she could hope to attain the pious object which she had in view. Whither to take her was the next puzzle. The only place where she is not likely to meet those odious Rawdons is at church, and that won't amuse her, Mrs. Bute justly felt. "We must go and visit our beautiful suburbs of London," she then thought. "I hear they are the most picturesque in the world;" and so she had a sudden interest for Hampstead, and Hornsey, and found that Dulwich had great charms for her, and getting her victim into her carriage, drove her to those rustic spots, beguiling the little journeys with conversations about Rawdon and his wife, and telling every story to the old lady which could add to her indignation against this pair of reprobates.

Perhaps Mrs. Bute pulled the string unnecessarily tight. For though she worked up Miss Crawley to a proper dislike of her disobedient nephew, the invalid had a great hatred and secret terror of her victimizer, and panted to escape from her. After a brief space, she rebelled against Highgate and Hornsey utterly. She would go into the Park. Mrs. Bute knew they would meet the abominable Rawdon there, and she was right. One day in the ring, Rawdon's stanhope came in sight; Rebecca was seated by him. In the enemy's equipage Miss Crawley occupied her usual place, with Mrs. Bute on her left, the poodle and Miss Briggs on the back seat. It was a nervous moment, and Rebecca's heart beat quick as she recognized the carriage, and as the two vehicles crossed each other in a line, she clasped her hands, and looked towards the spinster with a face of agonized attachment and devotion. Rawdon himself trembled, and his face grew purple behind his dyed mustachios. Only old Briggs was moved in the other carriage, and cast her great eyes nervously towards her old friends. Miss Crawley's bonnet was resolutely turned towards the Serpentine. Mrs. Bute happened to be in ecstasies with the poodle, and was calling him a little darling, and a sweet little zoggy, and a pretty pet. The carriages moved on, each in his line.

"Done, by Jove," Rawdon said to his wife.

"Try once more, Rawdon," Rebecca answered. "Could not you lock your wheels into theirs, dearest?"

Rawdon had not the heart for that manœuvre. When the carriages met again, he stood up in his stanhope; he raised his hand ready to doff his hat; he looked with all his eyes. But this time Crawley's face was not turned away; she and Mrs. Bute looked him full in the face, and cut their nephew pitilessly. He sank back in his seat with an oath, and striking out of the ring, dashed away desperately homewards.

It was a gallant and decided triumph for Mrs. Bute. But she felt the danger of many such meetings, as she saw the evident nervousness of Miss Crawley; and she determined that it was most necessary for her dear friend's health, that they should leave town for a while, and recommended Brighton very strongly.

CHAPTER XX

In Which Captain Dobbin Acts as the Messenger of Hymen

WITHOUT knowing how, Captain William Dobbin found himself the great promoter, arranger, and manager of the match between George Osborne and Amelia. But for him it never would have taken place: he could not but confess as much to himself, and smiled rather bitterly as he thought that he of all men in the world should be the person upon whom the care of this marriage had fallen. But though indeed the conducting of this negotiation was about as painful a task as could be set to him, yet when he had a duty to perform, Captain Dobbin was accustomed to go through it without many words or much hesitation: and, having made up his mind completely, that if Miss Sedley was balked of her husband she would die of the disappointment, he was determined to use all his best endeavours to keep her alive.

I forbear to enter into minute particulars of the interview between George and Amelia, when the former was brought back to the feet (or should we venture to say the arms?) of his young mistress by the intervention of his friend honest William. A much harder heart than George's would have melted at the sight of that sweet face so sadly ravaged by grief and despair, and at the simple tender accents in which she told her little broken-hearted story: but as she did not faint when her mother, trembling, brought Osborne to her; and as she only gave relief to her overcharged grief, by laying her head on her lover's shoulder and there weeping for a while the most tender, copious, and refreshing tears— old Mrs. Sedley, too greatly relieved, thought it was best to leave the young persons to themselves; and so quitted Emmy crying over George's hand, and kissing it humbly as if he were her supreme chief and master, and as if she were quite a guilty and unworthy person needing every favour and grace from him.

This prostration and sweet unrepining obedience exquisitely touched and flattered George Osborne. He saw a slave before him in that simple yielding faithful creature, and his soul within him thrilled secretly somehow at the knowledge of his power. He would be generous-minded, Sultan as he was, and raise up this kneeling Esther and make a queen of her: besides, her sadness and beauty touched him as much as her submission, and so he cheered her, and raised her up and forgave her, so to speak. All her hopes and feelings, which were dying and withering, this her sun having been removed from her, bloomed again and at once, its light being restored. You would scarcely have recognized the beaming little face upon Amelia's pillow that night as the one that was laid there the night before, so wan, so lifeless, so careless of all round about. The honest Irish maid-servant, delighted with the change, asked leave to kiss the face that had grown all of a sudden so rosy. Amelia put her arms round the girl's neck and kissed her with all her heart, like a child. She was little more. She had that night a sweet refreshing sleep, like one—and what a spring of inexpressible happiness as she woke in the morning sunshine!

"He will be here again to day," Amelia thought. "He is the greatest and best of men." And the fact is, that George thought he was one of the generousest creatures alive: and that he was making a tremendous sacrifice in marrying this young creature.

While she and Osborne were having their delightful tête-à-tête above stairs, old Mrs. Sedley and Captain Dobbin were conversing below upon the state of the affairs, and the chances and future arrangements of the young people. Mrs. Sedley having brought the two lovers together and left them embracing each other with all their might, like a true woman, was of opinion that no power on earth would induce Mr. Sedley to consent to the match between his daughter and the son of a man who had so shamefully, wickedly, and monstrously treated him. And she told a long story about happier days and their earlier splendours, when Osborne lived in a very humble way in the New Road, and his wife was *too glad* to receive some of Jos's little baby things, with which Mrs. Sedley accommodated her at the birth of one of Osborne's own children. The fiendish ingratitude of that man, she was sure, had broken Mr. S.'s heart: and as for a marriage, he would never, never, never, *never* consent.

"They must run away together, Ma'am," Dobbin said, laughing, "and follow the example of Captain Rawdon Crawley, and Miss Emmy's friend the little governess." Was it possible? Well she never! Mrs. Sedley was all excitement about this news. She wished that Blenkinsop were here to hear it: Blenkinsop always mistrusted that Miss Sharp.—What an escape Jos had had! and she described the already well-known love-passages between Rebecca and the Collector of Boggley Wollah.

It was not, however, Mr. Sedley's wrath which Dobbin feared, so much as that of the other parent concerned, and he owned that he had a very considerable doubt and anxiety respecting the behaviour of the black-browed old tyrant of a Russia merchant in Russell Square. He has forbidden the match peremptorily, Dobbin thought. He knew what a savage determined man Osborne was, and how he stuck by his word. "The only chance George has of reconcilement," argued his friend, "is by distinguishing himself in the coming campaign. If he dies they both go together. If he fails in distinction—what then? He has some money from his mother, I have heard—enough to purchase his majority—or he must sell out and go and dig in Canada, or rough it in a cottage in the country." With such a partner Dobbin thought he would not mind Siberia—and, strange to say, this absurd and utterly imprudent young fellow never for a moment considered that the want of means to keep a nice carriage and horses, and of an income which should enable its possessors to entertain their friends genteelly, ought to operate as bars to the union of George and Miss Sedley.

It was these weighty considerations which made him think too that the marriage should take place as quickly as possible. Was he anxious himself, I wonder, to have it over?—as people, when death has occurred, like to press forward the funeral, or when a parting is resolved upon, hasten it. It is certain that Mr. Dobbin, having taken the matter in hand, was most extraordinarily eager in the conduct of it. He urged on George the necessity of immediate action: he showed the chances of reconciliation with his father, which a favourable mention of his name in the *Gazette* must bring about. If need were he would go himself and brave both the fathers in the business. At all events, he besought George to go through with it before the orders came, which everybody expected, for the departure of the regiment from England on foreign service.

Bent upon these hymeneal projects, and with the applause and consent of Mrs. Sedley, who did not care to break the matter personally to her husband, Mr. Dobbin went to seek John Sedley at his house of call in the City, the Tapioca Coffee-house, where, since his own offices were shut up, and fate had overtaken him, the poor broken-down old gentleman used to betake himself daily, and write letters and receive them, and tie them up into mysterious bundles, several of which he carried in the flaps of his coat. I don't know anything more dismal than that business and bustle and mystery of a ruined man: those letters from the wealthy which he shows you: those worn greasy documents promising support and offering condolence which he places wistfully before you, and on which he builds his hopes of restoration and future fortune. My beloved reader has no doubt in the course of his experience been waylaid by many such a luckless companion. He takes you into the corner; he has his bundle of papers out of his gaping coat pocket; and the tape off, and the string in his mouth, and the favourite letters selected and laid before you; and who does not know the sad eager half-crazy look which he fixes on you with his hopeless eyes?

Changed into a man of this sort, Dobbin found the once florid, jovial, and prosperous John Sedley. His coat, that used to be so glossy and trim, was white at the seams, and the buttons showed the copper. His face had fallen in. and was unshorn; his frill and neck-cloth hung limp under his bagging waistcoat. When he used to treat the boys in old days at a coffee-house, he would shout and laugh louder than anybody there, and have all the waiters skipping round him; it was quite painful to see how humble and civil he was to John of the Tapioca, a blear-eyed old attendant in dingy stockings and cracked pumps, whose business it was to serve glasses of wafers, and bumpers of ink in pewter, and slices of paper to the frequenters of this dreary house of entertainment, where nothing else seemed to be consumed. As for William Dobbin, whom he had tipped repeatedly in his youth, and who had been the old gentleman's butt on a thousand occasions, old Sedley gave his hand to him in a very hesitating humble manner now, and called him "Sir." A feeling of shame and remorse took possession of William Dobbin as the broken old man so received and addressed him, as if he himself had been somehow guilty of the misfortunes which had brought Sedley so low.

"I am very glad to see you, Captain Dobbin, sir," says he, after a skulking look or two at his visitor (whose lanky figure and military appearance caused some excitement likewise to twinkle in the blear eyes of the waiter in the cracked dancing pumps, and awakened the old lady in black, who dozed among the mouldy old coffee-cups in the bar). "How is the worthy alderman, and my lady, your excellent mother, sir?" He looked round at the waiter as he said, "My lady," as much as to say, "Hark ye, John, I have friends still, and persons of rank and reputation, too." "Are you come to do anything in my way, sir? My young friends Dale and Spiggot do all my business for me now, until my new offices are ready; for I'm only here temporarily, you know, Captain. What can we do for you, sir? Will you like to take anything?"

Dobbin, with a great deal of hesitation and stuttering, protested that he was not in the least hungry or thirsty; that he had no business to transact; that he only came to ask if Mr. Sedley was well, and to shake hands with an old friend; and, he added, with a desperate perversion of truth, "My mother is very well—that is, she's been very unwell, and is only waiting for the first fine day to go out and call upon Mrs. Sedley. How is Mrs. Sedley, sir? I hope she's quite well." And here he paused, reflecting on his own consummate hypocrisy; for the day was as fine, and the sunshine as bright as it ever is in Coffin Court, where the Tapioca Coffee-house is situated: and Mr. Dobbin remembered that he had seen Mrs. Sedley himself only an hour before, having driven Osborne down to Fulham in his gig, and left him there *tête-à-tête* with Miss Amelia.

"My wife will be very happy to see her ladyship," Sedley replied, pulling out his papers. "I've a very kind letter here from your father, sir, and beg my respectful compliments to him. Lady D. will find us in rather a smaller house than we were accustomed to receive our friends in; but it's snug, and the change of air does good to my daughter, who was suffering in town rather—you remember little Emmy, sir?—yes, suffering a good deal." The old gentleman's eyes were wandering as he spoke, and he was thinking of something else, as he sate thrumming on his papers and fumbling at the worn red tape.

"You're a military man," he went on; "I ask you, Bill Dobbin, could any man ever have speculated upon the return of that Corsican scoundrel from Elba? When the allied sovereigns were here last year, and we gave 'em that dinner in the City, sir, and we saw the Temple of Concord, and the fireworks, and the Chinese bridge in St. James's Park, could any sensible man suppose that peace wasn't really concluded, after we'd actually sung *Te Deum* for it, sir? I ask you, William, could I suppose that the Emperor of Austria was a damned traitor—a traitor, and nothing more? I don't mince words—a double-faced infernal traitor and schemer, who meant to have his son-in-law back all along. And I say that the escape of Boney from Elba was a damned imposition and plot, sir, in which half the powers of Europe were concerned, to bring the funds down, and to ruin this country. That's why I'm here, William. That's why my name's in the *Gazette*. Why, sir?—because I trusted the Emperor of Russia and the Prince Regent. Look here. Look at my papers. Look what the funds were on the 1st of March—what the French fives were when I bought for the account. And what they're at now. There was collusion, sir, or that villain never would have escaped. Where was the English Commissioner who allowed him to get away? He ought to be shot, sir—brought to a court-martial, and shot, by Jove."

"We're going to hunt Boney out, sir," Dobbin said, rather alarmed at the fury of the old man, the veins of whose forehead began to swell, and who sate drumming his papers with his clenched fist. "We are going to hunt him out, sir—the Duke's in Belgium already, and we expect marching orders every day."

"Give him no quarter. Bring back the villain's head, sir. Shoot the coward down, sir," Sedley roared. "I'd enlist myself, by ——; but I'm a broken old man—ruined by that damned scoundrel—and by a parcel of swindling thieves in this country whom I made, sir, and who are rolling in their carriages now," he added, with a break in his voice.

Dobbin was not a little affected by the sight of this once kind old friend, crazed almost with misfortune and raving with senile anger. Pity the fallen gentleman: you to whom money and fair repute are the chiefest good; and so, surely, are they in Vanity Fair.

"Yes," he continued, "there are some vipers that you warm, and they sting you afterwards. There are some beggars that you put on horseback, and they're the first to ride you down. You know whom I mean, William Dobbin, my boy. I mean a purse-proud villain in Russell Square, whom I knew without a shilling, and whom I pray and hope to see a beggar as he was when I befriended him."

"I have heard something of this, sir, from my friend George," Dobbin said, anxious to come to his point. "The quarrel between you and his father has cut him up a great deal, sir. Indeed, I'm the bearer of a message from him."

"O, *that's* your errand, is it?" cried the old man, jumping up. "What! perhaps he condoles with me, does he? Very kind of him, the stiff-backed prig, with his dandified airs and West-end swagger. He's hankering about my house, is he still? If my son had the courage of a man, he'd shoot him. He's as big a villain as his father. I won't have his name mentioned in my house. I curse the day that ever I let him into it; and I'd rather see my daughter dead at my feet than married to him."

"His father's harshness is not George's fault, sir. Your daughter's love for him is as much your doing as his. Who are you, that you are to play with two young people's affections and break their hearts at your will?"

"Recollect it's not his father that breaks the match off," old Sedley cried out. "It's I that forbid it. That family and mine are separated for ever. I'm fallen low, but not so low as that: no, no. And so you may tell the whole race—son, and father, and sisters, and all."

"It's my belief, sir, that you have not the power or the right to separate those two," Dobbin answered in a low voice; "and that if you don't give your daughter your consent it will be her duty to marry without it. There's no reason she should die or live miserably because you are wrong-headed. To my thinking, she's just as much married as if the banns had been read in all the churches in London. And what better answer can there be to Osborne's charges against you, as charges there are, than that his son claims to enter your family and marry your daughter?"

A light of something like satisfaction seemed to break over old Sedley as this point was put to him: but he still persisted that with his consent the marriage between Amelia and George should never take place.

"We must do it without," Dobbin said, smiling, and told Mr. Sedley, as he had told Mrs. Sedley in the day, before, the story of Rebecca's elopement with Captain Crawley. It evidently amused the old gentleman. "You're terrible fellows, you Captains," said he, tying up his papers; and his face wore something like a smile upon it, to the astonishment of the blear-eyed waiter who now entered, and had never seen such an expression upon Sedley's countenance since he had used the dismal coffee-house.

The idea of hitting his enemy Osborne such a blow soothed, perhaps, the old gentleman: and, their colloquy presently ending, he and Dobbin parted pretty good friends.

"My sisters say she has diamonds as big as pigeons' eggs," George said laughing. "How they must set off her complexion! A perfect illumination it must be when her jewels are on her neck. Her jet-black hair is as curly as Sambo's. I dare say she wore a nose ring when she went to court; and with a plume of feathers in her top-knot she would look a perfect Belle Sauvage."

George, in conversation with Amelia, was rallying the appearance of a young lady of whom his father and sisters had lately made the acquaintance, and who was an object of vast respect to the Russell Square family. She was reported to have I don't know how many plantations in the West Indies; a deal of money in the funds; and three stars to her name in the East India stockholders' list. She had a mansion in Surrey, and a house in Portland Place. The name of the rich West India heiress had been mentioned with applause in the *Morning Post*. Mrs. Haggistoun, Colonel Haggistoun's widow, her relative, "chaperoned" her, and kept her house. She was just from school, where she had completed her education, and George and his sisters had met her at an evening party at old Hulker's house, Devonshire Place (Hulker, Bullock, and Co. were long the correspondents of her house in the West Indies), and the girls had made the most cordial advances to her, which the heiress had received with great good humour. An orphan in her position—with her money—so interesting! the Misses Osborne said. They were full of their new friend when they returned from the Hulker ball to Miss Wirt, their companion; they had made arrangements for continually meeting, and had the carriage and drove to see her the very next day. Mrs. Haggistoun, Colonel Haggistoun's widow, a relation of Lord Binkie, and always talking of him, struck the dear unsophisticated girls as rather haughty, and too much inclined to talk about her great relations: but Rhoda was everything they could wish—the frankest, kindest, most agreeable creature—wanting a little polish, but so good-natured. The girls Christian-named each other at once.

"You should have seen her dress for court, Emmy," Osborne cried, laughing. "She came to my sisters to show it off, before she was presented in state by my Lady Binkie, the Haggistoun's kinswoman. She's related to everyone, that Haggistoun. Her diamonds blazed out like Vauxhall on the night we were there. (Do you remember Vauxhall, Emmy, and Jos singing to his dearest diddle diddle darling?) Diamonds and mahogany, my dear! think what an advantageous contrast—and the white feathers in her hair—I mean in her wool. She had ear-rings like chandeliers; you might have lighted 'em up, by Jove—and a yellow satin train that streeled after her like the tail of a comet."

"How old is she?" asked Emmy, to whom George was rattling away regarding this dark paragon, on the morning of their re-union—rattling away as no other man in the world surely could.

"Why the Black Princess, though she has only just left school, must be two or three and twenty. And you should see the hand she writes! Mrs. Colonel Haggistoun usually writes her letters, but in a moment of confidence, she put pen to paper for my sisters; she spelt satin satting, and Saint James's, Saint Jams."

"Why, surely it must be Miss Swartz, the parlour boarder," Emmy said, remembering that good-natured young mulatto girl, who had been so hysterically affected when Amelia left Miss Pinkerton's academy.

"The very name," George said. "Her father was a German Jew—a slave-owner they say—connected with the Cannibal Islands in some way or other. He died last year, and Miss Pinkerton has finished her education. She can play two pieces on the piano; she knows three songs; she can write when Mrs. Haggistoun is by to spell for her; and Jane and Maria already have got to love her as a sister."

"I wish they would have loved me," said Emmy, wistfully. "They were always very cold to me."

"My dear child, they would have loved you if you had had two hundred thousand pounds," George replied. "That is the way in which they have been brought up. Ours is a ready-money society. We live among bankers and City big-wigs, and be hanged to them, and every man, as he talks to you, is jingling his guineas in his pocket. There is that jackass Fred Bullock is going to marry Maria —there's Goldmore, the East India Director, there's Dipley, in the tallow trade—*our* trade," George said, with an uneasy laugh and a blush. "Curse the whole pack of money-grubbing vulgarians! I fall asleep at their great heavy dinners. I feel ashamed in my father's great stupid parties. I've been accustomed to live with gentlemen, and men of the world and fashion, Emmy, not with a parcel of turtle-fed tradesmen. Dear little woman, you are the only person of our set who ever looked, or thought, or spoke like a lady: and you do it because you're an angel and can't help it. Don't remonstrate. Your *are* the only lady. Didn't Miss Crawley remark it, who has lived in the best company in Europe? And as for Crawley, of the Life Guards, hang it, he's a fine fellow: and I like him for marrying the girl he had chosen."

Amelia admired Mr. Crawley very much, too, for this; and trusted Rebecca would be happy with him, and hoped (with a laugh) Jos would be consoled. And so the pair went on prattling, as in quite early days. Amelia's confidence being perfectly restored to her, though she expressed a great deal of petty jealousy about Miss Swartz, and professed to be dreadfully frightened—like a hypocrite as she was—lest George should forget her for the heiress and her money and her estates in Saint Kitt's. But the fact is, she was a great deal too happy to have fears or doubts or misgivings of any sort: and having George at her side again, was not afraid of any heiress or beauty, or indeed of any sort of danger.

When Captain Dobbin came back in the afternoon to these people—which he did with a great deal of sympathy for them—it did his heart good to see how Amelia had grown young again—how she laughed, and chirped, and sang familiar old songs at the piano, which were only interrupted by the bell from without proclaiming Mr. Sedley's return from the City, before whom George received a signal to retreat.

Beyond the first smile of recognition—and even that was an hypocrisy, for she thought his arrival rather provoking—Miss Sedley did not once notice Dobbin during his visit. But he was content, so that he saw her happy; and thankful to have been the means of making her so.

CHAPTER XXI

A Quarrel About an Heiress

LOVE may be felt for any young lady endowed with such qualities as Miss Swartz possessed; and a great dream of ambition entered into old Mr. Osborne's soul, which she was to realize. He encouraged, with the utmost enthusiasm and friendliness, his daughters' amiable attachment to the young heiress, and protested that it gave him the sincerest pleasure as a father to see the love of his girls so well disposed.

"You won't find," he would say to Miss Rhoda, "that splendour and rank to which you are accustomed at the West End, my dear Miss, at our humble mansion in Russell Square. My daughters are plain, disinterested girls, but their hearts are in the right place, and they've conceived an attachment for you which does them honour—I say, which does them honour. I'm a plain, simple, humble British merchant—an honest one, as my respected friends Hulker and Bullock will vouch, who were the correspondents of your late lamented father. You'll find us a united, simple, happy, and I think I may say respected, family—a plain table, a plain people, but a warm welcome, my dear Miss Rhoda—Rhoda, let me say, for my heart warms to you, it does really. I'm a frank man, and I like you. A glass of Champagne! Hicks, Champagne to Miss Swartz."

There is little doubt that old Osborne believed all he said, and that the girls were quite earnest in their protestations of affection for Miss Swartz. People in Vanity Fair fasten on to rich folks quite naturally. If the simplest people are disposed to look not a little kindly on great Prosperity (for I defy any member of the British public to say that the notion of Wealth has not something awful and pleasing to him; and you, if you are told that the man next you at dinner has got half a million, not to look at

227

him with a certain interest;)—if the simple look benevo-
lently on money, how much more do your old worldlings
regard it! Their affections rush out to meet and welcome
money. Their kind sentiments awaken spontaneously towards the interesting possessors of it. I know some respectable people who don't consider themselves at liberty to indulge
in friendship for any individual who has not a certain competency, or place in society. They give a loose to their
feelings on proper occasions. And the proof is, that the
major part of the Osborne family, who had not, in fifteen
years, been able to get up a hearty regard for Amelia
Sedley, became as fond of Miss Swartz in the course of a
single evening as the most romantic advocate of friendship
at first sight could desire.

What a match for George she'd be (the sisters and Miss
Wirt agreed), and how much better than that insignificant
little Amelia! Such a dashing young fellow as he is, with
his good looks, rank, and accomplishments, would be the
very husband for her. Visions of balls in Portland Place,
presentations at Court, and introductions to half the peerage, filled the minds of the young ladies; who talked of
nothing but George and his grand acquaintances to their
beloved new friend.

Old Osborne thought she would be a great match, too,
for his son. He should leave the army; he should go to
Parliament; he should cut a figure in the fashion and in
the state. His blood boiled with honest British exultation,
as he saw the name of Osborne ennobled in the person of
his son, and thought that he might be the progenitor of a
glorious line of baronets. He worked in the City and on
'Change, until he knew everything relating to the fortune
of the heiress, how her money was placed, and where her
estates lay. Young Fred Bullock, one of his chief inform-
ants, would have liked to make a bid for her himself (it
was so the young banker expressed it) only he was booked
to Maria Osborne. But not being able to secure her as a
wife, the disinterested Fred quite approved of her as a sister-
in-law. "Let George cut in directly and win her," was
his advice. "Strike while the iron's hot, you know—while
she's fresh to the town: in a few weeks some d—— fellow

from the West End will come in with a title and a rotten
rent-roll and cut all us City men out, as Lord Fitzrufus did
last year with Miss Grogram, who was actually engaged to
Podder, of Podder & Brown's. The sooner it is done the
better, Mr. Osborne; them's my sentiments," the wag said;
though, when Osborne had left the bank parlour, Mr.
Bullock remembered Amelia, and what a pretty girl she
was, and how attached to George Osborne; and he gave
up at least ten seconds of his valuable time to regretting
the misfortune which had befallen that unlucky young
woman.

While thus George Osborne's good feelings, and his good
friend and genius, Dobbin, were carrying back the truant to
Amelia's feet, George's parent and sisters were arranging
this splendid match for him, which they never dreamed he
would resist.

When the elder Osborne gave what he called "a hint,"
there was no possibility for the most obtuse to mistake his
meaning. He called kicking a footman down-stairs, a hint
to the latter to leave his service. With his usual frankness
and delicacy he told Mrs. Haggistoun that he would give
her a cheque for five thousand pounds on the day his son
was married to her ward; and called that proposal a hint,
and considered it a very dexterous piece of diplomacy. He
gave George finally such another hint regarding the heiress;
and ordered him to marry her out of hand, as he would
have ordered his butler to draw a cork, or his clerk to write
a letter.

This imperative hint disturbed George a good deal. He
was in the very first enthusiasm and delight of his second
courtship of Amelia, which was inexpressibly sweet to him.
The contrast of her manners and appearance with those of
the heiress, made the idea of a union with the latter appear
doubly ludicrous and odious. Carriages and opera-boxes,
thought he; fancy being seen in them by the side of such a
mahogany charmer as that! Add to all, that the junior
Osborne was quite as obstinate as the senior: when he
wanted a thing, quite as firm in his resolution to get it; and
quite as violent when angered, as his father in his most
stern moments.

On the first day when his father formally gave him the hint that he was to place his affections at Miss Swartz's feet, George temporised with the old gentleman. "You should have thought of the matter sooner, sir," he said. "It can't be done now, when we're expecting every day to go on foreign service. Wait until my return, if I do return;" and then he represented, that the time when the regiment was daily expecting to quit England, was exceedingly ill-chosen: that the few days or weeks during which they were still to remain at home, must be devoted to business and not to love-making: time enough for that when he came home with his majority; "for, I promise you," said he, with a satisfied air, "that one way or other you shall read the name of George Osborne in the *Gazette*."

The father's reply to this was founded upon the information which he had got in the City: that the West End chaps would infallibly catch hold of the heiress if any delay took place; that if he didn't marry Miss S., he might at least have an engagement in writing, to come into effect when he returned to England; and that a man who could get ten thousand a year by staying at home, was a fool to risk his life abroad.

"So that you would have me shown up as a coward, sir, and our name dishonoured for the sake of Miss Swartz's money," George interposed.

This remark staggered the old gentleman; but as he had to reply to it, and as his mind was nevertheless made up, he said, "You will dine here to-morrow, sir, and every day Miss Swartz comes, you will be here to pay your respects to her. If you want for money, call upon Mr. Chopper." Thus a new obstacle was in George's way, to interfere with his plans regarding Amelia; and about which he and Dobbin had more than one confidential consultation. His friend's opinion respecting the line of conduct which he ought to pursue, we know already. And as for Osborne, when he was once bent on a thing, a fresh obstacle or two only rendered him the more resolute.

The dark object of the conspiracy into which the chiefs of the Osborne family had entered, was quite ignorant of all their plans regarding her (which, strange to say, her friend and chaperon did not divulge), and, taking all the young ladies' flattery for genuine sentiment, and being, as we have before had occasion to show, of a very warm and impetuous nature, responded to their affection with quite a tropical ardour. And if the truth may be told, I dare say that she too had some selfish attraction in the Russell Square house; and in a word, thought George Osborne a very nice young man. His whiskers had made an impression upon her, on the very first night she beheld them at the ball at Messrs. Hulkers; and, as we know, she was not the first woman who had been charmed by them. George had an air at once swaggering and melancholy, languid and fierce. He looked like a man who had passions, secrets, and private harrowing griefs and adventures. His voice was rich and deep. He would say it was a warm evening, or ask his partner to take an ice, with a tone as sad and confidential as if he were breaking her mother's death to her, or preluding a declaration of love. He trampled over all the young bucks of his father's circle, and was the hero among those third-rate men. Some few sneered at him and hated him. Some, like Dobbin, fanatically admired him. And his whiskers had begun to do their work, and to curl themselves round the affections of Miss Swartz.

Whenever there was a chance of meeting him in Russell Square, that simple and good-natured young woman was quite in a flurry to see her dear Misses Osborne. She went to great expenses in new gowns, and bracelets, and bonnets, and in prodigious feathers. She adorned her person with her utmost skill to please the Conqueror, and exhibited all her simple accomplishments to win his favour. The girls would ask her, with the greatest gravity, for a little music, and she would sing her three songs and play her two little pieces as often as ever they asked, and with an always increasing pleasure to herself. During these delectable entertainments, Miss Wirt and the chaperon sate by, and conned over the peerage, and talked about the nobility.

The day after George had his hint from his father, and a short time before the hour of dinner, he was lolling upon a sofa in the drawing-room in a very becoming and perfectly natural attitude of melancholy. He had been, at his father's request, to Mr. Chopper in the City, (the old gentleman, though he gave great sums to his son, would never specify any fixed allowance for him, and rewarded him only as he was in the humour). He had then been to pass three hours with Amelia, his dear little Amelia, at Fulham; and he came home to find his sisters spread in starched muslin in the drawing-room, the dowagers cackling in the background, and honest Swartz in her favourite amber-coloured satin, with turquoise bracelets, countless rings, flowers, feathers, and all sorts of tags and gimcracks, about as elegantly decorated as a she chimney-sweep on Mayday.

The girls, after vain attempts to engage him in conversation, talked about fashions and the last drawing-room until he was perfectly sick of their chatter. He contrasted their behaviour with little Emmy's—their shrill voices with her tender ringing tones; their attitudes and their elbows and their starch, with her humble soft movements and modest graces. Poor Swartz was seated in a place where Emmy had been accustomed to sit. Her bejewelled hands lay sprawling in her amber satin lap. Her tags and ear-rings twinkled, and her big eyes rolled about. She was doing nothing with perfect contentment, and thinking herself charming. Anything so becoming as the satin the sisters had never seen.

"Dammy," George said to a confidential friend, "she looked like a China doll, which has nothing to do all day but to grin and wag its head. By Jove, Will, it was all I could do to prevent myself from throwing the sofa-cushion at her." He restrained that exhibition of sentiment, however.

The sisters began to play the Battle of Prague. "Stop that d—— thing," George howled out in a fury from the sofa. "It makes me mad. *You* play us something, Miss Swartz, do. Sing something, anything but the Battle of Prague."

"Shall I sing Blue Eyed Mary, or the air from the Cabinet?" Miss Swartz asked.

"That sweet thing from the Cabinet," the sisters said.

"We've had that," replied the misanthrope on the sofa.

"I can sing Fluvy du Tajy," Swartz said, in a meek voice, "if I had the words." It was the last of the worthy young woman's collection.

"O, Fleuve du Tage," Miss Maria cried; "we have the song," and went off to fetch the book in which it was.

Now it happened that this song, then in the height of the fashion, had been given to the young ladies by a young friend of theirs, whose name was on the title, and Miss Swartz, having concluded the ditty with George's applause, (for he remembered that it was a favourite of Amelia's,) was hoping for an encore perhaps, and fiddling with the leaves of the music, when her eye fell upon the title, and she saw "Amelia Sedley" written in the corner.

"Lor!" cried Miss Swartz, spinning swiftly round on the music-stool, "is it *my* Amelia? Amelia that was at Miss P.'s at Hammersmith? I know it is. It's her, and —Tell me about her—where is she?"

"Don't mention her," Miss Maria Osborne said hastily. "Her family has disgraced itself. Her father cheated papa, and as for her, she is never to be mentioned *here.*" This was Miss Maria's return for George's rudeness about the Battle of Prague.

"Are you a friend of Amelia's?" George said, bouncing up. "God bless you for it, Miss Swartz. Don't believe what the girls say. *She's* not to blame at any rate. She's the best—"

"You know you're not to speak about her, George," cried Jane. "Papa forbids it."

"Who's to prevent me?" George cried out. "I *will* speak of her. I say she's the best, the kindest, the gentlest, the sweetest girl in England; and that, bankrupt or no, my sisters are not fit to hold candles to her. If you like her, go and see her, Miss Swartz; she wants friends now; and I say, God bless everybody who befriends her. Anybody who speaks kindly of her is my friend; anybody who speaks against her is my enemy. Thank you, Miss Swartz;" and he went up and wrung her hand.

"George! George!" one of the sisters cried imploringly.

"I say," George said fiercely, "I thank everybody who loves Amelia Sed—" He stopped. Old Osborne was in the room with a face livid with rage, and eyes like hot coals.

Though George had stopped in his sentence, yet, his blood being up, he was not to be cowed by all the generations of Osborne; rallying instantly, he replied to the bullying look of his father, with another so indicative of resolution and defiance, that the elder man quailed in his turn, and looked away. He felt that the tussle was coming. "Mrs. Haggistoun, let me take you down to dinner," he said. "Give your arm to Miss Swartz, George," and they marched.

"Miss Swartz, I love Amelia, and we've been engaged almost all our lives," Osborne said to his partner; and during all the dinner, George rattled on with a volubility which surprised himself, and made his father doubly nervous for the fight which was to take place as soon as the ladies were gone.

The difference between the pair was, that while the father was violent and a bully, the son had thrice the nerve and courage of the parent, and could not merely make an attack, but resist it; and finding that the moment was now come when the contest between him and his father was to be decided, he took his dinner with perfect coolness and appetite before the engagement began. Old Osborne, on the contrary, was nervous, and drank much. He floundered in his conversation with the ladies, his neighbours: George's coolness only rendering him more angry. It made him half mad to see the calm way in which George, flapping his napkin, and with a swaggering bow, opened the door for the ladies to leave the room; and filling himself a glass of wine, smacked it, and looked his father full in the face, as if to say, "Gentlemen of the Guard, fire first." The old man also took a supply of ammunition, but his decanter clinked against the glass as he tried to fill it.

After giving a great heave, and with a purple choking face, he then began. "How dare you, sir, mention that person's name before Miss Swartz to-day, in my drawing-room? I ask you, sir, how dare you do it?"

"Stop, sir," says George, "don't say dare, sir. Dare isn't a word to be used to a Captain in the British Army."

"I shall say what I like to my son, sir. I can cut him off with a shilling if I like. I can make him a beggar if I I like. I *will* say what I like," the elder said.

"I'm a gentleman though I *am* your son, sir," George answered haughtily. "Any communications which you have to make to me, or any orders which you may please to give, I beg may be couched in that kind of language which I am accustomed to hear."

Whenever the lad assumed his haughty manner, it always created either great awe or great irritation in the parent. Old Osborne stood in secret terror of his son as a better gentleman than himself; and perhaps my readers may have remarked in their experience of this Vanity Fair of ours, that there is no character which a low-minded man so much mistrusts, as that of a gentleman.

"My father didn't give me the education you have had, nor the advantages you have had, nor the money you have had. If I had kept the company *some* folks have had through *my means,* perhaps my son wouldn't have any reason to brag, sir, of his *superiority* and *West End airs* (these words were uttered in the elder Osborne's most sarcastic tones). But it wasn't considered the part of a gentleman, in *my* time, for a man to insult his father. If I'd done any such thing, mine would have kicked me downstairs, sir."

"I never insulted you, sir. I said I begged you to remember your son was a gentleman as well as yourself. I know very well that you give me plenty of money," said George (fingering a bundle of notes which he had got in the morning from Mr. Chopper). "You tell it me often enough, sir. There's no fear of my forgetting it."

"I wish you'd remember other things as well, sir," the sire answered. "I wish you'd remember that in this house —so long as you choose to *honour* it with your *company,* Captain—I'm the master, and that name, and that that— that you—that I say—"

"That what sir?" George asked, with scarcely a sneer, filling another glass of claret.

"————!" burst out his father with a screaming oath —"that the name of those Sedleys never be mentioned here, sir—not one of the whole damned lot of 'em, sir."

"It wasn't I, sir, that introduced Miss Sedley's name. It was my sisters who spoke ill of her to Miss Swartz; and by Jove I'll defend her wherever I go. Nobody shall speak lightly of that name in my presence. Our family has done her quite enough injury already, I think, and may leave off reviling her now she's down. I'll shoot any man but you who says a word against her."

"Go on, sir, go on," the old gentleman said, his eyes starting out of his head.

"Go on about what, sir? about the way in which we've treated that angel of a girl? Who told me to love her? It was your doing. I might have chosen elsewhere, and looked higher, perhaps, than your society: but I obeyed you. And now that her heart's mine you give me orders to fling it away, and punish her, kill her perhaps—for the faults of other people. It's a shame, by Heavens," said George, working himself up into passion and enthusiasm as he proceeded, "to play at fast and loose with a young girl's affections—and with such an angel as that—one so superior to the people amongst whom she lived, that she might have excited envy, only she was so good and gentle, that it's wonder anybody dared to hate her. If I desert her, sir, do you suppose she forgets me?"

"I ain't going to have any of this dam sentimental nonsense and humbug here, sir," the father cried out. "There shall be no beggar-marriages in my family. If you choose to fling away eight thousand a year, which you may have for the asking, you may do it: but by Jove you take your pack and walk out of this house, sir. Will you do as I tell you, once for all, sir, or will you not?"

"Marry that mulatto woman?" George said, pulling up his shirt-collars. "I don't like the colour, sir. Ask the black that sweeps opposite Fleet Market, sir. *I'm* not going to marry a Hottentot Venus."

Mr. Osborne pulled frantically at the cord by which he was accustomed to summon the butler when he wanted wine —and almost black in the face, ordered that functionary to call a coach for Captain Osborne.

"I've done it," said George, coming into the Slaughters' an hour afterwards, looking very pale.

"What, my boy?" says Dobbin.

George told what had passed between his father and himself.

"I'll marry her to-morrow," he said with an oath. "I love her more every day, Dobbin."

CHAPTER XXII

A Marriage and Part of a Honeymoon

ENEMIES the most obstinate and courageous can't hold out against starvation: so the elder Osborne felt himself pretty easy about his adversary in the encounter we have just described; and as soon as George's supplies fell short, confidently expected his unconditional submission. It was unlucky, to be sure, that the lad should have secured a stock of provisions on the very day when the first encounter took place; but this relief was only temporary, old Osborne thought, and would but delay George's surrender. No communication passed between father and son for some days. The former was sulky at this silence, but not disquieted; for, as he said, he knew where he could put the screw upon George, and only waited the result of that operation. He told the sisters the upshot of the dispute between them, but ordered them to take no notice of the matter, and welcome George on his return as if nothing had happened. His cover was laid as usual every day, and perhaps the old gentleman rather anxiously expected him; but he never came. Some one inquired at the Slaughters' regarding him, where it was said that he and his friend Captain Dobbin had left town.

One gusty, raw day at the end of April,—the rain whipping the pavement of that ancient street where the old Slaughters' Coffee-house was once situated, — George Osborne came into the coffee-room, looking very haggard and pale; although dressed rather smartly in a blue coat and brass buttons, and a neat buff waistcoat of the fashion of those days. Here was his friend Captain Dobbin, in blue and brass too, having abandoned the military frock and French-gray trowsers, which were the usual coverings of his lanky person.

Dobbin had been in the coffee-room for an hour or more. He had tried all the papers, but could not read them. He

238

had looked at the clock many scores of times; and at the
street, where the rain was pattering down, and the people as
they clinked by in patterns, left long reflections on the shining stone: he tattooed at the table: he bit his nails most completely, and nearly to the quick (he was accustomed to ornament his great big hands in this way): he balanced the tea-
spoon dexterously on the milk jug: upset it, &c., &c.; and in
fact showed those signs of disquietude, and practised those
desperate attempts at amusement, which men are accustomed
to employ when very anxious, and expectant, and perturbed
in mind.

Some of his comrades, gentlemen who used the room, joked
him about the splendour of his costume and his agitation of
manner. One asked him if he was going to be married?
Dobbin laughed, and said he would send his acquaintance
(Major Wagstaff of the Engineers) a piece of cake when
that event took place. At length Captain Osborne made his
appearance, very smartly dressed, but very pale and agitated
as we have said. He wiped his pale face with a large yellow
bandanna pocket-handkerchief that was prodigiously scented.
He shook hands with Dobbin, looked at the clock, and told
John, the waiter, to bring him some curaçoa. Of this cordial
he swallowed off a couple of glasses with nervous eagerness.
His friend asked with some interest about his health.

"Couldn't get a wink of sleep till daylight, Dob," said he.
"Infernal headache and fever. Got up at nine, and went
down to the Hummums for a bath. I say, Dob, I feel just
as I did on the morning I went out with Rocket at Quebec."

"So do I," William responded. "I was a deuced deal
more nervous than you were that morning. You made a
famous breakfast, I remember. Eat something now."

"You're a good old fellow, Will. I'll drink your health,
old boy, and farewell to—"

"No, no; two glasses are enough," Dobbin interrupted
him. "Here, take away the liqueurs, John. Have some
cayenne-pepper with your fowl. Make haste though, for it
is time we were there."

It was about half-an-hour from twelve when this brief
meeting and colloquy took place between the two captains.
A coach, into which Captain Osborne's servant put his mas-

ter's desk and dressing-case, had been in waiting for some time; and into this the two gentlemen hurried under an umbrella, and the valet mounted on the box, cursing the rain and the dampness of the coachman who was steaming beside him. "We shall find a better trap than this at the church-door," says he; "that's a comfort." And the carriage drove on, taking the road down Piccadilly, where Apsley House and St. George's Hospital wore red jackets still; where there were oil-lamps; where Achilles was not yet born; nor the Pimlico arch raised; nor the hideous equestrian monster which pervades it and the neigbourhood;—and so they drove down by Brompton to a certain chapel near the Fulham-road there.

A chariot was in waiting with four horses; likewise a coach of the kind called glass coaches. Only a very few idlers were collected on account of the dismal rain.

"Hang it!" said George, "I said only a pair."

"My master would have four," said Mr. Joseph Sedley's servant, who was in waiting; and he and Mr. Osborne's man agreed as they followed George and William into the church, that it was a "reg'lar shabby turn hout; and with scarce so much as a breakfast or a wedding faviour."

"Here you are," said our old friend, Jos Sedley, coming forward. "You're five minutes late, George, my boy. What a day, eh? Demmy, it's like the commencement of the rainy season in Bengal. But you'll find my carriage is water-tight. Come along, my mother and Emmy are in the vestry."

Jos Sedley was splendid. He was fatter than ever. His shirt collars were higher; his face was redder; his shirt-frill flaunted gorgeously out of his variegated waistcoat. Var-nished boots were not invented as yet; but the Hessians on his beautiful legs shone so that they must have been the identical pair in which the gentleman in the old picture used to shave himself; and on his light green coat there bloomed a fine wedding favour, like a great white spreading magnolia.

In a word, George had thrown the great cast. He was going to be married. Hence his pallor and nervousness—his sleepless night and agitation in the morning. I have heard people who have gone through the same thing own to the same emotion. After three or four ceremonies, you get accustomed to it, no doubt; but the first dip, everybody allows, is awful.

The bride was dressed in a brown silk pelisse (as Captain Dobbin has since informed me), and wore a straw bonnet with a pink ribbon; over the bonnet she had a veil of white Chantilly lace, a gift from Mr. Joseph Sedley, her brother. Captain Dobbin himself had asked leave to present her with a gold chain and watch, which she sported on this occasion; and her mother gave her her diamond brooch—almost the only trinket which was left to the old lady. As the service went on, Mrs. Sedley sat and whimpered a great deal in a pew, consoled by the Irish maid-servant and Mrs. Clapp from the lodgings. Old Sedley would not be present. Jos acted for his father, giving away the bride whilst Captain Dobbin stepped up as groom's-man to his friend George.

There was nobody in the church besides the officiating persons and the small marriage party and their attendants. The two valets sat aloof superciliously. The rain came rattling down on the windows. In the intervals of the service you heard it, and the sobbing of old Mrs. Sedley in the pew. The parson's tones echoed sadly through the empty walls. Osborne's "I will" was sounded in very deep bass. Emmy's response came fluttering up to her lips from her heart, but was scarcely heard by anybody except Captain Dobbin.

When the service was completed, Jos Sedley came forward and kissed his sister, the bride, for the first time for many months—George's look of gloom had gone, and he seemed quite proud and radiant. "It's your turn, William," says he. putting his hand fondly upon Dobbin's shoulder; and Dobbin went up and touched Amelia on the cheek.

Then they went into the vestry and signed the register. "God bless you, Old Dobbin," George said, grasping him by the hand, with something very like moisture glistening in his eyes. William replied only by nodding his head. His heart was too full to say much.

"Write directly, and come down as soon as you can, you know," Osborne said. After Mrs. Sedley had taken an hysterical adieu of her daughter, the pair went off to the carriage. "Get out of the way, you little devils," George cried to a small crowd of damp urchins, that were hanging about the chapel-door. The rain drove into the bride and bride-groom's faces as they passed to the chariot. The postilions' favours draggled on their dripping jackets. The few children made a dismal cheer, as the carriage, splashing mud, drove away.

William Dobbin stood in the church-porch, looking at it, a queer figure. The small crew of spectators jeered him. He was not thinking about them or their laughter.

"Come home and have some tiffin, Dobbin," a voice cried behind him; as a pudgy hand was laid on his shoulder, and the honest fellow's reverie was interrupted. But the Captain had no heart to go a feasting with Jos Sedley. He put the weeping old lady and her attendants into the carriage with Jos, and left them without any farther words passing. This carriage, too, drove away, and the urchins gave another sar-castical cheer.

"Here, you little beggars," Dobbins said, giving some six-pences amongst them, and then went off by himself through the rain. It was all over. They were married, and happy, he prayed God. Never since he was a boy had he felt so miserable and so lonely. He longed with a heartsick yearn-ing for the first few days to be over, that he might see her again.

Some ten days after the above ceremony, three young men of our acquaintance were enjoying that beautiful prospect of bow windows on the one side and blue sea on the other, which Brighton affords to the traveller. Sometimes it is towards the ocean—smiling with countless dimples, speckled with white sails, with a hundred bathing-machines kissing the skirt of his blue garment—that the Londoner looks en-raptured; sometimes, on the contrary, a lover of human nature rather than of prospects of any kind, it is towards the bow windows that he turns, and that swarm of human life which they exhibit. From one issue the notes of a piano, which a young lady in ringlets practises six hours daily, to the delight of the fellow-lodgers; at another, lovely Polly, the nursemaid, may be seen dandling Master Omnium in her arms: whilst Jacob, his papa, is beheld eating prawns, and devouring the *Times* for breakfast, at the window below. Yonder are the Misses Leery, who are looking out for the

young officers of the Heavies, who are pretty sure to be pacing the cliff; or again it is a City man, with a nautical turn
and a telescope, the size of a six-pounder, who has his instrument pointed seawards, so as to command every pleasure-
boat, herring-boat, or bathing-machine that comes to, or
quits, the shore, &c., &c. But have we any leisure for a description of Brighton?—for Brighton, a clean Naples with
genteel lazzaroni—for Brighton, that always looks brisk, gay,
and gaudy, like a harlequin's jacket—for Brighton, which
used to be seven hours distant from London at the time of
our story; which is now only a hundred minutes off; and
which may approach who knows how much nearer, unless
Joinville comes and untimely bombards it?

"What a monstrous fine girl that is in the lodgings over
the milliner's," one of these three promenaders remarked to
the other; "Gad, Crawley, did you see what a wink she gave
me as I passed?"

"Don't break her heart, Jos, you rascal," said another.
"Don't trifle with her affections, you Don Juan!"

"Get away," said Jos Sedley, quite pleased, and leering up
at the maid-servant in question with a most killing ogle. Jos
was even more splendid at Brighton than he had been at his
sister's marriage. He had brilliant under-waistcoats, any one
of which would have set up a moderate buck. He sported a
military frock-coat, ornamented with frogs, knobs, black buttons, and meandering embroidery. He had affected a military appearance and habits of late; and he walked with his
two friends, who were of that profession, clinking his boot-
spurs, swaggering prodigiously, and shooting death-glances
at all the servant girls who were worthy to be slain.

"What shall we do, boys, till the ladies return?" the buck
asked. The ladies were out to Rottingdean in his carriage
on a drive.

"Let's have a game at billiards," one of his friends said—
the tall one, with lacquered mustachios.

"No, dammy; no, Captain," Jos replied rather alarmed.
"No billiards to-day, Crawley, my boy; yesterday was
enough."

"You play very well," said Crawley, laughing. "Don't he,
Osborne? How well he made that five stroke, eh?"

"Famous," Osborne said. "Jos is a devil of a fellow at billiards, and at everything else, too. I wish there were any tiger-hunting about here! we might go and kill a few before dinner. (There goes a fine girl! what an ankle, eh, Jos?) Tell us that story about the tiger-hunt, and the way you did for him in the jungle—it's a wonderful story that, Crawley." Here George Osborne gave a yawn. "It's rather slow work," said he, "down here; what *shall* we do?"

"Shall we go and look at some horses that Snaffler's just brought from Lewes fair?" Crawley said.

"Suppose we go and have some jellies at Dutton's," said the rogue Jos, willing to kill two birds with one stone. "Devilish fine gal at Dutton's."

"Suppose we go and see the Lightning come in, it's just about time?" George said. This advice prevailing over the stables and the jelly, they turned towards the coach-office to witness the Lightning's arrival.

As they passed, they met the carriage—Jos Sedley's open carriage, with its magnificent armorial bearings—that splendid conveyance in which he used to drive about to Cheltenham, majestic and solitary, with his arms folded, and his hat cocked; or, more happy, with ladies by his side.

Two were in the carriage now: one a little person, with light hair, and dressed in the height of the fashion; the other in a brown silk pelisse, and a straw bonnet with pink ribbons, with a rosy, round, happy face, that did you good to behold. She checked the carriage as it neared the three gentlemen, after which exercise of authority she looked rather nervous, and then began to blush most absurdly. "We have had a delightful drive, George," she said, "and—and we're so glad to come back; and, Joseph, don't let him be late."

"Don't be leading our husbands into mischief, Mr. Sedley, you wicked, wicked man, you," Rebecca said, shaking at Jos a pretty little finger covered with the neatest French kid glove. "No billiards, no smoking, no naughtiness!"

"My dear Mrs. Crawley—Ah, now! upon my honour!" was all Jos could ejaculate by way of reply; but he managed to fall into a tolerable attitude, with his head lying on his shoulder, grinning upwards at his victim, with one hand at his back, which he supported on his cane, and the other hand (the one with the diamond ring) fumbling in his shirt-frill and among his under-waistcoats. As the carriage drove off he kissed the diamond hand to the fair ladies within. He wished all Cheltenham, all Chowringhee, all Calcutta, could see him in that position, waving his hand to such a beauty, and in company with such a famous buck as Rawdon Crawley of the Guards.

Our young bride and bridegroom had chosen Brighton as the place where they would pass the first few days after their marriage; and having engaged apartments at the Ship Inn, enjoyed themselves there in great comfort and quietude, until Jos presently joined them. Nor was he the only companion they found there. As they were coming into the Hotel from a sea-side walk one afternoon, on whom should they light but Rebecca and her husband. The recognition was immediate. Rebecca flew into the arms of her dearest friend. Crawley and Osborne shook hands together cordially enough; and Becky, in the course of a very few hours, found means to make the latter forget that little unpleasant passage of words which had happened between them. "Do you remember the last time we met at Miss Crawley's, when I was so rude to you, dear Captain Osborne? I thought you seemed careless about dear Amelia. It was that made me angry: and so pert: and so unkind: and so ungrateful. Do forgive me!" Rebecca said, and she held out her hand with so frank and winning a grace, that Osborne could not but take it. By humbly and frankly acknowledging yourself to be in the wrong, there is no knowing, my son, what good you may do. I knew once a gentleman and very worthy practitioner in Vanity Fair, who used to do little wrongs to his neighbours on purpose, and in order to apologise for them in an open and manly way afterwards—and what ensued? My friend Crocky Doyle was liked everywhere, and deemed to be rather impetuous—but the honestest fellow. Becky's humility passed for sincerity with George Osborne.

These two young couples had plenty of tales to relate to each other. The marriages of either were discussed; and their prospects in life canvassed with the greatest frankness and interest on both sides. George's marriage was to be made known to his father by his friend Captain Dobbin; and young Osborne trembled rather for the result of that communication. Miss Crawley, on whom all Rawdon's hopes depended, still held out. Unable to make an entry into her house in Park Lane, her affectionate nephew and niece had followed her to Brighton, where they had emissaries continually planted at her door.

"I wish you could see some of Rawdon's friends who are always about *our* door," Rebecca said laughing. "Did you ever see a dun, my dear; or a bailiff and his man? Two of the abominable wretches watched all last week at the greengrocer's opposite, and we could not get away until Sunday. If aunty does not relent, what *shall* we do?"

Rawdon, with roars of laughter, related a dozen amusing anecdotes of his duns, and Rebecca's adroit treatment of them. He vowed with a great oath, that there was no woman in Europe who could talk a creditor over as she could. Almost immediately after their marriage, her practice had begun, and her husband found the immense value of such a wife.

They had credit in plenty, but they had bills also in abundance, and laboured under a scarcity of ready money. Did these debt-difficulties affect Rawdon's good spirits? No. Everybody in Vanity Fair must have remarked how well those live who are comfortably and thoroughly in debt; how they deny themselves nothing; how jolly and easy they are in their minds. Rawdon and his wife had the very best apartments at the inn at Brighton; the landlord, as he brought in the first dish, bowed before them as to his greatest customers: and Rawdon abused the dinners and wine with an audacity which no grandee in the land could surpass. Long custom, a manly appearance, faultless boots and clothes, and a happy fierceness of manner, will often help a man as much as a great balance at the banker's.

The two wedding parties met constantly in each other's apartments. After two or three nights the gentlemen of an evening had a little piquet, as their wives sate and chatted apart.

This pastime, and the arrival of Jos Sedley who made his appearance in his grand open carriage, and who played a few games at billiards with Captain Crawley, replenished

Rawdon's purse somewhat, and gave him the benefit of that ready money for which the greatest spirits are sometimes at a stand-still.

So the three gentlemen walked down to see the Lightning coach come in. Punctual to the minute, the coach crowded inside and out, the guard blowing his accustomed tune on the horn—the Lightning came tearing down the street, and pulled up at the coach-office.

"Hullo! there's old Dobbin," George cried, quite delighted to see his old friend perched on the roof; and whose promised visit to Brighton had been delayed until now. "How are you, old fellow? Glad you're come down. Emmy 'll be delighted to see you," Osborne said, shaking his comrade warmly by the hand as soon as his descent from the vehicle was effected—and then he added, in a lower and agitated voice, "What's the news? Have you been in Russell Square? What does the governor say? Tell me everything."

Dobbin looked very pale and grave. "I've seen your father," said he. "How's Amelia—Mrs. George? I'll tell you all the news presently: but I've brought the great news of all: and that is——"

"Out with it, old fellow," George said.

"We're ordered to Belgium. All the army goes—Guards and all. Heavytop's got the gout, and is mad at not being able to move. O'Dowd goes in command, and we embark from Chatham next week." This news of war could not but come with a shock upon our lovers, and cause all these gentlemen to look very serious.

CHAPTER XXIII

Captain Dobbin Proceeds on His Canvass

WHAT is the secret mesmerism which friendship possesses, and under the operation of which a person ordinarily sluggish, or cold, or timid, becomes wise, active, and resolute, in another's behalf? As Alexis, after a few passes from Dr. Elliotson, despises pain, reads with the back of his head, sees miles off, looks into next week, and performs other wonders, of which, in his own private normal condition, he is quite incapable; so you see, in the affairs of the world and under the magnetism of friendship, the modest man become bold, the shy confident, the lazy active, or the impetuous prudent and peaceful. What is it, on the other hand, that makes the lawyer eschew his own cause, and call in his learned brother as an adviser? And what causes the doctor, when ailing, to send for his rival, and not sit down and examine his own tongue in the chimney glass, or write his own prescription at his study-table? I throw out these queries for intelligent readers to answer, who know, at once, how credulous we are, and how sceptical, how soft and how obstinate, how firm for others and how diffident about ourselves: meanwhile, it is certain that our friend William Dobbin, who was personally of so complying a disposition that if his parents had pressed him much, it is probably he would have stepped down into the kitchen and married the cook, and who, to further his own interests, would have found the most insuperable difficulty in walking across the street, found himself as busy and eager in the conduct of George Osborne's affairs, as the most selfish tactician could be in the pursuit of his own.

Whilst our friend George and his young wife were enjoying the first blushing days of the honeymoon at Brighton, honest William was left as George's plenipotentiary in London, to transact all the business part of the marriage.

His duty it was to call upon old Sedley and his wife, and to keep the former in good humour: to draw Jos and his brother-in-law nearer together, so that Jos's position and dignity, as collector of Boggley Wollah, might compensate for his father's loss of station, and tend to reconcile old Osborne to the alliance: and finally, to communicate it to the latter in such a way as should least irritate the old gentleman.

Now, before he faced the head of the Osborne house with the news which it was his duty to tell, Dobbin bethought him that it would be politic to make friends of the rest of the family, and, if possible, have the ladies on his side. They can't be angry in their hearts, thought he. No woman ever was really angry at a romantic marriage. A little crying out, and they must come round to their brother: when the three of us will lay siege to old Mr. Osborne. So this Machiavellian captain of infantry cast about him for some happy means of stratagem by which he could gently and gradually bring the Misses Osborne to a knowledge of their brother's secret.

By a little inquiry regarding his mother's engagements, he was pretty soon able to find out by whom of her ladyship's friends parties were given at that season; where he would be likely to meet Osborne's sisters; and, though he had that abhorrence of routs and evening parties, which many sensible men, alas! entertain, he soon found one where the Misses Osborne were to be present. Making his appearance at the ball, where he danced a couple of sets with both of them, and was prodigiously polite, he actually had the courage to ask Miss Osborne for a few minutes' conversation at an early hour the next day, when he had, he said, to communicate to her news of the very greatest interest.

What was it that made her start back, and gaze upon him for a moment, and then on the ground at her feet, and make as if she would faint on his arm, had he not by opportunely treading on her toes, brought the young lady back to self-control? Why was she so violently agitated at Dobbin's request? This can never be known. But when he came the next day, Maria was not in the drawing-room

with her sister, and Miss Wirt went off for the purpose
of fetching the latter, and the Captain and Miss Osborne
were left together. They were both so silent that the tick-
tock of the Sacrifice of Iphigenia clock on the mantel-piece
became quite rudely audible.

"What a nice party it was last night," Miss Osborne at
length began, encouragingly; "and—and how you're improved in your dancing, Captain Dobbin. Surely somebody
has taught you," she added, with amiable archness.

"You should see me dance a reel with Mrs. Major
O'Dowd of ours; and a jig—did you ever see a jig? But
I think anybody could dance with *you*, Miss Osborne, who
dance so well."

"Is the Major's lady young and beautiful, Captain?"
the fair questioner continued. "Ah, what a terrible thing
it must be to be a soldier's wife! I wonder they have any
spirits to dance, and in these dreadful times of war, too!
O Captain Dobbin, I tremble sometimes when I think of our
dearest George, and the dangers of the poor soldier. Are
there many married officers of the —th, Captain Dobbin?"

"Upon my word, she's playing her hand rather too
openly," Miss Wirt thought; but this observation is merely
parenthetic, and was not heard through the crevice of the
door at which the governess uttered it.

"One of our young men is just married," Dobbin said,
now coming to the point. "It was a very old attachment,
and the young couple are as poor as church mice."

"O, how delightful! O, how romantic!" Miss Osborne
cried, as the Captain said "old attachment" and "poor."
Her sympathy encouraged him.

"The finest young fellow in the regiment," he continued.
"Not a braver or handsomer officer in the army; and such
a charming wife! How you would like her! how you *will*
like her when you know her, Miss Osborne." The young
lady thought the actual moment had arrived, and that Dobbin's nervousness which now came on and was visible in
many twitchings of his face, in his manner of beating the
ground with his great feet, in the rapid buttoning and un-
buttoning of his frock-coat, &c.—Miss Osborne, I say,
thought that when he had given himself a little air, he

would unbosom himself entirely, and prepared eagerly to listen. And the clock, in the altar on which Iphigenia was situated, beginning, after a preparatory convulsion, to toll twelve, the mere tolling seemed as if it would last until one, so prolonged was the knell to the anxious spinster.

"But it's not about marriage that I came to speak—that is that marriage—that is—no, I mean—my dear Miss Osborne, it's about our dear friend George," Dobbin said.

"About George?" she said in a tone so discomfited that Maria and Miss Wirt laughed at the other side of the door, and even that abandoned wretch of a Dobbin felt inclined to smile himself; for he was not altogether unconscious of the state of affairs: George having often bantered him gracefully and said, "Hang it, Will, why don't you take old Jane? She'll have you if you ask her. I'll bet you five to two she will."

"Yes, about George, then," he continued. "There has been a difference between him and Mr. Osborne. And I regard him so much—for you know we have been like brothers—that I hope and pray the quarrel may be settled. We must go abroad, Miss Osborne. We may be ordered off at a day's warning. Who knows what may happen in the campaign? Don't be agitated, dear Miss Osborne; and those two at least should part friends."

"There has been no quarrel, Captain Dobbin, except a little usual scene with papa," the lady said. "We are expecting George back daily. What papa wanted was only for his good. He has but to come back, and I'm sure all will be well; and dear Rhoda, who went away from here in sad, sad anger, I know will forgive him. Woman forgives but too readily, Captain."

"Such an angel as *you* I am sure would," Mr. Dobbin said, with atrocious astuteness. "And no man can pardon himself for giving a woman pain. What would you feel, if a man were faithless to you?"

"I should perish—I should throw myself out of window —I should take poison—I should pine and die. I know I should," Miss Osborne cried, who had nevertheless gone through one or two affairs of the heart without any idea of suicide.

"And there are others," Dobbin continued, "as true and as kind-hearted as yourself. I'm not speaking about the West Indian heiress, Miss Osborne, but about a poor girl whom George once loved, and who was bred from her childhood to think of nobody but him. I've seen her in her poverty uncomplaining, broken-hearted, without a fault. It is of Miss Sedley I speak. Dear Miss Osborne, can your generous heart quarrel with your brother for being faithful to her? Could his own conscience ever forgive him if he deserted her? Be her friend—she always loved you—and —and I am come here charged by George to tell you that he holds his engagement to her as the most sacred duty he has; and to entreat *you,* at least, to be on his side."

When any strong emotion took possession of Mr. Dobbin, and after the first word or two of hesitation, he could speak with perfect fluency, and it was evident that his eloquence on this occasion made some impression upon the lady whom he addressed.

"Well," said she, "this is—most surprising—most painful —most extraordinary—what will papa say?—that George should fling away such a superb establishment as was offered to him,—but at any rate he has found a very brave champion in you, Captain Dobbin. It is of no use, however," she continued, after a pause; "I feel for poor Miss Sedley, most certainly—most sincerely, you know. We never thought the match a good one, though we were always very kind to her here—very. But papa will never consent, I am sure. And a well brought up young woman, you know,—with a well-regulated mind, must—George must give her up, Captain Dobbin, indeed he must."

"Ought a man to give up the woman he loved, just when misfortune befel her?" Dobbin said, holding out his hand. "Dear Miss Osborne, is this the counsel I hear from *you?* My dear young lady! you must befriend her. He can't give her up. He must not give her up. Would a man, think you, give *you* up if you were poor?"

This adroit question touched the heart of Miss Jane Osborne not a little. "I don't know whether we poor girls ought to believe what you men say, Captain," she said. "There is that in woman's tenderness which induces her **to**

believe too easily. I'm afraid you are cruel, cruel deceivers,"
—and Dobbin certainly thought he felt a pressure of the
hand which Miss Osborne had extended to him.

He dropped it in some alarm. "Deceivers!" said he.
"No, dear Miss Osborne, all men are not; your brother is
not; George has loved Amelia Sedley ever since they were
children; no wealth would make him marry any but her.
Ought he to forsake her? Would you counsel him to do
so?"

What could Miss Jane say to such a question, and with
her own peculiar views? She could not answer it, so she
parried it by saying, "Well, if you are not a deceiver, at
least you are *very* romantic;" and Captain William let this
observation pass without challenge.

At length when, by the help of farther polite speeches,
he deemed that Miss Osborne was sufficiently prepared to
receive the whole news, he poured it into her ear. "George
could not give up Amelia—George was married to her"—
and then he related the circumstances of the marriage as
we know them already; how the poor girl would have died
had not her lover kept his faith: how old Sedley had refused
all consent to the match, and a license had been got: and
Jos Sedley had come from Cheltenham to give away the
bride: how they had gone to Brighton in Jos's chariot and
four to pass the honeymoon: and how George counted on
his dear kind sisters to befriend him with their father, as
women—so true and tender as they were—assuredly would
do. And so, asking permission (readily granted) to see her
again, and rightly conjecturing that the news he had brought
would be told in the next five minutes to the other ladies,
Captain Dobbin made his bow and took his leave.

He was scarcely out of the house, when Miss Maria and
Miss Wirt rushed in to Miss Osborne, and the whole wonderful secret was imparted to them by that lady. To do
them justice, neither of the sisters was very much displeased.
There is something about a runaway match with which few
ladies can be seriously angry, and Amelia rather rose in
their estimation, from the spirit which she had displayed in
consenting to the union. As they debated the story, and
prattled about it, and wondered what papa would do and say,

came a loud knock as of an avenging thunder-clap, at the door, which made these conspirators start. It must be papa, they thought. But it was not he. It was only Mr. Frederick Bullock, who had come from the City according to appointment, to conduct the ladies to a flower-show.

This gentleman, as may be imagined, was not kept long in ignorance of the secret. But his face, when he heard it, showed an amazement which was very different to that look of sentimental wonder which the countenances of the sisters wore. Mr. Bullock was a man of the world, and a junior partner of a wealthy firm. He knew what money was, and the value of it: and a delightful throb of expectation lighted up his little eyes, and caused him to smile on his Maria, as he thought that by this piece of folly of Mr. George's she might be worth thirty thousand pounds more than he had ever hoped to get with her.

"Gad! Jane," said he, surveying even the elder sister with some interest, "Eels will be sorry he cried off. You may be a fifty thousand pounder yet."

The sisters had never thought of the money question up to that moment, but Fred Bullock bantered them with graceful gaiety about it during their forenoon's excursion; and they had risen not a little in their own esteem by the time when, the morning amusement over, they drove back to dinner. And do not let my respected reader exclaim against this selfishness as unnatural. It was but this present morning, as he rode on the omnibus from Richmond; while it changed horses, this present chronicler, being on the roof, marked three little children playing in a puddle below, very dirty, and friendly, and happy. To these three presently came another little one. *"Polly,"* says she, *"your sister's got a penny."* At which the children got up from the puddle instantly, and ran off to pay their court to Peggy. And as the omnibus drove off, I saw Peggy with the infantine procession at her tail, marching with great dignity towards the stall of a neighbouring lollipop-woman.

CHAPTER XXIV

In Which Mr. Osborne Takes Down the Family Bible

SO having prepared the sisters, Dobbin hastened away to the City to perform the rest and more difficult part of the task which he had undertaken. The idea of facing old Osborne rendered him not a little nervous, and more than once he thought of leaving the young ladies to communicate the secret, which, as he was aware, they could not long retain. But he had promised to report to George upon the manner in which the elder Osborne bore the intelligence; so going into the City to the paternal countinghouse in Thames Street, he despatched thence a note to Mr. Osborne begging for a half-hour's conversation relative to the affairs of his son George. Dobbin's messenger returned from Mr. Osborne's house of business, with the compliments of the latter, who would be very happy to see the Captain immediately, and away accordingly Dobbin went to confront him.

The Captain, with a half-guilty secret to confess, and with the prospect of a painful and stormy interview before him, entered Mr. Osborne's offices with a most dismal countenance and abashed gait, and, passing through the outer room where Mr. Chopper presided, was greeted by that functionary from his desk with a waggish air which farther discomfited him. Mr. Chopper winked and nodded and pointed his pen towards his patron's door, and said, "You'll find the governor all right," with the most provoking good humour.

Osborne rose too, and shook him heartily by the hand, and said, "How do, my dear boy?" with a cordiality that made poor George's ambassador feel doubly guilty. His hand lay as if dead in the old gentleman's grasp. He felt that he, Dobbin, was more or less the cause of all that had happened. It was he had brought back George to Amelia:

it was he had applauded, encouraged, transacted almost the marriage which he was come to reveal to George's father: and the latter was receiving him with smiles of welcome; patting him on the shoulder, and calling him "Dobbin, my dear boy." The envoy had indeed good reason to hang his head.

Osborne fully believed that Dobbin had come to announce his son's surrender. Mr. Chopper and his principal were talking over the matter between George and his father, at the very moment when Dobbin's messenger arrived. Both agreed that George was sending in his submission. Both had been expecting it for some days—and "Lord! Chopper, what a marriage we'll have!" Mr. Osborne said to his clerk, snapping his big fingers, and jingling all the guineas and shillings in his great pockets as he eyed his subordinate with a look of triumph.

With similar operations conducted in both pockets, and a knowing jolly air, Osborne from his chair regarded Dobbin seated blank and silent opposite to him. "What a bumpkin he is for a Captain in the army," old Osborne thought. "I wonder George hasn't taught him better manners."

At last Dobbin summoned courage to begin. "Sir," said he, "I've brought you some very grave news. I have been at the Horse Guards this morning, and there's no doubt that our regiment will be ordered abroad, and on its way to Belgium before the week is over. And you know, sir, that we shan't be home again before a tussle which may be fatal to many of us."

Osborne looked grave. "My s——, the regiment will do its duty, sir, I daresay," he said.

"The French are very strong, sir," Dobbin went on. "The Russians and Austrians will be a long time before they can bring their troops down. We shall have the first of the fight, sir; and depend on it Boney will take care that it shall be a hard one."

"What are you driving at, Dobbin?" his interlocutor said, uneasy and with a scowl. "I suppose no Briton's afraid of any d—— Frenchman, hay?"

"I only mean, that before we go, and considering the great and certain risk that hangs over every one of us—if there are any differences between you and George—it would be as well, sir, that—that you should shake hands: wouldn't it? Should anything happen to him, I think you would never forgive yourself if you hadn't parted in charity."

As he said this, poor William Dobbin blushed crimson, and felt and owned that he himself was a traitor. But for him, perhaps, this severance need never have taken place. Why had not George's marriage been delayed? What call was there to press it on so eagerly? He felt that George would have parted from Amelia at any rate without a mortal pang. Amelia, too, *might* have recovered the shock of losing him. It was his counsel had brought about this marriage, and all that was to ensue from it. And why was it? Because he loved her so much that he could not bear to see her unhappy; or because his own sufferings of suspense were so unendurable that he was glad to crush them at once—as we hasten a funeral after a death, or, when a separation from those we love is imminent, cannot rest until the parting be over.

"You are a good fellow, William," said Mr. Osborne in a softened voice; "and me and George shouldn't part in anger, that is true. Look here. I've done for him as much as any father ever did. He's had three times as much money from me, as I warrant your father ever gave you. But I don't brag about that. How I've toiled for him, and worked and employed my talents and energy, *I* won't say. Ask Chopper. Ask himself. Ask the City of London. Well, I proposed to him such a marriage as any nobleman in the land might be proud of—the only thing in life I ever asked him—and he refuses me. Am *I* wrong? Is the quarrel *my* making? What do I seek but his good, for which I've been toiling like a convict ever since he was born? Nobody can say there's anything selfish in *me*. Let him come back. I say, here's my hand. I say, forget and forgive. As for marrying now, it's out of the question. Let him and Miss S. make it up, and make out the marriage afterwards, when he comes back a Colonel; for he shall be a Colonel, by G—— he shall, if money can do it. I'm glad you've brought him round. I know it's you Dobbin. You've took him out of many a scrape before.

Let his come. *I* shan't be hard. Come along, and dine in Russell Square to-day: both of you. The old shop, the old hour. You'll find a neck of venison, and no questions asked."

This praise and confidence smote Dobbin's heart very keenly. Every moment the colloquy continued in this tone, he felt more and more guilty. "Sir," said he, "I fear you deceive yourself. I am sure you do. George is much too high-minded a man ever to marry for money. A threat on your part that you would disinherit him in case of disobedience would only be followed by resistance on his."

"Why, hang it, man, you don't call offering him eight or ten thousand a year threatening him?" Mr. Osborne said, with still provoking good humour. "Gad, if Miss S. will have me, I'm her man. *I* ain't particular about a shade or so of tawny." And the old gentleman gave his knowing grin and coarse laugh.

"You forget, sir, previous engagements into which Captain Osborne had entered," the ambassador said, gravely.

"What engagements? What the devil do you mean? You don't mean," Mr. Osborne continued, gathering wrath and astonishment as the thought now first came upon him; "you don't mean that he's such a d—— fool as to be still hankering after that swindling old bankrupt's daughter? You've not come here for to make me suppose that he wants to marry *her?* Marry *her,* that *is* a good one. My son and heir marry a beggar's girl out of a gutter. D—— him. if he does, let him buy a broom and sweep a crossing. She was always dangling and ogling after him, 1 recollect now; and I've no doubt she was put on by her old sharper of a father."

"Mr. Sedley was your very good friend, sir," Dobbin interposed, almost pleased at finding himself growing angry. "Time was you called him better names than rogue and swindler. The match was of your making. George had no right to play fast and loose——"

"Fast and loose!" howled out old Osborne. "Fast and loose! Why, hang me, those are the very words my gentleman used himself when he gave himself airs, last Thursday was. a fortnight, and talked about the British army to

his father who made him. What, it's you who have been
a setting of him up—is it? and my service to you, *Captain.*
It's you who want to introduce beggars into my family.
Thank you for nothing, Captain. Marry *her* indeed—he,
he! why should he? I warrant you she'd go to him fast
enough without."

"Sir," said Dobbin, starting up in undisguised anger;
"no man shall abuse that lady in my hearing, and you
least of all."

"O, your're a going to call me out, are you? Stop, let
me ring the bell for pistols for two. Mr. George sent you
here to insult his father, did he?" Osborne said, pulling at
the bell-cord.

"Mr. Osborne," said Dobbin, with a faltering voice, "it's
you who are insulting the best creature in the world. You
had best spare her, sir, for she's your son's wife."

And with this, feeling that he could say no more Dobbin went away, Osborne sinking back in his chair, and
looking wildly after him. A clerk came in, obedient to
the bell; and the Captain was scarcely out of the court
where Mr. Osborne's offices were, when Mr. Chopper the
chief clerk came rushing hatless after him.

"For God's sake, what is it?" Mr. Chopper said, catching the Captain by the skirt. "The governor's in a fit.
What has Mr. George been doing?"

"He married Miss Sedley five days ago," Dobbin replied.
"I was his groomsman, Mr. Chopper, and you must stand
his friend."

The old clerk shook his head. "If that's your news, Captain, it's bad. The governor will never forgive him."

Dobbin begged Chopper to report progress to him at the
hotel where he was stopping, and walked off moodily west-
wards, greatly perturbed as to the past and the future.

When the Russell Square family came to dinner that
evening, they found the father of the house seated in his
usual place, but with that air of gloom on his face, which,
whenever it appeared there, kept the whole circle silent.
The ladies, and Mr. Bullock who dined with them, felt
that the news had been communicated to Mr. Osborne.
His dark looks affected Mr. Bullock so far as to render him

still and quiet: but he was usually bland and attentive to Miss Maria, by whom he sat, and to her sister presiding at the head of the table.

Miss Wirt, by consequence, was alone on her side of the board, a gap being left between her and Miss Jane Osborne. Now this was George's place when he dined at home; and his cover, as we said, was laid for him in expectation of that truant's return. Nothing occurred during dinner-time except smiling Mr. Frederick's flagging confidential whispers, and the clinking of plate and china, to interrupt the silence of the repast. The servants went about stealthily doing their duty. Mutes at funerals could not look more glum than the domestics of Mr. Osborne. The neck of venison of which he had invited Dobbin to partake, was carved by him in perfect silence; but his own share went away almost untasted, though he drank much, and the butler assiduously, filled his glass.

At last, just at the end of the dinner, his eyes, which had been staring at everybody in turn, fixed themselves for a while upon the plate laid for George. He pointed to it presently with his left hand. His daughters looked at him and did not comprehend, or choose to comprehend, the signal; nor did the servants at first understand it.

"Take that plate away," at last he said, getting up with an oath—and with this pushing his chair back, he walked into his own room.

Behind Mr. Osborne's dining-room was the usual apartment which went in his house by the name of the study; and was sacred to the master of the house. Hither Mr. Osborne would retire of a Sunday forenoon when not minded to go to church; and here pass the morning in his crimson leather chair, reading the paper. A couple of glazed bookcases were here, containing standard works in stout gilt bindings. The "Annual Register," the "Gentleman's Magazine," "Blair's Sermons," and "Hume and Smollett." From year's end to year's end he never took one of these volumes from the shelf; but there was no member of the family that would dare for his life to touch one of the books, except upon those rare Sunday evenings when there was no dinner-party, and when the great scarlet Bible and

Prayer-book were taken out from the corner where they stood beside his copy of the Peerage, and the servants being rung up to the dining parlour, Osborne read the evening service to his family in a loud grating pompous voice. No member of the household, child, or domestic, ever entered that room without a certain terror. Here he checked the housekeeper's accounts, and overhauled the butler's cellar-book. Hence he could command, across the clean gravel court-yard, the back entrance of the stables with which one of his bells communicated, and into this yard the coachman issued from his premises as into a dock, and Osborne swore at him from the study window. Four times a year Miss Wirt entered this apartment to get her salary; and his daughters to receive their quarterly allowance. George as a boy had been horse-whipped in this room many times; his mother sitting sick on the stair listening to the cuts of the whip. The boy was scarcely ever known to cry under the punishment; the poor woman used to fondle and kiss him secretly, and give him money to soothe him when he came out.

There was a picture of the family over the mantel-piece, removed thither from the front room after Mrs. Osborne's death—George was on a pony, the elder sister holding him up a bunch of flowers; the younger led by her mother's hand; all with red cheeks and large red mouths, simpering on each other in the approved family-portrait manner. The mother lay underground now, long since forgotten—the sisters and brother had a hundred different interests of their own, and, familiar still, were utterly estranged from each other. Some few score of years afterwards, when all the parties represented are grown old, what bitter satire there is in those flaunting childish family-portraits, with their farce of sentiment and smiling lies, and innocence so self-conscious and self-satisfied. Osborne's own state portrait, with that of his great silver inkstand and arm-chair, had taken the place of honour in the dining-room, vacated by the family-piece.

To this study old Osborne retired then, greatly to the relief of the small party whom he left. When the servants had withdrawn, they began to talk for a while volubly but very low; then they went upstairs quietly, Mr. Bullock accompanying them stealthily on his creaking shoes. He had no heart to sit alone drinking wine, and so close to the terrible old gentleman in the study hard at hand.

An hour at least after dark, the butler, not having received any summons, ventured to tap at his door and take him in wax candles and tea. The master of the house sate in his chair, pretending to read the paper, and when the servant, placing the lights and refreshment on the table by him, retired, Mr. Osborne got up and locked the door after him. This time there was no mistaking the matter; all the household knew that some great catastrophe was going to happen which was likely direly to affect Master George.

In the large shining mahogany escritoire Mr. Osborne had a drawer especially devoted to his son's affairs and papers. Here he kept all the documents relating to him ever since he had been a boy: here were his prize copy-books and drawing-books, all bearing George's hand, and that of the master: here were his first letters in large round-hand sending his love to papa and mamma, and conveying his petitions for a cake. His dear godpapa Sedley was more than once mentioned in them. Curses quivered on old Osborne's livid lips, and horrid hatred and disappointment writhed in his heart, as looking through some of these papers he came on that name. They were all marked and docketed, and tied with red tape. It was—"From Georgy, requesting 5s., April 23, 18—; answered, April 25,"—or "Georgy about a pony, October 13,"—and so forth. In another packet were "Dr. S.'s accounts"—"G.'s tailor's bills and outfits, drafts on me by G. Osborne, jun." &c., —his letters from the West Indies—his agent's letters, and the newspapers containing his commissions: here was a whip he had when a boy, and in a paper a locket containing his hair, which his mother used to wear.

Turning one over after another, and musing over these memorials, the unhappy man passed many hours. His dearest vanities, ambitious hopes, had all been here. What pride he had in his boy! He was the handsomest child ever seen. Everybody said he was like a nobleman's son.

A royal princess had remarked him, and kissed him, and asked his name in Kew Gardens. What City man could show such another? Could a prince have been better cared for? Anything that money could buy had been his son's. He used to go down on speech-days with four horses and new liveries, and scatter new shillings among the boys at the school where George was: when he went with George to the depôt of his regiment, before the boy embarked for Canada, he gave the officers such a dinner as the Duke of York might have sat down to. Had he ever refused a bill when George drew one? There they were—paid without a word. Many a general in the army couldn't ride the horses he had! He had the child before his eyes, on a hundred different days when he remembered George—after dinner, when he used to come in as bold as a lord and drink off his glass by his father's side, at the head of the table—on the pony at Brighton, when he cleared the hedge and kept up with the huntsman—on the day when he was presented to the Prince Regent at the levee, when all Saint James's couldn't produce a finer young fellow. And this, this was the end of all!—to marry a bankrupt and fly in the face of duty and fortune! What humiliation and fury: what pangs of sickening rage, balked ambition and love; what wounds of outraged vanity, tenderness even, had this old worldling now to suffer under!

Having examined these papers, and pondered over this one and the other, in that bitterest of all helpless woe, with which miserable men think of happy past times— George's father took the whole of the documents out of the drawer in which he had kept them so long, and locked them into a writing-box, which he tied, and sealed with his seal. Then he opened the book-case, and took down the great red Bible we have spoken of—a pompous book, seldom looked at, and shining all over with gold. There was a frontispiece to the volume, representing Abraham sacrificing Isaac. Here, according to custom, Osborne had recorded on the fly-leaf and in his large clerk-like hand, the dates of his marriage and his wife's death, and the births and Christian names of his children. Jane came first, then George Sedley Osborne, then Maria Frances,

and the days of the christening of each. Taking a pen,
he carefully obliterated George's names from the page; and
when the leaf was quite dry, restored the volume to the
place from which he had moved it. Then he took a document out of another drawer, where his own private papers
were kept; and having read it, crumpled it up and lighted
it at one of the candles, and saw it burn entirely away in
the grate. It was his will; which being burned, he sate
down and wrote off a letter, and rang for his servant, whom
he charged to deliver it in the morning. It was morning
already: as he went up to bed, the whole house was alight
with the sunshine; and the birds were singing among the
fresh green leaves in Russell Square.

Anxious to keep all Mr. Osborne's family and dependants in good humour, and to make as many friends as possible for George in his hour of adversity, William Dobbin,
who knew the effect which good dinners and good wines
have upon the soul of man, wrote off immediately on his
return to his inn the most hospitable of invitations to
Thomas Chopper, Esquire, begging that gentleman to dine
with him at the Slaughters' next day. The note reached
Mr. Chopper before he left the City, and the instant reply
was, that "Mr. Chopper presents his respectful compliments, and will have the honour and pleasure of waiting on
Captain D." The invitation and the rough draft of the
answer were shown to Mrs. Chopper and her daughters on
his return to Somers' Town that evening, and they talked
about military gents and West End men with great exultation as the family sate and partook of tea. When the girls
had gone to rest, Mr. and Mrs. C. discoursed upon the
strange events which were occurring in the governor's
family. Never had the clerk seen his principal so moved.
When he went in to Mr. Osborne, after Captain Dobbin's
departure, Mr. Chopper found his chief black in the face,
and all but in a fit: some dreadful quarrel, he was certain,
had occurred between Mr. O. and the young Captain.
Chopper had been instructed to make out an account of all
sums paid to Captain Osborne within the last three years.
"And a precious lot of money he has had too," the chief
clerk said, and respected his old and young master the

more, for the liberal way in which the guineas had been
flung about. The dispute was something about Miss Sedley. Mrs. Chopper vowed and declared she pitied that
poor young lady to lose such a handsome young fellow as
the Capting. As the daughter of an unlucky speculator,
who had paid a very shabby dividend, Mr. Chopper had
no great regard for Miss Sedley. He respected the house
of Osborne before all others in the City of London: and
his hope and wish was that Captain George should marry a
nobleman's daughter. The clerk slept a great deal sounder
than his principal that night; and, cuddling his children
after breakfast (of which he partook with a very hearty
appetite, though his modest cup of life was only sweet-
ened with brown sugar), he set off in his best Sunday
suit and frilled shirt for business, promising his admiring
wife not to punish Captain D.'s port too severely that
evening.

Mr. Osborne's countenance, when he arrived in the City
at his usual time, struck those dependents who were accustomed, for good reasons, to watch its expression, as peculiarly ghastly and worn. At twelve o'clock Mr. Higgs
(of the firm of Higgs & Blatherwick, solicitors, Bedford
Row,) called by appointment, and was ushered into the
governor's private room, and closeted there for more than
an hour. At about one Mr. Chopper received a note brought
by Captain Dobbin's man, and containing an inclosure
for Mr. Osborne, which the clerk went in and delivered.
A short time afterwards Mr. Chopper and Mr. Birch,
the next clerk, were summoned, and requested to witness
a paper. "I've been making a new will," Mr. Osborne
said, to which these gentlemen appended their names accordingly. No conversation passed. Mr. Higgs looked
exceedingly grave as he came into the outer rooms, and
very hard in Mr. Chopper's face; but there were not any
explanations. It was remarked that Mr. Osborne was particularly quiet and gentle all day, to the surprise of those
who had augured ill from his darkling demeanour. He
called no man names that day, and was not heard to swear
once. He left business early; and before going away,
summoned his chief clerk once more, and having given him

general instructions, asked him, after some seeming hesitation and reluctance to speak, if he knew whether Captain Dobbin was in town?

Chopper said he believed he was. Indeed both of them knew the fact perfectly.

Osborne took a letter directed to that officer, and giving it to the clerk, requested the latter to deliver it into Dobbin's own hands immediately.

"And now, Chopper," says he, taking his hat, and with a strange look, "my mind will be easy." Exactly as the clock struck two (there was no doubt an appointment between the pair,) Mr. Frederick Bullock called, and he and Mr. Osborne walked away together.

The Colonel of the —th regiment, in which Messieurs Dobbin and Osborne had companies, was an old General who had made his first campaign under Wolfe at Quebec, and was long since quite too old and feeble for command; but he took some interest in the regiment of which he was the nominal head, and made certain of his young officers welcome at his table, a kind of hospitality which I believe is not now common amongst his brethren. Captain Dobbin was an especial favourite of this old General. Dobbin was versed in the literature of his profession, and could talk about the great Frederick, and the Empress Queen, and their wars, almost as well as the General himself, who was indifferent to the triumphs of the present day, and whose heart was with the tacticians of fifty years back. This officer sent a summons to Dobbin to come and breakfast with him, on the morning when Mr. Osborne altered his will and Mr. Chopper put on his best shirt frill, and then informed his young favourite, a couple of days in advance, of that which they were all expecting—a marching order to go to Belgium. The order for the regiment to hold itself in readiness would leave the Horse Guards in a day or two; and as transports were in plenty, they would get their route before the week was over. Recruits had come in during the stay of the regiment at Chatham; and the old General hoped that the regiment which had helped to beat Montcalm in Canada, and to rout Mr. Washington on Long Island, would prove itself worthy of its historical reputa-

tion on the oft-trodden battle-grounds of the Low Countries. "And so, my good friend, if you have any *affaire
là,*" said the old General, taking a pinch of snuff with his
trembling white old hand, and then pointing to the spot of
his *robe de chambre* under which his heart was still feebly
beating, "if you have any Phillis to console, or to bid farewell to papa and mamma, or any will to make, I recommend you to set about your business without delay." With
which the General gave his young friend a finger to shake,
and a good-natured nod of his powdered and pig-tailed
head; and the door being closed upon Dobbin, sate down
to pen a *poulet* (he was exceedingly vain of his French)
to Mademoiselle Aménaide of His Majesty's Theatre.

This news made Dobbin grave, and he thought of our
friends at Brighton, and then he was ashamed of himself
that Amelia was always the first thing in his thoughts (always before anybody—before father and mother, sisters
and duty—always at waking and sleeping indeed, and all
day long); and returning to his hotel, he sent off a brief
note to Mr. Osborne acquainting him with the information
which he had received, and which might tend farther, he
hoped, to bring about a reconciliation with George.

This note, despatched by the same messenger who had
carried the invitation to Chopper on the previous day,
alarmed the worthy clerk not a little. It was inclosed to
him, and as he opened the letter he trembled lest the dinner should be put off on which he was calculating. His
mind was inexpressibly relieved when he found that the
envelope was only a reminder for himself. ("I shall expect you at half-past five," Captain Dobbin wrote.) He
was very much interested about his employer's family; but,
que voulez-vous? a grand dinner was of more concern to
him than the affairs of any other mortal.

Dobbin was quite justified in repeating the General's
information to any officers of the regiment whom he should
see in the course of his peregrinations; accordingly he imparted it to Ensign Stubble, whom he met at the agent's,
and who—such was his military ardour—went off instantly
to purchase a new sword at the accoutrement-maker's.
Here this young fellow, who, though only seventeen years

of age, and about sixty-five inches high, with a constitution naturally rickety and much impaired by premature brandy and water, had an undoubted courage and a lion's heart, poised, tried, bent, and balanced a weapon such as he thought would do execution amongst Frenchmen. Shouting "Ha, ha!" and stamping his little feet with tremendous energy, he delivered the point twice or thrice at Captain Dobbin, who parried the thrust laughingly with his bamboo walking-stick.

Mr. Stubble, as may be supposed from his size and slenderness, was of the Light Bobs. Ensign Spooney, on the contrary was a tall youth, and belonged to (Captain Dobbin's) the Grenadier Company, and he tried on a new bearskin cap, under which he looked savage beyond his years. Then these two lads went off to the Slaughters' and having ordered a famous dinner, sat down and wrote off letters to the kind anxious parents at home—letters full of love and heartiness, and pluck and bad spelling. Ah! there were many anxious hearts beating through England at that time; and mothers' prayers and tears flowing in many homesteads.

Seeing young Stubble engaged in composition at one of the coffee-room tables at the Slaughters', and the tears trickling down his nose on to the paper (for the youngster was thinking of his mamma, and that he might never see her again,) Dobbin, who was going to write off a letter to George Osborne, relented, and locked up his desk. "Why should I?" said he. "Let her have this night happy. I'll go and see my parents early in the morning, and go down to Brighton myself to-morrow."

So he went up and laid his big hand on young Stubble's shoulder, and backed up that young champion, and told him if he would leave off brandy and water he would be a good soldier, as he always was a gentlemanly good-hearted fellow. Young Stubble's eyes brightened up at this, for Dobbin was greatly respected in the regiment, as the best officer and the cleverest man in it.

"Thank you, Dobbin," he said, rubbing his eyes with his knuckles, "I was just—just telling her I would. And, O Sir, she's so *dam* kind to me." The water pumps were at work again, and I am not sure that the soft-hearted Captain's eyes did not also twinkle.

The two ensigns, the Captain, and Mr. Chopper, dined together in the same box. Chopper brought the letter from Mr. Osborne, in which the latter briefly presented his compliments to Captain Dobbin, and requested him to forward the inclosed to Captain George Osborne. Chopper knew nothing further; he described Mr. Osborne's appearance, it is true, and his interview with his lawyer, wondered how the governor had sworn at nobody, and—especially as the wine circled round—abounded in speculations and conjectures. But these grew more vague with every glass, and at length became perfectly unintelligible. At a late hour Captain Dobbin put his guest into a hackney coach, in a hiccupping state, and swearing that he would be the kick—the kick—Captain's friend for ever and ever.

When Captain Dobbin took leave of Miss Osborne we have said that he asked leave to come and pay her another visit, and the spinster expected him for some hours the next day, when, perhaps, had he come, and had he asked her that question which she was prepared to answer, she would have declared herself as her brother's friend, and a reconciliation might have been effected between George and his angry father. But though she waited at home the Captain never came. He had his own affairs to pursue; his own parents to visit and console; and at an early hour of the day to take his place on the Lightning coach, and go down to his friends at Brighton. In the course of the day Miss Osborne heard her father give orders that that meddling scoundrel, Captain Dobbin, should never be admitted within his doors again, and any hopes in which she may have indulged privately were thus abruptly brought to an end. Mr. Frederick Bullock came, and was particularly affectionate to Maria, and attentive to the broken-spirited old gentleman. For though he said his mind would be easy, the means which he had taken to secure quiet did not seem to have succeeded as yet, and the events of the past two days had visibly shattered him.

CHAPTER XXV

IN WHICH ALL THE PRINCIPAL PERSONAGES THINK FIT TO LEAVE BRIGHTON

CONDUCTED to the ladies, at the Ship Inn, Dobbin assumed a jovial and rattling manner, which proved that this young officer was becoming a more consummate hypocrite every day of his life. He was trying to hide his own private feelings, first upon seeing Mrs. George Osborne in her new condition, and secondly to mask the apprehensions he entertained as to the effect which the dismal news brought down by him would certainly have upon her.

"It is my opinion, George," he said, "that the French Emperor will be upon us, horse and foot, before three weeks are over, and will give the Duke such a dance as shall make the Peninsula appear mere child's play. But you need not say that to Mrs. Osborne, you know. There mayn't be any fighting on our side after all, and our business in Belgium may turn out to be a mere military occupation. Many persons think so; and Brussels is full of fine people and ladies of fashion." So it was agreed to represent the duty of the British army in Belgium in this harmless light to Amelia.

This plot being arranged, the hypocritical Dobbin saluted Mrs. George Osborne quite gaily, tried to pay her one or two compliments relative to her new position as a bride (which compliments, it must be confessed, were exceedingly clumsy and hung fire woefully), and then fell to talking about Brighton, and the sea-air, and the gaieties of the place, and the beauties of the road and the merits of the Lightning coach and horses,—all in a manner quite incomprehensible to Amelia, and very amusing to Rebecca, who was watching the Captain, as indeed she watched every one near whom she came.

Little Amelia, it must be owned, had rather a mean opinion of her husband's friend, Captain Dobbin. He lisped—he was very plain and homely-looking: and exceedingly awkward and ungainly. She liked him for his attachment to her husband (to be sure there was very little merit in that), and she thought George was most generous and kind in extending his friendship to his brother officer.

George had mimicked Dobbin's lisp and queer manners many times to her, though to do him justice, he always spoke most highly of his friend's good qualities. In her little day of triumph, and not knowing him intimately as yet, she made light of honest William—and he knew her opinions of him quite well, and acquiesced in them very humbly. A time came when she knew him better, and changed her notions regarding him; but that was distant as yet.

As for Rebecca, Captain Dobbin had not been two hours in the ladies' company before she understood his secret perfectly. She did not like him, and feared him privately; nor was he very much prepossessed in her favour. He was so honest, that her arts and cajoleries did not affect him, and he shrank from her with instinctive repulsion. And, as she was by no means so far superior to her sex as to be above jealousy, she disliked him the more for his adoration of Amelia. Nevertheless, she was very respectful and cordial in her manner towards him. A friend to the Osbornes! a friend to her dearest benefactors! She vowed she should always love him sincerely: she remembered him quite well on the Vauxhall night, as she told Amelia archly, and she made a little fun of him when the two ladies went to dress for dinner. Rawdon Crawley paid scarcely any attention to Dobbin, looking upon him as a good-natured nincompoop, an underbred City man. Jos patronised him with much dignity.

When George and Dobbin were alone in the latter's room, to which George had followed him, Dobbin took from his desk the letter which he had been charged by Mr. Osborne to deliver to his son. "It's not in my father's hand-writing," said George, looking rather alarmed; nor was it: the letter was from Mr. Osborne's lawyer, and to the following effect:—

BEDFORD ROW, *May 7*, 1815.
"SIR,

"I am commissioned by Mr. Osborne to inform you, that he abides by the determination which he before expressed to you, and that in consequence of the marriage which you have been pleased to contract, he ceases to consider you henceforth as a member of his family. This determination is final and irrevocable.

"Although the monies expended upon you in your minority, and the bills which you have drawn upon him so unsparingly of late years, far exceed in amount the sum to which you are entitled in your own right (being the third part of the fortune of your mother, the late Mrs. Osborne and which reverted to you at her decease, and to Miss Jane Osborne and Miss Maria Frances Osborne); yet I am instructed by Mr. Osborne to say, that he waives all claim upon your estate, and that the sum of 2,000*l*. 4 per cent. annuities, at the value of the day (being your one-third share of the sum of 6,000*l*.), shall be paid over to yourself or your agents upon your receipt for the same, by

"Your obedient Servt.,
"S. HIGGS.

"P. S.—Mr. Osborne desires me to say, once for all, that he declines to receive any messages, letters, or communications from you on this or any other subject."

"A pretty way you have managed the affair," said George, looking savagely at William Dobbin. "Look there, Dobbin," and he flung over to the latter his parent's letter. "A beggar, by Jove, and all in consequence of my d—d sentimentality. Why couldn't we have waited? A ball might have done for me in the course of the war, and may still, and how will Emmy be bettered by being left a beggar's widow? It was all your doing. You were never easy until you had got me married and ruined. What the deuce am I to do with two thousand pounds? Such a sum won't last two years. I've lost a hundred and forty to Crawley at cards and billiards since I've been down here. A pretty manager of a man's matters *you* are, forsooth."

"There's no denying that the position is a hard one," Dobbin replied, after reading over the letter with a blank countenance; "and as you say, it is partly of my making. There are some men who wouldn't mind changing with you," he added, with a bitter smile. "How many captains in the regiment have two thousand pounds to the fore, think you? You must live on your pay till your father relents, and if you die, you leave your wife a hundred a year."

"Do you suppose a man of my habits can live on his pay and a hundred a year?" George cried out in great anger. "You must be a fool to talk so, Dobbin. How the deuce am I to keep up my position in the world upon such a pitiful pittance? I can't change my habits. I *must* have my comforts. *I* wasn't brought up on porridge, like Mac-Whirter, or on potatoes, like old O'Dowd. Do you expect my wife to take in soldiers' washing, or ride after the regiment in a baggage waggon?"

"Well, well," said Dobbin, still good-naturedly, "we'll get her a better conveyance. But try and remember that you are only a dethroned prince now, George, my boy; and be quiet whilst the tempest lasts. It won't be for long. Let your name be mentioned in the *Gazette,* and I'll engage the old father relents towards you."

"Mentioned in the *Gazette!*" George answered. "And in what part of it? Among the killed and wounded returns, and at the top of the list, very likely."

"Psha! It will be time enough to cry out when we are hurt," Dobbin said. "And if anything happens, you know, George, I have got a little, and I am not a marrying man, and I shall not forget my godson in my will," he added, with a smile. Whereupon the dispute ended—as many scores of such conversations between Osborne and his friend had concluded previously—by the former declaring there was no possibility of being angry with Dobbin long, and forgiving him very generously after abusing him without cause.

"I say, Becky," cried Rawdon Crawley out of his dressing-room, to his lady, who was attiring herself for dinner in her own chamber.

"What?" said Becky's shrill voice. She was looking over her shoulder in the glass. She had put on the neatest and freshest white frock imaginable, and with bare shoulders and a little necklace, and a light blue sash, she looked the image of youthful innocence and girlish happiness.

"I say, what'll Mrs. O. do, when O. goes out with the regiment?" Crawley said coming into the room, performing a duet on his head with two huge hair-brushes, and looking out from under his hair with admiration on his pretty little wife.

"I suppose she'll cry her eyes out," Becky answered. "She has been whimpering half-a-dozen times, at the very notion of it, already to me."

"*You* don't care, I suppose?" Rawdon said, half angry at his wife's want of feeling.

"You wretch! don't you know that I intend to go with you," Becky replied. "Besides, you're different. You go as General Tufto's aide-de-camp. *We* don't belong to the line," Mrs. Crawley said, throwing up her head with an air that so enchanted her husband that he stooped down and kissed it.

"Rawdon dear—don't you think—you'd better get that —money from Cupid, before he goes?" Becky continued, fixing on a killing bow. She called George Osborne, Cupid. She had flattered him about his good looks a score of times already. She watched over him kindly at écarté of a night when he would drop in to Rawdon's quarters for a half hour before bed-time.

She had often called him a horrid dissipated wretch, and threatened to tell Emmy of his wicked ways and naughty extravagant habits. She brought his cigar and lighted it for him; she knew the effect of that manœuvre, having practised it in former days upon Rawdon Crawley. He thought her gay, brisk, arch, destinguée, delightful. In their little drives and dinners, Becky, of course, quite outshone poor Emmy, who remained very mute and timid while Mrs. Crawley and her husband rattled away together, and Captain Crawley (and Jos after he joined the young married people) gobbled in silence.

Emmy's mind somehow misgave her about her friend. Rebecca's wit, spirits, and accomplishments troubled her with a rueful disquiet. They were only a week married, and here was George already suffering ennui, and eager for others' society! She trembled for the future. How shall I be a companion for him, she thought,—so clever and so

brilliant, and I such a humble foolish creature? How
noble it was of him to marry me—to give up everything
and stoop down to me! I ought to have refused him, only
I had not the heart. I ought to have stopped at home and
taken care of poor papa. And her neglect of her parents
(and indeed there was some foundation for this charge
which the poor child's uneasy conscience brought against
her) was now remembered for the first time, and caused
her to blush with humiliation. Oh! thought she, I have
been very wicked and selfish—selfish in forgetting them in
their sorrows—selfish in forcing George to marry me. I
know I'm not worthy of him—I know he would have been
happy without me—and yet—I tried, I tried to give him up.

It is hard when before seven days of marriage are over,
such thoughts and confessions as these force themselves on
a little bride's mind. But so it was, and the night before
Dobbin came to join these young people—on a fine brilliant
moonlight night of May—so warm and balmy that the
windows were flung open to the balcony, from which George
and Mrs. Crawley were gazing upon the calm ocean spread
shining before them, while Rawdon and Jos were engaged
at backgammon within—Amelia couched in a great chair
quite neglected, and watching both these parties, felt a despair and remorse such as were bitter companions for that
tender lonely soul. Scarce a week was past, and it was
come to this! The future, had she regarded it, offered a
dismal prospect; but Emmy was too shy, so to speak, to
look to that, and embark alone on that wide sea, and unfit
to navigate it without a guide and protector. I know Miss
Smith has a mean opinion of her. But how many, my
dear Madam, are endowed with your prodigious strength of
mind?

"Gad, what a fine night, and how bright the moon is!"
George said, with a puff of his cigar, which went soaring
up skywards.

"How delicious they smell in the open air! I adore
them. Who'd think the moon was two hundred and thirty-
six thousand eight hundred and forty-seven miles off?"
Becky added, gazing at that orb with a smile. "Isn't it
clever of me to remember that? Pooh! we learned it all

at Miss Pinkerton's! How calm the sea is, and how clear everything. I declare I can almost see the coast of France!" and her bright green eyes streamed out, and shot into the night as if they *could* see through it.

"Do you know what I intend to do one morning?" she said; "I find I can swim beautifully, and some day, when my Aunt Crawley's companion—old Briggs, you know— you remember her—that hook-nosed woman, with the long wisps of hair—when Briggs goes out to bathe, I intend to dive under her awning, and insist on a reconciliation in the water. Isn't that a stratagem?"

George burst out laughing at the idea of this aquatic meeting. "What's the row there, you two?" Rawdon shouted out, rattling the box. Amelia was making a fool of herself in an absurd hysterical manner, and retired to her own room to whimper in private.

Our history is destined in this chapter to go backwards and forwards in a very irresolute manner seemingly, and having conducted our story to to-morrow presently, we shall immediately again have occasion to step back to yesterday, so that the whole of the tale may get a hearing. As you behold at her Majesty's drawing-room, the ambassadors' and high dignitaries' carriages whisk off from a private door, while Captain Jones's ladies are waiting for their fly: as you see in the Secretary of the Treasury's antechamber, a half-dozen of petitioners waiting patiently for their audience, and called out one by one, when suddenly an Irish member or some eminent personage enters the apartment, and instantly walks in to Mr. Under-Secretary over the heads of all the people present: so in the conduct of a tale, the romancer is obliged to exercise this most partial sort of justice. Although all the little incidents must be heard, yet they must be put off when the great events make their appearance; and surely such a circumstance as that which brought Dobbin to Brighton, viz., the ordering out of the Guards and the line of Belgium, and the mustering of the allied armies in that country under the command of his Grace the Duke of Wellington —such a dignified circumstance as that, I say, was entitled to the *pas* over all minor occurrences wherof this history is composed mainly, and hence a little trifling disarrangement and disorder was excusable and becoming. We have only now advanced in time so far beyond Chapter XXII, as to have got our various characters up into their dressing-rooms before the dinner, which took place as usual on the day of Dobbin's arrival.

George was too humane or too much occupied with the tie of his neckcloth to convey at once all the news to Amelia which his comrade had brought with him from London. He came into her room, however, holding the attorney's letter in his hand, and with so solemn and important an air that his wife, always ingeniously on the watch for calamity, thought the worst was about to befall, and running up to her husband, besought her dearest George to tell her everything—he was ordered abroad; there would be a battle next week—she knew there would.

Dearest George parried the question about foreign service, and with a melancholy shake of the head said, "No, Emmy; it isn't that: it's not myself I care about: it's you. I have had bad news from my father. He refuses any communication with me; he has flung us off; and leaves us to poverty. *I* can rough it well enough; but you, my dear, how will you bear it? read here." And he handed her over the letter.

Amelia, with a look of tender alarm in her eyes, listened to her noble hero as he uttered the above generous sentiments, and sitting down on the bed, read the letter which George gave her with such a pompous martyr-like air. Her face cleared up as she read the document, however. The idea of sharing poverty and privation in company with the beloved object is, as we have before said, far from being disagreeable to a warm-hearted woman. The notion was actually pleasant to little Amelia. Then, as usual, she was ashamed of herself for feeling happy at such an indecorous moment, and checked her pleasure, saying demurely, "O, George, how your poor heart must bleed at the idea of being separated from your papa!"

"It does," said George, with an agonised countenance.

"But he can't be angry with you long," she continued. "Nobody could, I'm sure. He must forgive you, my dearest, kindest husband. O, I shall never forgive myself if **he** does not."

"What vexes me, my poor Emmy, is not *my* misfortune, but yours," George said. "I don't care for a little poverty; and I think, without vanity, I've talents enough to make my own way."

"That you have," interposed his wife, who thought that war should cease, and her husband should be made a general instantly.

"Yes, I shall make my way as well as another," Osborne went on; "but you, my dear girl, how can I bear your being deprived of the comforts and station in society which my wife had a right to expect? My dearest girl in barracks; the wife of a soldier in a marching regiment; subject to all sorts of annoyance and privation! It makes me miserable."

Emmy, quite at ease, as this was her husband's only cause of disquiet, took his hand, and with a radiant face and smile began to warble that stanza from the favourite song of "Wapping Old Stairs," in which the heroine, after rebuking her Tom for inattention, promises "his trowsers to mend, and his grog too to make," if he will be constant and kind, and not forsake her. "Besides," she said, after a pause, during which she looked as pretty and happy as any young woman need, "isn't two thousand pounds an immense deal of money, George?"

George laughed at her naïveté; and finally they went down to dinner, Amelia clinging to George's arm, still warbling the tune of "Wapping Old Stairs," and more pleased and light of mind than she had been for some days past.

Thus the repast, which at length came off, instead of being dismal, was an exceedingly brisk and merry one. The excitement of the campaign counteracted in George's mind the depression occasioned by the disinheriting letter. Dobbin still kept up his character of rattle. He amused the company with accounts of the army in Belgium, where nothing but fêtes and gaiety and fashion were going on. Then, having a particular end in view, this dexterous captain proceeded to describe Mrs. Major O'Dowd packing her own and her Major's wardrobe, and how his best epaulets had been stowed into a tea canister, whilst her own famous yellow turban, with the bird of paradise wrapped in brown paper, was locked up in the Major's tin cocked-hat case, and wondered what effect it would have at the French king's court at Ghent, or the great military balls at Brussels.

"Ghent! Brussels!" cried out Amelia with a sudden shock and start. "Is the regiment ordered away, George,—is it ordered away?" A look of terror came over the sweet smiling face, and she clung to George as by an instinct.

"Don't be afraid, dear," he said good-naturedly; "it is but a twelve hours' passage. It won't hurt you. You shall go, too, Emmy."

"*I* intend to go," said Becky. "I'm on the staff. General Tufto is a great flirt of mine. Isn't he, Rawdon?"

Rawdon laughed out with his usual roar. William Dobbin flushed up quite red. "She can't go," he said; "think of the—of the danger," he was going to add; but had not all this conversation during dinner-time tended to prove there was none? He became very confused and silent.

"I must and will go," Amelia cried with the greatest spirit; and George, applauding her resolution, patted her under the chin, and asked all the persons present if they ever saw such a termagant of a wife, and agreed that the lady should bear him company. "We'll have Mrs. O'Dowd to chaperon you," he said. What cared she so long as her husband was near her? Thus somehow the bitterness of a parting was juggled away. Though war and danger were in store, war and danger might not befall for months to come. There was a respite at any rate, which made the timid little Amelia almost as happy as a full reprieve would have done, and which even Dobbin owned in his heart was very welcome. For, to be permitted to see her was now the greatest privilege and hope of his life, and he thought with himself secretly how he would watch and protect her. I wouldn't have let her go if I had been married to her, he thought. But George was the master, and his friend did not think fit to remonstrate.

Putting her arm round her friend's waist, Rebecca at length carried Amelia off from the dinner-table where so much business of importance had been discussed, and left the gentlemen in a highly exhilarated state, drinking and talking very gaily.

In the course of the evening Rawdon got a little family-note from his wife, which, although he crumpled it up and burnt it instantly in the candle, we had the good luck to read over Rebecca's shoulder. "Great news," she wrote. "Mrs. Bute is gone. Get the money from Cupid to-night, as he'll be off to-morrow most likely. Mind this.—R." So when the little company was about adjourning to coffee in the women's apartment, Rawdon touched Osborne on the elbow, and said gracefully, "I say, Osborne, my boy, if quite convenient, I'll trouble you for that 'ere small trifle." It was not quite convenient, but nevertheless George gave him a considerable present instalment in bank-notes from his pocket-book, and a bill on his agents at a week's date, for the remaining sum.

This matter arranged, George, and Jos, and Dobbin, held a council of war over their cigars, and agreed that a general move should be made for London in Jos's open carriage the next day. Jos, I think, would have preferred staying until Rawdon Crawley quitted Brighton, but Dobbin and George overruled him, and he agreed to carry the party to town, and ordered four horses, as became his dignity. With these they set off in state, after breakfast, the next day. Amelia had risen very early in the morning, and packed her little trunks with the greatest alacrity, while Osborne lay in bed deploring that she had not a maid to help her. She was only too glad, however, to perform this office for herself. A dim uneasy sentiment about Rebecca filled her mind already; and although they kissed each other most tenderly at parting, yet we know what jealousy is; and Mrs. Amelia possessed that among other virtues of her sex.

Besides these characters who are coming and going away, we must remember that there were some other old friends of ours at Brighton; Miss Crawley, namely, and the suite in attendance upon her. Now, although Rebecca and her husband were but at a few stones' throw of the lodgings which the invalid Miss Crawley occupied, the old lady's door remained as pitilessly closed to them as it had been heretofore in London. As long as she remained by the side of her sister-in-law, Mrs. Bute Crawley took care that her beloved Matilda should not be agitated by a meeting with her nephew. When the spinster took her drive, the faithful Mrs. Bute sate beside her in the carriage. When Miss Crawley took the air in a chair, Mrs. Bute marched on one side of the vehicle, whilst honest Briggs occupied the other wing. And if they met Rawdon and his wife by chance—although the former constantly and obsequiously took off his hat, the Miss-Crawley party passed him by with such a frigid and killing indifference, that Rawdon began to despair.

"We might as well be in London as here," Captain Rawdon often said, with a downcast air.

"A comfortable inn in Brighton is better than a spunging-house in Chancery Lane," his wife answered, who was of a more cheerful temperament. "Think of those two aides-de-camp of Mr. Moses, the sheriff's officer, who watched our lodging for a week. Our friends here are very stupid, but Mr. Jos and Captain Cupid are better companions than Mr. Moses's men, Rawdon, my love."

"I wonder the writs haven't followed me down here," Rawdon continued, still desponding.

"When they do, we'll find means to give them the slip," said dauntless little Becky, and further pointed out to her husband the great comfort and advantage of meeting Jos and Osborne, whose acquaintance had brought to Rawdon Crawley a most timely little supply of ready money.

"It will hardly be enough to pay the inn bill," grumbled the Guardsman.

"Why need we pay it?" said the lady, who had an answer for everything.

Through Rawdon's valet, who still kept up a trifling acquaintance with the male inhabitants of Miss Crawley's servants' hall, and was instructed to treat the coachman to drink whenever they met, old Miss Crawley's movements were pretty well known by our young couple; and Rebecca luckily bethought herself of being unwell, and of calling in the same apothecary who was in attendance upon the spinster, so that their information was on the whole tolerably complete. Nor was Miss Briggs, although forced to adopt a hostile attitude, secretly inimical to Rawdon and his wife. She was naturally of a kindly and forgiving disposition. Now that the cause of jealousy was removed, her dislike for Rebecca disappeared also, and she remembered the latter's invariable good words and good humour. And, indeed, she and Mrs. Firkin, the lady's-maid, and the whole of Miss Crawley's household, groaned under the tyranny of the triumphant Mrs. Bute.

As often will be the case, that good but imperious woman pushed her advantages too far, and her successes quite unmercifully. She had in the course of a few weeks brought the invalid to such a state of helpless docility, that the poor soul yielded herself entirely to her sister's orders, and did not even dare to complain of her slavery to Briggs or Firkin. Mrs. Bute measured out the glasses of wine which Miss Crawley was daily allowed to take, with irresistible accuracy, greatly to the annoyance of Firkin and the butler, who found themselves deprived of control over even the sherry-bottle. She apportioned the sweet-breads, jellies, chickens; their quantity and order. Night and noon and morning she brought the abominable drinks ordained by the Doctor, and made her patient swallow them with so affecting an obedience, that Firkin said "my poor Missus du take her physic like a lamb." She prescribed the drive in the carriage or the ride in the chair, and, in a word, ground down the old lady in her convalescence in such a way as only belongs to your proper-managing, motherly moral woman. If ever the patient faintly resisted, and pleaded for a little bit more dinner or a little drop less medicine, the nurse threatened her with instantaneous death, when Miss Crawley instantly gave in. "She's no spirit left in her," Firkin remarked to Briggs; "she aint ave called me a fool these three weeks." Finally, Mrs. Bute had made up her mind to dismiss the aforesaid honest lady's-maid, Mr. Bowls the large confidential man, and Briggs herself, and to send for her daughters from the Rectory, previous to removing the dear invalid bodily to Queen's

Crawley, when an odious accident happened which called
her away from duties so pleasing. The Reverend Bute
Crawley, her husband, riding home one night, fell with his
horse and broke his collar-bone. Fever and inflammatory
symptoms set in, and Mrs. Bute was forced to leave Sussex
for Hampshire. As soon as ever Bute was restored, she
promised to return to her dearest friend, and departed,
leaving the strongest injunctions with the household regarding their behaviour to their mistress; and as soon as she
got into the Southampton coach, there was such a jubilee
and sense of relief in all Miss Crawley's house, as the company of persons assembled there had not experienced for
many a week before. That very day Miss Crawley left off
her afternoon dose of medicine: that afternoon Bowls
opened an independent bottle of sherry for himself and
Mrs. Firkin: that night Miss Crawley and Miss Briggs indulged in a game of piquet instead of one of Porteus's
sermons. It was as in the old nursery-story, when the stick
forgot to beat the dog, and the whole course of events un-
derwent a peaceful and happy revolution.

At a very early hour in the morning, twice or thrice a
week, Miss Briggs used to betake herself to a bathing-
machine, and disport in the water in a flannel gown and an
oilskin cap. Rebecca, as we have seen, was aware of this
circumstance, and though she did not attempt to storm
Briggs as she had threatened, and actually dive into that
lady's presence and surprise her under the sacredness of
the awning, Mrs. Rawdon determined to attack Briggs as
she came away from her bath, refreshed and invigorated
by her dip, and likely to be in good humour.

So getting up very early the next morning, Becky brought
the telescope in their sitting-room, which faced the sea, to
bear upon the bathing-machines on the beach; saw Briggs
arrive, enter her box, and put out to sea; and was on the
shore just as the nymph of whom she came in quest stepped
out of the little caravan on to the shingles.

It was a pretty picture: the beach; the bathing-women's
faces; the long line of rocks and buildings were blushing
and bright in the sunshine. Rebecca wore a kind, tender
smile on her face, and was holding out her pretty white

hand as Briggs emerged from the box. What could Briggs do but accept the salutation?

"Miss Sh—, Mrs. Crawley," she said.

Mrs. Crawley seized her hand, pressed it to her heart, and with a sudden impulse, flinging her arms round Briggs, kissed her affectionately. "Dear, dear friend!" she said, with a touch of such natural feeling, that Miss Briggs of course at once began to melt, and even the bathing-woman was mollified.

Rebecca found no difficulty in engaging Briggs in a long, intimate, and delightful conversation. Everything that had passed since the morning of Becky's sudden departure from Miss Crawley's house in Park Lane up to the present day, and Mrs. Bute's happy retreat, was discussed and described by Briggs. All Miss Crawley's symptoms, and the particulars of her illness and medical treatment, were narrated by the confidante with that fulness and accuracy which women delight in. About their complaints and their doctors do ladies ever tire of talking to each other? Briggs did not on this occasion; nor did Rebecca weary of listening. She was thankful, truly thankful, that the dear kind Briggs, that the faithful, the invaluable Firkin, had been permitted to remain with their benefactress through her illness. Heaven bless her! though she, Rebecca, had seemed to act undutifully towards Miss Crawley; yet was not her fault a natural and excusable one? Could she help giving her hand to the man who had won her heart? Briggs, the sentimental, could only turn up her eyes to heaven at this appeal, and heave a sympathetic sigh, and think that she, too, had given away her affections long years ago, and own that Rebecca was no very great criminal.

"Can I ever forget her who so befriended the friendless orphan? No, though she has cast me off," the latter said, "I shall never cease to love her, and I would devote my life to her service. As my own benefactress, as my beloved Rawdon's adored relative, I love and admire Miss Crawley, dear Miss Briggs, beyond any woman in the world, and next to her I love all those who are faithful to her. *I* would never have treated Miss Crawley's faithful friends as that odious designing Mrs. Bute has done. Rawdon, who was all heart," Rebecca continued, "although his outward manners might seem rough and careless, had said a hundred times, with tears in his eyes, that he blessed Heaven for sending his dearest Aunty two such admirable nurses as her attached Firkin and her admirable Miss Briggs. Should the machinations of the horrible Mrs. Bute end, as she too much feared they would, in banishing everybody that Miss Crawley loved from her side, and leaving that poor lady a victim to those harpies at the Rectory, Rebecca besought her (Miss Briggs) to remember that her own home, humble as it was, was always open to receive Briggs. Dear friend," she exclaimed, in a transport of enthusiasm, "*some* hearts can *never* forget benefits; *all* women are not Bute Crawleys! Though why should I complain of her," Rebecca added; "though I have been her tool and the victim to her arts, do I not owe my dearest Rawdon to her?" And Rebecca unfolded to Briggs all Mrs. Bute's conduct at Queen's Crawley, which, though unintelligible to her then, was clearly enough explained by the events now,—now that the attachment had sprung up which Mrs. Bute had encouraged by a thousand artifices,—now that two innocent people had fallen into the snares which she had laid for them, and loved and married and been ruined through her schemes.

It was all very true. Briggs saw the stratagems as clearly as possible. Mrs. Bute had made the match between Rawdon and Rebecca. Yet, though the latter was a perfectly innocent victim, Miss Briggs could not disguise from her friend her fear that Miss Crawley's affections were hopelessly estranged from Rebecca, and that the old lady would never forgive her nephew for making so imprudent a marriage.

On this point Rebecca had her own opinion, and still kept up a good heart. If Miss Crawley did not forgive them at present, she might at least relent on a future day. Even now, there was only that puling, sickly Pitt Crawley between Rawdon and a baronetcy; and should anything happen to the former, all would be well. At all events, to have Mrs. Bute's designs exposed, and herself well abused, was a satisfaction, and might be advantageous to Rawdon's interests; and Rebecca, after an hour's chat with her re-covered friend, left her with the most tender demonstra-tions of regard, and quite assured that the conversation they had had together would be reported to Miss Crawley before many hours were over.

This interview ended, it became full time for Rebecca to return to her inn, where all the party of the previous day were assembled at a farewell breakfast. Rebecca took such a tender leave of Amelia as became two women who loved each other as sisters; and having used her handkerchief plentifully, and hung on her friend's neck as if they were parting for ever, and waved the handkerchief (which was quite dry, by the way) out of window, as the carriage drove off, she came back to the breakfast table, and ate some prawns with a good deal of appetite, considering her emo-tion; and while she was munching these delicacies, ex-plained to Rawdon what had occurred in her morning walk between herself and Briggs. Her hopes were very high: she made her husband share them. She generally succeeded in making her husband share all her opinions, whether melancholy or cheerful.

"You will now, if you please, my dear, sit down at the writing-table and pen me a pretty little letter to Miss Crawley, in which you say that you are a good boy, and that sort of thing." So Rawdon sate down, and wrote off, "Brighton, Thursday," and "My dear Aunt," with great rapidity: but there the gallant officer's imagination failed him. He mumbled the end of his pen, and looked up in his wife's face. She could not help laughing at his rueful countenance, and marching up and down the room with her hands behind her, the little woman began to dictate a letter, which he took down.

"Before quitting the country and commencing a campaign, which very possibly may be fatal,"

"What?" said Rawdon, rather surprised, but took the humour of the phrase, and presently wrote it down with a grin.

"Which very possibly may be fatal, I have come hither—"

"Why not say come here, Becky? come here's grammar," the dragoon interposed.

"I have come hither," Rebecca insisted, with a stamp of her foot, "to say farewell to my dearest and earliest friend. I beseech you before I go, not perhaps to return, once more to let me press the hand from which I have received nothing but kindnesses all my life."

"Kindnesses all my life," echoed Rawdon, scratching down the words, and quite amazed at his own facility of composition.

"I ask nothing from you but that we should part not in anger. I have the pride of my family on some points, though not on all. I married a painter's daughter, and am not ashamed of the union."

"No, run me through the body if I am!" Rawdon ejaculated.

"You old booby," Rebecca said, pinching his ear and looking over to see that he made no mistakes in spelling— "beseech is not spelt with an *a*, and earliest is." So he altered these words, bowing to the superior knowledge of his little Missis.

"I thought that you were aware of the progress of my attachment," Rebecca continued: "I knew that Mrs. Bute Crawley confirmed and encouraged it. But I make no reproaches. I married a poor woman, and am content to abide by what I have done. Leave your property, dear Aunt, as you will. *I* shall never complain of the way in which you dispose of it. I would have you believe that I love you for yourself, and not for money's sake. I want to be reconciled to you ere I leave England. Let me, let me see you before I go. A few weeks or months hence it may be too late, and I cannot bear the notion of quitting the country without a kind word of farewell from you."

"She won't recognise my style in *that*," said Becky. "I have made the sentences short and brisk on purpose." And this authentic missive was despatched under cover to Miss Briggs.

Old Miss Crawley laughed when Briggs, with great mystery, handed her over this candid and simple statement. "We may read it now Mrs. Bute is away," she said. "Read it to me, Briggs."

When Briggs had read the epistle out, her patroness laughed more. "Don't you see, you goose," she said to Briggs, who professed to be much touched by the honest affection which pervaded the composition, "Don't you see that Rawdon never wrote a word of it. He never wrote to me without asking for money in his life, and all his letters are full of bad spelling, and dashes and bad grammar. It is that little serpent of a governess who rules him." They are all alike, Miss Crawley thought in her heart. They all want me dead, and are hankering for my money.

"I don't mind seeing Rawdon," she added, after a pause, and in a tone of perfect indifference. "I had just as soon shake hands with him as not. Provided there is no scene, why shouldn't we meet? I don't mind. But human patience has its limits; and mind, my dear, I respectfully decline to receive Mrs. Rawdon—I can't support *that* quite"—and Miss Briggs was fain to be content with this half-message of conciliation; and thought that the best method of bringing the old lady and her nephew together, was to warn Rawdon to be in waiting on the Cliff, when Miss Crawley went out for her air in her chair.

There they met. I don't know whether Miss Crawley had any private feeling of regard or emotion upon seeing her old favourite; but she held out a couple of fingers to him with as smiling and good-humoured an air, as if they had met only the day before. And as for Rawdon, he turned as red as scarlet, and wrung off Briggs's hand, so great was his rapture and his confusion at the meeting. Perhaps it was interest that moved him: or perhaps affection: perhaps he was touched by the change which the illness of the last weeks had wrought in his aunt.

"The old girl has always acted like a trump to me," he said to his wife, as he narrated the interview, "and I felt, you know, rather queer, and that sort of thing. I walked by the side of the what-dy'e-call-'em, you know, and to her own door, where Bowls came to help her in. And I wanted to go in very much, only—"

"*You didn't go in,* Rawdon!" screamed his wife.

"No, my dear; I'm hanged if I wasn't afraid when it came to the point."

"You fool! you ought to have gone in, and never come out again," Rebecca said.

"Don't call me names," said the big Guardsman, sulkily. "Perhaps I *was* a fool, Becky, but you shouldn't say so;" and he gave his wife a look, such as his countenance could wear when angered, and such as was not pleasant to face.

"Well, dearest, to-morrow you must be on the look-out, and go and see her, mind, whether she asks you or no," Rebecca said, trying to soothe her angry yoke-mate. On which he replied, that he would do exactly as he liked, and would just thank her to keep a civil tongue in her head—and the wounded husband went away, and passed the forenoon at the billiard-room, sulky, silent, and suspicious.

But before the night was over he was compelled to give in, and own, as usual, to his wife's superior prudence and foresight, by the most melancholy confirmation of the presentiments which she had regarding the consequences of the mistake which he had made. Miss Crawley *must* have had some emotion upon seeing him and shaking hands with him after so long a rupture. She mused upon the meeting a considerable time. "Rawdon is getting very fat and old, Briggs," she said to her companion. "His nose has become red, and he is exceedingly coarse in appearance. His marriage to that woman has hopelessly vulgarised him. Mrs. Bute always said they drank together; and I have no doubt they do. Yes: he smelt of gin abominably. I remarked it. Didn't you?"

In vain Briggs interposed that Mrs. Bute spoke ill of everybody: and, as far as a person in *her* humble position could judge, was an—

"An artful, designing woman? Yes, so she is, and she does speak ill of every one,—but I am certain that woman has made Rawdon drink. All those low people do—"

"He was very much affected at seeing you, ma'am," the companion said; "and I am sure, when you remember that he is going to the field of danger—"

"How much money has he promised you, Briggs?" the old spinster cried out, working herself into a nervous rage —"there now, of course you begin to cry. I hate scenes.

Why am I always to be worried? Go and cry up in your own room, and send Firkin to me,—no, stop, sit down and blow your nose, and leave off crying, and write a letter to Captain Crawley." Poor Briggs went and placed herself obediently at the writing-book. Its leaves were blotted all over with relics of the firm, strong, rapid writing of the spinster's late amanuensis, Mrs. Bute Crawley.

"Begin 'My dear sir,' or, 'Dear sir,' that will be better, and say you are desired by Miss Crawley—no, by Miss Crawley's medical man, by Mr. Creamer, to state, that my health is such that all strong emotions would be dangerous in my present delicate condition—and that I must decline any family discussions or interviews whatever. And thank him for coming to Brighton, and so forth, and beg him not to stay any longer on my account. And, Miss Briggs, you may add that I wish him a *bon voyage,* and that if he will take the trouble to call upon my lawyers in Gray's Inn Square, he will find there a communication for him. Yes, that will do; and that will make him leave Brighton." The benevolent Briggs penned this sentence with the utmost satisfaction.

"To seize upon me the very day after Mrs. Bute was gone," the old lady prattled on; "it was too indecent. Briggs, my dear, write to Mrs. Crawley, and say *she* needn't come back. No—she needn't—and she shan't—and I won't be a slave in my own house—and I won't be starved and choked with poison. They all want to kill me—all—all"—and with this the lonely old woman burst into a scream of hysterical tears.

The last scene of her dismal Vanity Fair comedy was fast approaching; the tawdry lamps were going out one by one; and the dark curtain was almost ready to descend.

That final paragraph, which referred Rawdon to Miss Crawley's solicitor in London, and which Briggs had written so good-naturedly, consoled the dragoon and his wife somewhat, after their first blank disappointment, on reading the spinster's refusal of a reconciliation. And it effected the purpose for which the old lady had caused it to be written, by making Rawdon very eager to get to London.

Out of Jos's losings and George Osborne's bank-notes, he paid his bill at the inn, the landlord whereof does not probably know to this day how doubtfully his account once stood. For, as a general sends his baggage to the rear before an action, Rebecca had wisely packed up all their chief valuables and sent them off under care of George's servant, who went in charge of the trunks on the coach back to London. Rawdon and his wife returned by the same conveyance next day.

"I should have liked to see the old girl before we went," Rawdon said. "She looks so cut up and altered that I'm sure she can't last long. I wonder what sort of a cheque I shall have at Waxy's. Two hundred—it can't be less than two hundred,—hey, Becky?"

In consequence of the repeated visits of the aides-de-camp of the Sheriff of Middlesex, Rawdon and his wife did not go back to their lodgings at Brompton, but put up at an inn. Early the next morning, Rebecca had an opportunity of seeing them as she skirted that suburb on her road to old Mrs. Sedley's house at Fulham, whither she went to look for her dear Amelia and her Brighton friends. They were all off to Chatham, thence to Harwich, to take shipping for Belgium with the regiment—kind old Mrs. Sedley very much depressed and tearful, solitary. Returning from this visit, Rebecca found her husband, who had been off to Gray's Inn, and learnt his fate. He came back furious.

"By Jove, Becky," says he, "she's only given me twenty pound!"

Though it told against themselves, the joke was too good, and Becky burst out laughing at Rawdon's discomfiture.

CHAPTER XXVI

BETWEEN LONDON AND CHATHAM

ON quitting Brighton, our friend George, as became a person of rank and fashion travelling in a barouche with four horses, drove in state to a fine hotel in Cavendish Square, where a suite of splendid rooms, and a table magnificently furnished with plate and surrounded by a half-dozen of black and silent waiters, was ready to receive the young gentleman and his bride. George did the honours of the place with a princely air to Jos and Dobbin; and Amelia, for the first time, and with exceeding shyness and timidity, presided at what George called her own table.

George pooh-poohed the wine and bullied the waiters royally, and Jos gobbled the turtle with immense satisfaction. Dobbin helped him to it; for the lady of the house, before whom the tureen was placed, was so ignorant of the contents, that she was going to help Mr. Sedley without bestowing upon him either calipash or calipee.

The splendour of the entertainment, and the apartments in which it was given, alarmed Mr. Dobbin, who remonstrated after dinner, when Jos was asleep in the great chair. But, in vain he cried out against the enormity of turtle and champagne that was fit for an archbishop. "I've always been accustomed to travel like a gentleman," George said, "and, damme, my wife shall travel like a lady. As long as there's a shot in the locker, *she* shall want for nothing," said the generous fellow, quite pleased with himself for his magnificence of spirit. Nor did Dobbin try and convince him that Amelia's happiness was not centred in turtle-soup.

A while after dinner, Amelia timidly expressed a wish to go and see her mamma, at Fulham: which permission George granted her with some grumbling. And she tripped away to her enormous bedroom, in the centre of which stood the enormous funereal bed "that the Emperor Halixander's sister slep in when the allied sufferings was here," and put on her little bonnet and shawl with the utmost eagerness and pleasure. George was still drinking claret when she returned to the dining-room, and made no signs of moving. "Ar'n't you coming with me, dearest?" she asked him. No; the "dearest" had "business" that night. His man should get her a coach and go with her. And the coach being at the door of the hotel, Amelia made George a little disappointed curtsey after looking vainly into his face once or twice, and went sadly down the great stair-case, Captain Dobbin after, who handed her into the vehicle, and saw it drive away to its destination. The very valet was ashamed of mentioning the address to the hackney-coachman before the hotel waiters, and promised to instruct him when they got further on.

Dobbin walked home to his old quarters at the Slaughters' thinking very likely that it would be delightful to be in that hackney-coach, along with Mrs. Osborne. George was evidently of quite a different taste; for when he had taken wine enough, he went off to half-price at the play, to see Mr. Kean perform in Shylock. Captain Osborne was a great lover of the drama, and had himself performed high-comedy characters with great distinction in several garrison theatrical entertainments. Jos slept on until long after dark, when he woke up with a start at the motions of his servant, who was removing and emptying the decanters on the table; and the hackney-coach stand was again put into requisition for a carriage to convey this stout hero to his lodgings and bed.

Mrs. Sedley, you may be sure, clasped her daughter to her heart with all maternal eagerness and affection, running out of the door as the carriage drew up before the little garden-gate, to welcome the weeping, trembling, young bride. Old Mr. Clapp, who was in his shirt-sleeves, trimming the garden-plot, shrank back alarmed. The Irish servant-lass rushed up from the kitchen and smiled a "God bless you." Amelia could hardly walk along the flags and up the steps into the parlour.

How the floodgates were opened, and mother and daughter wept, when they were together embracing each other in this sanctuary, may readily be imagined by every reader who possesses the least sentimental turn. When don't ladies weep? At what occasion of joy, sorrow, or other business of life? and, after such an event as a marriage, mother and daughter were surely at liberty to give way to a sensibility which is as tender as it is refreshing. About a question of marriage I have seen women who hate each other kiss and cry together quite fondly. How much more do they feel when they love! Good mothers are married over again at their daughters' weddings: and as for subsequent events, who does not know how ultra-maternal grandmothers are?—in fact a woman, until she is a grandmother, does not often really know what to be a mother is. Let us respect Amelia and her mamma whispering and whimpering and laughing and crying in the parlour and the twilight. Old Mr. Sedley did. *He* had not divined who was in the carriage when it drove up. He had not flown out to meet his daughter, though he kissed her very warmly when she entered the room (where he was occupied, as usual, with his papers and tapes and statements of accounts), and after sitting with the mother and daughter for a short time, he very wisely left the little apartment in their possession.

George's valet was looking on in a very supercilious manner at Mr. Clapp in his shirt-sleeves, watering his rose-bushes. He took off his hat, however, with much condescension to Mr. Sedley, who asked news about his son-in-law, and about Jos's carriage, and whether his horses had been down to Brighton, and about that infernal traitor Bonaparty, and the war; until the Irish maid-servant came with a plate and a bottle of wine, from which the old gentleman insisted upon helping the valet. He gave him a half-guinea too, which the servant pocketed with a mixture of wonder and contempt. "To the health of your master and mistress, Trotter," Mr. Sedley said, "and here's something to drink your health when you get home, Trotter."

There were but nine days past since Amelia had left that little cottage and home—and yet how far off the time seemed since she had bidden it farewell. What a gulf lay between her and that past life. She could look back to it from her present standing-place, and contemplate, almost as another being, the young unmarried girl absorbed in her love, having no eyes but for one special object, receiving parental affection if not ungratefully, at least indifferently, and as if it were her due—her whole heart and thoughts bent on the accomplishment of one desire. To review those days, so lately gone yet so far away, touched her with shame; and the aspect of the kind parents filled her with tender remorse. Was the prize gained—the heaven of life—and the winner still doubtful and unsatisfied? As his hero and heroine pass the matrimonial barrier, the novelist generally drops the curtain, as if the drama were over then: the doubts and struggles of life ended: as if, once landed in the marriage country, all were green and pleasant there: and wife and husband had nothing to do but to link each other's arms together, and wander gently downwards towards old age in happy and perfect fruition. But our little Amelia was just on the bank of her new country, and was already looking anxiously back towards the sad friendly figures waving farewell to her across the stream, from the other distant shore.

In honour of the young bride's arrival, her mother thought it necessary to prepare I don't know what festive entertainment, and after the first ebullition of talk, took leave of Mrs. George Osborne for a while, and dived down to the lower regions of the house to a sort of kitchen-parlour (occupied by Mr. and Mrs. Clapp, and in the evening, when her dishes were washed and her curl-papers removed, by Miss Flannigan, the Irish servant), there to take measures for the preparing of a magnificent ornamented tea. All people have their ways of expressing kindness, and it seemed to Mrs. Sedley that a muffin and a quantity of orange marmalade spread out in a little cut-glass saucer would be peculiarly agreeable refreshments to Amelia in her most interesting situation.

While these delicacies were being transacted below, Amelia, leaving the drawing-room, walked up stairs and found herself, she scarce knew how, in the little room which she had occupied before her marriage, and in that very chair in which she had passed so many bitter hours. She sank back in its arms as if it were an old friend; and fell to thinking over the past week, and the life beyond it. Already to be looking sadly and vaguely back: always to be pining for something which, when obtained, brought doubt and sadness rather than pleasure; here was the lot of our poor little creature, and harmless lost wanderer in the great struggling crowds of Vanity Fair.

Here she sate, and recalled to herself fondly that image of George to which she had knelt before marriage. Did she own to herself how different the real man was from that superb young hero whom she had worshipped? It requires many, many years—and a man must be very bad indeed—before a woman's pride and vanity will let her own to such a confession. Then Rebecca's twinkling green eyes and baleful smile lighted upon her, and filled her with dismay. And so she sate for awhile indulging in her usual mood of selfish brooding, in that very listless melancholy attitude in which the honest maid-servant had found her, on the day when she brought up the letter in which George renewed his offer of marriage.

She looked at the little white bed, which had been hers a few days before, and thought she would like to sleep in it that night, and wake, as formerly, with her mother smiling over her in the morning. Then she thought with terror of the great funereal damask pavilion in the vast and dingy state bed-room, which was awaiting her at the grand hotel in Cavendish Square. Dear little white bed! how many a long night had she wept on its pillow! How she had despaired and hoped to die there; and now were not all her wishes accomplished, and the lover of whom she had despaired her own for ever? Kind mother! how patiently and tenderly she had watched round that bed! She went and knelt down by the bed-side; and there this wounded and timorous, but gentle and loving soul, sought for consolation where as yet, it must be owned, our little girl had but seldom looked for it. Love had been her faith hitherto; and the sad, bleeding disappointed heart began to feel the want of another consoler.

Have we a right to repeat or to overhear her prayers? These, brother, are secrets, and out of the domain of Vanity Fair, in which our story lies.

But this may be said, that when the tea was finally announced, our young lady came downstairs a great deal more cheerful; that she did not despond, or deplore her fate, or think about George's coldness, or Rebecca's eyes, as she had been wont to do of late. She went downstairs, and kissed her father and mother, and talked to the old gentleman, and made him more merry than he had been for many a day. She sate down at the piano which Dobbin had bought for her, and sang over all her father's favourite old songs. She pronounced the tea to be excellent, and praised the exquisite taste in which the marmalade was arranged in the saucers. And in determining to make everybody else happy, she found herself so; and was sound asleep in the great funereal pavilion, and only woke up with a smile when George arrived from the theatre.

For the next day, George had more important "business" to transact than that which took him to see Mr. Kean in Shylock. Immediately on his arrival in London he had written off to his father's solicitors, signifying his royal pleasure that an interview should take place between them on the morrow. His hotel bill, losses at billiards and cards to Captain Crawley had almost drained the young man's purse, which wanted replenishing before he set out on his travels, and he had no resource but to infringe upon the two thousand pounds which the attorneys were commissioned to pay over to him. He had a perfect belief in his own mind that his father would relent before very long. How could any parent be obdurate for a length of time against such a paragon as he was? If his mere past and personal merits did not succeed in mollifying his father, George determined that he would distinguish himself so prodigiously in the ensuing campaign that the old gentleman must give in to him. And if not? Bah! the world was before him. His luck might change at cards, and there was a deal of spending in two thousand pounds.

So he sent off Amelia once more in a carriage to her mamma, with strict orders and carte blanche to the two ladies to purchase everything requisite for a lady of Mrs. George Osborne's fashion, who was going on a foreign tour. They had but one day to complete the outfit, and it may

be imagined that their business therefore occupied them
pretty fully. In a carriage once more, bustling about from
milliner to linen-draper, escorted back to the carriage by
obsequious shopmen or polite owners, Mrs. Sedley was herself again almost, and sincerely happy for the first time
since their misfortunes. Nor was Mrs. Amelia at all above
the pleasure of shopping, and bargaining, and seeing and
buying pretty things. (Would any man, the most philo-
sophic, give twopence for a woman who was?) She gave
herself a little treat, obedient to her husband's orders, and
purchased a quantity of lady's gear, showing a great deal
of taste and elegant discernment, as all the shopfolks said.

And about the war that was ensuing, Mrs. Osborne was
not much alarmed; Bonaparty was to be crushed almost
without a struggle. Margate packets were sailing every
day, filled with men of fashion and ladies of note, on their
way to Brussels and Ghent. People were going not so much
to a war as to a fashionable tour. The newspapers laughed
the wretched upstart and swindler to scorn. Such a Corsican wretch as that withstand the armies of Europe and
the genius of the immortal Wellington! Amelia held him
in utter contempt; for it needs not to be said that this soft
and gentle creature took her opinions from those people
who surrounded her, such fidelity being much too humble-
minded to think for itself. Well, in a word, she and her
mother performed a great day's shopping, and she acquitted
herself with considerable liveliness and credit on this her
first appearance in the genteel world of London.

George meanwhile, with his hat on one side, his elbows
squared, and his swaggering martial air, made for Bedford
Row, and stalked into the attorney's offices as if he was
lord of every pale-faced clerk who was scribbling there.
He ordered somebody to inform Mr. Higgs that Captain
Osborne was waiting, in a fierce and patronizing way, as if
the *pékin* of an attorney, who had thrice his brains, fifty
times his money, and a thousand times his experience, was
a wretched underling who should instantly leave all his
business in life to attend on the Captain's pleasure. He
did not see the sneer of contempt which passed all round
the room, from the first clerk to the articled gents, from

the articled gents to the ragged writers and white-faced
runners, in clothes too tight for them, as he sate there tap-
ping his boot with his cane, and thinking what a parcel of
miserable poor devils these were. The miserable poor devils
knew all about his affairs. They talked about them over
their pints of beer at their public-house clubs to other clerks
of a night. Ye Gods, what do not attorneys and attorneys'
clerks know in London! Nothing is hidden from their in-
quisition, and their familiars mutely rule our city.

Perhaps George expected, when he entered Mr. Higg's
apartment, to find that gentleman commissioned to give him
some message of compromise or conciliation from his
father; perhaps his haughty and cold demeanour was
adopted as a sign of his spirit and resolution; but if so,
his fierceness was met by a chilling coolness and indifference on the attorney's part, that rendered swaggering absurd.
He pretended to be writing at a paper, when the Captain
entered. "Pray, sit down, sir," said he, "and I will attend
to your little affair in a moment. Mr. Poe, get the release
papers, if you please;" and then he fell to writing again.

Poe having produced those papers, his chief calculated
the amount of two thousand pounds stock at the rate of
the day; and asked Captain Osborne whether he would take
the sum in a cheque upon the bankers, or whether he should
direct the latter to purchase stock to that amount. "One
of the late Mrs. Osborne's trustees is out of town," he said
indifferently, "but my client wishes to meet your wishes,
and have done with the business as quick as possible."

"Give me a cheque, sir," said the Captain very surlily.
"Damn the shillings and halfpence, sir," he added, as the
lawyer was making out the amount of the draft, and, flattering himself that by this stroke of magnanimity he had
put the old quiz to the blush, he stalked out of the office
with the paper in his pocket.

"That chap will be in gaol in two years," Mr. Higgs said
to Mr. Poe.

"Won't O. come round, sir, don't you think?"

"Won't the monument come round," Mr. Higgs replied.

"He's going it pretty fast," said the clerk. "He's only
married a week, and I saw him and some other military

chaps handing Mrs. Highflyer to her carriage after the play."
And then another case was called, and Mr. George Osborne
thenceforth dismissed from these worthy gentlemen's
memory.

The draft was upon our friends Hulker and Bullock of
Lombard Street, to whose house, still thinking he was doing
business, George bent his way, and from whom he received
his money.   Frederick Bullock, Esq., whose yellow face
was over a ledger, at which sate a demure clerk, happened
to be in the banking-room when George entered. His yellow
face turned to a more deadly colour when he saw the
Captain, and he slunk back guiltily into the inmost parlour.
George was too busy gloating over the money (for he had
never had such a sum before), to mark the countenance or
flight of the cadaverous suitor of his sister.

Fred Bullock told old Osborne of his son's appearance
and conduct, "He came in as bold as brass," said Frederick.
"He has drawn out every shilling.   How long will a few
hundred pounds last such a chap as that?"   Osborne swore
with a great oath that he little cared when or how soon he
spent it.   Fred dined every day in Russell Square now.   But
altogether, George was highly pleased with his day's business.   All his own baggage and outfit was put into a state
of speedy preparation, and he paid Amelia's purchases with
cheques on his agents, and with the splendour of a lord.

CHAPTER XXVII

In Which Amelia Joins Her Regiment

WHEN Jos's fine carriage drove up to the inn door at Chatham, the first face which Amelia recognized was the friendly countenance of Captain Dobbin, who had been pacing the street for an hour past in expectation of his friends' arrival. The Captain, with shells on his frock-coat, and a crimson sash and sabre, presented a military appearance, which made Jos quite proud to be able to claim such an acquaintance, and the stout civilian hailed him with a cordiality very different from the reception which Jos vouchsafed to his friend in Brighton and Bond Street.

Along with the Captain was Ensign Stubble; who, as the barouche neared the inn, burst out with an exclamation of "By Jove! what a pretty girl;" highly applauding Osborne's choice. Indeed, Amelia dressed in her wedding-pelisse and pink ribbons, with a flush in her face, occasioned by rapid travel through the open air, looked so fresh and pretty, as fully to justify the Ensign's compliment. Dobbin liked him for making it. As he stepped forward to help the lady out of the carriage, Stubble saw what a pretty little hand she gave him, and what a sweet pretty little foot came tripping down the step. He blushed profusely, and made the very best bow of which he was capable; to which Amelia, seeing the number of the —th regiment embroidered on the Ensign's cap, replied with a blushing smile, and a curtsey on her part; which finished the young Ensign on the spot. Dobbin took most kindly to Mr. Stubble from that day, and encouraged him to talk about Amelia in their private walks, and at each other's quarters. It became the fashion, indeed, among all the honest young fellows of the —th to adore and admire Mrs. Osborne. Her simple artless behaviour, and modest kindness of demeanour, won all their unsophisticated hearts; all of which simplicity and sweetness are quite impossible to describe in print. But who has not beheld these among women, and recognised the presence of all sorts of qualities in them, even though they say no more to you than that they are engaged to dance the next quadrille, or that it is very hot weather? George, always the champion of his regiment, rose immensely in the opinion of the youth of the corps, by his gallantry in marrying this portionless young creature, and by his choice of such a pretty, kind partner.

In the sitting-room which was awaiting the travellers, Amelia, to her surprise, found a letter addressed to Mrs. Captain Osborne. It was a triangular billet, on pink paper, and sealed with a dove and an olive branch, and a profusion of light blue sealing wax, and it was written in a very large, though undecided female hand.

"It's Peggy O'Dowd's fist," said George, laughing. "I know it by the kisses on the seal." And in fact, it was a note from Mrs. Major O'Dowd, requesting the pleasure of Mrs. Osborne's company that very evening to a small friendly party. "You must go," George said. "You will make acquaintance with the regiment there. O'Dowd goes in command of the regiment, and Peggy goes in command of O'Dowd."

But they had not been for many minutes in the enjoyment of Mrs. O'Dowd's letter, when the door was flung open, and a stout jolly lady, in a riding habit, followed by a couple of officers of Ours, entered the room.

"Sure, I couldn't stop till tay-time. Present me, Garge, my dear fellow, to your lady. Madam, I'm deloighted to see ye; and to present to you me husband, Meejor O'Dowd;" and with this, the jolly lady in the riding-habit grasped Amelia's hand very warmly, and the latter knew at once that the lady was before her whom her husband had so often laughed at.

"You've often heard of me from that husband of yours," said the lady, with great vivacity.

"You've often heard of her," echoed her husband, the Major.

Amelia answered, smiling, "that she had."

"And small good he's told you of me," Mrs. O'Dowd replied; adding that "George was a wicked divvle."

"That I'll go bail for," said the Major, trying to look knowing, at which George laughed; and Mrs. O'Dowd, with a tap of her whip, told the Major to be quiet; and then requested to be presented in form to Mrs. Captain Osborne.

"This, my dear," said George with great gravity, "is my very good, kind, and excellent friend Auralia Margaretta otherwise called Peggy."

"Faith, you're right," interposed the Major.

"Otherwise called Peggy, lady of Major Michael O'Dowd, of our regiment, and daughter of Fitzjurld Ber'sford de Burgo Malony of Glenmalony, County Kildare."

"And Muryan Squeer, Doblin," said the lady with calm superiority.

"And Muryan Square, sure enough," the Major whispered.

" 'Twas there ye coorted me, Meejor dear," the lady said, and the Major assented to this as to every other proposition which was made generally in company.

Major O'Dowd, who had served his sovereign in every quarter of the world, and had paid for every step in his profession by some more than equivalent act of daring and gallantry, was the most modest, silent, sheep-faced and meek of little men, and as obedient to his wife as if he had been her tay-boy. At the mess-table he sat silently, and drank a great deal. When full of liquor, he reeled silently home. When he spoke, it was to agree with everybody on every conceivable point; and he passed through life in perfect ease and good-humour. The hottest suns of India never heated his temper; and the Walcheren ague never shook it. He walked up to a battery with just as much indifference as to a dinner-table; had dined on horse-flesh and turtle with equal relish and appetite; and had an old mother, Mrs. O'Dowd of O'Dowdstown indeed, whom he had never disobeyed but when he ran away and enlisted, and when he persisted in marrying that odious Peggy Malony.

Peggy was one of five sisters, and eleven children of the noble house of Glenmalony; but her husband, though her own cousin, was of the mother's side, and so had not the inestimable advantage of being allied to the Malonys, whom she believed to be the most famous family in the world. Having tried nine seasons at Dublin and two at Bath and Chel-

tenham, and not finding a partner for life, Miss Malony ordered her cousin Mick to marry her when she was about
thirty-three years of age; and the honest fellow obeying,
carried her off to the West Indies, to preside over the ladies
of the —th regiment, into which he had just exchanged.

Before Mrs. O'Dowd was half an hour in Amelia's (or
indeed in anybody else's) company, this amiable lady told all
her birth and pedigree to her new friend. "My dear," said
she, good-naturedly, "it was my intention that Garge should
be a brother of my own, and my sister Glorvina would have
suited him entirely. But as bygones are bygones, and he was
engaged to yourself, why, I'm determined to take you as a
sister instead, and to look upon you as such, and to love you
as one of the family. Faith, you've got such a nice good-
natured face and way widg you, that I'm sure we'll agree;
and that you'll be an addition to our family any way."

" 'Deed and she will," said O'Dowd, with an approving air,
and Amelia felt herself not a little amused and grateful to
be thus suddenly introduced to so large a party of relations.

"We're all good fellows here," the Major's lady continued.
"There's not a regiment in the service where you'll find a
more united society nor a more agreeable mess-room. There's
no quarrelling, bickering, slandthering, nor small talk
amongst *us*. We all love each other."

"Especially Mrs. Magenis," said George, laughing.

"Mrs. Captain Magenis and me has made up, though her
treatment of me would bring me gray hairs with sorrow to
the grave."

"And you with such a beautiful front of black, Peggy, my
dear," the Major cried.

"Hould your tongue, Mick, you booby. Them husbands
are always in the way, Mrs. Osborne, my dear; and as for my
Mick, I often tell him he should never open his mouth but
to give the word of command, or to put meat and drink into
it. I'll tell you about the regiment, and warn you when we're
alone. Introduce me to your brother now; sure he's a
mighty fine man, and reminds me of me cousin, Dan Malony
(Malony of Ballymalony, my dear, you know, who mar'ied
Ophalia Scully, of Oysterstown, own cousin to Lord Pol-
doody). Mr. Sedley, sir, I'm deloighted to be made known

te ye. I suppose you'll dine at the mess to-day. (Mind that divvle of a docther, Mick, and whatever ye du, keep yourself sober for me party this evening.)"

"It's the 150th gives us a farewell dinner, my love," interposed the Major, "but we'll easy get a card for Mr. Sedley."

"Run Simple (Ensign Simple, of Ours, my dear Amelia. I forgot to introjuce him to ye). Run in a hurry, with Mrs. Major O'Dowd's compliments to Colonel Tavish, and Captain Osborne has brought his brothernlaw down, and will bring him to the 150th mess at five o'clock sharp—when you and I, my dear, will take a snack here, if you like." Before Mrs. O'Dowd's speech was concluded, the young Ensign was trotting downstairs on his commission.

"Obedience is the soul of the army. We will go to our duty while Mrs. O'Dowd will stay and enlighten you, Emmy," Captain Osborne said; and the two gentlemen, taking each a wing of the Major, walked out with that officer, grinning at each other over his head.

And, now having her new friend to herself, the impetuous Mrs. O'Dowd proceeded to pour out such a quantity of information as no poor little woman's memory could ever tax itself to bear. She told Amelia a thousand particulars relative to the very numerous family of which the amazed young lady found herself a member. "Mrs. Heavytop, the Colonel's wife, died in Jamaica of the yellow faver and a broken heart comboined, for the horrud old Colonel, with a head as bald as a cannon ball, was making sheep's eyes at a half-caste girl there. Mrs. Magenis, though without education, was a good woman, but she had the divvle's tongue, and would cheat her own mother at whist. Mrs. Captain Kirk must turn up her lobster eyes forsooth at the idea of an honest round game, (wherein me fawther, as pious a man as ever went to church, me uncle Dane Malony, and our cousin the Bishop, took a hand at loo, or whist, every night of their lives). Nayther of 'em's goin' with the regiment this time," Mrs. O'Dowd added. "Fanny Magenis stops with her mother, who sells small coal and potatoes, most likely, in Islington-town, hard by London, though she's always bragging of her father's ships, and pointing them out to us as they go up the river: and Mrs. Kirk and her children will stop here in Bethesda Place, to be nigh to her favourite preacher, Dr. Ramshorn. Mrs. Bunny's in an interesting situation—faith, and she always is, then—and has given the Lieutenant seven already. And Ensign Posky's wife, who joined two months before you, my dear, has quarl'd with Tom Posky a score of times, till you can hear 'em all over the bar'ck (they say they're come to broken pleets, and Tom never accounted for his black oi,) and she'll go back to her mother, who keeps a ladies' siminary at Richmond,—bad luck to her for running away from it! Where did ye get your finishing, my dear? I had moin, and no expince spared, at Madame Flanahan's, at Ilyssus Grove, Booterstown, near Dublin wid a Marchioness to teach us the true Parisian pronunciation, and a retired Mejor-General of the French service to put us through the exercise."

Of this incongruous family our astonished Amelia found herself all of a sudden a member: with Mrs. O'Dowd as an elder sister. She was presented to her other female relations at tea-time, on whom, as she was quiet, good-natured, and not too handsome, she made rather an agreeable impression until the arrival of the gentlemen from the mess of the 150th, who all admired her so, that her sisters began, of course, to find fault with her.

"I hope Osborne has sown his wild oats," said Mrs. Magenis to Mrs. Bunny. "If a reformed rake makes a good husband, sure it's she will have the fine chance with Garge," Mrs. O'Dowd remarked to Posky, who had lost her position as bride in the regiment, and was quite angry with the usurper. And as for Mrs. Kirk: that disciple of Dr. Ramshorn put one or two leading professional questions to Amelia, to see whether she was awakened, whether she was a professing Christian and so forth, and finding from the simplicity of Mrs. Osborne's replies that she was yet in utter darkness, put into her hands three little penny books with pictures, viz., the "Howling Wilderness," the "Washerwoman of Wandsworth Common," and the "British Soldier's best Bayonet," which, bent upon awakening her before she slept, Mrs. Kirk begged Amelia to read that night ere she went to bed.

But all the men, like good fellows as they were, rallied round their comrade's pretty wife, and paid her their court with soldierly gallantry. She had a little triumph, which flushed her spirits and made her eyes sparkle. George was proud of her popularity, and pleased with the manner (which was very gay and graceful, though naïve and a little timid) with which she received the gentlemen's attentions, and answered their compliments. And he in his uniform—how much handsomer he was than any man in the room! She felt that he was affectionately watching her, and glowed with pleasure at his kindness. "I will make all his friends welcome," she resolved in her heart. "I will love all as I love him. I will always try and be gay and good-humoured and make his home happy."

The regiment indeed adopted her with acclamation. The Captains approved, the Lieutenants applauded, the Ensigns admired. Old Cutler, the Doctor, made one or two jokes, which, being professional, need not be repeated; and Cackle, the Assistant M.D. of Edinburgh, condescended to examine her upon leeterature, and tried her with his three best French quotations. Young Stubble went about from man to man whispering, "Jove, isn't she a pretty gal?" and never took his eyes off her except when the negus came in.

As for Captain Dobbin, he never so much as spoke to her during the whole evening. But he and Captain Porter of the 150th took home Jos to the hotel, who was in a very maudlin state, and had told his tiger-hunt story with great effect, both at the mess-table and at the *soirée*, to Mrs. O'Dowd in her turban and bird of paradise. Having put the Collector into the hands of his servant, Dobbin loitered about, smoking his cigar before the inn door. George had meanwhile very carefully shawled his wife, and brought her away from Mrs. O'Dowd's after a general handshaking from the young officers, who accompanied her to the fly, and cheered that vehicle as it drove off. So Amelia gave Dobbin her little hand as she got out of the carriage, and rebuked him smilingly for not having taken any notice of her all night.

The Captain continued that deleterious amusement of smoking, long after the inn and the street were gone to bed. He watched the lights vanish from George's sitting-room windows, and shine out in the bedroom close at hand. It was almost morning when he returned to his own quarters. He could hear the cheering from the ships in the river, where the transports were already taking in their cargoes preparatory to dropping down the Thames.

CHAPTER XXVIII

In Which Amelia Invades the Low Countries

THE regiment with its officers was to be transported in ships provided by His Majesty's government for the occasion: and in two days after the festive assembly at Mrs. O'Dowd's apartments, in the midst of cheering from all the East India ships in the river, and the military on shore, the band playing "God save the King," the officers waving their hats, and the crews hurrahing gallantly, the transports went down the river and proceeded under convoy to Ostend. Meanwhile the gallant Jos had agreed to escort his sister and the Major's wife, the bulk of whose goods and chattels, including the famous bird of paradise and turban, were with the regimental baggage: so that our two heroines drove pretty much unencumbered to Ramsgate, where there were plenty of packets plying, in one of which they had a speedy passage to Ostend.

That period of Jos's life which now ensued was so full of incident, and it served him for conversation for many years after, and even the tiger-hunt story was put aside for more stirring narratives which he had to tell about the great campaign of Waterloo. As soon as he had agreed to escort his sister abroad, it was remarked that he ceased shaving his upper lip. At Chatham he followed the parades and drills with great assiduity. He listened with the utmost attention to the conversation of his brother officers (as he called them in after days sometimes), and learned as many military names as he could. In these studies the excellent Mrs. O'Dowd was of great assistance to him; and on the day finally when they embarked on board the Lovely Rose, which was to carry them to their destination, he made his appearance in a braided frock-coat and duck trousers, with a foraging cap ornamented with a smart gold band. Having his carriage with him, and informing everybody on board confidentially that he was going to join the Duke of Wellington's army, folks mistook him for a great personage, a commissary-general, or a government courier at the very least.

He suffered hugely on the voyage, during which the ladies were likewise prostrate; but Amelia was brought to life again as the packet made Ostend, by the sight of the transports conveying her regiment, which entered the harbour almost at the same time with the Lovely Rose. Jos went in a collapsed state to an inn, while Captain Dobbin escorted the ladies, and then busied himself in freeing Jos's carriage and luggage from the ship and the custom-house, for Mr. Jos was at present without a servant, Osborne's man and his own pampered menial having conspired together at Chatham, and refused point-blank to cross the water. This revolt, which came very suddenly, and on the last day, so alarmed Mr. Sedley, junior, that he was on the point of giving up the expedition, but Captain Dobbin (who made himself immensely officious in the business, Jos said), rated him and laughed at him soundly: the mustachios were grown in advance, and Jos finally was persuaded to embark. In place of the well-bred and well-fed London domestics, who could only speak English, Dobbin procured for Jos's party a swarthy little Belgian servant who could speak no language at all; but who, by his bustling behaviour, and by invariably addressing Mr. Sedley as "My lord," speedily acquired that gentleman's favour. Times are altered at Ostend now; of the Britons who go thither, very few look like lords, or act like those members of our hereditary aristocracy. They seem for the most part shabby in attire, dingy of linen, lovers of billiards and brandy, and cigars and greasy ordinaries.

But it may be said as a rule, that every Englishman in the Duke of Wellington's army paid his way. The remembrance of such a fact surely becomes a nation of shopkeepers. It was a blessing for a commerce-loving country to be overrun by such an army of customers; and to have such creditable warriors to feed. And the country which they came to protect is not military. For a long period of history they have let other people fight there. When the present writer went to survey with eagle glance the field of Water-

loo, we asked the conductor of the diligence, a portly war-
like-looking veteran, whether he had been at the battle.
"Pas si bête"—such an answer and sentiment as no Frenchman would own to—was his reply. But, on the other hand,
the postilion who drove us was a *Viscount,* a son of some
bankrupt Imperial General, who accepted a pennyworth of
beer on the road. The moral is surely a good one.

This flat, flourishing, easy country never could have
looked more rich and prosperous than in that opening summer of 1815, when its green fields and quiet cities were
enlivened by multiplied red-coats: when its wide *chaussées*
swarmed with brilliant English equipages: when its great
canal-boats, gliding by rich pastures and pleasant quaint
old villages, by old châteaux lying amongst old trees, were
all crowded with well-to-do English travellers: when the
soldier who drank at the village inn, not only drank, but
paid his score; and Donald, the Highlander,[1] billeted in
the Flemish farm-house, rocked the baby's cradle, while
Jean and Jeannette were out getting in the hay. As our
painters are bent on military subjects just now, I throw
out this as a good subject for the pencil, to illustrate the
principle of an honest English war. All looked as brilliant
and harmless as a Hyde Park review. Meanwhile, Napoleon, screened behind his curtain of frontier-fortresses, was
preparing for the outbreak which was to drive all these
orderly people into fury and blood; and lay so many of them
low.

Everybody had such a perfect feeling of confidence in
the leader (for the resolute faith which the Duke of Wellington had inspired in the whole English nation was as
intense as that more frantic enthusiasm with which at one
time the French regarded Napoleon), the country seemed
in so perfect a state of orderly defence, and the help at
hand in case of need so near and overwhelming, that alarm
was unknown, and our travellers, among whom two were
naturally of a very timid sort, were, like all the other multiplied English tourists, entirely at ease. The famous
regiment, with so many of whose officers we have made

[1] This incident is mentioned in Mr. Gleig's "Story of the Battle of
Waterloo."

acquaintance, was drafted in canal-boats to Bruges and Ghent, thence to march to Brussels. Jos accompanied the ladies in the public boats; the which all old travellers in Flanders must remember for the luxury and accommodation they afforded. So prodigiously good was the eating and drinking on board these sluggish but most comfortable vessels, that there are legends extant of an English traveller, who, coming to Belgium for a week, and travelling in one of these boats, was so delighted with the fare there that he went backwards and forwards from Ghent to Bruges perpetually until the railroads were invented, when he drowned himself on the last trip of the passage-boat. Jos's death was not to be of this sort, but his comfort was exceeding, and Mrs. O'Dowd insisted that he only wanted her sister Glorvina to make his happiness complete. He sate on the roof of the cabin all day drinking Flemish beer, shouting for Isidor, his servant, and talking gallantly to the ladies.

His courage was prodigious. "Boney attack *us*," he cried. "My dear creature, my poor Emmy, don't be frightened. There's no danger. The allies will be in Paris in two months, I tell you; when I'll take you to dine in the Palais Royal, by Jove! There are three hundred thousand Rooshians, I tell you, now entering France by Mayence and the Rhine— three hundred thousand under Wittgenstein and Barclay de Tolly, my poor love. You don't know military affairs, my dear. I do, and I tell you there's no infantry in France can stand against Rooshian infantry, and no general of Boney's that's fit to hold a candle to Wittgenstein. Then there are the Austrians, they are five hundred thousand if a man, and they are within ten marches of the frontier by this time, under Schwartzenberg and Prince Charles. Then there are the Prooshians under the gallant Prince Marshal. Show me a cavalry chief like him now that Murat is gone. Hey, Mrs. O'Dowd? Do you think our little girl here need be afraid? Is there any cause for fear, Isidor? Hey, sir? Get some more beer."

Mrs. O'Dowd said that her "Glorvina was not afraid of any man alive, let alone a Frenchman," and tossed off a glass of beer with a wink which expressed her liking for the beverage.

Having frequently been in presence of the enemy, or, in other words, faced the ladies at Cheltenham and Bath, our friend, the Collector, had lost a great deal of his pristine timidity, and was now, especially when fortified with liquor, as talkative as might be. He was rather a favourite with the regiment, treating the young officers with sumptuosity, and amusing them by his military airs. And as there is one well-known regiment of the army which travels with a goat heading the column, whilst another is led by a deer, George said with respect to his brother-in-law, that his regiment marched with an elephant.

Since Amelia's introduction to the regiment, George began to be rather ashamed of some of the company to which he had been forced to present her; and determined, as he told Dobbin (with what satisfaction to the latter it need not be said,) to exchange into some better regiment soon, and to get his wife away from those damned vulgar women. But this vulgarity of being ashamed of one's society is much more common among men than women (except very great ladies of fashion, who, to be sure, indulge in it); and Mrs. Amelia, a natural and unaffected person, had none of that artificial shamefacedness which her husband mistook for delicacy on his own part. Thus Mrs. O'Dowd had a cock's plume in her hat, and a very large "repayther" on her stomach, which she used to ring on all occasions, narrating how it had been presented to her by her fawther, as she stipt into the car'ge after her mar'ge; and these ornaments, with other outward peculiarities of the Major's wife, gave excruciating agonies to Captain Osborne, when his wife and the Major's came in contact; whereas Amelia was only amused by the honest lady's eccentricities, and not in the least ashamed of her company.

As they made that well-known journey, which almost every Englishman of middle rank has travelled since, there might have been more instructive, but few more entertaining, companions than Mrs. Major O'Dowd. "Talk about kenal boats, my dear! Ye should see the kenal boats between Dublin and Ballinasloe. It's there the rapid travelling is; and the beautiful cattle. Sure me fawther got a goold medal (and his Excellency himself eat a slice of it,

and said never was finer mate in his loif) for a four-year-
old heifer, the like of which ye never saw in *this* country
any day." And Jos owned with a sigh "that for good
streaky beef, really mingled with fat and lean, there was
no country like England."

"Except Ireland, where all your best mate comes from,"
said the Major's lady; proceeding, as is not unusual with
patriots of her nation, to make comparisons greatly in
favour of her own country. The idea of comparing the
market at Bruges with those of Dublin, although she had
suggested it herself, caused immense scorn and derision on
her part. "I'll thank ye tell me what they mean by that
old gazabo on the top of the market-place," said she, in a
burst of ridicule fit to have brought the old tower down.
The place was full of English soldiery as they passed.
English bugles woke them in the morning; at night-fall
they went to bed to the note of the British fife and drum:
all the country and Europe was in arms, and the greatest
event of history pending: and honest Peggy O'Dowd, whom
it concerned as well as another, went on prattling about
Ballinafad, and the horses in the stables at Glenmalony,
and the clar't drunk there; and Jos Sedley interposed about
curry and rice at Dumdum; and Amelia thought about her
husband, and how best she should show her love for him;
as if these were the great topics of the world.

Those who like to lay down the History-book, and to
speculate upon what *might* have happened in the world, but
for the fatal occurrence of what actually did take place (a
most puzzling, amusing, ingenious, and profitable kind of
meditation), have no doubt often thought to themselves what
a specially bad time Napoleon took to come back from Elba,
and to let loose his eagle from Gulf San Juan to Notre Dame.
The historians on our side tell us that the armies of the allied
powers were all providentially on a war-footing, and ready to
bear down at a moment's notice upon the Elban Emperor.
The august jobbers assembled at Vienna, and carving out the
kingdoms of Europe according to their wisdom, had such
causes of quarrel among themselves as might have set the
armies which had overcome Napoleon to fight against each
other, but for the return of the object of unanimous hatred

and fear. This monarch had an army in full force because he had jobbed to himself Poland, and was determined to keep it: another had robbed half Saxony, and was bent upon maintaining his acquisition: Italy was the object of a third's solicitude. Each was protesting against the rapacity of the other; and could the Corsican but have waited in prison until all these parties were by the ears, he might have returned and reigned unmolested. But what would have become of our story and all our friends, then? If all the drops in it were dried up, what would become of the sea?

In the meanwhile the business of life and living, and the pursuits of pleasure, especially, went on as if no end were to be expected to them, and no enemy in front. When our travellers arrived at Brussels, in which their regiment was quartered, a great piece of good fortune, as all said, they found themselves in one of the gayest and most brilliant little capitals in Europe, and where all the Vanity Fair booths were laid out with the most tempting liveliness and splendour. Gambling was here in profusion, and dancing in plenty: feasting was there to fill with delight that great gourmand of a Jos; there was a theatre where a miraculous Catalani was delighting all hearers: beautiful rides, all enlivened with martial splendour; a rare old city, with strange costumes and wonderful architecture, to delight the eyes of little Amelia, who had never before seen a foreign country, and fill her with charming surprises: so that now and for a few weeks' space in a fine handsome lodging, whereof the expenses were borne by Jos and Osborne, who was flush of money and full of kind attentions to his wife —for about a fortnight, I say, during which her honeymoon ended, Mrs. Amelia was as pleased and happy as any little bride out of England.

Every day during this happy time there was novelty and amusement for all parties. There was a church to see, or a picture-gallery—there was a ride, or an opera. The bands of the regiments were making music at all hours. The greatest folks of England walked in the Park—there was a perpetual military festival. George, taking out his wife to a new jaunt or junket every night, was quite pleased with himself as usual, and swore he was becoming quite a

domestic character. And a jaunt or a junket with *him!*
Was it not enough to set this little heart beating with joy?
Her letters home to her mother were filled with delight and
gratitude at this season. Her husband bade her buy laces,
millinery, jewels, and gimcracks of all sorts. Oh, he was
the kindest, best, and most generous of men!

The sight of the very great company of lords and ladies
and fashionable persons who thronged the town, and appeared in every public place, filled George's truly British
soul with intense delight. They flung off that happy fri-
gidity and insolence of demeanour which occasionally char-
acterises the great at home, and appearing in numberless
public places, condescended to mingle with the rest of the
company whom they met there. One night at a party given
by the general of the division to which George's regiment
belonged, he had the honour of dancing with Lady Blanche
Thistlewood, Lord Bareacres' daughter; he bustled for ices
and refreshments for the two noble ladies; he pushed and
squeezed for Lady Bareacres' carriage; he bragged about
the Countess when he got home, in a way which his own
father could not have surpassed. He called upon the ladies
the next day; he rode by their side in the Park; he asked
their party to a great dinner at a restaurateur's, and was
quite wild with exultation when they agreed to come. Old
Bareacres, who had not much pride and a large appetite,
would go for a dinner anywhere.

"I hope there will be no women besides our own party,"
Lady Bareacres said, after reflecting upon the invitation
which had been made, and accepted with too much precipi-
tancy.

"Gracious Heaven, Mamma—you don't suppose the man
would bring his wife," shrieked Lady Blanche, who had
been languishing in George's arms in the newly-imported
waltz for hours the night before. "The men are bearable,
but their women—"

"Wife, just married, dev'lish pretty woman, I hear," the
old Earl said.

"Well, my dear Blanche," said the mother, "I suppose,
as Papa wants to go, we must go; but we needn't know
them in England, you know." And so, determined to cut

their new acquaintance in Bond street, these great folks went to eat his dinner at Brussels, and condescending to make him pay for their pleasure, showed their dignity by making his wife uncomfortable, and carefully excluding her from the conversation. This is a species of dignity in which the high-bred British female reigns supreme. To watch the behaviour of a fine lady to other and humbler women, is a very good sport for a philosophical frequenter of Vanity Fair.

This festival, on which honest George spent a great deal of money, was the very dismallest of all the entertainments which Amelia had in her honeymoon. She wrote the most piteous accounts of the feast home to her mamma: how the Countess of Bareacres would not answer when spoken to; how Lady Blanche stared at her with her eye-glass; and what a rage Captain Dobbin was in at their behaviour; and how my lord, as they came away from the feast, asked to see the bill, and pronounced it a d— bad dinner, and d— dear. But though Amelia told all these stories, and wrote home regarding her guests' rudeness, and her own discomfiture, old Mrs. Sedley was mightily pleased nevertheless, and talked about Emmy's friend, the Countess of Bareacres, with such assiduity that the news how his son was entertaining Peers and Peeresses actually came to Osborne's ears in the City.

Those who know the present Lieutenant-General Sir George Tufto, K.C.B., and have seen him, as they may on most days in the season, padded and in stays, strutting down Pall Mall with a rickety swagger on his high-heeled lacquered boots, leering under the bonnets of passers-by, or riding a showy chestnut, and ogling broughams in the Park —those who know the present Sir George Tufto would hardly recognise the daring Peninsular and Waterloo officer. He has thick curling brown hair and black eyebrows now, and his whiskers are of the deepest purple. He was light-haired and bald in 1815, and stouter in the person and in the limbs, which especially have shrunk very much of late. When he was about seventy years of age (he is now nearly eighty,) his hair, which was very scarce and quite white, suddenly grew thick, and brown, and curly, and his whiskers and eyebrows took their present colour. Ill-natured people say that his chest is all wool, and that his hair, because it never grows, is a wig. Tom Tufto, with whose father he quarrelled ever so many years ago, declares that Mademoiselle de Jaisey, of the French theatre, pulled his grandpapa's hair off in the green-room; but Tom is notoriously spiteful and jealous; and the General's wig has nothing to do with our story.

One day, as some of our friends of the —th were sauntering in the flower-market of Brussels, having been to see the Hôtel de Ville, which Mrs. Major O'Dowd declared was not near so large or handsome as her fawther's mansion of Glenmalony, an officer of rank, with an orderly behind him, rode up to the market, and descending from his horse, came amongst the flowers, and selected the very finest bouquet which money could buy. The beautiful bundle being tied up in a paper, the officer remounted, giving the nosegay into the charge of his military groom, who carried it with a grin, following his chief, who rode away in great state and self-satisfaction.

"You should see the flowers at Glenmalony," Mrs. O'Dowd was remarking. "Me fawther has three Scotch garners with nine helpers. We have an acre of hot-houses, and pines as common as pays in the sayson. Our greeps weighs six pounds every bunch of 'em and upon me honour and conscience I think our magnolias is as big as tay-kettles."

Dobbin, who never used to "draw out" Mrs. O'Dowd as that wicked Osborne delighted in doing (much to Amelia's terror, who implored him to spare her), fell back in the crowd, crowing and sputtering until he reached a safe distance, when he exploded amongst the astonished market-people with shrieks of yelling laughter.

"Hwhat's that gawky guggling about?" said Mrs. O'Dowd. "Is it his nose bleedn? He always used to say 'twas his nose bleedn, till he must have pomped all the blood out of 'um. An't the magnolias at Glenmalony as big as tay-kettles, O'Dowd?"

"Deed then they are, and bigger, Peggy," the Major said. When the conversation was interrupted in the manner

stated by the arrival of the officer who purchased the bouquet.

"Devlish fine horse,—who is it?" George asked.

"You should see me brother Molloy Malony's horse, Molasses, that won the cup at the Curragh," the Major's wife
was exclaiming, and was continuing the family history,
when her husband interrupted her by saying—

"It's General Tufto, who commands the —— cavalry division;" adding quietly, "he and I were both shot in the
same leg at Talavera."

"Where you got your step," said George with a laugh.
"General Tufto! Then, my dear, the Crawleys are come."

Amelia's heart fell,—she knew not why. The sun did
not seem to shine so bright. The tall old roofs and gables
looked less picturesque all of a sudden, though it was a
brilliant sunset, and one of the brightest and most beautiful days at the end of May.

CHAPTER XXIX

BRUSSELS

MR. JOS had hired a pair of horses for his open carriage, with which cattle, and the smart London vehicle, he made a very tolerable figure in the drives about Brussels. George purchased a horse for his private riding, and he and Captain Dobbin would often accompany the carriage in which Jos and his sister took daily excursions of pleasure. They went out that day in the park for their accustomed diversion, and there, sure enough, George's remark with regard to the arrival of Rawdon Crawley and his wife proved to be correct. In the midst of a little troop of horsemen, consisting of some of the very greatest persons in Brussels, Rebecca was seen in the prettiest and tightest of riding-habits, mounted on a beautiful little Arab, which she rode to perfection (having acquired the art at Queen's Crawley, where the Baronet, Mr. Pitt, and Rawdon himself had given her many lessons), and by the side of the gallant General Tufto.

"Sure it's the Juke himself," cried Mrs. Major O'Dowd to Jos, who began to blush violently; "and that's Lord Uxbridge on the bay. How elegant he looks! Me brother, Molloy Malony, is as like him as two pays."

Rebecca did not make for the carriage; but as soon as she perceived her old acquaintance Amelia seated in it, acknowledged her presence by a gracious nod and smile, and by kissing and shaking her fingers playfully in the direction of the vehicle. Then she resumed her conversation with General Tufto, who asked "who the fat officer was in the gold-laced cap?" on which Becky replied, "that he was an officer in the East Indian service." But Rawdon Crawley rode out of the ranks of his company, and came up and shook hands heartily with Amelia, and said to Jos, "Well, old boy, how are you?" and stared in Mrs. O'Dowd's

320

face and at the black cock's feathers until she began to think she had made a conquest of him

George, who had been delayed behind, rode up almost immediately with Dobbin, and they touched their caps to the august personages, among whom Osborne at once perceived Mrs. Crawley. He was delighted to see Rawdon leaning over his carriage familiarly and talking to Amelia, and met the aide-de-camp's cordial greeting with more than corresponding warmth. The nods between Rawdon and Dobbin were of the very faintest specimens of politeness.

Crawley told George where they were stopping with General Tufto at the Hôtel du Parc, and George made his friend promise to come speedily to Osborne's own residence. "Sorry I hadn't seen you three days ago," George said. "Had a dinner at the Restaurateur's—rather a nice thing. Lord Bareacres, and the Countess, and Lady Blanche were good enough to dine with us—wish we'd had you." Having thus let his friend know his claims to be a man of fashion, Osborne parted from Rawdon, who followed the august squadron down an alley into which they cantered, while George and Dobbin resumed their places, one on each side of Amelia's carriage.

"How well the Juke looked," Mrs. O'Dowd remarked. "The Wellesleys and Malonys are related; but, of course, poor I would never dream of introjuicing myself unless his Grace thought proper to remember our family-tie"

"He's a great soldier," Jos said, much more at ease now the great man was gone. "Was there ever a battle won like Salamanca? Hey Dobbin? But where was it he learnt his art? In India, my boy! The jungle's the school for a general, mark me that. I knew him myself, too, Mrs. O'Dowd: we both of us danced the same evening with Miss Cutler, daughter of Cutler of the Artillery, and a devilish fine girl, at Dumdum"

The apparition of the great personages held them all in talk during the drive; and at dinner; and until the hour came when they were all to go to the Opera.

It was almost like Old England. The house was filled with familiar British faces, and those toilettes for which the British female has long been celebrated. Mrs. O'Dowd's was not the least splendid amongst these, and she had a curl on her forehead, and a set of Irish diamonds and Cairngorms, which outshone all the decorations in the house, in her notion. Her presence used to excruciate Osborne; but go she would upon all parties of pleasure on which she heard her young friends were bent. It never entered into her thought but that they must be charmed with her company.

"She's been useful to you, my dear," George said to his wife, whom he could leave alone with less scruple when she had this society. "But what a comfort it is that Rebecca's come; you will have her for a friend, and we may get rid now of this damn'd Irishwoman." To this Amelia did not answer, yes or no: and how do we know what her thoughts were?

The *coup-d'œil* of the Brussels opera-house did not strike Mrs. O'Dowd as being so fine as the theatre in Fishamble Street, Dublin, nor was French music at all equal, in her opinion, to the melodies of her native country. She favoured her friends with these and other opinions in a very loud tone of voice, and tossed about a great clattering fan she sported, with the most splendid complacency.

"Who is that wonderful woman with Amelia, Rawdon, love?" said a lady in an opposite box (who, almost always civil to her husband in private, was more fond than ever of him in company).

"Don't you see that creature with a yellow thing in her turban, and a red satin gown, and a great watch?"

"Near the pretty little woman in white?" asked a middle-aged gentleman seated by the querist's side, with orders in his button, and several under-waistcoats, and a great, choky, white stock.

"That pretty woman in white is Amelia, General: you are remarking all the pretty women, you naughty man."

"Only one, begad, in the world!" said the General, delighted, and the lady gave him a tap with a large bouquet which she had.

"Bedad it's him," said Mrs. O'Dowd; "and that's the very bokay he bought in the Marshy aux Flures!" and when Rebecca, having caught her friend's eye, performed the

little hand-kissing operation once more, Mrs. Major O'D.,
taking the compliment to herself, returned the salute with
a gracious smile, which sent that unfortunate Dobbin shrieking out of the box again.

At the end of the act, George was out of the box in a
moment, and he was even going to pay his respects to Rebecca in her *loge*. He met Crawley in the lobby, however,
where they exchanged a few sentences upon the occurrences
of the last fortnight.

"You found my cheque all right at the agent's?" George
said, with a knowing air.

"All right, my boy," Rawdon answered. "Happy to give
you your revenge. Governor come round?"

"Not yet," said George, "but he will; and you know I've
some private fortune through my mother. Has Aunty relented?"

"Sent me twenty pound, damned old screw. When shall
we have a meet? The General dines out on Tuesday. Can't
you come Tuesday? I say, make Sedley cut off his moustache. What the devil does a civilian mean with a moustache and those infernal frogs to his coat? By-bye. Try
and come on Tuesday;" and Rawdon was going off with
two brilliant young gentlemen of fashion, who were, like
himself, on the staff of a general officer.

George was only half pleased to be asked to dinner on
that particular day when the General was *not* to dine. "I
will go in and pay my respects to your wife," said he; at
which Rawdon said, "Hm, as you please," looking very
glum, and at which the two young officers exchanged knowing glances. George parted from them and strutted down
the lobby to the General's box, the number of which he
had carefully counted.

"*Entrez*," said a clear little voice, and our friend found
himself in Rebecca's presence; who jumped up, clapped
her hands together, and held out both of them to George,
so charmed was she to see him. The General, with the
orders in his button, stared at the new comer with a sulky
scowl, as much as to say, who the devil are you?

"My dear Captain George!" cried little Rebecca in an
ecstasy. "How good of you to come. The general and I

were moping together *tête-à-tête*. General, this is my Captain George of whom you heard me talk."

"Indeed," said the General, with a very small bow; "of what regiment is Captain George?"

George mentioned the —th; how he wished he could have said it was a crack cavalry corps.

"Come home lately from the West Indies, I believe. Not seen much service in the late war. Quartered here, Captain George?"—the General went on with killing haughtiness.

"Not Captain George, you stupid man; Captain Osborne," Rebecca said. The General all the while was looking savagely from one to the other.

"Captain Osborne, indeed! Any relation to the L— Osbornes?"

"We bear the same arms," George said, as indeed was the fact; Mr. Osborne having consulted with a herald in Long Acre, and picked the L— arms out of the peerage, when he set up his carriage fifteen years before. The General made no reply to this announcement; but took up his opera-glass—the double-barrelled lorgnon was not invented in those days—and pretended to examine the house, but Rebecca saw that his disengaged eye was working round in her direction, and shooting out blood-shot glances at her and George.

She redoubled in cordiality. "How is dearest Amelia? But I needn't ask: how pretty she looks! And who is that nice good-natured looking creature with her—a flame of yours? O, you wicked man! And there is Mr. Sedley eating ice, I declare: how he seems to enjoy it! General, why have we not had any ices?"

"Shall I go and fetch you some?" said the General bursting with wrath.

"Let *me* go, I entreat you," George said.

"No, I will go to Amelia's box. Dear, sweet girl! Give me your arm, Captain George;" and so saying, and with a nod to the General, she tripped into the lobby. She gave George the queerest knowingest look, when they were together, a look which might have been interpreted, "Don't you see the state of affairs, and what a fool I'm

making of him?" But he did not perceive it. He was thinking of his own plans, and lost in pompous admiration of his
own irresistible powers of pleasing.

The curses to which the General gave a low utterance,
as soon as Rebecca and her conqueror had quitted him,
were so deep, that I am sure no compositor would venture
to print them were they written down. They came from
the General's heart; and a wonderful thing it is to think
that the human heart is capable of generating such produce, and can throw out, as occasion demands, such a supply
of lust and fury, rage and hatred.

Amelia's gentle eyes, too, had been fixed anxiously on
the pair, whose conduct had so chafed the jealous General;
but when Rebecca entered her box, she flew to her friend
with an affectionate rapture which showed itself, in spite
of the publicity of the place; for she embraced her dearest
friend in the presence of the whole house, at least in full
view of the General's glass, now brought to bear upon the
Osborne party. Mrs. Rawdon saluted Jos, too, with the
kindliest greeting: she admired Mrs. O'Dowd's large Cairn-
gorm brooch and superb Irish diamonds, and wouldn't
believe that they were not from Golconda direct. She bustled, she chattered, she turned and twisted, and smiled
upon one, and smirked on another, all in full view of
the jealous opera-glass opposite. And when the time
for the ballet came (in which there was no dancer that
went through her grimaces or performed her comedy of
action better), she skipped back to her own box, leaning
on Captain Dobbin's arm this time. No, she would not have
George's: he must stay and talk to his dearest, best, little
Amelia.

"What a humbug that woman is!" honest old Dobbin
mumbled to George, when he came back from Rebecca's
box, whither he had conducted her in perfect silence, and
with a countenance as glum as an undertaker's. "She
writhes and twists about like a snake. All the time she
was here, didn't you see, George, how she was acting at
the General over the way?"

"Humbug—acting! Hang it, she's the nicest little woman
in England," George replied, showing his white teeth, and

giving his ambrosial whiskers a twirl. "You ain't a man of the world, Dobbin. Dammy, look at her now, she's talked over Tufto in no time. Look how he's laughing! Gad, what a shoulder she has! Emmy, why didn't you have a bouquet? Everybody has a bouquet."

"Faith, then, why didn't you *boy* one?" Mrs. O'Dowd said; and both Amelia and William Dobbin thanked her for this timely observation. But beyond this neither of the ladies rallied. Amelia was overpowered by the flash and the dazzle and the fashionable talk of her worldly rival. Even the O'Dowd was silent and subdued after Becky's brilliant apparition, and scarcely said a word more about Glenmalony all the evening.

"When do you intend to give up play, George, as you have promised me, any time these hundred years?" Dobbin said to his friend a few days after the night at the Opera.

"When do you intend to give up sermonising?" was the other's reply. "What the deuce, man, are you alarmed about? We play low; I won last night. You don't suppose Crawley cheats? With fair play it comes to pretty much the same thing at the year's end."

"But I don't think he could pay if he lost," Dobbin said; and his advice met with the success which advice usually commands. Osborne and Crawley were repeatedly together now. General Tufto dined abroad almost constantly. George was always welcome in the apartments (very close indeed to those of the General) which the Aide-de-camp and his wife occupied in the hotel.

Amelia's manners were such when she and George visited Crawley and his wife at these quarters, that they had very nearly come to their first quarrel; that is, George scolded his wife violently for her evident unwillingness to go, and the high and mighty manner in which she comported herself towards Mrs. Crawley, her old friend; and Amelia did not say one single word in reply; but with her husband's eye upon her and Rebecca scanning her, as she felt, was, if possible, more bashful and awkward on the second visit which she paid to Mrs. Rawdon, than on her first call.

Rebecca was doubly affectionate, of course, and would not take notice, in the least, of her friend's coolness. "I think Emmy has become prouder since her father's name was in the —, since Mr. Sedley's *misfortunes*," Rebecca said, softening the phrase charitably for George's ear.

"Upon my word, I thought when we were at Brighton she was doing me the honour to be jealous of me; and now I suppose she is scandalised because Rawdon, and I, and the General live together. Why my dear creature, how could we, with our means, live at all, but for a friend to share expenses? And do you suppose that Rawdon is not big enough to take care of my honour? But I'm very much obliged to Emmy, very," Mrs. Rawdon said.

"Pooh, jealousy!" answered George, "all women are jealous."

"And all men too. Weren't you jealous of General Tufto, and the General of you, on the night of the Opera? Why, he was ready to eat me for going with you to visit that foolish little wife of yours; as if I care a pin for either of you," Crawley's wife said, with a pert toss of her head. "Will you dine here? The dragon dines with the Commander-in-Chief. Great news is stirring. They say the French have crossed the frontier. We shall have a quiet dinner."

George accepted the invitation, although his wife was a little ailing. They were now not quite six weeks married. Another woman was laughing or sneering at her expense, and he not angry. He was not even angry with himself, this good-natured fellow. It is a shame, he owned to himself; but hang it, if a pretty woman *will* throw herself in your way, why, what can a fellow do, you know? I *am* rather free about women, he had often said, smiling and nodding knowingly to Stubble and Spooney, and other comrades of the mess-table; and they rather respected him than otherwise for this prowess. Next to conquering in war, conquering in love has been a source of pride, time out of mind, amongst men in Vanity Fair, or how should school-boys brag of their amours, or Don Juan be popular?

So Mr. Osborne, having a firm conviction in his own mind that he was a woman-killer and destined to conquer, did not run counter to his fate, but yielded himself up to it quite complacently. And as Emmy did not say much or plague him with her jealousy, but merely became unhappy and pined over it miserably in secret, he chose to fancy that she was not suspicious of what all his acquaintance were perfectly aware—namely, that he was carrying on a desperate flirtation with Mrs. Crawley. He rode with her whenever she was free. He pretended regimental business to Amelia (by which falsehood she was not in the least deceived), and consigning his wife to solitude or her brother's society, passed his evenings in the Crawleys' company; losing money to the husband and flattering himself that the wife was dying of love for him. It is very likely that this worthy couple never absolutely conspired and agreed together in so many words: the one to cajole the young gentleman, whilst the other won his money at cards; but they understood each other perfectly well, and Rawdon let Osborne come and go with entire good humour.

George was so occupied with his new acquaintances that he and William Dobbin were by no means so much together as formerly. George avoided him in public and in the regiment, and as we see, did not like those sermons which his senior was disposed to inflict upon him. If some parts of his conduct made Captain Dobbin exceedingly grave and cool; of what use was it to tell George that, though his whiskers were large, and his own opinion of his knowingness great, he was as green as a school-boy? that Rawdon was making a victim of him as he had done of many before, and as soon as he had used him would fling him off with scorn? He would not listen: and so, as Dobbin, upon those days when he visited the Osborne house, seldom had the advantage of meeting his old friend, much painful and unavailing talk between them was spared. Our friend George was in the full career of the pleasures of Vanity Fair.

There never was, since the days of Darius, such a brilliant train of camp-followers as hung around the Duke of Wellington's army in the Low Countries, in 1815; and led it dancing and feasting, as it were, up to the very brink of battle. A certain ball which a noble Duchess gave at Brussels on the 15th of June in the above-named year is historical. All Brussels had been in a state of excitement about it, and I have heard from ladies who were in that town at the period, that the talk and interest of persons of their own sex regarding the ball was much greater even than in respect of the enemy in their front. The struggles, intrigues, and prayers to get tickets were such as only English ladies will employ, in order to gain admission to the society of the great of their own nation.

Jos and Mrs. O'Dowd, who were panting to be asked, strove in vain to procure tickets; but others of our friends were more lucky. For instance, through the interest of my Lord Bareacres, and as a set-off for the dinner at the restaurateur's, George got a card for Captain and Mrs. Osborne; which circumstance greatly elated him. Dobbin, who was a friend of the General commanding the division in which their regiment was, came laughing one day to Mrs. Osborne, and displayed a similar invitation, which made Jos envious, and George wonder how the deuce *he* should be getting into society. Mr. and Mrs. Rawdon, finally, were of course invited; as became the friends of a General commanding a cavalry brigade.

On the appointed night, George, having commanded new dresses and ornaments of all sorts for Amelia, drove to the famous ball, where his wife did not know a single soul. After looking about for Lady Bareacres, who cut him, thinking the card was quite enough—and after placing Amelia on a bench he left her to her own cogitations there, thinking, on his own part, that he had behaved very handsomely in getting her new clothes, and bringing her to the ball, where she was free to amuse herself as she liked. Her thoughts were not of the pleasantest, and nobody except honest Dobbin came to disturb them.

Whilst her appearance was an utter failure (as her husband felt with a sort of rage,) Mrs. Rawdon Crawley's *début* was, on the contrary, very brilliant. She arrived very late. Her face was radiant; her dress perfection. In the midst of the great persons assembled, and the eyeglasses directed to her, Rebecca seemed to be as cool and collected as when she used to marshal Miss Pinkerton's little girls to church. Numbers of the men she knew already, and the dandies thronged round her. As for the ladies, it was whispered among them that Rawdon had run away with her from out of a convent, and that she was a relation of the Montmorency family. She spoke French so perfectly that there might be some truth in this report, and it was agreed that her manners were fine, and her air *distingué*. Fifty would-be partners thronged round her at once, and pressed to have the honour to dance with her. But she said she was engaged, and only going to dance very little; and made her way at once to the place where Emmy sat quite unnoticed, and dismally unhappy. And so, to finish the poor child at once, Mrs. Rawdon ran and greeted affectionately her dearest Amelia, and began forthwith to patronise her. She found fault with her friend's dress, and her hair-dresser, and wondered how she could be so *chaussée*, and vowed that she must send her *corsetière* the next morning. She vowed that it was a delightful ball; that there was everybody that every one knew, and only a *very* few nobodies in the whole room. It is a fact, that in a fortnight, and after three dinners in general society, this young woman had got up the genteel jargon so well, that a native could not speak it better; and it was only from her French being so good, that you could know she was not a born woman of fashion.

George, who had left Emmy on her bench on entering the ballroom, very soon found his way back when Rebecca was by her dear friend's side. Becky was just lecturing Mrs. Osborne upon the follies which her husband was committing. "For God's sake, stop him from gambling, my dear," she said, "or he will ruin himself. He and Rawdon are playing at cards every night, and you know he is very poor, and Rawdon will win every shilling from him if he does not take care. Why don't you prevent him, you little careless creature? Why don't you come to us of an evening, instead of moping at home with that Captain Dobbin. I dare say he is *très aimable;* how could one love a man with feet of such size? Your husband's feet are darlings—Here he comes. Where have you been, wretch? Here is Emmy crying her eyes out for you. Are you coming to fetch me for the quadrille?" And she left her bouquet and shawl by Amelia's side, and tripped off with George to dance. Women only know how to wound so. There is a poison on the tips of their little shafts, which stings a thousand times more than a man's blunter weapon. Our poor Emmy, who had never hated, never sneered all her life, was powerless in the hands of her remorseless little enemy.

George danced with Rebecca twice or thrice—how many times Amelia scarcely knew. She sat quite unnoticed in her corner, except when Rawdon came up with some words of clumsy conversation: and later in the evening, when Captain Dobbin made so bold as to bring her refreshments and sit beside her. He did not like to ask her why she was so sad; but as a pretext for the tears which were filling in her eyes, she told him that Mrs. Crawley had alarmed her by telling her that George would go on playing.

"It is curious, when a man is bent upon play, by what clumsy rogues he will allow himself to be cheated," Dobbin said; and Emmy said, "Indeed." She was thinking of something else. It was not the loss of the money that grieved her.

At last George came back for Rebecca's shawl and flowers. She was going away. She did not even condescend to come back and say good-bye to Amelia. The poor girl let her husband come and go without saying a word, and her head fell on her breast. Dobbin had been called away and was whispering deep in conversation with the General of the division, his friend, and had not seen this last parting. George went away then with the bouquet; but when he gave it to the owner, there lay a note, coiled like a snake among the flowers. Rebecca's eye caught it at once. She had been used to deal with notes in early life. She put out her hand and took the nosegay. He saw by her eyes as they met, that she was aware what she should find there. Her husband hurried her away, still too intent upon his own thoughts, seemingly, to take note of any marks of recognition which might pass between his friend and his wife. These were, however, but trifling. Rebecca gave George her hand with one of her usual quick knowing glances, and made a curtsey and walked away. George bowed over the hand, said nothing in reply to a remark of Crawley's, did not hear it even, his brain was so throbbing with triumph and excitement, and allowed them to go away without a word.

His wife saw the one part at least of the bouquet-scene. It was quite natural that George should come at Rebecca's request to get her her scarf and flowers: it was no more than he had done twenty times before in the course of the last few days; but now it was too much for her. "William," she said, suddenly clinging to Dobbin, who was near her, "you've always been very kind to me—I'm—I'm not well. Take me home." She did not know she called him by his Christian name, as George was accustomed to do. He went away with her quickly. Her lodgings were hard by; and they threaded through the crowd without, where everything seemed to be more astir than even in the ball-room within.

George had been angry twice or thrice at finding his wife up on his return from the parties which he frequented: so she went straight to bed now; but although she did not sleep, and although the din and clatter, and the galloping of horsemen were incessant, she never heard any of these noises, having quite other disturbances to keep her awake.

Osborne meanwhile, wild with elation, went off to a play-table, and began to bet frantically. He won repeatedly. "Everything succeeds with me to-night," he said. But his luck at play even did not cure him of his restlessness, and he started up after awhile, pocketing his winnings, and went to a buffet, where he drank off many bumpers of wine.

Here, as he was rattling away to the people around, laughing loudly and wild with spirits, Dobbin found him. He had been to the card-tables to look there for his friend. Dobbin looked as pale and grave as his comrade was flushed and jovial.

"Hullo, Dob! Come and drink, old Dob! The Duke's wine is famous. Give me some more, you sir;" and he held out a trembling glass for the liquor.

"Come out, George," said Dobbin, still gravely; "don't drink."

"Drink! there's nothing like it. Drink yourself, and light up your lantern jaws, old boy. Here's to you."

Dobbin went up and whispered something to him, at which George, giving a start and a wild hurray, tossed off his glass, clapped it on the table, and walked away speedily on his friend's arm. "The enemy has passed the Sambre," William said, "and our left is already engaged. Come away. We are to march in three hours."

Away went George, his nerves quivering with excitement at the news so long looked for, so sudden when it came. What were love and intrigue now? He thought about a thousand things but these in his rapid walk to his quarters —his past life and future chances—the fate which might be before him—the wife, the child perhaps, from whom unseen he might be about to part. Oh, how he wished that night's work undone! and that with a clear conscience at least he might say farewell to the tender and guileless being by whose love he had set such little store!

He thought over his brief married life. In those few weeks he had frightfully dissipated his little capital. How wild and reckless he had been! Should any mischance befall him; what was then left for her? How unworthy he was of her. Why had he married her? He was not fit for marriage. Why had he disobeyed his father, who had been always so generous to him?

Hope, remorse, ambition, tenderness, and selfish regret filled his heart. He sat down and wrote to his father, remembering what he had said once before, when he was engaged to fight a duel. Dawn faintly streaked the sky as he closed this farewell letter. He sealed it, and kissed the superscription. He thought how he had deserted that generous father, and of the thousand kindnesses which the stern old man had done him.

He had looked into Amelia's bed-room when he entered; she lay quiet, and her eyes seemed closed, and he was glad that she was asleep. On arriving at his quarters from the ball, he had found his regimental servant already making preparations for his departure: the man had understood his signal to be still, and these arrangements were very quickly and silently made. Should he go in and wake Amelia, he thought, or leave a note for her brother to break the news of departure to her? He went in to look at her once again.

She had been awake when he first entered her room, but had kept her eyes closed, so that even her wakefulness should not seem to reproach him. But when he had returned, so soon after herself, too, this timid little heart had felt more at ease, and turning towards him as he stepped softly out of the room, she had fallen into a light sleep. George came in and looked at her again, entering still more softly. By the pale night-lamp he could see her sweet, pale face—the purple eyelids were fringed and closed, and one round arm, smooth and white, lay outside of the coverlet. Good God, how pure she was; how gentle, how tender, and how friendless! and he, how selfish, brutal, and black with crime! Heart-stained, and shame-stricken, he stood at the bed's foot, and looked at the sleeping girl. How dared he— who was he, to pray for one so spotless! God bless her! God bless her! He came to the bed-side, and looked at the hand, the little soft hand, lying asleep; and he bent over the pillow noiselessly towards the gentle pale face.

Two fair arms closed tenderly round his neck as he stooped down. "I am awake, George," the poor child said, with a sob fit to break the little heart that nestled so closely by his own. She was awake, poor soul, and to what? At that moment a bugle from the Place of Arms began sounding clearly, and was taken up through the town; and amidst the drums of the infantry, and the shrill pipes of the Scotch, the whole city awoke.

CHAPTER XXX

"The Girl I Left Behind Me"

WE do not claim to rank among the military novelists. Our place is with the non-combatants. When the decks are cleared for action we go below and wait meekly. We should only be in the way of the manœuvres that the gallant fellows are performing overhead. We shall go no farther with the —th than to the city gate : and leaving Major O'Dowd to his duty, come back to the Major's wife, and the ladies and the baggage.

Now the Major and his lady, who had not been invited to the ball at which in our last chapter other of our friends figured, had much more time to take their wholesome natural rest in bed, than was accorded to people who wished to enjoy pleasure as well as to do duty. "It's my belief, Peggy, my dear," said he, as he placidly pulled his nightcap over his ears, "that there will be such a ball danced in a day or two as some of 'em has never heard the chune of;" and he was much more happy to retire to rest after partaking of a quiet tumbler, than to figure at any other sort of amusement. Peggy, for her part, would have liked to have shown her turban and bird of paradise at the ball, but for the information which her husband had given her, and which made her very grave.

"I'd like ye wake me about half an hour before the assembly beats," the Major said to his lady. "Call me at half-past one, Peggy dear, and see me things is ready. Maybe I'll not come back to breakfast, Mrs. O'D." With which words, which signified his opinion that the regiment would march the next morning, the Major ceased talking, and fell asleep.

Mrs. O'Dowd, the good housewife, arrayed in curl-papers and a camisole, felt that her duty was to act, and not to sleep, at this juncture. "Time enough for that," she said, "when Mick's gone;" and so she packed his travelling valise ready for the march, brushed his cloak, his cap, and other warlike habiliments, set them out in order for him; and stowed away in the cloak pockets a light package of portable refreshments, and a wicker-covered flask or pocket-pistol, containing near a pint of a remarkably sound Cognac brandy, of which she and the Major approved very much; and as soon as the hands of the "repayther" pointed to half-past one, and its interior arrangements (it had a tone quite equal to a cathaydral, its fair owner considered) knelled forth that fatal hour, Mrs. O'Dowd woke up her Major, and had as comfortable a cup of coffee prepared for him as any made that morning in Brussels. And who is there will deny that this worthy lady's preparations betokened affection as much as the fits of tears and hysterics by which more sensitive females exhibited their love, and that their partaking of this coffee, which they drank together while the bugles were sounding the turn-out and the drums beating in the various quarters of the town, was not more useful and to the purpose than the outpouring of any mere sentiment could be? The consequence was, that the Major appeared on parade quite trim, fresh, and alert—his well-shaved rosy countenance, as he sat on horseback, giving cheerfulness and confidence to the whole corps. All the officers saluted her when the regiment marched by the balcony on which this brave woman stood, and waved them a cheer as they passed; and I daresay it was not from want of courage, but from a sense of female delicacy and propriety, that she refrained from leading the gallant —th personally into action.

On Sundays, and at periods of a solemn nature, Mrs. O'Dowd used to read with great gravity out of a large volume of her uncle the Dean's sermons. It had been of great comfort to her on board the transport as they were coming home, and were very nearly wrecked, on their return from the West Indies. After the regiment's departure she betook herself to this volume for meditation; perhaps she did not understand much of what she was reading, and her thoughts were elsewhere: but the sleep project, with poor Mick's nightcap there on the pillow, was quite a vain one. So it is in the world. Jack or Donald marches away to

glory with his knapsack on his shoulder, stepping out briskly
to the tune of "The Girl I left Behind me." It is she who
remains and suffers,—and has the leisure to think, and brood,
and remember.

Knowing how useless regrets are, and how the indulgence
of sentiment only serves to make people more miserable,
Mrs. Rebecca wisely determined to give way to no vain
feelings of sorrow, and bore the parting from her husband
with quite a Spartan equanimity. Indeed Captain Rawdon
himself was much more affected at the leave-taking than
the resolute little woman to whom he bade farewell. She
had mastered this rude coarse nature; and he loved and
worshipped her with all his faculties of regard and admiration. In all his life he had never been so happy, as, during
the past few months, his wife had made him. All former
delights of turf, mess, hunting-field, and gambling-table;
all previous loves and courtships of milliners, opera-dancers,
and the like easy triumphs of the clumsy military Adonis,
were quite insipid when compared to the lawful matrimonial pleasures which of late he had enjoyed. She had
known perpetually how to divert him; and he had found
his house and her society a thousand times more pleasant
than any place or company which he had ever frequented
from his childhood until now. And he cursed his past
follies and extravagances, and bemoaned his vast outlying
debts above all, which must remain forever as obstacles to
prevent his wife's advancement in the world. He had often
groaned over these in midnight conversations with Rebecca,
although as a bachelor they had never given him any disquiet. He himself was struck with this phenomenon. "Hang
it," he would say (or perhaps use a still stronger expression
out of his simple vocabulary), "before I was married I
didn't care what bills I put my name to, and so long as
Moses would wait or Levy would renew for three months,
I kept on never minding. But since I'm married, except
renewing, of course, I give you my honour I've not touched
a bit of stamped paper."

Rebecca always knew how to conjure away these moods of
melancholy. "Why, my stupid love," she would say, "we
have not done with your aunt yet. If she fails us, isn't there

what you call the *Gazette?* or, stop, when your uncle Bute's life drops, I have another scheme. The living has always belonged to the younger brother, and why shouldn't you sell out and go into the Church?" The idea of this conversion set Rawdon into roars of laughter: you might have heard the explosion through the hotel at midnight, and the haw-haws of the great dragoon's voice. General Tufto heard him from his quarters on the first floor above them; and Rebecca acted the scene with great spirit, and preached Rawdon's first sermon, to the immense delight of the General at breakfast.

But these were mere by-gone days and talk. When the final news arrived that the campaign was opened, and the troops were to march, Rawdon's gravity became such that Becky rallied him about it in a manner which rather hurt the feelings of the Guardsman. "You don't suppose I'm afraid, Becky, I should think," he said, with a tremor in his voice. "But I'm a pretty good mark for a shot, and you see if it brings me down, why I leave one and perhaps two behind me whom I should wish to provide for, as I brought 'em into the scrape. It is no laughing matter *that,* Mrs. C., anyways."

Rebecca by a hundred caresses and kind words tried to soothe the feelings of the wounded lover. It was only when her vivacity and sense of humour got the better of this sprightly creature (as they would do under most circumstances of life indeed) that she would break out with her satire, but she could soon put on a demure face. "Dearest love," she said, "do you suppose I feel nothing?" and hastily dashing something from her eyes, she looked up in her husband's face with a smile.

"Look here," said he. "If I drop, let us see what there is for you. I have had a pretty good run of luck here, and here's two hundred and thirty pounds. I have got ten Napoleons in my pocket. That is as much as I shall want; for the General pays everything like a prince; and if I'm hit, why, you know I cost nothing. Don't cry, little woman; I may live to vex you yet. Well, I shan't take either of my horses, but shall ride the General's grey charger: it's cheaper, and I told him mine was lame. If I'm done, those two ought to fetch you something. Grigg offered ninety for the mare

yesterday, before this confounded news came, and like a fool
I wouldn't let her go under the two o's. Bullfinch will fetch
his price any day, only you'd better sell him in this country,
because the dealers have so many bills of mine, and so I'd
rather he shouldn't go back to England. Your little mare
the General gave you will fetch something, and there's no
d—d livery stable bills here as there are in London," Rawdon
added, with a laugh. "There's that dressing-case cost me two
hundred,—that is, I owe two for it; and the gold tops and
bottles must be worth thirty or forty. Please to put *that* up
the spout, ma'am, with my pins, and rings, and watch and
chain, and things. They cost a precious lot of money. Miss
Crawley, I know, paid a hundred down for the chain and
ticker. Gold tops and bottles, indeed! dammy, I'm sorry I
didn't take more now. Edwards pressed on me a silver-gilt
boot-jack, and I might have had a dressing-case fitted up
with a silver warming-pan, and a service of plate. But we
must make the best of what we've got, Becky, you know."

And so, making his last dispositions, Captain Crawley,
who had seldom thought about anything but himself, until
the last few months of his life, when Love had obtained the
mastery over the dragoon, went through the various items
of his little catalogue of effects, striving to see how they
might be turned into money for his wife's benefit, in case any
accident should befall him. He pleased himself by noting
down with a pencil, in his big school-boy handwriting, the
various items of his portable property which might be sold
for his widow's advantage—as, for example, "My double-
barril by Manton, say 40 guineas; my driving cloak, lined
with sable fur, £50; my duelling pistols in rosewood case
(same which I shot Captain Marker), £20; my regulation
saddle-holsters and housings; my Laurie ditto," and so forth,
over all of which articles he made Rebecca the mistress.

Faithful to his plan of economy, the Captain dressed himself in his oldest and shabbiest uniform and epaulets, leaving
the newest behind, under his wife's (or it might be his
widow's) guardianship. And this famous dandy of Windsor
and Hyde Park went off on his campaign with a kit as modest as that of a sergeant, and with something like a prayer
on his lips for the woman he was leaving. He took her up

from the ground, and held her in his arms for a minute, tight pressed against his strong-beating heart. His face was purple and his eyes dim, as he put her down and left her. He rode by his General's side, and smoked his cigar in silence as they hastened after the troops of the General's brigade, which preceded them; and it was not until they were some miles on their way that he left off twirling his moustache and broke silence.

And Rebecca, as we have said, wisely determined not to give way to unavailing sentimentality on her husband's departure. She waved him an adieu from the window, and stood there for a moment looking out after he was gone. The cathedral towers and the full gables of the quaint old houses were just beginning to blush in the sunrise. There had been no rest for her that night. She was still in her pretty ball-dress, her fair hair hanging somewhat out of curl on her neck, and the circles round her eyes dark with watching. "What a fright I seem," she said, examining herself in the glass, "and how pale this pink makes one look!" So she divested herself of this pink raiment; in doing which a note fell out from her corsage, which she picked up with a smile, and locked into her dressing-box. And then she put her bouquet of the ball into a glass of water, and went to bed, and slept very comfortably.

The town was quite quiet when she woke up at ten o'clock, and partook of coffee, very requisite and comforting after the exhaustion and grief of the morning's occurrences.

This meal over, she resumed honest Rawdon's calculations of the night previous, and surveyed her position. Should the worst befall, all things considered, she was pretty well to do. There were her own trinkets and trousseau, in addition to those which her husband had left behind. Rawdon's generosity, when they were first married, has already been described and lauded. Besides these, and the little mare, the General, her slave and worshipper, had made her many very handsome presents, in the shape of cashmere shawls bought at the auction of a bankrupt French general's lady, and numerous tributes from the jewellers' shops, all of which betokened her admirer's taste and wealth. As for "tickers," as poor Rawdon called watches, her apartments were alive with their clicking. For, happening to mention one night that hers, which Rawdon had given to her, was of English workmanship, and went ill, on the very next morning there came to her a little bijou marked Leroy, with a chain and cover charmingly set with turquoises, and another signed Breguet, which was covered with pearls, and yet scarcely bigger than a half-crown. General Tufto had bought one, and Captain Osborne had gallantly presented the other. Mrs. Osborne had no watch, though, to do George justice, she might have had one for the asking, and the Honourable Mrs. Tufto in England had an old instrument of her mother's that might have served for the plate warming-pan which Rawdon talked about. If Messrs. Howell and James were to publish a list of the purchasers of all the trinkets which they sell, how surprised would some families be: and if all these ornaments went to gentlemen's lawful wives and daughters, what a profusion of jewellery there would be exhibited in the genteelest homes of Vanity Fair!

Every calculation made of these valuables Mrs. Rebecca found, not without a pungent feeling of triumph and self-satisfaction, that should circumstances occur, she might reckon on six or seven hundred pounds at the very least, to begin the world with; and she passed the morning disposing, ordering, looking out, and locking up her properties in the most agreeable manner. Among the notes in Rawdon's pocket-book, was a draft for twenty pounds on Osborne's banker. This made her think about Mrs. Osborne. "I will go and get the draft cashed," she said, "and pay a visit afterwards to poor little Emmy." If this is a novel without a hero, at least let us lay claim to a heroine. No man in the British army which has marched away, not the great Duke himself, could be more cool or collected in the presence of doubts and difficulties, than the indomitable little aide-de-camp's wife.

And there was another of our acquaintances who was also to be left behind, a non-combatant, and whose emotions and behaviour we have therefore a right to know. This was our friend the ex-collector of Boggley Wollah, whose rest was broken, like other people's, by the sounding of the bugles in the early morning. Being a great sleeper, and fond of his bed, it is possible he would have snoozed on until his usual hour of rising in the forenoon, in spite of all the drums, bugles, and bagpipes in the British army, but for an interruption, which did not come from George Osborne, who shared Jos's quarters with him, and was as usual occupied too much with his own affairs or with grief at parting with his wife, to think of taking leave of his slumbering brother-in-law—it was not George, we say, who interposed between Jos Sedley and sleep, but Captain Dobbin, who came and roused him up, insisting on shaking hands with him before his departure.

"Very kind of you," said Jos, yawning, and wishing the Captain at the deuce.

"I—I didn't like to go off without saying good-bye, you know," Dobbin said in a very incoherent manner; "because you know some of us mayn't come back again, and I like to see you all well, and—and that sort of thing, you know."

"What do you mean?" Jos asked, rubbing his eyes. The Captain did not in the least hear him or look at the stout gentleman in the nightcap, about whom he professed to have such a tender interest. The hypocrite was looking and listening with all his might in the direction of George's apartments, striding about the room, upsetting the chairs, beating the tattoo, biting his nails, and showing other signs of great inward emotion.

Jos had always had rather a mean opinion of the Captain, and now began to think his courage was somewhat equivocal. "What is it I can do for you, Dobbin?" he said, in a sarcastic tone.

"I tell you what you can do," the Captain replied, coming up to the bed; "we march in a quarter of an hour, Sedley, and neither George nor I may ever come back. Mind you, you are not to stir from this town until you ascertain how things go. You are to stay here and watch over your sister, and comfort her, and see that no harm comes to her. If anything happens to George, remember she has no one but you in the world to look to. If it goes wrong with the army, you'll see her safe back to England; and you will promise me on

your word that you will never desert her. I know you won't:
as far as money goes, you were always free enough with that.
Do you want any? I mean, have you enough gold to take
you back to England in case of a misfortune?"

"Sir," said Jos, majestically, "when I want money, I know
where to ask for it. And as for my sister, *you* needn't tell
me how I ought to behave to her."

"You speak like a man of spirit, Jos," the other answered
good-naturedly, "and I am glad that George can leave her
in such good hands. So I may give him your word of honour, may I, that in case of extremity you will stand by her?"

"Of course, of course," answered Mr. Jos, whose generosity in money matters Dobbin estimated quite correctly.

"And you'll see her safe out of Brussels in the event of a
defeat?"

"A defeat! D— it, sir, it's impossible. Don't try and
frighten *me,*" the hero cried from his bed; and Dobbin's
mind was thus perfectly set at ease now that Jos had spoken
out so resolutely respecting his conduct to his sister. "At
least," thought the Captain, "there will be a retreat secured
for her in case the worst should ensue."

If Captain Dobbin expected to get any personal comfort
and satisfaction from having one more view of Amelia before the regiment marched away, his selfishness was pun-
ished just as such odious egotism deserved to be. The door
of Jos's bed-room opened into the sitting-room which was
common to the family party, and opposite this door was
that of Amelia's chamber. The bugles had wakened everybody: there was no use in concealment now. George's
servant was packing in this room: Osborne coming in and
out of the contiguous bed-room, flinging to the man such
articles as he thought fit to carry on the campaign. And
presently Dobbin had the opportunity which his heart cov-
eted, and he got sight of Amelia's face once more. But
what a face it was! So white, so wild and despair stricken,
that the remembrance of it haunted him afterwards like a
crime, and the sight smote him with inexpressible pangs of
longing and pity.

She was wrapped in a white morning dress, her hair falling on her shoulders, and her large eyes fixed and without

light. By way of helping on the preparations for the departure, and showing that she too could be useful at a moment
so critical, this poor soul had taken up a sash of George's
from the drawers whereon it lay, and followed him to and fro
with the sash in her hand, looking on mutely as his packing
proceeded. She came out and stood, leaning at the wall,
holding this sash against her bosom, from which the heavy
net of crimson dropped like a large stain of blood. Our
gentle-hearted Captain felt a guilty shock as he looked at her.
"Good God," thought he, "and is it grief like this I dared
to pry into?" And there was no help: no means to soothe
and comfort this helpless, speechless misery. He stood for a
moment and looked at her, powerless and torn with pity, as
a parent regards an infant in pain.

At last, George took Emmy's hand, and led her back into
the bed-room, from whence he came out alone. The parting
had taken place in that moment, and he was gone.

"Thank Heaven that is over," George thought, bounding
down the stair, his sword under his arm, as he ran swiftly
to the alarm ground, where the regiment was mustered, and
whither trooped men and officers hurrying from their billets;
his pulse was throbbing and his cheeks flushed: the great
game of war was going to be played, and he one of the
players. What a fierce excitement of doubt, hope, and
pleasure! What tremendous hazards of loss or gain! What
were all the games of chance he had ever played compared
to this one? Into all contests requiring athletic skill and
courage, the young man, from his boyhood upwards, had
flung himself with all his might. The champion of his school
and his regiment, the bravos of his companions had followed
him everywhere; from the boy's cricket-match to the garrison
races, he had won a hundred of triumphs; and wherever he
went, women and men had admired and envied him. What
qualities are there for which a man gets so speedy a return
of applause, as those of bodily superiority, activity, and
valour? Time out of mind strength and courage have been
the theme of bards and romances; and from the story
of Troy down to to-day, poetry has always chosen a soldier
for a hero. I wonder is it because men are cowards in
heart that they admire bravery so much, and place military

valour so far beyond every other quality for reward and worship?

So, at the sound of that stirring call to battle, George jumped away from the gentle arms in which he had been dallying; not without a feeling of shame (although his wife's hold on him had been but feeble), that he should have been detained there so long. The same feeling of eagerness and excitement was amongst all those friends of his of whom we have had occasional glimpses, from the stout senior Major, who led the regiment into action, to little Stubble, the Ensign, who was to bear its colours on that day.

The sun was just rising as the march began—it was a gallant sight—the band led the column, playing the regimental march—then came the Major in command, riding upon Pyramus, his stout charger—then marched the grenadiers, their Captain at their head; in the centre were the colours, borne by the senior and junior Ensigns—then George came marching at the head of his company. He looked up, and smiled at Amelia, and passed on; and even the sound of the music died away.

CHAPTER XXXI

In Which Jos Sedley Takes Care of His Sister

THUS all the superior officers being summoned on duty elsewhere, Jos Sedley was left in command of the little colony at Brussels, with Amelia invalided, Isidor, his Belgian servant, and the *bonne,* who was maid-of-all-work for the establishment, as a garrison under him. Though he was disturbed in spirit, and his rest destroyed by Dobbin's interruption and the occurrences of the morning, Jos nevertheless remained for many hours in bed, wakeful and rolling about there until his usual hour of rising had arrived. The sun was high in the heavens, and our gallant friends of the —th miles on their march, before the civilian appeared in his flowered dressing-gown at breakfast.

About George's absence, his brother-in-law was very easy in mind. Perhaps Jos was rather pleased in his heart that Osborne was gone, for during George's presence, the other had played but a very secondary part in the household, and Osborne did not scruple to show his contempt for the stout civilian. But Emmy had always been good and attentive to him. It was she who ministered to his comforts, who superintended the dishes that he liked, who walked or rode with him (as she had many, too many, opportunities of doing, for where was George?) and who interposed her sweet face between his anger and her husband's scorn. Many timid remonstrances had she uttered to George in behalf of her brother, but the former in his trenchant way cut these entreaties short. "I'm an honest man," he said, "and if I have a feeling I show it, as an honest man will. How the deuce, my dear, would you have me behave respectfully to such a fool as your brother?" So Jos was pleased with George's absence. His plain hat, and gloves on a sideboard, and the idea that the owner was away, caused Jos I don't know what secret thrill of pleasure. "*He* won't be troubling me this morning," Jos thought, "with his dandified airs and his impudence."

"Put the Captain's hat into the ante-room," he said to Isidor, the servant.

"Perhaps he won't want it again," replied the lackey, looking knowingly at his master. He hated George too, whose insolence towards him was quite of the English sort.

"And ask if Madame is coming to breakfast," Mr. Sedley said with great majesty, ashamed to enter with a servant upon the subject of his dislike for George. The truth is, he had abused his brother to the valet a score of times before.

Alas! Madame could not come to breakfast, and cut the *tartines* that Mr. Jos liked. Madame was a great deal too ill, and had been in a frightful state ever since her husband's departure, so her *bonne* said. Jos showed his sympathy, by pouring her out a large cup of tea. It was his way of exhibiting kindness: and he improved on this; he not only sent her breakfast, but he bethought him what delicacies she would most like for dinner.

Isidor, the valet, had looked on very sulkily, while Osborne's servant was disposing of his master's baggage previous to the Captain's departure: for in the first place he hated Mr. Osborne, whose conduct to him, and to all inferiors, was generally overbearing, (nor does the continental domestic like to be treated with insolence as our own better-tempered servants do:) and secondly, he was angry that so many valuables should be removed from under his hands, to fall into other people's possession when the English discomfiture should arrive. Of this defeat he and a vast number of other persons in Brussels and Belgium did not make the slightest doubt. The almost universal belief was, that the Emperor would divide the Prussian and English armies, annihilate one after the other, and march into Brussels before three days were over: when all the moveables of his present masters, who would be killed, or fugitives, or prisoners, would lawfully become the property of Monsieur Isidor.

As he helped Jos through his toilsome and complicated daily toilette, this faithful servant would calculate what he should do with the very articles with which he was decorating his master's person. He would make a present of the silver essence-bottles and toilet knicknacks to a young lady of whom he was fond; and keep the English cutlery and the large ruby pin for himself. It would look very smart upon one of the fine frilled shirts, which, with the gold-laced cap and the frogged frock coat, that might easily be cut down to suit his shape, and the Captain's gold-headed cane, and the great double ring with the rubies, which he would have made into a pair of beautiful earrings, he calculated would make a perfect Adonis of himself, and render Mademoiselle Reine an easy prey. "How those sleeve-buttons will suit me!" thought he, as he fixed a pair on the fat pudgy wrists of Mr. Sedley. "I long for sleeve-buttons; and the Captain's boots with brass spurs, in the next room, *corbleu!* what an effect they will make in the Allée Verte!" So while Monsieur Isidor with bodily fingers was holding on to his master's nose, and shaving the lower part of Jos's face, his imagination was rambling along the Green Avenue, dressed out in a frogged coat and lace, and in company with Mademoiselle Reine; he was loitering in spirit on the banks, and examining the barges sailing slowly under the cool shadows of the trees by the canal, or refreshing himself with a mug of Faro at the bench of a beer-house on the road to Laeken.

But Mr. Joseph Sedley, luckily for his own peace, no more knew what was passing in his domestic's mind than the respected reader, and I suspect what John or Mary, whose wages we pay, think of ourselves. What our servants think of us!—Did we know what our intimates and dear relations thought of us, we should live in a world that we should be glad to quit, and in a frame of mind and a constant terror, that would be perfectly unbearable. So Jos's man was marking his victim down, as you see one of Mr. Paynter's assistants in Leadenhall-street ornament an unconscious turtle with a placard on which is written, "Soup to-morrow."

Amelia's attendant was much less selfishly disposed. Few dependants could come near that kind and gentle creature without paying their usual tribute of loyalty and affection

to her sweet and affectionate nature. And it is a fact that
Pauline, the cook, consoled her mistress more than anybody
whom she saw on this wretched morning; for when she
found how Amelia remained for hours, silent, motionless,
and haggard, by the windows in which she had placed herself
to watch the last bayonets of the column as it marched away,
the honest girl took the lady's hand, and said, *Tenez, Madame,
est-ce qu'il n'est pas aussi à l'armée, mon homme à moi?*
with which she burst into tears, and Amelia falling into her
arms, did likewise, and so each pitied and soothed the other.

Several times during the forenoon Mr. Jos's Isidor went
from his lodgings into the town, and to the gates of the
hotels and lodging-houses round about the Parc, where the
English were congregated, and there mingled with other
valets, couriers, and lackeys, gathered such news as was
abroad, and brought back bulletins for his master's information. Almost all these gentlemen were in heart partisans
of the Emperor, and had their opinions about the speedy
end of the campaign. The Emperor's proclamation from
Avesnes had been distributed everywhere plentifully in
Brussels. "Soldiers!" it said, "this is the anniversary of
Marengo and Friedland, by which the destinies of Europe
were twice decided. Then, as after Austerlitz, as after
Wagram, we were too generous. We believed in the oaths
and promises of princes whom we suffered to remain upon
their thrones. Let us march once more to meet them. We
and they, are we not still the same men? Soldiers! these
same Prussians who are so arrogant to-day, were three to
one against you at Jena, and six to one at Montmirail.
Those among you who were prisoners in England can tell
their comrades what frightful torments they suffered on
board the English hulks. Madmen! a moment of prosperity has blinded them, and if they enter into France it
will be to find a grave there!" But the partisans of the
French prophesied a more speedy extermination of the
Emperor's enemies than this; and it was agreed on all
hands that Prussians and British would never return except
as prisoners in the rear of the conquering army.

These opinions in the course of the day were brought to
operate upon Mr. Sedley. He was told that the Duke of

Wellington had gone to try and rally his army, the advance
of which had been utterly crushed the night before.

"Crushed, psha!" said Jos, whose heart was pretty stout
at breakfast-time. "The Duke has gone to beat the Emperor as he has beaten all his generals before."

"His papers are burned, his effects are removed, and his
quarters are being got ready for the Duke of Dalmatia,"
Jos's informant replied. "I had it from his own *maître
d'hôtel*. Milor Duc de Richemont's people are packing up
everything. His Grace has fled already, and the Duchess
is only waiting to see the plate packed to join the King of
France at Ostend."

"The King of France is at Ghent, fellow," replied Jos,
affecting incredulity.

"He fled last night to Bruges, and embarks to-day from
Ostend. The Duc de Berri is taken prisoner. Those who
wish to be safe had better go soon, for the dykes will be
opened to-morrow, and who can fly when the whole country
is under water?"

"Nonsense, sir, we are three to one, sir, against any
force Boney can bring into the field," Mr. Sedley objected;
"The Austrians and the Russians are on their march. He
must, he shall be crushed," Jos said, slapping his hand on
the table.

"The Prussians were three to one at Jena, and he took
their army and kingdom in a week. They were six to one
at Montmirail, and he scattered them like sheep. The
Austrian army *is* coming, but with the Empress and the
King of Rome at its head; and the Russians, bah! the
Russians will withdraw. No quarter is to be given to the
English, on account of their cruelty to our braves on board
the infamous pontoons. Look here, here it is in black and
white. Here's the proclamation of his Majesty the Emperor and King," said the now declared partisan of Napoleon, and taking the document from his pocket, Isidor sternly
thrust it into his master's face, and already looked upon the
frogged coat and valuables as his own spoil.

Jos was, if not seriously alarmed as yet, at least considerably disturbed in mind. "Give me my coat and cap, sir,"
said he, "and follow me. I will go myself and learn the

truth of these reports." Isidor was furious as Jos put on the braided frock. "Milor had better not wear that military coat," said he; "the Frenchmen have sworn not to give quarter to a single British soldier."

"Silence, sirrah!" said Jos, with a resolute countenance still, and thrust his arm into the sleeve with indomitable resolution, in the performance of which heroic act he was found by Mrs. Rawdon Crawley, who at this juncture came up to visit Amelia, and entered without ringing at the ante-chamber door.

Rebecca was dressed very neatly and smartly, as usual: her quiet sleep after Rawdon's departure had refreshed her, and her pink smiling cheeks were quite pleasant to look at, in a town and on a day when everybody else's countenance wore the appearance of the deepest anxiety and gloom. She laughed at the attitude in which Jos was discovered, and the struggles and convulsions with which the stout gentleman thrust himself into the braided coat.

"Are you preparing to join the army, Mr. Joseph?" she said. "Is there to be nobody left in Brussels to protect us poor women?"

Jos succeeded in plunging into the coat, and came forward blushing and stuttering out excuses to his fair visitor. "How was she after the events of the morning—after the fatigues of the ball the night before?" Monsieur Isidor disappeared into his master's adjacent bed-room, bearing off the flowered dressing-gown.

"How good of you to ask," said she, pressing one of his hands in both her own. "How cool and collected you look when everybody else is frightened! How is our dear little Emmy? It must have been an awful, awful parting."

"Tremendous," Jos said.

"You men can bear anything," replied the lady. "Parting or danger are nothing to you. Own now that you were going to join the army and leave us to our fate. I know you were—something tells me you were. I was so frightened, when the thought came into my head (for I do sometimes think of you when I am alone, Mr. Joseph), that I ran off immediately to beg and entreat you not to fly from us."

This speech might be interpreted, "My dear sir, should an accident befall the army, and a retreat be necessary, you have a very comfortable carriage, in which I propose to take a seat." I don't know whether Jos understood the words in this sense. But he was profoundly mortified by the lady's inattention to him during their stay at Brussels.

He had never been presented to any of Rawdon Crawley's great acquaintances; he had scarcely been invited to Rebecca's parties; for he was too timid to play much, and his presence bored George and Rawdon equally, who neither of them, perhaps, liked to have a witness of the amusements in which the pair chose to indulge. "Ah!" thought Jos, "now she wants me she comes to me. When there is nobody else in the way she can think about old Joseph Sedley!" But besides these doubts he felt flattered at the idea Rebecca expressed of his courage.

He blushed a good deal, and put on an air of importance. "I should like to see the action," he said. "Every man of any spirit would, you know. I've seen a little service in India, but nothing on this grand scale."

"You men would sacrifice any thing for a pleasure," Rebecca answered. "Captain Crawley left me this morning as gay as if he were going to a hunting party. What does he care? What do any of you care for the agonies and tortures of a poor forsaken woman? (I wonder whether he *could* really have been going to the troops, this great lazy gourmand?) Oh! dear Mr. Sedley, I have come to you for comfort—for consolation. I have been on my knees all the morning. I tremble at the frightful danger into which our husbands, our friends, our brave troops and allies, are rushing. And I come here for shelter, and find another of my friends—the last remaining to me—bent upon plunging into the dreadful scene!"

"My dear madam," Jos replied, now beginning to be quite soothed, "don't be alarmed. I only said I should like to go—what Briton would not? But my duty keeps me here: I can't leave that poor creature in the next room." And he pointed with his finger to the door of the chamber in which Amelia was.

"Good noble brother!" Rebecca said, putting her handkerchief to her eyes, and smelling the eau-de-cologne with
which it was scented. "I have done you injustice; you
have got a heart. I thought you had not."

"O, upon my honour!" Jos said, making a motion as
if he would lay his hand upon the spot in question. "You
do me injustice, indeed you do—my dear Mrs. Crawley."

"I do, now your heart is true to your sister. But I remember two years ago—when it was false to me!" Rebecca
said, fixing her eyes upon him for an instant, and then
turning away into the window.

Jos blushed violently. That organ which he was accused
by Rebecca of not possessing began to thump tumultuously.
He recalled the days when he had fled from her, and the
passion which had once inflamed him—the days when he
had driven her in his curricle: when she had knit the green
purse for him: when he had sat enraptured gazing at her
white arms and bright eyes.

"I know you think me ungrateful," Rebecca continued,
coming out of the window, and once more looking at him
and addressing him in a low tremulous voice. "Your coldness, your averted looks, your manner when we have met
of late—when I came in just now, all proved it to me.
But were there no reasons why I should avoid you? Let
your own heart answer that question. Do you think my
husband was too much inclined to welcome you? The only
unkind words I have ever had from him (I will do Captain Crawley that justice) have been about you—and most
cruel, cruel words they were."

"Good gracious! what have I done?" asked Jos in a
flurry of pleasure and perplexity; "what have I done—to
—to—?"

"Is jealousy nothing?" said Rebecca. "He makes me
miserable about you. And whatever it might have been
once—my heart is all his. I am innocent now. Am I not,
Mr. Sedley?"

All Jos's blood tingled with delight, as he surveyed this
victim to his attractions. A few adroit words, one or two
knowing tender glances of the eyes, and his heart was inflamed again and his doubts and suspicions forgotten. From

Solomon downwards, have not wiser men than he been cajoled and befooled by women? "If the worst comes to the worst," Becky thought, "my retreat is secure; and I have a right-hand seat in the barouche."

There is no knowing into what declarations of love and ardour the tumultuous passions of Mr. Joseph might have led him, if Isidor the valet had not made his re-appearance at this minute, and begun to busy himself about the domestic affairs. Jos, who was just going to gasp out an avowal, choked almost with the emotion that he was obliged to restrain. Rebecca too bethought her that it was time she should go in and comfort her dearest Amelia. *"Au revoir,"* she said, kissing her hand to Mr. Joseph, and tapped gently at the door of his sister's apartment. As she entered and closed the door on herself, he sank down in a chair, and gazed and sighed and puffed portentously.

"That coat is very tight for Milor," Isidor said, still having his eye on the frogs; but his master heard him not: his thoughts were elsewhere: now glowing, maddening, upon the contemplation of the enchanting Rebecca: anon shrinking guiltily before the vision of the jealous Rawdon Crawley, with his curling, fierce mustachios, and his terrible duelling pistols loaded and cocked.

Rebecca's appearance struck Amelia with terror, and made her shrink back. It recalled her to the world and the remembrance of yesterday. In the overpowering fears about to-morrow she had forgotten Rebecca,—jealousy—everything except that her husband was gone and was in danger. Until this dauntless worldling came in and broke the spell, and lifted the latch, we too have forborne to enter into that sad chamber. How long had that poor girl been on her knees! what hours of speechless prayer and bitter prostration had she passed there! The war-chroniclers who write brilliant stories of fight and triumph scarcely tell us of these. These are too mean parts of the pageant: and you don't hear widows' cries or mothers' sobs in the midst of the shouts and jubilation in the great Chorus of Victory. And yet when was the time, that such have not cried out: heart-broken, humble Protestants, unheard in the uproar of the triumph!

After the first movement of terror in Amelia's mind—when Rebecca's green eyes lighted upon her, and rustling in her fresh silks and brilliant ornaments, the latter tripped up with extended arms to embrace her—a feeling of anger succeeded, and from being deadly pale before, her face flushed up red, and she returned Rebecca's look after a moment with a steadiness which surprised and somewhat abashed her rival.

"Dearest Amelia, you are very unwell," the visitor said, putting forth her hand to take Amelia's. "What is it? I could not rest until I knew how you were."

Amelia drew back her hand—never since her life began had that gentle soul refused to believe or to answer any demonstration of good-will or affection. But she drew back her hand, and trembled all over. "Why are you here, Rebecca?" she said, still looking at her solemnly with her large eyes. These glances troubled her visitor.

"She must have seen him give me the letter at the ball," Rebecca thought. "Don't be agitated, dear Amelia," she said, looking down. "I came but to see if I could—if you were well."

"Are you well?" said Amelia "I dare say you are. You don't love your husband. You would not be here if you did. Tell me, Rebecca, did I ever do you anything but kindness?"

"Indeed, Amelia, no," the other said, still hanging down her head

"When you were quite poor, who was it that befriended you? Was I not a sister to you? You saw us all in happier days before he married me. I was all in all then to him; or would he have given up his fortune, his family, as he nobly did to make me happy? Why did you come between my love and me? Who sent you to separate those whom God joined, and take my darling's heart from me—my own husband? Do you think you could love him as I did? His love was everything to me. You knew it, and wanted to rob me of it. For shame, Rebecca; bad and wicked woman—false friend and false wife."

"Amelia, I protest before God, I have done my husband no wrong," Rebecca said, turning from her.

"Have you done *me* no wrong, Rebecca? You did not succeed, but you tried. Ask your heart if you did not."

She knows nothing, Rebecca thought.

"He came back to me. I knew he would. I knew no falsehood, no flattery, could keep him from me long. I knew he would come. I prayed so that he should."

The poor girl spoke these words with a spirit and volubility which Rebecca had never before seen in her, and before which the latter was quite dumb. "But what have I done to you," she continued in a more pitiful tone, "that you should try and take him from me? I had him but for six weeks. You might have spared me those, Rebecca. And yet, from the very first day of our wedding, you came and blighted it. Now he is gone, are you come to see how unhappy I am?" she continued. "You made me wretched enough for the past fortnight: you might have spared me to-day."

"I—I never came here," interposed Rebecca, with unlucky truth.

"No. You didn't come. You took him away. Are you come to fetch him from me?" she continued in a wilder tone. "He was here, but he is gone now. There on that very sofa he sate. Don't touch it. We sate and talked there. I was on his knee, and my arms were round his neck, and we said 'Our Father.' Yes, he was here: and they came and took him away, but he promised me to come back."

"He will come back, my dear," said Rebecca, touched in spite of herself.

"Look," said Amelia, "this is his sash—isn't it a pretty colour?" and she took up the fringe and kissed it. She had tied it round her waist at some part of the day. She had forgotten her anger, her jealousy, the very presence of her rival seemingly. For she walked silently and almost with a smile on her face, towards the bed, and began to smooth down George's pillow.

Rebecca walked, too, silently away. "How is Amelia?" asked Jos, who still held his position in the chair.

"There should be somebody with her," said Rebecca. "I think she is very unwell;" and she went away with a very grave face, refusing Mr. Sedley's entreaties that she would stay and partake of the early dinner which he had ordered.

Rebecca was of a good-natured and obliging disposition; and she liked Amelia rather than otherwise. Even her hard words, reproachful as they were, were complimentary —the groans of a person stinging under defeat. Meeting Mrs. O'Dowd, whom the Dean's sermons had by no means comforted, and who was walking very disconsolately in the Parc, Rebecca accosted the latter, rather to the surprise of the Major's wife, who was not accustomed to such marks of politeness from Mrs. Rawdon Crawley, and informing her that poor little Mrs. Osborne was in a desperate condition, and almost mad with grief, sent off the good-natured Irishwoman straight to see if she could console her young favourite.

"I've cares of my own enough," Mrs. O'Dowd said, gravely, "and I thought poor Amelia would be little wanting for company this day. But if she's so bad as you say, and you can't attend to her, who used to be so fond of her, faith I'll see if I can be of service. And so good marning to ye, Madam;" with which speech and a toss of her head the lady of the repayther took a farewell of Mrs. Crawley, whose company she by no means courted.

Becky watched her marching off, with a smile on her lip. She had the keenest sense of humour, and the Parthian look which the retreating Mrs. O'Dowd flung over her shoulder almost upset Mrs. Crawley's gravity. "My service to ye, me fine Madam, and I'm glad to see ye so cheerful," thought Peggy. "It's not *you* that will cry your eyes out with grief, anyway." And with this she passed on, and speedily found her way to Mrs. Osborne's lodgings.

The poor soul was still at the bedside where Rebecca had left her, and stood almost crazy with grief. The Major's wife, a strong-minded woman, endeavoured her best to comfort her young friend. "You must bear up, Amelia, dear," she said kindly, "for he mustn't find you ill when he sends for you after the victory. It's not you are the only woman that are in the hands of God this day."

"I know that. I am very wicked, very weak," Amelia said. She knew her own weakness well enough. The presence of the more resolute friend checked it, however; and she was the better of this control and company. They went on until two o'clock; their hearts were with the column as it marched farther and farther away. Dreadful doubt and anguish—prayers and fears and griefs unspeakable—followed the regiment. It was the women's tribute to the war. It taxes both alike, and takes the blood of the men, and the tears of the women.

At half-past two, an event occurred of daily importance to Mr. Joseph: the dinner-hour arrived. Warriors may fight and perish, but he must dine. He came into Amelia's room to see if he could coax her to share that meal. "Try," said he; "the soup is very good. Do try, Emmy," and he kissed her hand. Except when she was married, he had not done so much for years before. "You are very good and kind, Joseph," she said. "Everybody is, but if you please, I will stay in my room to-day."

The savour of the soup, however, was agreeable to Mrs. O'Dowd's nostrils: and she thought she would bear Mr. Jos company. So the two sate down to their meal. "God bless the meat," said the Major's wife, solemnly: she was thinking of her honest Mick, riding at the head of his regiment: "'Tis but a bad dinner those poor boys will get to-day," she said, with a sigh, and then, like a philosopher, fell to.

Jos's spirits rose with his meal. He would drink the regiment's health; or, indeed, take any other excuse to indulge in a glass of champagne. "We'll drink to O'Dowd and the brave —th," said he, bowing gallantly to his guest. "Hey, Mrs. O'Dowd? Fill Mrs. O'Dowd's glass, Isidor."

But all of a sudden, Isidor started, and the Major's wife laid down her knife and fork. The windows of the room were open, and looked southward, and a dull distant sound came over the sun-lighted roofs from that direction. "What is it?" said Jos. "Why don't you pour, you rascal?"

"*C'est le feu!*" said Isidor, running to the balcony.

"God defend us; it's cannon!" Mrs. O'Dowd cried, starting up, and followed too to the window. A thousand pale and anxious faces might have been seen looking from other casements. And presently it seemed as if the whole population of the city rushed into the streets.

CHAPTER XXXII

In Which Jos Takes Flight, and the War Is Brought to a Close

WE of peaceful London City have never beheld—and please God never shall witness—such a scene of hurry and alarm, as that which Brussels presented. Crowds rushed to the Namur gate, from which direction the noise proceeded, and many rode along the level *chaussée,* to be in advance of any intelligence from the army. Each man asked his neighbour for news; and even great English lords and ladies condescended to speak to persons whom they did not know. The friends of the French went abroad, wild with excitement, prophesying the triumph of their Emperor. The merchants closed their shops, and came out to swell the general chorus of alarm and clamour. Women rushed to the churches, and crowded the chapels, and knelt and prayed on the flags and steps. The dull sound of the cannon went on rolling, rolling. Presently carriages with travellers began to leave the town, galloping away by the Ghent barrier.

The prophecies of the French partisans began to pass for facts. "He has cut the armies in two," it was said. "He is marching straight on Brussels. He will overpower the English, and be here to-night." "He will overpower the English," shrieked Isidor to his master, "and will be here to-night." The man bounded in and out from the lodgings to the street, always returning with some fresh particulars of disaster. Jos's face grew paler and paler. Alarm began to take entire possession of the stout civilian. All the champagne he drank brought no courage to him. Before sunset he was worked up to such a pitch of nervousness as gratified his friend Isidor to behold, who now counted surely upon the spoils of the owner of the laced coat.

The women were away all this time. After hearing the firing for a moment, the stout Major's wife bethought her of her friend in the next chamber, and ran in to watch, and if possible to console, Amelia. The idea that she had that helpless and gentle creature to protect, gave additional strength to the natural courage of the honest Irishwoman. She passed five hours by her friend's side, sometimes in remonstrance, sometimes talking cheerfully, oftener in silence, and terrified mental supplication. "I never let go her hand once," said the stout lady afterwards, "until after sunset, when the firing was over." Pauline, the *bonne*, was on her knees at church hard by, praying for *son homme à elle*.

When the noise of the cannonading was over, Mrs. O'Dowd issued out of Amelia's room into the parlour adjoining, where Jos sate with two emptied flasks, and courage entirely gone. Once or twice he had ventured into his sister's bed-room, looking very much alarmed, and as if he would say something. But the Major's wife kept her place, and he went away without disburthening himself of his speech. He was ashamed to tell her that he wanted to fly.

But when she made her appearance in the dining-room, where he sate in the twilight in the cheerless company of his empty champagne bottles, he began to open his mind to her.

"Mrs. O'Dowd," he said, "hadn't you better get Amelia ready?"

"Are you going to take her out for a walk?" said the Major's lady; "sure she's too weak to stir."

"I—I've ordered the carriage," he said, "and—and post-horses; Isidor is gone for them," Jos continued.

"What do you want with driving to-night?" answered the lady. "Isn't she better on her bed? I've just got her to lie down."

"Get her up," said Jos; "she must get up, I say:" and he stamped his foot energetically. "I say the horses are ordered —yes, the horses are ordered. It's all over, and—"

"And what?" asked Mrs. O'Dowd.

"I'm off for Ghent," Jos answered. "Everybody is going; there's a place for you! We shall start in half-an-hour."

The Major's wife looked at him with infinite scorn. "I don't move till O'Dowd gives me the route," said she. "You may go if you like, Mr. Sedley; but, faith, Amelia and I stop here."

"She *shall* go," said Jos, with another stamp of his foot. Mrs. O'Dowd put herself with arms akimbo before the bedroom door.

"Is it her mother you're going to take her to?" she said; "or do you want to go to Mamma yourself, Mr. Sedley? Good marning—a pleasant journey to ye, sir. *Bon voyage,* as they say, and take my counsel, and shave off them mustachios, or they'll bring you into mischief."

"D—n!" yelled out Jos, wild with fear, rage, and mortification; and Isidor came in at this juncture, swearing in his turn. *"Pas de chevaux, sacrebleu!"* hissed out the furious domestic. All the horses were gone. Jos was not the only man in Brussels seized with panic that day.

But Jos's fears, great and cruel as they were already, were destined to increase to an almost frantic pitch before the night was over. It has been mentioned, how Pauline, the *bonne,* had *son homme à elle* also in the ranks of the army that had gone out to meet the Emperor Napoleon. This lover was a native of Brussels, and a Belgian hussar. The troops of his nation signalised themselves in this war for anything but courage, and young Van Cutsum, Pauline's admirer, was too good a soldier to disobey his Colonel's orders to run away. Whilst in garrison at Brussels young Regulus (he had been born in the revolutionary times) found his great comfort, and passed almost all his leisure moments, in Pauline's kitchen; and it was with pockets and holsters crammed full of good things from her larder, that he had taken leave of his weeping sweetheart, to proceed upon the campaign a few days before.

As far as his regiment was concerned, this campaign was over now. They had formed a part of the division under the command of his Sovereign apparent, the Prince of Orange, and as respected length of swords and mustachios, and the richness of uniform and equipments, Regulus and his comrades looked to be as gallant a body of men as ever trumpet sounded for.

When Ney dashed upon the advance of the allied troops, carrying one position after the other, until the arrival of the great body of the British army from Brussels changed the aspect of the combat of Quatre Bras, the squadrons among which Regulus rode showed the greatest activity in retreating before the French, and were dislodged from one post and another which they occupied with perfect alacrity on their part. Their movements were only checked by the advance of the British in their rear. Thus forced to halt, the enemy's cavalry (whose bloodthirsty obstinacy cannot be too severely reprehended), had at length an opportunity of coming to close quarters with the brave Belgians before them; who preferred to encounter the British rather than the French, and at once turning tail rode through the English regiments that were behind them, and scattered in all directions. The regiment in fact did not exist any more. It was nowhere. It had no head-quarters. Regulus found himself galloping many miles from the field of action, entirely alone; and whither should he fly for refuge so naturally as to that kitchen and those faithful arms in which Pauline had so often welcomed him?

At some ten o'clock the clinking of a sabre might have been heard up the stair of the house where the Osbornes occupied a storey in the continental fashion. A knock might have been heard at the kitchen door; and poor Pauline, come back from church, fainted almost with terror as she opened it and saw before her her haggard hussar. He looked as pale as the midnight dragoon who came to disturb Leonora. Pauline would have screamed, but that her cry would have called her masters, and discovered her friend. She stifled her scream, then, and leading her hero into the kitchen, gave him beer, and the choice bits from the dinner, which Jos had not had the heart to taste. The hussar showed he was no ghost by the prodigious quantity of flesh and beer which he devoured—and during the mouthfuls he told his tale of disaster.

His regiment had performed prodigies of courage, and had withstood for a while the onset of the whole French army. But they were overwhelmed at last, as was the whole British army by this time. Ney destroyed each regiment as it came up. The Belgians in vain interposed to prevent the butchery of the English. The Brunswickers were routed and had fled—their Duke was killed. It was a general *débâcle.* He sought to drown his sorrow for the defeat in floods of beer.

Isidor, who had come into the kitchen, heard the conversation and rushed out to inform his master. "It is all over," he shrieked to Jos. "Milor Duke is a prisoner; the Duke of Brunswick is killed; the British army is in full flight; there is only one man escaped, and he is in the kitchen now—come and hear him." So Jos tottered into that apartment where Regulus still sate on the kitchen table, and clung fast to his flagon of beer. In the best French which he could muster, and which was in sooth of a very ungrammatical sort, Jos besought the hussar to tell his tale. The disasters deepened as Regulus spoke. He was the only man of his regiment not slain on the field. He had seen the Duke of Brunswick fall, the black hussars fly, and the Ecossais pounded down by the cannon.

"And the —th?" gasped Jos.

"Cut in pieces," said the hussar—upon which Pauline cried out, "O my mistress, *ma bonne petite dame,*" went off fairly into hysterics, and filled the house with her screams.

Wild with terror, Mr. Sedley knew not how or where to seek for safety. He rushed from the kitchen back to the sitting-room, and cast an appealing look at Amelia's door, which Mrs. O'Dowd had closed and locked in his face; but he remembered how scornfully the latter had received him, and after pausing and listening for a brief space at the door, he left it, and resolved to go into the street, for the first time that day. So, seizing a candle, he looked about for his gold-laced cap, and found it lying in its usual place, on a console-table, in the anteroom, placed before a mirror at which Jos used to coquet, always giving his side-locks a twirl, and his cap the proper cock over his eye, before he went forth to make appearance in public. Such is the force of habit, that even in the midst of his terror he began mechanically to twiddle with his hair, and arrange the cock of his hat. Then he looked amazed at the pale face in the glass before him, and especially at his mustachios, which had attained a rich growth in the course of near seven weeks, since they had come into the world. They *will* mistake me for a military man, thought he, remembering Isidor's warning, as to the massacre with which all the defeated British army was threatened; and staggering back to his bed-chamber, he began wildly pulling the bell which summoned his valet.

Isidor answered that summons. Jos had sunk in a chair —he had torn off his neckcloths, and turned down his collars, and was sitting with both his hands lifted to his throat.

"Coupez-moi, Isidor," shouted he; *"vite! Coupez-moi!"*

Isidor thought for a moment he had gone mad, and that he wished his valet to cut his throat.

"Les moustaches," gasped Jos; *"les moustaches—coupy, rasy, vite!*—his French was of this sort—voluble, as we have said, but not remarkable for grammar.

Isidor swept off the mustachios in no time with the razor, and heard with inexpressible delight his master's orders that he should fetch a hat and a plain coat. *"Ne porty ploo—habit militair—bonny—bonny avoo, prenny dehors"* —were Jos's words,—the coat and cap were at last his property.

This gift being made, Jos selected a plain black coat and waistcoat from his stock, and put on a large white neckcloth, and a plain beaver. If he could have got a shovel-hat he would have worn it. As it was, you would have fancied he was a flourishing, large parson of the Church of England.

"Venny maintenong," he continued, *"sweevy—ally—party —dong la roo."* And so having said, he plunged swiftly down the stairs of the house and passed into the street.

Although Regulus had vowed that he was the only man of his regiment or of the allied army, almost, who had escaped being cut to pieces by Ney, it appeared that his statement was incorrect, and that a good number more of the supposed victims had survived the massacre. Many scores of Regulus's comrades had found their way back to Brussels, and —all agreeing that they had run away—filled the whole

town with an idea of the defeat of the allies. The arrival
of the French was expected hourly; the panic continued,
and preparations for flight went on everywhere. No horses!
thought Jos, in terror. He made Isidor inquire of scores
of persons, whether they had any to lend or sell, and his
heart sank within him, at the negative answers returned
everywhere. Should he take the journey on foot? Even
fear could not render that ponderous body so active.

Almost all the hotels occupied by the English in Brussels
face the Parc, and Jos wandered irresolutely about in this
quarter, with crowds of other people, oppressed as he was
by fear and curiosity. Some families he saw more happy
than himself, having discovered a team of horses, and rattling through the streets in retreat; others again there were
whose case was like his own, and who could not for any
bribes or entreaties procure the necessary means of flight.
Amongst these would-be fugitives, Jos remarked the Lady
Bareacres and her daughter, who sate in their carriage in
the *porte-cochère* of their hotel, all their imperials packed,
and the only drawback to whose flight was the same want
of motive power which kept Jos stationary.

Rebecca Crawley occupied apartments in this hotel; and
had before this period had sundry hostile meetings with
the ladies of the Bareacres family. My Lady Bareacres cut
Mrs. Crawley on the stairs when they met by chance; and
in all places where the latter's name was mentioned, spoke
perseveringly ill of her neighbour. The Countess was
shocked at the familiarity of General Tufto with the aide-de-
camp's wife. The Lady Blanche avoided her as if she had
been an infectious disease. Only the Earl himself kept up
a sly occasional acquaintance with her, when out of the
jurisdiction of his ladies.

Rebecca had her revenge now upon these insolent enemies.
It became known in the hotel that Captain Crawley's horses
had been left behind, and when the panic began, Lady
Bareacres condescended to send her maid to the Captain's
wife with her Ladyship's compliments, and a desire to know
the price of Mrs. Crawley's horses. Mrs. Crawley returned
a note with her compliments, and an intimation that it was
not her custom to transact bargains with ladies' maids.

This curt reply brought the Earl in person to Becky's apartment; but he could get no more success than the first ambassador. "Send a lady's maid to *me!*" Mrs. Crawley cried in great anger; "why didn't my Lady Bareacres tell me to go and saddle the horses! Is it her Ladyship that wants to escape, or her ladyship's *femme de chambre?*" And this was all the answer that the Earl bore back to his Countess.

What will not necessity do? The Countess herself actually came to wait upon Mrs. Crawley on the failure of her second envoy. She entreated her to name her own price; she even offered to invite Becky to Bareacres House, if the latter would but give her the means of returning to that residence. Mrs. Crawley sneered at her.

"I don't want to be waited on by bailiffs in livery," she said; "you will never get back though most probably—at least not you and your diamonds together. The French will have those. They will be here in two hours, and I shall be half way to Ghent by that time. I would not sell you my horses, no, not for the two largest diamonds that your Ladyship wore at the ball." Lady Bareacres trembled with rage and terror. The diamonds were sewed into her habit, and secreted in my Lord's padding and boots.

"Woman, the diamonds are at the banker's, and I *will* have the horses," she said. Rebecca laughed in her face. The infuriate Countess went below, and sate in her carriage; her maid, her courier, and her husband were sent once more through the town, each to look for cattle; and woe betide those who came last! Her Ladyship was resolved on departing the very instant the horses arrived from any quarter—with her husband or without him.

Rebecca had the pleasure of seeing her Ladyship in the horseless carriage, and keeping her eyes fixed upon her, and bewailing, in the loudest tone of voice, the Countess's perplexities. "Not to be able to get horses!" she said, "and to have all those diamonds sewed into the carriage cushions! What a prize it will be for the French when they come!— the carriage and the diamonds, I mean; not the lady!" She gave this information to the landlord, to the servants, to the guests, and the innumerable stragglers about the court-yard. Lady Bareacres could have shot her from the carriage window.

It was while enjoying the humiliation of her enemy that Rebecca caught sight of Jos, who made towards her directly he perceived her.

That altered, frightened, fat face, told his secret well enough. He too wanted to fly, and was on the look-out for the means of escape. "*He* shall buy my horses," thought Rebecca, "and I'll ride the mare."

Jos walked up to his friend, and put the question for the hundredth time during the past hour, "Did she know where horses were to be had?"

"What, *you* fly?" said Rebecca, with a laugh. "I thought you were the champion of all the ladies, Mr. Sedley."

"I—I'm not a military man," gasped he.

"And Amelia?—Who is to protect that poor little sister of yours?" asked Rebecca. "You surely would not desert her?"

"What good can I do her, suppose—suppose the enemy arrive?" Jos answered. "They'll spare the women; but my man tells me that they have taken an oath to give no quarter to the men—the dastardly cowards."

"Horrid!" cried Rebecca, enjoying his perplexity.

"Besides, I don't want to desert her," cried the brother. "She *shan't* be deserted. There is a seat for her in my carriage, and one for you, dear Mrs. Crawley, if you will come; and if we can get horses—" sighed he—

"I have two to sell," the lady said. Jos could have flung himself into her arms at the news. "Get the carriage, Isidor," he cried: "we've found them—we have found them."

"My horses never were in harness," added the lady. "Bullfinch would kick the carriage to pieces, if you put him in the traces."

"But he is quiet to ride?" asked the civilian.

"As quiet as a lamb and as fast as a hare," answered Rebecca.

"Do you think he is up to my weight?" Jos said. He was already on his back, in imagination, without ever so much as a thought for poor Amelia. What person who loved a horse-speculation could resist such a temptation?

In reply, Rebecca asked him to come into her room, whither he followed her quite breathless to conclude the bargain. Jos seldom spent a half-hour in his life which cost him so much money. Rebecca, measuring the value of the goods which she had for sale by Jos's eagerness to purchase, as well as by the scarcity of the article, put upon her horses a price so prodigious as to make even the civilian draw back. "She would sell both or neither," she said, resolutely. Rawdon had ordered her not to part with them, for a price less than that which she specified. Lord Bareacres below would give her the same money—and with all her love and regard for the Sedley family, her dear Mr. Joseph must conceive that poor people must live—nobody, in a word, could be more affectionate, but more firm about the matter of business.

Jos ended by agreeing, as might be supposed of him. The sum he had to give her was so large that he was obliged to ask for time; so large as to be a little fortune to Rebecca, who rapidly calculated that with this sum, and the sale of the residue of Rawdon's effects, and her pension as a widow should he fall, she would now be absolutely independent of the world, and might look her weeds steadily in the face.

Once or twice in the day she certainly had herself thought about flying. But her reason gave her better counsel. "Suppose the French do come," thought Becky, "what can they do to a poor officer's widow? Bah! the times of sacks and sieges are over. We shall be let to go home quietly, or I may live pleasantly abroad with a snug little income."

Meanwhile Jos and Isidor went off to the stables to inspect the newly-purchased cattle. Jos bade his man saddle the horses at once. He would ride away that very night, that very hour. And he left the valet busy in getting the horses ready, and went homewards himself to prepare for his departure. It must be secret. He would go to his chamber by the back entrance. He did not care to face Mrs. O'Dowd and Amelia, and own to them that he was about to run.

By that time Jos's bargain with Rebecca was completed, and his horses had been visited and examined, it was almost morning once more. But though midnight was long passed, there was no rest for the city; the people were up, the doors, and the streets were busy. Rumours of various natures went still from mouth to mouth: one report averred that the Prussians had been utterly defeated; another that it was the English who had been attacked and conquered: a third that the latter had held their ground. This last rumour gradually got strength. No Frenchmen had made their appearance. Stragglers had come in from the army bringing reports more and more favourable: at last an aide-de-camp actually reached Brussels with despatches for the Commandant of the place, who placarded presently through the town an official announcement of the success of the allies at Quatre Bras, and the entire repulse of the French under Ney after a six hours' battle. The aide-de-camp must have arrived sometime while Jos and Rebecca were making their bargain together, or the latter was inspecting his purchase. When he reached his own hotel, he found a score of its numerous inhabitants on the threshold discoursing of the news; there was no doubt as to its truth. And he went up to communicate it to the ladies under his charge. He did not think it was necessary to tell them how he had intended to take leave of them, how he had bought horses, and what a price he had paid for them.

But success or defeat was a minor matter to them, who had only thought for the safety of those they loved. Amelia, at the news of the victory, became still more agitated even than before. She was for going that moment to the army. She besought her brother with tears to conduct her thither. Her doubts and terrors reached their paroxysm; and the poor girl, who for many hours had been plunged into stupor, raved and ran hither and thither in hysteric insanity—a piteous sight. No man writhing in pain on the hard-fought field fifteen miles off, where lay, after their struggles, so many of the brave—no man suffered more keenly than this poor harmless victim of the war. Jos could not bear the sight of her pain. He left his sister in the charge of her stouter female companion, and descended once more to the threshold of the hotel, where everybody still lingered, and talked, and waited for more news.

It grew to be broad daylight as they stood here, and fresh news began to arrive from the war, brought by men who had been actors in the scene. Wagons and long country carts laden with wounded came rolling into the town; ghastly groans came from within them, and haggard faces looked up sadly from out of the straw. Jos Sedley was looking at one of these carriages with a painful curiosity —the moans of the people within were frightful—the wearied horses could hardly pull the cart. "Stop! stop!" a feeble voice cried from the straw, and the carriage stopped opposite Mr. Sedley's hotel.

"It is George, I know it is!" cried Amelia, rushing in a moment to the balcony, with a pallid face and loose flowing hair. It was not George, however, but it was the next best thing: it was news of him.

It was poor Tom Stubble, who had marched out of Brussels so gallantly twenty-four hours before, bearing the colours of the regiment which he had defended very gallantly upon the field. A French lancer had speared the young ensign in the leg, who fell, still bravely holding to his flag. At the conclusion of the engagement, a place had been found for the poor boy in a cart, and he had been brought back to Brussels.

"Mr. Sedley, Mr. Sedley!" cried the boy, faintly, and Jos came up almost frightened at the appeal. He had not at first distinguished who it was that called him.

Little Tom Stubble held out his hot and feeble hand. "I'm to be taken in here," he said. "Osborne—and—and Dobbin said I was; and you are to give the man two napoleons: my mother will pay you." This young fellow's thoughts, during the long feverish hours passed in the cart, had been wandering to his father's parsonage which he had quitted only a few months before, and he had sometimes forgotten his pain in that delirium.

The hotel was large, and the people kind, and all the inmates of the cart were taken in and placed on various couches. The young ensign was conveyed upstairs to Osborne's quarters. Amelia and the Major's wife had rushed down to him, when the latter had recognized him from the balcony. You may fancy the feelings of these women when they were told that the day was over, and both their husbands were safe; in what mute rapture Amelia fell on her good friend's neck, and embraced her; in what a grateful passion of prayer she fell on her knees, and thanked the Power which had saved her husband.

Our young lady, in her fevered and nervous condition, could have had no more salutary medicine prescribed for her by any physician than that which chance put in her way. She and Mrs. O'Dowd watched incessantly by the wounded lad, whose pains were very severe, and in the duty thus forced upon her, Amelia had not time to brood over her personal anxieties, or to give herself up to her own fears and forebodings after her wont. The young patient told in his simple fashion the events of the day, and the actions of our friends of the gallant —th. They had suffered severely. They had lost very many officers and men. The Major's horse had been shot under him as the regiment charged, and they all thought that O'Dowd was gone, and that Dobbin had got his majority, until on their return from the charge to their old ground, the Major was discovered seated on Pyramus's carcase, refreshing himself from a case-bottle. It was Captain Osborne that cut down the French lancer who had speared the ensign. Amelia turned so pale at the notion, that Mrs. O'Dowd stopped the young ensign in this story. And it was Captain Dobbin who at the end of the day, though wounded himself, took up the lad in his arms and carried him to the surgeon, and thence to the cart which was to bring him back to Brussels. And it was he who promised the driver two louis if he would make his way to Mr. Sedley's hotel in the city; and tell Mrs. Captain Osborne that the action was over, and that her husband was unhurt and well.

"Indeed, but he has a good heart that William Dobbin," Mrs. O'Dowd said, "though he is always laughing at me."

Young Stubble vowed there was not such another officer in the army, and never ceased his praises of the senior captain, his modesty, his kindness, and his admirable coolness in the field. To these parts of the conversation, Amelia lent a very distracted attention: it was only when George was spoken of that she listened, and when he was not mentioned, she thought about him.

In tending her patient, and in thinking of the wonderful escapes of the day before, her second day passed away not too slowly with Amelia. There was only one man in the army for her: and as long as he was well, it must be owned that its movements interested her little. All the reports which Jos brought from the street fell very vaguely on her ears; though they were sufficient to give that timorous gentleman, and many other people then in Brussels, every disquiet. The French had been repulsed certainly, but it was after a severe and doubtful struggle, and with only a division of the French army. The Emperor, with the main body, was away at Ligny, where he had utterly annihilated the Prussians, and was now free to bring his whole force to bear upon the allies. The Duke of Wellington was retreating upon the capital, and a great battle must be fought under its walls probably, of which the chances were more than doubtful. The Duke of Wellington had but twenty thousand British troops on whom he could rely, for the Germans were raw militia, the Belgians disaffected; and with this handful his Grace had to resist a hundred and fifty thousand men that had broken into Belgium under Napoleon. Under Napoleon! What warrior was there, however famous and skilful, that could fight at odds with him?

Jos thought of all these things, and trembled. So did all the rest of Brussels—where people felt that the fight of the day before was but the prelude to the greater combat which was imminent. One of the armies opposed to the Emperor was scattered to the winds already. The few English that could be brought to resist him would perish at their posts, and the conqueror would pass over their bodies into the city. Woe be to those whom he found there! Addresses were prepared, public functionaries assembled and debated secretly, apartments were got ready, and tricoloured banners and triumphal emblems manufactured, to welcome the arrival of His Majesty the Emperor and King.

The emigration still continued, and wherever families could find means of departure, they fled. When Jos, on the afternon of the 17th of June, went to Rebecca's hotel, he found that the great Bareacres' carriage had at length rolled away from the *porte-cochère*. The Earl had procured a pair of horses somehow, in spite of Mrs. Crawley, and was rolling on the road to Ghent. Louis the Desired was getting ready his portmanteau in that city, too. It seemed as if Misfortune was never tired of worrying into motion that unwieldly exile.

Jos felt that the delay of yesterday had been only a respite, and that his dearly bought horses must of a surety be put into requisition. His agonies were very severe all this day. As long as there was an English army between Brussels and Napoleon, there was no need of immediate flight; but he had his horses brought from their distant stables, to the stables in the court-yard of the hotel where he lived; so that they might be under his own eyes, and beyond the risk of violent abduction. Isidor watched the stable-door constantly, and had the horses saddled, to be ready for the start. He longed intensely for that event.

After the reception of the previous day, Rebecca did not care to come near her dear Amelia. She clipped the bouquet which George had brought her, and gave fresh water to the flowers, and read over the letter which he had sent her. "Poor wretch," she said, twirling round the little bit of paper in her fingers, "how I could crush her with this!—and it is for a thing like this that she must break her heart, forsooth —for a man who is stupid—a coxcomb—and who does not care for her. My poor good Rawdon is worth ten of this creature." And then she fell to thinking what she should do if—if anything happened to poor good Rawdon, and what a great piece of luck it was that he had left his horses behind.

In the course of this day too, Mrs. Crawley, who saw not without anger the Bareacres party drive off, bethought her of the precaution which the Countess had taken, and did a little needlework for her own advantage; she stitched away the major part of her trinkets, bills and bank-notes about her person, and so prepared, was ready for any event —to fly if she thought fit, or to stay and welcome the conqueror, were he Englishman or Frenchman. And I am not sure that she did not dream that night of becoming a duchess and Madame la Maréchale, while Rawdon wrapped in his cloak, and making his bivouac under the rain at Mount Saint John, was thinking, with all the force of his heart, about the little wife whom he had left behind him.

The next day was a Sunday. And Mrs. Major O'Dowd had the satisfaction of seeing both her patients refreshed in health and spirits by some rest which they had taken during the night. She herself had slept on a great chair in Amelia's room, ready to wait upon her poor friend or the ensign, should either need her nursing. When morning came, this robust woman went back to the house where she and her Major had their billet; and here performed an elaborate and splendid toilette, befitting the day. And it is very possible that whilst alone in that chamber, which her husband had inhabited, and where his cap still lay on the pillow, and his cane stood in the corner, one prayer at least was sent up to Heaven for the welfare of the brave soldier, Michael O'Dowd.

When she returned she brought her prayer-book with her, and her uncle the Dean's famous book of sermons, out of which she never failed to read every Sabbath; not understanding all, haply, not pronouncing many of the words aright, which were long and abstruse—for the Dean was a learned man, and loved long Latin words—but with great gravity, vast emphasis, and with tolerable corrections in the main. How often has my Mick listened to these sermons, she thought, and me reading in the cabin of a calm! She proposed to resume this exercise on the present day, with Amelia and the wounded ensign for a congregation. The same service was read on that day in twenty thousand churches at the same hour; and millions of British men and women, on their knees, implored protection of the Father of all.

They did not hear the noise which disturbed our little congregation at Brussels. Much louder than that which had interrupted them two days previously, as Mrs. O'Dowd was reading the service in her best voice, the cannon of Waterloo began to roar.

When Jos heard that dreadful sound, he made up his mind that he would bear this perpetual recurrence of terrors no longer, and would fly at once. He rushed into the sick man's room, where our three friends had paused in their prayers, and further interrupted them by a passionate appeal to Amelia.

"I can't stand it any more, Emmy," he said; "I won't stand it; and you must come with me. I have bought a horse for you—never mind at what price—and you must dress and come with me, and ride behind Isidor."

"God forgive me, Mr. Sedley, but you are no better than a coward," Mrs. O'Dowd said, laying down the book.

"I say come, Amelia," the civilian went on; "never mind what she says; why are we to stop here and be butchered by the Frenchmen?"

"You forget the —th, my boy," said the little Stubble, the wounded hero, from his bed—"and—and you won't leave me, will you, Mrs. O'Dowd?"

"No, my dear fellow," said she, going up and kissing the boy. "No harm shall come to you while *I* stand by. I don't budge till I get the word from Mick. A pretty figure I'd be, wouldn't I, stuck behind that chap on a pillion?"

This image caused the young patient to burst out laughing in his bed, and even made Amelia smile. "I don't ask her," Jos shouted out—"I don't ask that—that Irishwoman, but you Amelia; once for all, will you come?"

"Without my husband, Joseph?" Amelia said, with a look of wonder, and gave her hand to the Major's wife. Jos's patience was exhausted.

"Good-bye, then," he said, shaking his fist in a rage, and slamming the door by which he retreated. And this time he really gave his order for march: and mounted in the court-yard. Mrs. O'Dowd heard the clattering hoofs of the horses as they issued from the gate; and looking on, made many scornful remarks on poor Joseph as he rode down the street with Isidor after him in the laced cap. The horses, which had not been exercised for some days, were lively, and sprang about the street. Joe, a clumsy and timid horseman, did not look to advantage in the saddle. "Look at him, Amelia dear, driving into the parlour window. Such a bull in a china-shop *I* never saw." And presently the pair of riders disappeared at a canter down the street leading in the direction of the Ghent road, Mrs. O'Dowd pursuing them with a fire of sarcasm so long as they were in sight.

All that day from morning until past sunset, the cannon never ceased to roar. It was dark when the cannonading stopped all of a sudden.

All of us have read of what occurred during that interval. The tale is in every Englishman's mouth; and you and I, who were children when the great battle was won and lost, are never tired of hearing the recounting the history of that famous action. Its remembrance rankles still in the bosoms of millions of the countrymen of those brave men who lost the day. They pant for an opportunity of revenging that humiliation; and if a contest, ending in a victory on their part, should ensue, elating them in their turn, and leaving its cursed legacy of hatred and rage behind to us, there is no end to the so-called glory and shame, and to the alterations of successful and unsuccessful murder, in which two high-spirited nations might engage. Centuries hence, we Frenchmen and Englishmen might be boasting and killing each other still, carrying out bravely the Devil's code of honour.

All our friends took their share and fought like men in the great field. All day long, whilst the women were praying ten miles away, the lines of the dauntless English infantry were receiving and repelling the furious charges of the French horsemen. Guns which were heard at Brussels were ploughing up their ranks, and comrades falling, and the resolute survivors closing in. Toward evening, the attack of the French, repeated and resisted so bravely, slackened in its fury. They had other foes besides the British to engage, or were preparing for a final onset. It came at last; the columns of the Imperial Guard marched up the hill of Saint Jean, at length and at once to sweep the English from the height which they had maintained all day, and spite of all: unscared by the thunder of the artillery, which hurled death from the English line—the dark rolling column pressed on and up the hill. It seemed almost to crest the eminence, when it began to wave and falter. Then it stopped, still facing the shot. Then at last the English troops rushed from the post from which no enemy had been able to dislodge them, and the Guard turned and fled.

No more firing was heard at Brussels—the pursuit rolled miles away. Darkness came down on the field and city: and Amelia was praying for George, who was lying on his face, dead, with a bullet through his heart. '

CHAPTER XXXIII

IN WHICH MISS CRAWLEY'S RELATIONS ARE VERY ANXIOUS ABOUT HER

THE kind reader must please to remember—while the army is marching from Flanders, and, after its heroic actions there, is advancing to take the fortifications on the frontiers of France, previous to an occupation of that country,—that there are a number of persons living peaceably in England who have to do with the history at present in hand, and must come in for their share of the chronicle. During the time of these battles and dangers, old Miss Crawley was living at Brighton, very moderately moved by the great events going on. The great events rendered the newspapers rather interesting, to be sure, and Briggs read out the *Gazette,* in which Rawdon Crawley's gallantry was mentioned with honour, and his promotion was presently recorded.

"What a pity that young man has taken such an irretrievable step in the world!" his aunt said; "with his rank and distinction he might have married a brewer's daughter with a quarter of a million—like Miss Grains; or have looked to ally himself with the best families in England. He would have had my money some day or other; or his children would—for I'm not in a hurry to go, Miss Briggs, although you may be in a hurry to be rid of me; and instead of that, he is a doomed pauper, with a dancing-girl for a wife."

"Will my dear Miss Crawley not cast an eye of compassion upon the heroic soldier, whose name is inscribed in the annals of his country's glory?" said Miss Briggs, who was greatly excited by the Waterloo proceedings, and loved speaking romantically when there was an occasion. "Has not the Captain—or the Colonel as I may now style him—done deeds which make the name of Crawley illustrious?"

"Briggs, you are a fool," said Miss Crawley: "Colonel Crawley has dragged the name of Crawley through the mud, Miss Briggs. Marry a drawing-master's daughter, indeed!— marry a *dame de compagnie*—for she was no better, Briggs; no, she was just what you are—only younger, and a great deal prettier and cleverer. Were you an accomplice of that abandoned wretch, I wonder, of whose vile arts he became a victim, and of whom you used to be such an admirer? Yes, I daresay you were an accomplice. But you will find yourself disappointed in my will, I can tell you: and you will have the goodness to write to Mr. Waxy, and say that I desire to see him immediately." Miss Crawley was now in the habit of writing to Mr. Waxy her solicitor almost every day in the week, for her arrangements respecting her property were all revoked, and her perplexity was great as to the future disposition of her money.

The spinster had, however, rallied considerably; as was proved by the increased vigour and frequency of her sarcasms upon Miss Briggs, all which attacks the poor companion bore with meekness, with cowardice, with a resignation that was half generous and half hypocritical—with the slavish submission, in a word, that women of her disposition and station are compelled to show. Who has not seen how women bully women? What tortures have men to endure, comparable to those daily repeated shafts of scorn and cruelty with which poor women are riddled by the tyrants of their sex? Poor victims! But we are starting from our proposition, which is, that Miss Crawley was always particularly annoying and savage when she was rallying from illness—as they say wounds tingle most when they are about to heal.

While thus approaching, as all hoped, to convalescence, Miss Briggs was the only victim admitted into the presence of the invalid; yet Miss Crawley's relatives afar off did not forget their beloved kinswoman, and by a number of tokens, presents, and kind affectionate messages, strove to keep themselves alive in her recollection.

In the first place, let us mention her nephew, Rawdon Crawley. A few weeks after the famous fight of Waterloo, and after the *Gazette* had made known to her the promotion and gallantry of that distinguished officer, the Dieppe packet brought over to Miss Crawley at Brighton, a box containing presents, and a dutiful letter, from the Colonel her nephew. In the box were a pair of French epaulets, a Cross of the Legion of Honour, and the hilt of a sword— relics from the field of battle: and the letter described with a good deal of humour how the latter belonged to a com- manding-officer of the Guard, who having sworn that "the Guard died, but never surrendered," was taken prisoner the next minute by a private soldier, who broke the Frenchman's sword with the butt of his musket, when Rawdon made himself master of the shattered weapon. As for the cross and epaulets, they came from a Colonel of French cavalry, who had fallen under the aide-de-camp's arm in the battle: and Rawdon Crawley did not know what better to do with the spoils than to send them to his kindest and most affec- tionate old friend. Should he continue to write to her from Paris, whither the army was marching? He might be able to give her interesting news from that capital, and of some of Miss Crawley's old friends of the emigration, to whom she had shown so much kindness during their distress.

The spinster caused Briggs to write back to the Colonel a gracious and complimentary letter, encouraging him to continue his correspondence. His first letter was so exces- sively lively and amusing that she should look with pleasure for its successors.—"Of course, I know," she explained to Miss Briggs, "that Rawdon could not write such a good letter any more than you could, my poor Briggs, and that it is that clever little wretch of a Rebecca, who dictates every word to him; but that is no reason why my nephew should not amuse me; and so I wish to let him understand that I am in high good-humour."

I wonder whether she knew that it was not only Becky who wrote the letters, but that Mrs. Rawdon actually took and sent home the trophies—which she bought for a few francs, from one of the innumerable pedlars who immedi- ately began to deal in relics of the war. The novelist, who knows everything, knows this also. Be this, however, as it may, Miss Crawley's gracious reply greatly encouraged our young friends, Rawdon and his lady, who hoped for the best from their aunt's evidently pacified humour: and they took care to entertain her with many delightful letters from Paris, whither, as Rawdon said, they had the good luck to go in the track of the conquering army.

To the rector's lady, who went off to tend her husband's broken collar-bone at the Rectory at Queen's Crawley, the spinster's communications were by no means so gracious. Mrs. Bute, that brisk, managing, lively, imperious woman, had committed the most fatal of all errors with regard to her sister-in-law. She had not merely oppressed her and her household—she had bored Miss Crawley; and if poor Miss Briggs had been a woman of any spirit, she might have been made happy by the commission which her principal gave her to write a letter to Mrs. Bute Crawley, saying that Miss Crawley's health was greatly improved since Mrs. Bute had left her, and begging the latter on no account to put herself to trouble, or quit her family for Miss Crawley's sake. This triumph over a lady who had been very haughty and cruel in her behaviour to Miss Briggs, would have rejoiced most women; but the truth is, Briggs was a woman of no spirit at all, and the moment her enemy was discomfited, she began to feel compassion in her favour.

"How silly I was," Mrs. Bute thought, and with reason, "ever to hint that I was coming, as I did, in that foolish letter when we sent Miss Crawley the guinea-fowls. I ought to have gone without a word to the poor dear doting old creature, and taken her out of the hands of that ninny Briggs, and that harpy of a *femme de chambre*. Oh! Bute, Bute, why did you break your collar-bone?"

Why, indeed? We have seen how Mrs. Bute, having the game in her hands, had really played her cards too well. She had ruled over Miss Crawley's household utterly and completely, to be utterly and completely routed when a favourable opportunity for rebellion came. She and her household, however, considered that she had been the victim of horrible selfishness and treason, and that her sacrifices in Miss Crawley's behalf had met with the most savage ingratitude. Rawdon's promotion, and the honourable mention made of his name in the *Gazette*, filled the good Christian lady also with alarm. Would his aunt relent towards him now that he was a Lieutenant-Colonel and a C. B.? and would that odious Rebecca once more get into favour? The Rector's wife wrote a sermon for her husband about the vanity of military glory and the prosperity of the wicked, which the worthy parson read in his best voice and without understanding one syllable of it. He had Pitt Crawley for one of his auditors—Pitt, who had come with his two half-sisters to church, which the old Baronet could now by no means be brought to frequent.

Since the departure of Becky Sharp, that old wretch had given himself up entirely to his bad courses, to the great scandal of the county and the mute horror of his son. The ribbons in Miss Horrock's cap became more splendid than ever. The polite families fled the hall and its owner in terror. Sir Pitt went about tippling at his tenants' houses; and drank rum-and-water with the farmers at Mudbury and the neighbouring places on market-days. He drove the family coach-and-four to Southampton with Miss Horrocks inside; and the county people expected every week, as his son did in speechless agony, that his marriage with her would be announced in the provincial paper. It was indeed a rude burthen for Mr. Crawley to bear. His eloquence was palsied at the missionary meetings, and other religious assemblies in the neighbourhood, where he had been in the habit of presiding, and of speaking for hours; for he felt, when he rose, that the audience said, "That is the son of the old reprobate Sir Pitt, who is very likely drinking at the public-houses at this very moment." And once when he was speaking of the benighted condition of the king of Timbuctoo, and the number of his wives who were likewise in darkness, some gipsy miscreant from the crowd asked, "How many is there at Queen's Crawley, Young Square-toes?" to the surprise of the platform, and the ruin of Mr. Pitt's speech. And the two daughters of the house of Queen's Crawley would have been allowed to run utterly wild (for Sir Pitt swore that no governess should ever enter into his doors again), had not Mr. Crawley, by threatening the old gentleman, forced the latter to send them to school.

Meanwhile, as we have said, whatever individual differences there might be between them all, Miss Crawley's dear

nephews and nieces were unanimous in loving her and
sending her tokens of affection. Thus Mrs. Bute sent
guinea-fowls, and some remarkably fine cauliflowers, and a
pretty purse or pincushion worked by her darling girls,
who begged to keep a little place in the recollection of their
dear aunt, while Mr. Pitt sent peaches and grapes and venison from the Hall. The Southampton coach used to carry
those tokens of affection to Miss Crawley at Brighton: it
used sometimes to convey Mr. Pitt thither too: for his differences with Sir Pitt caused Mr. Crawley to absent himself
a good deal from home now: and besides, he had an attraction at Brighton in the person of the Lady Jane Sheepshanks,
whose engagement to Mr. Crawley has been formerly mentioned in this history. Her Ladyship and her sisters lived
at Brighton with their mamma, the Countess Southdown,
that strong-minded woman so favourably known in the
serious world.

A few words ought to be said regarding her Ladyship and
her noble family, who are bound by ties of present and
future relationship to the house of Crawley. Respecting
the chief of the Southdown family, Clement William,
fourth Earl of Southdown, little need be told, except that
his Lordship came into Parliament (as Lord Wolsey) under
the auspices of Mr. Wilberforce, and for a time was a
credit to his political sponsor, and decidedly a serious
young man. But words cannot describe the feelings of
his admirable mother, when she learned, very shortly after
her noble husband's demise, that her son was a member
of several worldly clubs, had lost largely at play at Wattier's and the Cocoa Tree; that he had raised money on
post-obits, and encumbered the family estate; that he drove
four-in-hand, and patronised the ring; and that he actually
had an opera-box, where he entertained the most dangerous
bachelor company. His name was only mentioned with
groans in the dowager's circle.

The Lady Emily was her brother's senior by many years;
and took considerable rank in the serious world as author
of some of the delightful tracts before mentioned, and of
many hymns and spiritual pieces. A mature spinster, and
having but faint ideas of marriage, her love for the blacks

occupied almost all her feelings. It is to her, I believe,
we owe that beautiful poem—

> "Lead us to some sunny isle,
> Yonder in the western deep;
> Where the skies for ever smile,
> And the blacks for ever weep," &c.

She had correspondence with clerical gentlemen in most
of our East and West India possessions; and was secretly
attached to the Reverend Silas Hornblower, who was tat-
toed in the South Sea Islands.

As for the Lady Jane, on whom, as it has been said, Mr.
Pitt Crawley's affection had been placed, she was gentle,
blushing, silent, and timid. In spite of his falling away,
she wept for her brother, and was quite ashamed of loving
him still. Even yet she used to send him little hurried
smuggled notes, and pop them into the post in private. The
one dreadful secret which weighed upon her life was, that
she and the old housekeeper had been to pay Southdown a
furtive visit at his chambers in the Albany; and found him
—O the naughty dear abandoned wretch!—smoking a cigar
with a bottle of Curacoa before him. She admired her sister, she adored her mother, she thought Mr. Crawley the
most delightful and accomplished of men, after Southdown,
that fallen angel: and her mamma and sister, who were
ladies of the most superior sort, managed everything for
her, and regarded her with that amiable pity, of which
your really superior woman always has such a share to give
away. Her mamma ordered her dresses, her books, her
bonnets, and her ideas for her. She was made to take
pony-riding, or piano-exercise, or any other sort of bodily
medicament, according as my Lary Southdown saw meet;
and her ladyship would have kept her daughter in pinafores up to her present age of six-and-twenty, but that they
were thrown off when Lady Jane was presented to Queen
Charlotte.

When these ladies first came to their house at Brighton,
it was to them alone that Mr. Crawley paid his personal
visits, contenting himself by leaving a card at his aunt's
house, and making a modest inquiry of Mr. Bowls or his

assistant footman, with respect to the health of the invalid. When he met Miss Briggs coming home from the library with a cargo of novels under her arm, Mr. Crawley blushed in a manner quite unusual to him, as he stepped forward and shook Miss Crawley's companion by the hand. He introduced Miss Briggs to the lady with whom he happened to be walking, the Lady Jane Sheepshanks, saying, "Lady Jane, permit me to introduce to you my aunt's kindest friend and most affectionate companion, Miss Briggs, whom you know under another title, as authoress of the delightful 'Lyrics of the Heart,' of which you are so fond." Lady Jane blushed too as she held out a kind little hand to Miss Briggs and said something very civil and incoherent about mamma, and proposing to call on Miss Crawley, and being glad to be made known to the friends and relatives of Mr. Crawley; and with soft dove-like eyes saluted Miss Briggs as they separated, while Pitt Crawley treated her to a profound courtly bow, such as he had used to H.H. the Duchess of Pumpernickel, when he was attaché at that court.

The artful diplomatist and disciple of the Machiavellian Binkie! It was he who had given Lady Jane that copy of poor Briggs's early poems, which he remembered to have seen at Queen's Crawley, with a dedication from the poetess to his father's late wife; and he brought the volume with him to Brighton, reading it in the Southampton coach and marking it with his own pencil, before he presented it to the gentle Lady Jane.

It was he, too, who laid before Lady Southdown the great advantages which might occur from an intimacy between her family and Miss Crawley,—advantages both worldly and spiritual, he said: for Miss Crawley was now quite alone; the monstrous dissipation and alliance of his brother Rawdon had estranged her affections from that reprobate young man; the greedy tyranny and avarice of Mrs. Bute Crawley had caused the old lady to revolt against the exorbitant pretensions of that part of the family; and though he himself had held off all his life from cultivating Miss Crawley's friendship, with perhaps an improper pride, he thought now that every becoming means should be taken, both to save her soul from perdition, and to secure her fortune to himself as the head of the house of Crawley.

The strong-minded Lady Southdown quite agreed in both proposals of her son-in-law, and was for converting Miss Crawley off hand. At her own home, both at Southdown and at Trottermore Castle, this tall and awful missionary of the truth rode about the country in her barouche with outriders, launched packets of tracts among the cottagers and tenants, and would order Gaffer Jones to be converted, as she would order Goody Hicks to take a James's powder, without appeal, resistance, or benefit of clergy. My Lord Southdown, her late husband, an epileptic and simple-minded nobleman, was in the habit of approving of everything which his Matilda did and thought. So that whatever changes her own belief might undergo (and it accommodated itself to a prodigious variety of opinion, taken from all sorts of doctors among the Dissenters), she had not the least scruple in ordering all her tenants and inferiors to follow and believe after her. Thus whether she received the Reverend Saunders McNitre, the Scotch divine; or the Reverend Luke Waters, the mild Wesleyan; or the Reverend Giles Jowls, the illuminated Cobbler, who dubbed himself Reverend as Napoleon crowned himself Emperor—the household, children, tenantry of my Lady Southdown were expected to go down on their knees with her Ladyship, and say Amen to the prayers of either Doctor. During these exercises old Southdown, on account of his invalid condition, was allowed to sit in his own room, and have negus and the paper read to him. Lady Jane was the old Earl's favourite daughter, and tended and loved him sincerely; as for Lady Emily, the authoress of the "Washerwoman of Finchley Common," her denunciations of future punishment (at this period, for her opinions modified afterwards), were so awful that they used to frighten the timid old gentleman her father, and the physician declared his fits always occurred after one of her Ladyship's sermons.

"I will certainly call," said Lady Southdown then, in reply to the exhortation of her daughter's *prétendu*, Mr. Pitt Crawley—"Who is Miss Crawley's medical man?"

Mr. Crawley mentioned the name of Mr. Creamer.

"A most dangerous and ignorant practitioner, my dear
Pitt. I have providentially been the means of removing
him from several houses: though on one or two instances
I did no arrive in time. I could not save poor dear General Glanders, who was dying under the hands of that
ignorant man—dying. He rallied a little under the Podgers' pills which I administered to him; but alas! it was
too late. His death was delightful, however, and his change
was only for the better; Creamer, my dear Pitt, must leave
your aunt."

Pitt expressed his perfect acquiescence. He, too, had
been carried along by the energy of his noble kinswoman, and
future mother-in-law. He had been made to accept Saunders McNitre, Luke Waters, Giles Jowls, Podgers' Pills,
Rodgers' Pills, Pokey's Elixir, every one of her Ladyship's
remedies spiritual or temporal. He never left her house
without carrying respectfully away with him piles of her
quack theology and medicine. O, my dear brethren and
fellow-sojourners in Vanity Fair, which among you does not
know and suffer under such benevolent despots? It is in vain
you say to them, "Dear Madam, I took Podgers' specific
at your orders last year, and believe in it. Why, why am
I to recant and accept the Rodgers' article now?" There
is no help for it; the faithful proselytizer, if she cannot
convince by arguments, bursts into tears, and the recusant
finds himself, at the end of the contest, taking down the
bolus, and saying, "Well, well, Rodgers' be it."

"And as for her spiritual state," continued the Lady,
"that of course must be looked to immediately; with Creamer
about her, she may go off any day: and in what a condition,
my dear Pitt, in what a dreadful condition! I will send the
Reverend Mr. Irons to her instantly. Jane, write a line to
the Reverend Bartholomew Irons, in the third person, and
say that I desire the pleasure of his company this evening
at tea at half-past six. He is an awakening man; he ought
to see Miss Crawley before she rests this night. And Emily,
my love, get ready a packet of books for Miss Crawley. Put
up 'A voice from the Flames,' 'A Trumpet-warning to
Jericho,' and the 'Fleshpots Broken; or, the Converted
Cannibal.'"

"And the 'Washerwoman of Finchley Common,' Mamma," said Lady Emily. "It is as well to begin soothingly at first."

"Stop, my dear ladies," said Pitt, the diplomatist. "With every deference to the opinion of my beloved and respected Lady Southdown, I think it would be quite unadvisable to commence so early upon serious topics with Miss Crawley. Remember her delicate condition, and how little, how very little accustomed she has hitherto been to considerations connected with her immortal welfare."

"Can we then begin too early, Pitt?" said Lady Emily, rising with six little books already in her hand.

"If you begin abruptly, you will frighten her altogether. I know my aunt's worldly nature so well as to be sure that any abrupt attempt at conversion will be the very worst means that can be employed for the welfare of that unfortunate lady. You will only frighten and annoy her. She will very likely fling the books away, and refuse all acquaintance with the givers."

"You are as worldly as Miss Crawley, Pitt," said Lady Emily, tossing out of the room, her books in her hand.

"And I need not tell you, my dear Lady Southdown," Pitt continued, in a low voice, and without heeding the interruption, "how fatal a little want of gentleness and caution may be to any hopes which we may entertain with regard to the worldly possessions of my aunt. Remember she has seventy thousand pounds, think of her age, and her highly nervous and delicate condition; I know that she has destroyed the will which was made in my brother's (Colonel Crawley's) favour: it is by soothing that wounded spirit that we must lead it into the right path, and not by frightening it; and so I think you will agree with me that —that—"

"Of course, of course," Lady Southdown remarked. "Jane, my love, you need not send that note to Mr. Irons. If her health is such that discussions fatigue her, we will wait her amendment. I will call upon Miss Crawley to-morrow."

"And if I might suggest, my sweet lady," Pitt said in a bland tone, "it would be as well not to take our precious Emily, who is too enthusiastic; but rather that you should be accompanied by our sweet and dear Lady Jane."

"Most certainly, Emily would ruin everything," Lady Southdown said; and this time agreed to forego her usual practice, which was, as we have said, before she bore down personally upon any individual whom she proposed to subjugate, to fire in a quantity of tracts upon the menaced party (as a charge of the French was always preceded by a furious cannonade). Lady Southdown, we say, for the sake of the invalid's health, or for the sake of her soul's ultimate welfare, or for the sake of her money, agreed to temporise.

The next day, the great Southdown female family carriage, with the Earl's coronet and the lozenge (upon which the three lambs trottant argent upon the field vert of the Southdowns, were quartered with sable on a bend or, three snuff-mulls gules, the cognizance of the house of Binkie), drove up in state to Miss Crawley's door, and the tall serious footman handed into Mr. Bowls her Ladyship's cards for Miss Crawley, and one likewise for Miss Briggs. By way of compromise, Lady Emily sent in a packet in the evening for the latter lady, containing copies of the "Washerwoman," and other mild and favourite tracts for Miss B.'s own perusal; and a few for the servants' hall, viz.: "Crumbs from the Pantry," "The Frying Pan and the Fire," and "The Livery of Sin," of a much stronger kind.

CHAPTER XXXIV

James Crawley's Pipe Is Put Out

THE amiable behaviour of Mr. Crawley, and Lady
Jane's kind reception of her, highly flattered Miss
Briggs, who was enabled to speak a good word for
the latter, after the cards of the Southdown family had been
presented to Miss Crawley. A Countess's card left personally too for her, Briggs, was not a little pleasing to the poor
friendless companion. "What could Lady Southdown mean
by leaving a card upon *you*, I wonder, Miss Briggs?" said
the republican Miss Crawley; upon which the companion
meekly said "that she hoped there could be no harm in a lady
of rank taking notice of a poor gentlewoman," and she put
away this card in her work-box amongst her most cherished
personal treasures. Furthermore, Miss Briggs explained
how she had met Mr. Crawley walking with his cousin and
long affianced bride the day before: and she told how kind
and gentle-looking the lady was, and what a plain, not to
say common, dress she had, all the articles of which, from
the bonnet down to the boots, she described and estimated
with female accuracy.

Miss Crawley allowed Briggs to prattle on without inter-
rupting her too much. As she got well, she was pining for
society. Mr. Creamer, her medical man, would not hear
of her returning to her old haunts and dissipation in London.

The old spinster was too glad to find any companionship
at Brighton, and not only were the cards acknowledged
the very next day, but Pitt Crawley was graciously invited to come and see his aunt. He came, bringing with
him Lady Southdown and her daughter. The dowager did
not say a word about the state of Miss Crawley's soul; but
talked with much discretion about the weather: about the
war and the downfall of the monster Bonaparte: and above

all, about doctors, quacks, and the particular merits of Dr. Podgers, whom she then patronised.

During their interview Pitt Crawley made a great stroke, and one which showed that, had his diplomatic career not been blighted by early neglect, he might have risen to a high rank in his profession. When the Countess Dowager of Southdown fell foul of the Corsican upstart, as the fashion was in those days, and showed that he was a monster stained with every conceivable crime, a coward and a tyrant not fit to live, one whose fall was predicted, &c., Pitt Crawley suddenly took up the cudgels in favour of the man of Destiny. He described the First Consul as he saw him at Paris at the peace of Amiens; when he, Pitt Crawley, had the gratification of making the acquaintance of the great and good Mr. Fox, a statesman whom, however much he might differ with him, it was impossible not to admire fervently—a statesman who had always had the highest opinion of the Emperor Napoleon. And he spoke in terms of the strongest indignation of the faithless conduct of the allies towards this dethroned monarch, who, after giving himself generously up to their mercy, was consigned to an ignoble and cruel banishment, while a bigoted Popish rabble was tyrannising over France in his stead.

This orthodox horror of Romish superstition saved Pitt Crawley in Lady Southdown's opinion, whilst his admiration for Fox and Napoleon raised him immeasurably in Miss Crawley's eyes. Her friendship with that defunct British statesman was mentioned when we first introduced her in this history. A true Whig, Miss Crawley had been in opposition all through the war, and though, to be sure, the downfall of the Emperor did not very much agitate the old lady, or his ill-treatment tend to shorten her life or natural rest, yet Pitt spoke to her heart when he lauded both her idols; and by that single speech made immense progress in her favour.

"And what do you think, my dear?" Miss Crawley said to the young lady, for whom she had taken a liking at first sight, as she always did for pretty and modest young people; though it must be owned her affections cooled as rapidly as they rose.

Lady Jane blushed very much, and said "that she did not
understand politics, which she left to wiser heads than hers;
but though Mamma was, no doubt, correct, Mr. Crawley had
spoken beautifully." And when the ladies were retiring at
the conclusion of their visit, Miss Crawley hoped "Lady
Southdown would be so kind as to send her Lady Jane
sometimes, if she could be spared to come down and console
a poor sick lonely old woman." This promise was graciously
accorded, and they separated upon great terms of amity.

"Don't let Lady Southdown come again, Pitt," said the
old lady. "She is stupid and pompous, like all your mother's
family, whom I never could endure. But bring that nice
good-natured little Jane as often as ever you please." Pitt
promised that he would do so. He did not tell the Countess
of Southdown what opinion his aunt had formed of her
Ladyship, who, on the contrary, thought that she had made a
most delightful and majestic impression on Miss Crawley.

And so, nothing loth to comfort a sick lady, and perhaps
not sorry in heart to be freed now and again from the
dreary spouting of the Reverend Bartholomew Irons, and
the serious toadies who gathered round the footstool of the
pompous Countess, her mamma, Lady Jane became a pretty
constant visitor to Miss Crawley, accompanied her in her
drives, and solaced many of her evenings. She was so
naturally good and soft, that even Firkin was not jealous
of her; and the gentle Briggs thought her friend was less
cruel to her, when kind Lady Jane was by. Towards her
Ladyship Miss Crawley's manners were charming. The old
spinster told her a thousand anecdotes about her youth, talking to her in a very different strain from that in which she
had been accustomed to converse with the godless little
Rebecca; for there was that in Lady Jane's innocence which
rendered light talking impertinence before her, and Miss
Crawley was too much of a gentlewoman to offend such
purity. The young lady herself had never received kindness
except from this old spinster, and her brother and father:
and she repaid Miss Crawley's engoûment by artless sweetness and friendship.

In the autumn evenings (when Rebecca was flaunting at
Paris, the gayest among the gay conquerors there, and our

Amelia, our dear wounded Amelia, ah! where was she?)
Lady Jane would be sitting in Miss Crawley's drawing-room
singing sweetly to her, in the twilight, her little simple songs
and hymns, while the sun was setting and the sea was roaring on the beach. The old spinster used to wake up when
these ditties ceased, and ask for more. As for Briggs, and
the quantity of tears of happiness which she now shed as she
pretended to knit, and looked out at the splendid ocean
darkling before the windows, and the lamps of heaven beginning more brightly to shine—who, I say, can measure the
happiness and sensibility of Briggs?

Pitt meanwhile in the dining-room, with a pamphlet on
the Corn Laws or a Missionary Register by his side, took
that kind of recreation which suits romantic and unromantic
men after dinner. He sipped Madeira: built castles in the
air: thought himself a fine fellow: felt himself much more
in love with Jane than he had been any time these seven
years, during which their *liaison* had lasted without the
slightest impatience on Pitt's part—and slept a good
deal.

When the time for coffee came, Mr. Bowls used to enter
in a noisy manner, and summon Squire Pitt, who would be
found in the dark very busy with his pamphlet.

"I wish, my love, I could get somebody to play piquet
with me," Miss Crawley said one night when this functionary
made his appearance with the candles and the coffee. "Poor
Briggs can no more play than an owl, she is so stupid" (the
spinster always took an opportunity of abusing Briggs before
the servants); "and I think I should sleep better if I had
my game."

At this Lady Jane blushed to the tips of her little ears,
and down to the ends of her pretty fingers; and when Mr.
Bowls had quitted the room, and the door was quite shut,
she said:

"Miss Crawley, I can play a little. I used to—to play a
little with poor dear papa."

"Come and kiss me. Come and kiss me this instant, you
dear little soul," cried Miss Crawley in an ecstasy: and in
this picturesque and friendly occupation Mr. Pitt found the
old lady and the young one, when he came upstairs with his

pamphlet in his hand.   How she did blush all the evening,
that poor Lady Jane!

It must not be imagined that Mr. Pitt Crawley's artifices
escaped the attention of his dear relations at the Rectory
at Queen's Crawley.   Hampshire and Sussex lie very close
together, and Mrs. Bute had friends in the latter county
who took care to inform her of all, and a great deal more
than all, that passed at Miss Crawley's house at Brighton.
Pitt was there more and more.   He did not come for months
together to the Hall, where his abominable old father abandoned himself completely to rum-and-water, and the odious
society of the Horrocks family.   Pitt's success rendered
the Rector's family furious, and Mrs. Bute regretted
more (though she confessed less) than ever her monstrous
fault in so insulting Miss Briggs, and in being so haughty
and parsimonious to Bowls and Firkin, that she had not a
single person left in Miss Crawley's household to give her
information of what took place there.   "It was all Bute's
collar-bone," she persisted in saying; "if that had not broke,
I never would have left her.   I am a martyr to duty and to
your odious unclerical habit of hunting, Bute."

"Hunting; nonsense!   It was you that frightened her,
Barbara," the divine interposed.   "You're a clever woman,
but you've got a devil of a temper; and you're a screw with
your money, Barbara."

"You'd have been screwed in gaol, if I had not kept your
money."

"I know I would, my dear," said the rector, good-naturedly.
"You *are* a clever woman, but you manage too well, you
know:" and the pious man consoled himself with a big glass
of port.

"What the deuce can she find in that spooney of a Pitt
Crawley?" he continued.   "The fellow has not pluck enough
to say Bo to a goose.   I remember when Rawdon, who *is* a
man, and be hanged to him, used to flog him round the stables
as if he was a whipping-top: and Pitt would go howling home
to his ma—ha, ha!   Why, either of my boys would whop him
with one hand.   Jim says he's remembered at Oxford as Miss
Crawley still—the spooney."

"I say, Barbara," his reverence continued, after a pause.

"What?" said Barbara, who was biting her nails, and drumming the table.

"I say, why not send Jim over to Brighton to see if he can do anything with the old lady. He's very near getting his degree, you know. He's only been plucked twice—so was I—but he's had the advantages of Oxford and a university education. He knows some of the best chaps there He pulls stroke in the Boniface boat. He's a handsome feller. D— it, ma'am, let's put him on the old woman, hey; and tell him to thrash Pitt if he says anything. Ha, ha, ha!"

"Jim might go down and see her, certainly," the housewife said; adding with a sigh, "If we could but get one of the girls into the house; but she could never endure them, because they are not pretty!" Those unfortunate and well-educated women made themselves heard from the neighbouring drawing-room, where they were thrumming away, with hard fingers, an elaborate music-piece on the pianoforte, as their mother spoke; and indeed, they were at music, or at blackboard, or at geography, or at history, the whole day long. But what avail all these accomplishments, in Vanity Fair, to girls who are short, poor, plain, and have a bad complexion? Mrs. Bute could think of nobody but the Curate to take one of them off her hands; and Jim coming in from the stable at this minute, through the parlour window, with a short pipe stuck in his oil-skin cap, he and his father fell to talking about odds on the St. Leger, and the colloquy between the Rector and his wife ended.

Mrs. Bute did not augur much good to the cause from the sending of her son James as an ambassador, and saw him depart in rather a despairing mood. Nor did the young fellow himself, when told what his mission was to be, expect much pleasure or benefit from it; but he was consoled by the thought that possibly the old lady would give him some handsome remembrance of her, which would pay a few of his most pressing bills at the commencement of the ensuing Oxford term, and so took his place by the coach from Southampton, and was safely landed at Brighton on the same evening, with his portmanteau, his favorite bulldog Towzer, and an immense basket of farm and garden produce, from the dear Rectory folks to the dear Miss Crawley. Considering it was too late to disturb the invalid lady on the first night of his arrival, he put up at an inn, and did not wait upon Miss Crawley until a late hour in the noon of next day.

James Crawley, when his aunt had last beheld him, was a gawky lad, at that uncomfortable age when the voice varies between an unearthly treble and a preternatural bass: when the face not uncommonly blooms out with appearances for which Rowland's Kalydor is said to act as a cure; when boys are seen to shave furtively with their sister's scissors, and the sight of other young women produces intolerable sensations of terror in them; when the great hands and ankles protrude a long way from garments which have grown too tight for them; when their presence after dinner is at once frightful to the ladies, who are whispering in the twilight in the drawing-room, and inexpressibly odious to the gentlemen over the mahogany, who are restrained from freedom of intercourse and delightful interchange of wit by the presence of that gawky innocence; when at the conclusion of the second glass, papa says, "Jack, my boy, go out and see if the evening holds up," and the youth, willing to be free yet hurt at not being yet a man, quits the incomplete banquet. James, then a hobbadehoy, was now become a young man, having had the benefits of a university education, and acquired the inestimable polish which is gained by living in a fast set at a small college, and contracting debts, and being rusticated, and being plucked.

He was a handsome lad, however, when he came to present himself to his aunt at Brighton, and good looks were always a title to the fickle old lady's favour. Nor did his blushes and awkwardness take away from it: she was pleased with these healthy tokens of the young gentleman's ingenuousness.

He said "he had come down for a couple of days to see a man of his college, and—and to pay my respects to you, Ma'am, and my father's and mother's, who hope you are well."

Pitt was in the room with Miss Crawley when the lad was announced, and looked very blank when his name was mentioned. The old lady had plenty of humour, and enjoyed her correct nephew's perplexity. She asked after all the people at the Rectory with great interest; and said she was thinking of paying them a visit. She praised the lad to his face, and said he was well-grown and very much improved, and that it was a pity his sisters had not some of his good looks; and finding, on inquiry, that he had taken up his quarters at an hotel, would not hear of his stopping there, but bade Mr. Bowls send for Mr. James Crawley's things instantly; "and hark ye, Bowls," she added, with great graciousness, "you will have the goodness to pay Mr. James's bill."

She flung Pitt a look of arch triumph, which caused that diplomatist almost to choke with envy. Much as he had ingratiated himself with his aunt, she had never yet invited him to stay under her roof, and here was a young whipper-snapper, who at first sight was made welcome there.

"I beg your pardon, Sir," says Bowls, advancing with a profound bow; "what 'otel, Sir, shall Thomas fetch the luggage from?"

"Oh, dam," said young James, starting up, as if in some alarm, "I'll go."

"What!" said Miss Crawley.

"The Tom Cribb's Arms," said James, blushing deeply.

Miss Crawley burst out laughing at this title. Mr. Bowls gave one abrupt guffaw, as a confidential servant of the family, but choked the rest of the volley; the diplomatist only smiled.

"I—I didn't know any better," said James, looking down. "I've never been here before; it was the coachman told me."

The young story-teller! The fact is, that on the Southampton coach, the day previous, James Crawley had met the Tutbury Pet, who was coming to Brighton to make a match with the Rottingdean Fibber; and enchanted by the Pet's conversation, had passed the evening in company with that scientific man and his friends, at the inn in question.

"I—I'd best go and settle the score," James continued. "Couldn't think of asking you, Ma'am," he added, generously.

This delicacy made his aunt laugh the more.

"Go and settle the bill, Bowls," she said, with a wave of her hand, "and bring it to me."

Poor lady, she did not know what she had done! "There —there's a little *dawg*," said James, looking frightfully guilty. "I'd best go for him. He bites footmen's calves."

All the party cried out with laughing at this description; even Briggs and Lady Jane, who was sitting mute during the interview between Miss Crawley and her nephew: and Bowls, without a word, quitted the room.

Still, by way of punishing her elder nephew, Miss Crawley persisted in being gracious to the young Oxonian. There were no limits to her kindness or her compliments when they once began. She told Pitt he might come to dinner, and insisted that James should accompany her in her drive, and paraded him solemnly up and down the cliff, on the back seat of the barouche. During all this excursion, she condescended to say civil things to him: she quoted Italian and French poetry to the poor bewildered lad, and persisted that he was a fine scholar, and was perfectly sure he would gain a gold medal, and be a Senior Wrangler.

"Haw, haw," laughed James, encouraged by these compliments; "Senior Wrangler, indeed; that's at the other shop."

"What is the other shop, my dear child?" said the lady.

"Senior Wranglers at Cambridge, not Oxford," said the scholar, with a knowing air; and would probably have been more confidential, but that suddenly there appeared on the cliff in a tax-cart, drawn by a bang-up pony, dressed in white flannel coats, with mother-of-pearl buttons, his friends the Tutbury Pet and the Rottingdean Fibber, with three other gentlemen of their acquaintance, who all saluted poor James there in the carriage as he sate. This incident damped the ingenuous youth's spirits, and no word of yea or nay could he be induced to utter during the rest of the drive.

On his return he found his room prepared, and his portmanteau ready, and might have remarked that Mr. Bowls's countenance, when the latter conducted him to his apartments, wore a look of gravity, wonder, and compassion. But the thought of Mr. Bowls did not enter his head. He was deploring the dreadful predicament in which he found himself, in a house full of old women, jabbering French and Italian, and talking poetry to him. "Regularly up a tree, by jingo!" exclaimed the modest boy, who could not face the gentlest of her sex—not even Briggs—when she began to talk to him; whereas, put him at Iffley Lock, and he could out-slang the boldest bargeman.

At dinner, James appeared choking in a white neck-cloth, and had the honour of handing my Lady Jane downstairs, while Briggs and Mr. Crawley followed afterwards, conducting the old lady, with her apparatus of bundles, and shawls, and cushions. Half of Briggs's time at dinner was spent in superintending the invalid's comfort, and in cutting up chicken for her fat spaniel. James did not talk much, but he made a point of asking all the ladies to drink wine, and accepted Mr. Crawley's challenge, and consumed the greater part of a bottle of champagne which Mr. Bowls was ordered to produce in his honour. The ladies having withdrawn, and the two cousins being left together, Pitt, the ex-diplomatist, became very communicative and friendly. He asked after James's career at college—what his prospects in life were—hoped heartily he would get on; and, in a word, was frank and amiable. James's tongue unloosed with the port, and he told his cousin his life, his prospects, his debts, his troubles at the little-go, and his rows with the proctors, filling rapidly from the bottles before him, and flying from Port to Madeira with joyous activity.

"The chief pleasure which my aunt has," said Mr. Crawley, filling his glass, "is that people should do as they like in her house. This is Liberty Hall, James, and you can't do Miss Crawley a greater kindness than to do as you please, and ask for what you will. I know you have all sneered at me in the country for being a Tory. Miss Crawley is liberal enough to suit any fancy. She is a Republican in principle, and despises everything like rank or title."

"Why are you going to marry an Earl's daughter?" said James.

"My dear friend, remember it is not poor Lady Jane's fault that she is well born," Pitt replied, with a courtly air. "She cannot help being a lady. Besides, I am a Tory, you know."

"Oh, as for that," said Jim, "there's nothing like old blood; no, dammy, nothing like it. I'm none of your radicals. I know what it is to be a gentleman, dammy. See the chaps in a boat-race; look at the fellers in a fight; aye, look at a dawg killing rats,—which is it wins? the good-blooded ones. Get some more port, Bowls, old boy, whilst I buzz this bottle here. What was I saying?"

"I think you were speaking of dogs killing rats," Pitt remarked mildly, handling his cousin the decanter to "buzz."

"Killing rats was I? Well, Pitt, are you a sporting man? Do you want to see a dawg as *can* kill a rat? If you do, come down with me to Tom Corduroy's, in Castle Street Mews, and I'll show you such a bull-terrier as——Pooh! gammon," cried James, bursting out laughing at his own absurdity,—"you don't care about a dawg or rat; it's all nonsense. I'm blest if I think you know the difference between a dog and a duck."

"No; by the way," Pitt continued with increased blandness, "it was about blood you were talking, and the personal advantages which people derive from patrician birth. Here's the fresh bottle."

"Blood's the word," said James, gulping the ruby fluid down. "Nothing like blood, sir, in hosses, dawgs, and men. Why, only last term, just before I was rusticated, that is, I mean just before I had the measles, ha, ha,—there was me and Ringwood of Christchurch, Bob Ringwood, Lord Cinqbars' son, having our beer at the Bell at Blenheim, when the Banbury bargeman offered to fight either of us for a bowl of punch.

"I couldn't. My arm was in a sling; couldn't even take the drag down,—a brute of a mare of mine had fell with me only two days before, out with the Abingdon, and I thought my arm was broke. Well, sir, I couldn't finish him, but Bob had his coat off at once—he stood up to the Banbury man for three minutes, and polished him off in four rounds, easy. Gad, how he did drop, sir, and what was it? Blood, sir, all blood."

"You don't drink, James," the ex-attaché continued. "In my time at Oxford, the men passed round the bottle a little quicker than you young fellows seem to do."

"Come, come," said James, putting his hand to his nose and winking at his cousin with a pair of vinous eyes," no jokes, old boy; no trying it on on me. You want to trot me out, but it's no go. In vino veritas, old boy. Mars, Bacchus, Apollo virorum, hay? I wish my aunt would send down some of this to the governor; it's a precious good tap."

"You had better ask her," Machiavel continued, "or make the best of your time now. What says the bard? 'Nunc vino pellite curas, Cras ingens iterabimus æquor,'" and the Bacchanalian, quoting the above with a House of Commons air, tossed off nearly a thimbleful of wine with an immense flourish of his glass.

At the Rectory, when the bottle of port wine was opened after dinner, the young ladies had each a glass from a bottle of currant wine. Mrs. Bute took one glass of port, honest James had a couple commonly, but as his father grew very sulky if he made further inroads on the bottle, the good lad generally refrained from trying for more, and subsided either into the currant wine, or to some private gin-and-water in the stables, which he enjoyed in the company of the coachman and his pipe. At Oxford, the quantity of wine was unlimited, but the quality was inferior: but when quantity and quality united as at his aunt's house, James showed that he could appreciate them indeed; and hardly needed any of his cousin's encouragement in draining off the second bottle supplied by Mr. Bowls.

When the time for coffee came, however, and for a return to the ladies, of whom he stood in awe, the young gentleman's agreeable frankness left him, and he relapsed into his usual surly timidity; contenting himself by saying yes and no, by scowling at Lady Jane, and by upsetting one cup of coffee during the evening.

If he did not speak he yawned in a pitiable manner, and his presence threw a damp upon the modest proceedings of the evening, for Miss Crawley and Lady Jane at their piquet, and Miss Briggs at her work, felt that his eyes were widely fixed on them, and were uneasy under that maudlin look.

"He seems a very silent, awkward, bashful lad," said Miss Crawley to Mr. Pitt.

"He is more communicative in men's society than with ladies," Machiavel dryly replied: perhaps rather disappointed that the port wine had not made Jim speak more.

He had spent the early part of the next morning in writing home to his mother a most flourishing account of his reception by Miss Crawley. But ah! he little knew what evils the day was bringing for him, and how short his reign of favour was destined to be. A circumstance which Jim had forgotten—a trivial but fatal circumstance—had taken place at the Cribb's Arms on the night before he had come to his aunt's house. It was no other than this—Jim, who was always of a generous disposition, and when in his cups especially hospitable, had in the course of the night treated the Tutbury champion and the Rottingdean man, and their friends, twice or thrice to the refreshment of gin-and-water —so that no less than eighteen glasses of that fluid at eightpence per glass were charged in Mr. James Crawley's bill. It was not the amount of eight-pences, but the quantity of gin which told fatally against poor James's character, when his aunt's butler, Mr. Bowls, went down at his mistress's request to pay the young gentleman's bill. The landlord, fearing lest the account should be refused altogether, swore solemnly that the young gent had consumed personally every farthing's worth of the liquor: and Bowls paid the bill finally, and showed it on his return home to Mrs. Firkin, who was shocked at the frightful prodigality of gin; and took the bill to Miss Briggs as accountant-general; who thought it her duty to mention the circumstance to her principal, Miss Crawley.

Had he drunk a dozen bottles of claret, the old spinster could have pardoned him. Mr. Fox and Mr. Sheridan drank claret. Gentlemen drank claret. But eighteen glasses of gin consumed among boxers in an ignoble pothouse—it was an odious crime and not to be pardoned readily. Everything went against the lad: he came home perfumed from the stables, whither he had been to pay his dog Towzer a visit—and whence he was going to take his friend out for an airing, when he met Miss Crawley and her wheezy Blenheim spaniel, which Towzer would have eaten up had not the Blenheim fled squealing to the protection of Miss Briggs. while the atrocious master of the bulldog stood laughing at the horrible persecution.

This day too the unlucky boy's modesty had likewise forsaken him. He was lively and facetious at dinner. During the repast he levelled one or two jokes against Pitt Crawley: he drank as much wine as upon the previous day; and going quite unsuspiciously to the drawing-room, began to entertain the ladies there with some choice Oxford stories. He described the different pugilistic qualities of Molyneux and Dutch Sam, offered playfully to give Lady Jane the odds upon the Tutbury Pet against the Rottingdean man, or take them, as her Ladyship chose: and crowned the pleasantry by proposing to back himself against his cousin Pitt Crawley, either with or without gloves. "And that's a fair offer, my buck," he said, with a loud laugh, slapping Pitt on the shoulder, "and my father told me to make it too, and he'll go halves in the bet, ha, ha!" So saying, the engaging youth nodded knowingly at poor Miss Briggs, and pointed his thumb over his shoulder at Pitt Crawley in a jocular and exulting manner.

Pitt was not pleased altogether perhaps, but still not unhappy in the main. Poor Jim had his laugh out: and staggered across the room with his aunt's candle, when the old lady moved to retire, and offered to salute her with the blandest tipsy smile: and he took his own leave and went upstairs to his bed-room perfectly satisfied with himself, and with a pleased notion that his aunt's money would be left to him in preference to his father and all the rest of the family.

Once up in the bed-room, one would have thought he could not make matters worse; and yet this unlucky boy did. The moon was shining very pleasantly out on the sea, and Jim, attracted to the window by the romantic appearance of the ocean and the heavens, thought he would further enjoy them while smoking. Nobody would smell the tobacco, he thought, if he cunningly opened the window and kept his head and pipe in the fresh air. This he did: but being in an excited state, poor Jim had forgotten that his door was open all this time, so that the breeze blowing inwards and a fine thorough draught being established, the clouds of tobacco were carried downstairs, and arrived with quite undiminished fragrance to Miss Crawley and Miss Briggs.

The pipe of tobacco finished the business: and the Bute-Crawleys never knew how many thousand pounds it cost them. Firkin rushed downstairs to Bowls who was reading out the "Fire and the Frying Pan" to his aide-de-camp in a loud and ghostly voice. The dreadful secret was told to him by Firkin with so frightened a look, that for the first moment Mr. Bowls and his young man thought that robbers were in the house; the legs of whom had probably been discovered by the woman under Miss Crawley's bed.

When made aware of the fact, however—to rush upstairs at three steps at a time—to enter the unconscious James's apartment, calling out, "Mr. James," in a voice stifled with alarm, and to cry, "For Gawd's sake, sir, stop that 'ere pipe," was the work of a moment with Mr. Bowls. "O, Mr. James, what 'ave you done!" he said in a voice of the deepest pathos, as he threw the implement out of the window. "What 'ave you done, sir! Missis can't abide 'em."

"Missis needn't smoke," said James with a frantic misplaced laugh, and thought the whole matter an excellent joke.

But his feelings were very different in the morning, when Mr. Bowls's young man, who operated upon Mr. James's boots, and brought him his hot water to shave that beard which he was so anxiously expecting, handed a note in to Mr. James in bed, in the handwriting of Miss Briggs.

"Dear sir," it said, "Miss Crawley has passed an exceedingly disturbed night, owing to the shocking manner in which the house has been polluted by tobacco; Miss Crawley bids me say she regrets that she is too unwell to see you before you go—and above all that she ever induced you to remove from the ale-house, where she is sure you will be much more comfortable during the rest of your stay at Brighton."

And herewith honest James's career as a candidate for his aunt's favour ended. He *had* in fact, and without knowing it, done what he menaced to do. He had fought his cousin Pitt with the gloves.

Where meanwhile was he who had been once first favourite for this race for money? Becky and Rawdon, as we have seen, were come together after Waterloo, and were passing the winter of 1815 at Paris in great splendour and gaiety. Rebecca was a good economist, and the price poor Jos Sedley had paid for her two horses was in itself sufficient to keep their little establishment afloat for a year, at the least; there was no occasion to turn into money "my pistols, the same which I shot Captain Marker," or the gold dressing-case, or the cloak lined with sable. Becky had it made into a pelisse for herself, in which she rode in the Bois de Boulogne to the admiration of all: and you should have seen the scene between her and her delighted husband, whom she rejoined after the army had entered Cambray, and when she unsewed herself, and let out of her dress all those watches, knickknacks, bank-notes, cheques, and valuables, which she had secreted in the wadding, previous to her meditated flight from Brussels! Tufto was charmed, and Rawdon roared with delightful laughter, and swore that she was better than any play he ever saw, by Jove. And the way in which she jockeyed Jos, and which she described with infinite fun, carried up his delight to a pitch of quite insane enthusiasm. He believed in his wife as much as the French soldiers in Napoleon.

Her success in Paris was remarkable. All the French ladies voted her charming. She spoke their language admirably. She adopted at once their grace, their liveliness, their manner. Her husband was stupid certainly—all English are stupid—and, besides, a dull husband at Paris is always a point in a lady's favour. He was the heir of the rich and *spirituelle* Miss Crawley, whose house had been open to so many of the French noblesse during the emigration. They received the colonel's wife in their own hotels —"Why," wrote a great lady to Miss Crawley, who had bought her lace and trinkets at the Duchess's own price, and given her many a dinner during the pinching times after the Revolution—"Why does not our dear Miss come to her nephew and niece, and her attached friends in Paris? All the world *raffoles* of the charming Mistress and her *espigèle* beauty. Yes, we see in her the grace, the charm, the wit of our dear friend Miss Crawley! The King took notice of her yesterday at the Tuileries, and we are all jealous of the attention which Monsieur pays her. If you could have seen the spite of a certain stupid Miladi Bare-acres, (whose eagle-beak and toque and feathers may be seen peering over the heads of all assemblies,) when Ma-dame, the Duchess of Angoulême, the august daughter and companion of kings, desired especially to be presented to Mrs. Crawley, as your dear daughter and *protégée*, and thanked her in the name of France, for all your benevolence towards our unfortunates during their exile! She is of all the societies, of all the balls—of the balls—yes—of the dances, no; and yet how interesting and pretty this fair creature looks surrounded by the homage of the men, and so soon to be a mother! To hear her speak of you, her protectress, her mother, would bring tears to the eyes of ogres. How she loves you! how we all love our admira-ble, our respectable Miss Crawley!"

It is to be feared that this letter of the Parisian great lady did not by any means advance Mrs. Becky's interest with her admirable, her respectable, relative. On the con-trary, the fury of the old spinster was beyond bounds, when she found what was Rebecca's situation, and how audaciously she had made use of Miss Crawley's name, to get an *entrée* into Parisian society. Too much shaken in mind and body to compose a letter in the French language in reply to that of her correspondent, she dictated to Briggs a furious answer in her own native tongue, repudiating Mrs. Rawdon Crawley altogether, and warning the public to be-ware of her as a most artful and dangerous person. But as Madame the Duchess of X— had only been twenty years in England, she did not understand a single word of the language, and contented herself by informing Mrs. Rawdon Crawley at their next meeting, that she had received a charming letter from that *chère Mees,* and that it was full of benevolent things for Mrs. Crawley, who began seriously to have hopes that the spinster would relent.

Meanwhile, she was the gayest and most admired of Englishwomen: and had a little European congress on her reception-night. Prussians and Cossacks, Spanish and English—all the world was at Paris during this famous winter: to have seen the stars and cordons in Rebecca's humble saloon would have made all Baker Street pale with envy. Famous warriors rode by her carriage in the Bois, or crowded her modest little box at the opera. Rawdon was in the highest spirits. There were no duns in Paris as yet: there were parties every day at Véry's or Beauvilliers'; play was plentiful and his luck good. Tufto perhaps was sulky. Mrs. Tufto had come over to Paris at her own invitation, and besides this *contretemps,* there were a score of generals now round Becky's chair, and she might take her choice of a dozen bouquets when she went to the play. Lady Bareacres and the chiefs of the English society, stupid and irreproachable females, writhed with anguish at the success of the little upstart Becky, whose poisoned jokes quivered and rankled in their chaste breasts. But she had all the men on her side. She fought the women with indomitable courage, and they could not talk scandal in any tongue but their own.

So in *fêtes,* pleasures, and prosperity, the winter of 1815-16 passed away with Mrs. Rawdon Crawley, who accommodated herself to polite life as if her ancestors had been people of fashion for centuries past—and who from her wit, talent, and energy, indeed merited a place of honour in Vanity Fair. In the early spring of 1816, *Galignani's Journal* contained the following announcement in an interesting corner of the page: "On the 26th of March—the Lady of Lieutenant-Colonel Crawley, of the Life Guards Green—of a son and heir."

This event was copied into the London papers, out of which Miss Briggs read the statement to Miss Crawley, at breakfast, at Brighton. The intelligence, expected as it might have been, caused a crisis in the affairs of the Crawley family. The spinster's rage rose to its height, and sending instantly for Pitt, her nephew, and for the Lady

Southdown, from Brunswick Square, she requested an immediate celebration of the marriage which had been so long pending between the two families. And she announced that it was her intention to allow the young couple a thousand a year during her lifetime, at the expiration of which the bulk of her property would be settled upon her nephew and her dear niece, Lady Jane Crawley. Waxy came down to ratify the deeds—Lord Southdown gave away his sister —she was married by a Bishop, and not by the Rev. Bartholomew Irons—to the disappointment of the irregular prelate.

When they were married, Pitt would have liked to take a hymeneal tour with his bride, as became people of their condition. But the affection of the old lady towards Lady Jane had grown so strong, that she fairly owned she could not part with her favourite. Pitt and his wife came therefore and lived with Miss Crawley: and (greatly to the annoyance of poor Pitt, who conceived himself a most injured character—being subject to the humours of his aunt on one side, and of his mother-in-law on the other) Lady Southdown, from her neighbouring house, reigned over the whole family—Pitt, Lady Jane, Miss Crawley, Briggs, Bowls, Firkin, and all. She pitilessly dosed them with her tracts and her medicine, she dismissed Creamer, she installed Rodgers, and soon stripped Miss Crawley of even the semblance of authority. The poor soul grew so timid that she actually left off bullying Briggs any more, and clung to her niece, more fond and terrified every day. Peace to thee, kind and selfish, vain and generous old heathen!—We shall see thee no more. Let us hope that Lady Jane supported her kindly, and led her with gentle hand out of the busy struggle of Vanity Fair.

CHAPTER XXXV

WIDOW AND MOTHER

THE news of the great fights of Quatre Bras and
Waterloo reached England at the same time. The
Gazette first published the result of the two battles;
at which glorious intelligence all England thrilled with
triumph and fear. Particulars then followed; and after the
announcement of the victories came the list of the wounded
and the slain. Who can tell the dread with which that catalogue was opened and read! Fancy, at every village and
homestead almost through the three kingdoms, the great news
coming of the battles in Flanders, and the feelings of exultation and gratitude, bereavement and sickening dismay,
when the lists of the regimental losses were gone through,
and it became known whether the dear friend and relative
had escaped or fallen. Anybody who will take the trouble
of looking back to a file of the newspapers of the time, must,
even now, feel at second-hand this breathless pause of expectation. The lists of casualties are carried on from day
to day: you stop in the midst as in a story which is to be
continued in our next. Think what the feelings must have
been as those papers followed each other fresh from the
press; and if such an interest could be felt in our country,
and about a battle where but twenty thousand of our people
were engaged, think of the condition of Europe for twenty
years before, where people were fighting, not by thousands,
but by millions; each one of whom as he struck his enemy
wounded horribly some other innocent heart far away.

The news which that famous *Gazette* brought to the Osbornes gave a dreadful shock to the family and its chief.
The girls indulged unrestrained in their grief. The gloom-
stricken old father was still more borne down by his fate
and sorrow. He strove to think that a judgment was on
the boy for his disobedience. He dared not own that the

410

severity of the sentence frightened him, and that its fulfil-
ment had come too soon upon his curses. Sometimes a
shuddering terror struck him, as if he had been the author
of the doom which he had called down on his son. There
was a chance before of reconciliation. The boy's wife
might have died; or he might have come back and said,
Father I have sinned. But there was no hope now. He
stood on the other side of the gulf impassable, haunting
his parent with sad eyes. He remembered them once before so in a fever, when every one thought the lad was
dying, and he lay on his bed speechless, and gazing with a
dreadful gloom. Good God! how the father clung to the
doctor then; and with what a sickening anxiety he followed
him: what a weight of grief was off his mind when, after
the crisis of the fever, the lad recovered, and looked at his
father once more with eyes that recognised him. But now
there was no help or cure, or chance of reconcilement;
above all, there were no humble words to soothe vanity
outraged and furious, or bring to its natural flow the poisoned, angry blood. And it is hard to say which pang it
was that tore the proud father's heart most keenly—that
his son should have gone out of the reach of his forgiveness, or that the apology which his own pride expected
should have escaped him.

Whatever his sensations might have been, however, the
stern old man would have no confidant. He never mentioned his son's name to his daughters; but ordered the
elder to place all the females of the establishment in mourning; and desired that the male servants should be similarly
attired in deep black. All parties and entertainments, of
course, were to be put off. No communications were made
to his future son-in-law, whose marriage-day had been fixed;
but there was enough in Mr. Osborne's appearance to
prevent Mr. Bullock from making any inquiries, or in any
way pressing forward that ceremony. He and the ladies
whispered about it under their voices in the drawing-room
sometimes, whither the father never came. He remained
constantly in his own study; the whole front part of the
house being closed until some time after the completion of
the general mourning.

About three weeks after the 18th of June, Mr. Osborne's acquaintance, Sir William Dobbin, called at Mr. Osborne's house in Russell Square, with a very pale and agitated face, and insisted upon seeing that gentleman. Ushered into his room, and after a few words, which neither the speaker nor the host understood, the former produced from an inclosure a letter sealed with a large red seal. "My son, Major Dobbin," the Alderman said, with some hesitation, "despatched me a letter by an officer of the —th, who arrived in town to-day. My son's letter contains one for you, Osborne." The Alderman placed the letter on the table, and Osborne stared at him for a moment or two in silence. His looks frightened the ambassador, who after looking guiltily for a little time at the grief-stricken man, hurried away without another word.

The letter was in George's well-known bold hand-writing. It was that one which he had written before day-break on the 16th of June, and just before he took leave of Amelia. The great red seal was emblazoned with the sham coat of arms which Osborne had assumed from the Peerage, with "Pax in bello" for a motto; that of the ducal house with which the vain old man tried to fancy himself connected. The hand that signed it would never hold pen or sword more. The very seal that sealed it had been robbed from George's dead body as it lay on the field of battle. The father knew nothing of this, but sat and looked at the letter in terrified vacancy. He almost fell when he went to open it.

Have you ever had a difference with a dear friend? How his letters, written in the period of love and confidence, sicken and rebuke you! What a dreary mourning it is to dwell upon those vehement protests of dead affection! What lying epitaphs they make over the corpse of love! What dark, cruel comments upon Life and Vanities! Most of us have got or written drawers full of them. They are closet-skeletons which we keep and shun. Osborne trembled long before the letter from his dead son.

The poor boy's letter did not say much. He had been too proud to acknowledge the tenderness which his heart felt. He only said, that on the eve of a great battle, he

wished to bid his father farewell, and solemnly to implore
his good offices for the wife—it might be for the child—
whom he left behind him. He owned with contrition
that his irregularities and his extravagance had already
wasted a large part of his mother's little fortune. He
thanked his father for his former generous conduct; and
he promised him, that if he fell on the field or survived it,
he would act in a manner worthy of the name of George
Osborne.

His English habit, pride, awkwardness perhaps, had
prevented him from saying more. His father could not
see the kiss George had placed on the superscription of his
letter. Mr. Osborne dropped it with the bitterest, deadliest
pang of balked affection and revenge. His son was still
beloved and unforgiven.

About two months afterwards, however, as the young
ladies of the family went to church with their father, they
remarked how he took a different seat from that which he
usually occupied when he chose to attend divine worship;
and that from his cushion opposite, he looked up at the
wall over their heads. This caused the young women likewise to gaze in the direction towards which their father's
gloomy eyes pointed: and they saw an elaborate monument
upon the wall, where Britannia was represented weeping
over an urn, and a broken sword and a couchant lion indicated that the piece of sculpture had been erected in honour
of a deceased warrior. The sculptors of those days had
stocks of such funereal emblems in hand; as you may see
still on the walls of St. Paul's, which are covered with
hundreds of these braggart heathen allegories. There was
a constant demand for them during the first fifteen years
of the present century.

Under the memorial in question were emblazoned the
well-known and pompous Osborne arms; and the inscription said, that the monument was "Sacred to the memory
of George Osborne, Junior, Esq., late a Captain in his
Majesty's —th regiment of foot, who fell on the 18th of
June, 1815, aged 28 years, while fighting for his king and
country in the glorious victory of Waterloo. *Dulce et de-
sorum est pro patriâ mori.*"

The sight of that stone agitated the nerves of the sisters so much, that Miss Maria was compelled to leave the church. The congregation made way respectfully for those sobbing girls clothed in deep black, and pitied the stern old father seated opposite the memorial of the dead soldier. "Will he forgive Mrs. George?" the girls said to themselves as soon as their ebullition of grief was over. Much conversation passed too among the acquaintances of the Osborne family, who knew of the rupture between the son and father caused by the former's marriage, as to the chance of a reconciliation with the young widow. There were bets among the gentlemen both about Russell Square and in the City.

If the sisters had any anxiety regarding the possible recognition of Amelia as a daughter of the family, it was increased presently, and towards the end of the autumn, by their father's announcement that he was going abroad. He did not say whither, but they knew at once that his steps would be turned towards Belgium, and were aware that George's widow was still in Brussels. They had pretty accurate news indeed of poor Amelia from Lady Dobbin and her daughters. Our honest Captain had been promoted in consequence of the death of the second Major of the regiment on the field; and the brave O'Dowd, who had distinguished himself greatly here as upon all occasions where he had a chance to show his coolness and valour, was a Colonel and Companion of the Bath.

Very many of the brave —th, who had suffered severely upon both days of action, were still at Brussels in the autumn, recovering of their wounds. The city was a vast military hospital for months after the great battles; and as men and officers began to rally from their hurts, the gardens and places of public resort swarmed with maimed warriors, old and young, who, just rescued out of death, fell to gambling, and gaiety, and love-making, as people of Vanity Fair will do. Mr. Osborne found out some of the —th easily. He knew their uniform quite well, and had been used to follow all the promotions and exchanges in the regiment, and loved to talk about it and its officers as if he had been one of the number. On the day after his arrival at Brussels, and as he issued from his hotel, which faced the park, he saw a soldier in the well-known facings, reposing on a stone bench in the garden, and went and sate down trembling by the wounded convalescent man.

"Were you in Captain Osborne's company?" he said, and added, after a pause, "he was my son, sir."

The man was not of the Captain's company, but he lifted up his unwounded arm and touched his cap sadly and respectfully to the haggard broken-spirited gentleman who questioned him. "The whole army didn't contain a finer or a better officer," the soldier said. "The Sergeant of the Captain's company (Captain Raymond had it now), was in town, though, and was just well of a shot in the shoulder. His honour might see him if he liked, who could tell him anything he wanted to know about—about the —th's actions. But his honour had seen Major Dobbin, no doubt, the brave Captain's great friend; and Mrs. Osborne, who was here too, and had been very bad, he heard everybody say. They say she was out of her mind like for six weeks or more. But your honour knows all about that—and asking your pardon"—the man added.

Osborne put a guinea into the soldier's hand, and told him he should have another if he would bring the Sergeant to the Hôtel du Parc; a promise which very soon brought the desired officer to Mr. Osborne's presence. And the first soldier went away; and after telling a comrade or two how Captain Osborne's father was arrived, and what a free-handed generous gentleman he was, they went and made good cheer with drink and feasting, as long as the guineas lasted which had come from the proud purse of the mourning old father.

In the Sergeant's company, who was also just convalescent, Osborne made the journey of Waterloo and Quatre Bras, a journey which thousands of his countrymen were then taking. He took the Sergeant with him in his carriage, and went through both fields under his guidance. He saw the point of the road where the regiment marched into action on the 16th, and the slope down which they drove the French cavalry who were pressing on the retreating Belgians. There was the spot where the noble Captain cut down the French officer who was grappling with the young Ensign for the colours, the Colour-Sergeants having been shot down. Along this road they retreated on the next day, and here was the bank at which the regiment bivouacked under the rain of the night of the seventeenth. Further on was the position which they took and held during the day, forming time after time to receive the charge of the enemy's horsemen and lying down under the shelter of the bank from the furious French cannonade. And it was at this declivity when at evening the whole English line received the order to advance, as the enemy fell back after his last charge, that the Captain, hurraying and rushing down the hill waving his sword, received a shot and fell dead. "It was Major Dobbin who took back the Captain's body to Brussels," the Sergeant said, in a low voice, "and had him buried, as your honour knows." The peasants and relic-hunters about the place were screaming round the pair, as the soldier told his story, offering for sale all sorts of mementoes of the fight, crosses, and epaulets, and shattered cuirasses, and eagles.

Osborne gave a sumptuous reward to the Sergeant when he parted with him, after having visited the scenes of his son's last exploits. His burial-place he had already seen. Indeed, he had driven thither immediately after his arrival at Brussels. George's body lay in the pretty burial-ground of Laeken, near the city; in which place, having once visited it on a party of pleasure, he had lightly expressed a wish to have his grave made. And there the young officer was laid by his friend, in the unconsecrated corner of the garden, separated by a little hedge from the temples and towers and plantations of flowers and shrubs, under which the Roman Catholic dead repose. It seemed a humiliation to old Osborne to think that his son, an English gentleman, a captain in the famous British army, should not be found worthy to lie in ground where mere foreigners were buried. Which of us is there can tell how much vanity lurks in our warmest regard for others, and how selfish our love is? Old Osborne did not speculate much upon the mingled nature of his feelings, and how his instinct and selfishness were combating together. He firmly believed that everything he did was right, that he ought on all occasions to have his own way—and like the sting of a wasp or serpent his hatred rushed out armed and poisonous against anything like opposition. He was proud of his hatred as of everything else. Always to be right, always to trample forward, and never to doubt, are not these the great qualities with which dullness takes the lead in the world?

As after the drive to Waterloo, Mr. Osborne's carriage was nearing the gates of the city at sunset, they met another open barouche, in which were a couple of ladies and a gentleman, and by the side of which an officer was riding. Osborne gave a start back, and the Sergeant, seated with him, cast a look of surprise at his neighbour, as he touched his cap to the officer, who mechanically returned his salute. It was Amelia, with the lame young Ensign by her side, and opposite to her her faithful friend Mrs. O'Dowd. It was Amelia, but how changed from the fresh and comely girl Osborne knew. Her face was white and thin. Her pretty brown hair was parted under a widow's cap—the poor child. Her eyes were fixed, and looking nowhere. They stared blank in the face of Osborne, as the carriages crossed each other, but she did not know him; nor did he recognise her, until looking up, he saw Dobbin riding by her: and then he knew who it was. He hated her. He did not know how much until he saw her there. When her carriage had passed on, he turned and stared at the Sergeant, with a curse and defiance in his eye cast at his companion, who could not help looking at him—as much as to say "How dare *you* look at me? Damn you! I *do* hate her. It is she who has tumbled my hopes and all my pride down." "Tell the scoundrel to drive on quick," he shouted with an oath, to the lackey on the box. A minute afterwards, a horse came clattering over the pavement behind Osborne's carriage, and Dobbin rode up. His thoughts had been elsewhere as the carriages passed each other, and it was not until he had ridden some paces forward, that he remembered it was Osborne who had just passed him. Then he turned to examine if the sight of her father-in-law had made any impression on Amelia, but the poor girl did not know who had passed. Then William, who daily used to accompany her in his drives, taking out his watch, made some excuse about an engagement which he suddenly recollected, and so rode off. She did not remark that either; but sate looking before her, over the homely landscape towards the woods in the distance, by which George marched away.

"Mr. Osborne, Mr. Osborne!" cried Dobbin, as he rode up and held out his hand. Osborne made no motion to take it, but shouted out once more and with another curse to his servant to drive on.

Dobbin laid his hand on the carriage side. "I will see you, sir," he said. "I have a message for you."

"From that woman?" said Osborne, fiercely.

"No," replied the other, "from your son;" at which Osborne fell back into the corner of his carriage, and Dobbin allowing it to pass on, rode close behind it, and so through the town until they reached Mr. Osborne's hotel, and without a word. There he followed Osborne up to his apartments. George had often been in the rooms; they were the lodgings which the Crawleys had occupied during their stay in Brussels.

"Pray, have you any commands for me, Captain Dobbin, or, I beg your pardon, I should say *Major* Dobbin, since better men than you are dead, and you step into their *shoes?*" said Mr. Osborne, in that sarcastic tone which he sometimes was pleased to assume.

"Better men *are* dead," Dobbin replied. "I want to speak to you about one."

"Make it short, sir," said the other with an oath, scowling at his visitor.

"I am here as his closest friend," the Major resumed, "and the executor of his will. He made it before he went into action. Are you aware how small his means are, and of the straitened circumstances of his widow?"

"I don't know his widow, sir," Osborne said. "Let her go back to her father." But the gentleman whom he addressed was determined to remain in good temper, and went on without heeding the interruption.

"Do you know, sir, Mrs. Osborne's condition? Her life and her reason almost have been shaken by the blow which has fallen on her. It is very doubtful whether she will rally. There is a chance left for her, however, and it is about this I came to speak to you. She will be a mother soon. Will you visit the parent's offence upon the child's head? or will you forgive the child for poor George's sake?"

Osborne broke out into a rhapsody of self-praise and imprecations;—by the first, excusing himself to his own conscience for his conduct; by the second, exaggerating the undutifulness of George. No father in all England could have behaved more generously to a son, who had rebelled against him wickedly. He had died without even so much as confessing he was wrong. Let him take the consequences of his undutifulness and folly. As for himself, Mr. Osborne, he was a man of his word. He had sworn never to speak to that woman, or to recognize her as his son's wife. "And that's what you may tell her," he concluded with an oath; "and that's what I will stick to to the last day of my life."

There was no hope from that quarter then. The widow must live on her slender pittance, or on such aid as Jos could give her. "I might tell her, and she would not heed it," thought Dobbin, sadly: for the poor girl's thoughts were not here at all since her catastrophe, and, stupefied under the pressure of her sorrow, good and evil were alike indifferent to her.

So, indeed, were even friendship and kindness. She received them both uncomplainingly, and having accepted them, relapsed into her grief.

Suppose some twelve months after the above conversation took place to have passed in the life of our poor Amelia. She has spent the first portion of that time in a sorrow so profound and pitiable, that we who have been watching and describing some of the emotions of that weak and tender heart, must draw back in the presence of the cruel grief under which it is bleeding. Tread silently round the hapless couch of the poor prostrate soul. Shut gently the door of the dark chamber wherein she suffers, as those kind people did who nursed her through the first months of her pain, and never left her until heaven had sent her consolation. A day came—of almost terrified delight and wonder—when the poor widowed girl pressed a child upon her breast—a child, with the eyes of George who was gone— a little boy, as beautiful as a cherub. What a miracle it was to hear its first cry! How she laughed and wept over it—how love, and hope, and prayer woke again in her bosom as the baby nestled there. She was safe. The doctors who attended her, and had feared for her life or for her brain, had waited anxiously for this crisis before they could pronounce that either was secure. It was worth the long months of doubt and dread which the persons who had constantly been with her had passed, to see her eyes once more beaming tenderly upon them.

Our friend Dobbin was one of them. It was he who brought her back to England and to her mother's house; when Mrs. O'Dowd, receiving a peremptory summons from her Colonel, had been forced to quit her patient. To see Dobbin holding the infant, and to hear Amelia's laugh of triumph as she watched him, would have done any man good who had a sense of humour. William was the god-father of the child, and exerted his ingenuity in the pur-chase of cups, spoons, pap-boats, and corals for this little Christian.

How his mother nursed him, and dressed him, and lived upon him; how she drove away all nurses, and would scarce allow any hand but her own to touch him; how she considered that the greatest favour she could confer upon his godfather, Major Dobbin, was to allow the Major occa-sionally to dandle him, need not be told here. This child was her being. Her existence was a maternal caress. She enveloped the feeble and unconscious creature with love and worship. It was her life which the baby drank in from her bosom. Of nights, and when alone, she had stealthy and intense raptures of motherly love, such as God's marvellous care has awarded to the female instinct —joys how far higher and lower than reason—blind beauti-ful devotions which only women's hearts know. It was William Dobbin's task to muse upon these movements of Amelia's, and to watch her heart; and if his love made him divine almost all the feelings which agitated it, alas! he could see with a fatal perspicuity that there was no place there for him. And so, gently, he bore his fate, knowing it, and content to bear it.

I suppose Amelia's father and mother saw through the intentions of the Major, and were not ill-disposed to encourage him; for Dobbin visited their house daily, and stayed for hours with them, or with Amelia, or with the honest landlord, Mr. Clapp, and his family. He brought, on one pretext or another, presents to everybody, and almost every day; and went, with the landlord's little girl, who was rather a favourite with Amelia, by the name of Major Sugarplums. It was this little child who commonly acted as mistress of the ceremonies to introduce him to Mrs. Osborne. She laughed one day when Major Sugarplums' cab drove up to Fulham, and he descended from it, bringing out a wooden horse, a drum, a trumpet, and other warlike toys, for little Georgy, who was scarcely six months old, and for whom the articles in question were entirely premature.

The child was asleep. "Hush," said Amelia, annoyed, perhaps, at the creaking of the Major's boots; and she held out her hand; smiling because William could not take it until he had rid himself of his cargo of toys. "Go downstairs, little Mary," said he presently to the child, "I want to speak to Mrs. Osborne." She looked up rather astonished, and laid down the infant on its bed.

"I am come to say good-bye, Amelia," said he, taking her slender little white hand gently.

"Good-bye? and where are you going?" she said, with a smile.

"Send the letters to the agents," he said; "they will forward them; for you will write to me, won't you? I shall be away a long time."

"I'll write to you about Georgy," she said. "Dear William, how good you have been to him and to me. Look at him. Isn't he like an angel?"

The little pink hands of the child closed mechanically round the honest soldier's finger, and Amelia looked up in his face with bright maternal pleasure. The cruellest looks could not have wounded him more than that glance of hopeless kindness. He bent over the child and mother.

He could not speak for a moment. And it was only with all his strength that he could force himself to say a God bless you. "God bless you," said Amelia, and held up her face and kissed him.

"Hush! Don't wake Georgy!" she added, as William Dobbin went to the door with heavy steps. She did not hear the noise of his cab-wheels as he drove away: she was looking at the child, who was laughing in his sleep.